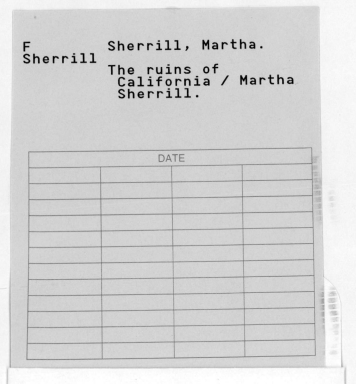

The Ruins of California

ALSO BY MARTHA SHERRILL

My Last Movie Star
The Buddha from Brooklyn

The Ruins of California

MARTHA SHERRILL

The Penguin Press
New York
2006

THE PENGUIN PRESS
Published by the Penguin Group
Penguin Group (USA) Inc., 375 Hudson Street, New York, New York 10014, U.S. A. • Penguin Group
(Canada), 90 Eglinton Avenue East, Suite 700, Toronto, Ontario, Canada M4P 2Y3 (a division of Pearson
Penguin Canada Inc.) • Penguin Books Ltd, 80 Strand, London WC2R 0RL, England • Penguin Ireland,
25 St Stephen's Green, Dublin 2, Ireland (a division of Penguin Books Ltd) • Penguin Books Australia
Ltd, 250 Camberwell Road, Camberwell, Victoria 3124, Australia (a division of Pearson Australia Group
Pty Ltd) • Penguin Books India Pvt Ltd, 11 Community Centre, Panchsheel Park, New Delhi – 110 017,
India • Penguin Group (NZ), Cnr Airborne and Rosedale Roads, Albany, Auckland 1310, New Zealand
(a division of Pearson New Zealand Ltd) • Penguin Books (South Africa) (Pty) Ltd, 24 Sturdee Avenue,
Rosebank, Johannesburg 2196, South Africa

Penguin Books Ltd, Registered Offices:
80 Strand, London WC2R 0RL, England

First published in 2006 by The Penguin Press,
a member of Penguin Group (USA) Inc.

Publisher's Note
This is a work of fiction. Names, characters, places, and incidents either are the product of the author's
imagination or are used fictitiously, and any resemblance to actual persons, living or dead, business
establishments, events, or locales is entirely coincidental.

Library of Congress Cataloging-in-Publication Data

Sherrill, Martha.
The ruins of California / Martha Sherrill.
p. cm.
ISBN 1-59420-080-7 (alk. paper)
1. California—Fiction. 2. Girls—Fiction. I. Title.
PS3619.H469R85 2006
813'.6—dc22   2005049343

Printed in the United States of America
10 9 8 7 6 5 4 3 2

Designed by Stephanie Huntwork

For Peter and Nathaniel and Liam
—with love and exasperation

CONTENTS

PROSPERO   Be collected.
   No more amazement. Tell your piteous heart
   There's no harm done.

MIRANDA   O, woe the day!

PROSPERO   No harm.

—William Shakespeare, *The Tempest*, Act 1, Scene 2

1969

Say Hello for Me

Two things always signaled that she was suffering: stage makeup worn during the day and loudness. She'd act too happy, like something was hiding beneath all her giddiness, something dank and unaired way down. My mother laughed, and sometimes she couldn't stop. Over the summer it had gotten worse—the shrieking jollity, the nonstop hardy-har-har—and she was always slipping away to watch more bad news on TV, turning it off when I wandered into the den. When the television tube faded out, it made a weird vibrating sound that grew fainter and fainter, and then she would yell out, "That's enough of that!"

Not listening was part of it. When she was upset, it seemed like a siren was blaring inside her head every few seconds and distracting her. She'd talk louder, over you. In June, after Bobby Kennedy was shot and that picture of him lying in a black pool of his own blood ran in a magazine (I looked at it for a very long time), it was as if a megaphone had attached itself to her mouth. She brayed. She bellowed. The walls of Abuelita's house shook with my mother's giddy remorse and hysteria. She would fake that everything was all right—her big trick—and then, putting me to bed one night, she broke down and whimpered, "What kind of world have I brought you into?"

What kind of world? I stood in the parking lot at Burbank Airport and watched her unload my pink Samsonite suitcase from the trunk of the car and wasn't inclined to ask. It's probably not fair to say I was the passive type. But maybe I was. I was receptive and quiet. I stood around a lot—waiting for balls to be pitched, orders to be given, situations to arise. While I slept, things came together: My clothes were laid out on my bed, my white orthopedic shoes polished, and in the morning plates of food appeared on the table before me. I ate everything on them. Hard to imagine now, but I was almost fat in those days—thick arms and legs, a belly that swelled where my waist would someday appear. Not that I paid much attention. My traveling outfit could be boiled down to three haphazard moves: a thin purple windbreaker, blue knee socks, and a pair of my special white shoes, which Doug Daley, one of the dumber boys at school, had recently called "clodhoppers." I was wild about the purple windbreaker. As for my belly, or the clods (a cure for a duck waddle), in my mind I was arrestingly beautiful and really quite grown up.

What kind of world? One of mystery and magic and endless possibilities for romance. My new pink Samsonite suitcase was packed with Coco, my deteriorating baby blanket, and everything else. Why, it was almost like I was running away.

> *Dearest Inez,*
> *Did I tell you that I had a wonderful time with you at Christmas?*
> *Well, I did. I felt like your father and your friend, and I enjoyed that*
> *so much I wanted to laugh and yell at the same time—have you ever*
> *had that feeling?*
> *All my love,*
> *F.G. (or, the Friendly Giant)*

On board I was a small figure at the front of the plane, but I felt large and super noticeable, almost famous. The stewardess kept turning up—

shooing away a tired guy in a business suit who sat down next to me. She fussed about my jumper, which wasn't worth fussing over, and she used a baby voice, the kind of voice that always put me on edge because nobody in my family spoke to me like that—nobody—and suddenly everything about the stewardess seemed completely fake and hammy. Her orange-and-pink Pacific Southwest Airlines uniform with the hot-air-balloon cap was ridiculous. The way she spoke into the airplane microphone was like a fake person on TV. Everybody knew how to lock and unlock seat belts, so why did she have to stand in the aisle with a set of them—little belts attached to nothing—and demonstrate fastening and unfastening?

I pulled out the airsickness bag, fascinated by how clean and sinister it was—and imagined having a vomiting spree next time the stewardess passed by. I tugged on my seat belt to make sure it was tight and checked the metal ashtrays at the end of the armrest for gems or coins. I looked at my ticket stub inside its pink-and-orange PSA folder. The stub said CHILD $15.00, and I returned it to my windbreaker pocket and then rested both my palms on the armrests—and looked out the window.

"Say hello for me," my mom said at the gate. Her voice had gone soft. Her face was weird and dreamy. She had shifted into a new position. Her mind was like a sail, and a new breeze was blowing. It wasn't only her. My father had a way of doing that to a person. Just when you'd decided that he didn't care about anybody but himself, he said something so sensitive and kind, or did something so generous, you couldn't get over it. Just when you'd decided he was a rat and a fink—my mother's words, not mine—it would dawn on you that he was a god and you loved him more than anybody. That's how he made us all feel. Uncertain, off kilter. You wanted more of him—but, at the same time, you weren't sure about that either.

I thought of him driving to meet me, the MG changing lanes all the way. I'd saunter down the aisle of my plane, disembark, and he'd be leaning against a wall near the arrival gate. Cool, elegant. That inky black hair. A crisp, starched white shirt. And when he'd smiled, it was a burst of fireworks—as if he had searched the world over and finally found a girl he liked most of all: me.

> *Sweet Inez,*
>
> *Thank you, darling, for your letter and the beautiful drawing. I put it up on my bulletin board for important messages, and I look at it a lot. Since Marisa is not "my girlfriend"—if you know what I mean—I don't have a picture of a beautiful girl for my desk. Why don't you send me your picture, and then I'll have a girl's picture to put up?*
>
> *All my love,*
> *Daddy*

The takeoff was scary and loud but the shrieking engine calmed and the plane floated upward, toward the clouds. I watched the airport get smaller. Down below, the patch of parking lot where my mother's blue Mustang was, along with my mother, vanished from view.

It was a short flight to San Francisco, maybe thirty minutes. I studied the irregular checkerboard fabric of the seats—oranges and golds and pinks—in front of me. I looked at the sharp afternoon sunlight and noticed a small hole in the window, a round worm tunnel at the bottom. There were two windows, really, with an interior slice of space in between. Beads of dew, or rain, were leaking into that space and stretching in one direction like a tiny trail of spit or tears.

Marisa was his friend. One weekend, when my father and I were together, she appeared at the botanical garden inside Golden Gate Park. I assumed it was a coincidence, the way he and I had stumbled upon this stunning woman inside the hothouse, among the bromeliads and plumeria. *Hey, Daddy knows somebody here.* Marisa was around after that. Whether or not she was his girlfriend—"if you know what I mean" (but I didn't)—she was, like him, a math person, a graduate student at the university where my father taught. She had wild curly hair and swimming-pool blue eyes and a kind of extreme figure like my mother's, with giant boobs exploding out in front.

Marisa and my father got along. I imagined that they had math in common, or maybe just numbers and ideas about numbers, because a great deal of their conversation was loopy and incomprehensible. But Marisa was warm to me, and welcoming, and never told me what to do. She had a soft personality and a soft voice, and being with her was like sinking into a big down pillow. You just wanted to stay in her company forever. Once, the summer before, I'd even met her parents, been to their rambling house in Encino and swum in their pool that hung over a canyon. Marisa's father was a doctor of some kind. My father was a doctor of some kind, too, but not the same kind. Didn't matter. Nobody talked about work. Everybody talked politics, made jokes about Ronald Reagan, our governor, and then my father did his Jerry Lewis impression and fell spastically into the pool. He wore his Polaroid wraparound sunglasses underwater and got more laughs—Marisa's parents seemed to like him, and they seemed to like me, too, although I'm not sure if I actually spoke that day. (People were always nice to me, especially if I didn't say anything.) At Christmas, Marisa had given me some beads and a *Get Smart* transistor wristwatch, which led me to believe that she wanted to be my mom someday, or maybe just my older sister.

I was missing a day of school this time. I'd taken the spelling test early, gotten an A (and I didn't study). There was a Bluebirds meeting in the afternoon that I'd be missing, but Robbie would fill me in. Robyn Morrison was my best friend in Van Dale. She was a strawberry blonde with a husky laugh. She was Mormon, and her parents weren't divorced or separated—nobody's in Van Dale were, except mine—but for some reason, even though Robbie was blond and Mormon and her parents were married, she and I understood each other. I felt sure our connection was fated and meant to be.

Van Dale. I belonged there, like I belonged with Robbie. There were other places, other towns, but it was hard to imagine them. Van Dale

stretched for miles—one way into Burbank, the other into Pasadena—
and it was a safe slice of air in between. We moved into Abuelita's house
in the summer before second grade. We moved in a hurry and my mother
talked like it was temporary, "until things get worked out," but school
started, and Robbie sat next to me in class and every time a discussion
rose up that suggested another change, or that we might get our own
place, or move to New York, where my mother might be able to work, I
grew silent. (My big trick.) Robbie and I were not going to be separated.
Van Dale and I were not going to be separated. Unlike anywhere else,
north or south, it was comprehensible. The summer was hot and dry and
smoggy. The autumn was largely invisible, except for the slow disappear-
ance of summer. The winter was temperate—you needed a jacket on
some days. Spring showed up promptly in March with an arrival of balmy
air, warm rains, brilliant green grass on the hills, and peeps of sharp sunlight in the late morning after the fog and haze had burned off. Van Dale
seemed regular to me, and I wanted regular.

Nothing too large or too small. Modest expectations, predictable out-
comes, a string of nice houses along the street, set back at exactly the
same distance from the sidewalk. There were rows of arching trees, rectangles of lawn grass, the fanning of fairy-tale sprinklers in the late afternoon, and sunken cement alleyways where the L.A. River trickled by or
dried up. There was silvery dew on the windshield of the blue Mustang
in the morning when my mother drove me to the same elementary school
where she herself had gone—how amazed people were by that—and
later, as I walked home, there were black earthworms on the sidewalk,
cooked flat by the sun. Robbie and I ascended the shady uphill streets
and felt safe, without question or worry, in spite of my mother's hysteria
about a mentally disturbed man prowling the streets. She said too much,
perhaps. We passed 31 Flavors and Hagen's Pharmacy, where we bought
Milk Duds or Necco Wafers, then passed quiet apartment buildings with
dry fountains and perfectly mowed lawns with all the brown cuttings removed. We walked on, slowly, dislodging the cooked earthworms with a

flick of our shoe tips. (Clods were exquisitely good at this.) And at the top of Central Avenue, we checked the metal lamppost to make sure our initials were still painted in red nail polish.

Robbie and I liked to talk on the phone after dinner—usually about our third-grade teacher, Mrs. Craig, who was very strict and had a wooden leg. (A story had been passed down, through generations of Van Dale public-school children: A boy had once thrown a dart at that leg.) We discussed other girls in Bluebirds, focusing our critical attention on Julie Brownlee, who was stuck up and "acted big." (Her father ran a barbecue pit.) We talked about Davy Mitchell or Pat McClarty—a natural athlete, tall, strong, funny, a couple of devastating moles on his neck. I liked how everybody's phone number in Van Dale started with the same three numbers: 2 4 6. My mind tended to dwell on unifying features of things and gravitated toward symmetry and pairs—patterns never seemed random to me. I liked harmony and sameness. I felt good with even numbers, not odd, and although sometimes my heart quickened when I saw doubles, like 33 and 66 and 88, I didn't dwell on the fact that there were no pairs in Abuelita's house or that my mother wasn't dancing anymore or that everybody in Van Dale seemed born with a religion except me.

On Sundays, Robbie was all busy with church. On Saturdays she was allowed to ride the bus into downtown and shop. This seemed to terrify my mother. It had taken an endless amount of time, weeks, before she consented to let me go downtown, too. My mother hated the bus, or seemed to, and said the word with the same tones of disapproval with which she said "bar" or "Las Vegas," as though public transportation were a magnet for perverts and criminals and God's castoffs, or the grown man in a garter belt whom the Van Dale police were trying to catch. But I finally ground my mother down. She was halfway ground down to begin with, so it didn't take much.

The business district of Van Dale was a stretch of several long blocks. There was Webb's, a family-owned department store where my mother bought her huge bras and girdles and other lingerie. There was Skiffing-ton's Shoe Shop, where my shoes were special-ordered twice a year from a skinny shoe salesman with a big Adam's apple that made him look like Super Chicken. There was an ancient Woolworth's and two old-time movie theaters with big marquees that played strange pairings in the mid-day. (*Planet of the Apes / Chitty Chitty Bang Bang.*) When I came home, my fingernails dirty and my breath smelling like hot tamales, I showed my mother and Abuelita all my purchases, things like a yellow rabbit's foot key chain, a bamboo back scratcher, Chapstick.

Abuelita asked about the bus in nostalgic tones. She knew all the lines, the stops, was eager to hear about the new fares. She drove to work in her own car now, a white Corvair, but she still kept bus schedules in her head. Sometimes when I was alone, like today when I was riding the plane, I thought about Abuelita traveling by herself to America all those years ago from her father's house in Peru and then traveling to work all those years—she was a housekeeper for David Feinman, a recording-industry executive, in Los Feliz Hills—moving from one dimension to an-other, from her small one-story house with its turquoise linoleum and beat-up toaster and handmade Peruvian place mats and flimsy paper napkins into another world of swimming pools and heavy linen and large glass windows, a land of views, of canyons, of expansive space and a sense that horizons were unlimited and not daunting, just an open stretch of blue sky that you could soar into and eat.

Inez Garcia Ruin. I was traveling through that sky. I was gliding from one zone of life to another. I was passing from mother to father, a baton of a girl flying in the distance between hands. I felt unburdened of my pink bedroom and my ceiling-tall stuffed giraffe, my Midge doll with its smooth nippleless breasts, the warm-biscuit smell of Dr. Guinea Pig and his cozy cage, the aquarium of translucent baby guppies, my diary with entries about the boys I had crushes on. I'd gotten engaged to Davy Mitchell in second grade. But when he used the word "ain't" in class, I buried the engagement ring he gave me in the side yard under Abuelita's avocado tree and near the fish graveyard area. I said it broke. He said he'd buy me another one. And I said, "Don't bother."

I felt unburdened of that ring now, and of Davy, and of the complications of living in a household of women where my mother was lost and loud, where my grandmother worked all the time, and where I was always wishing to stay forever and, at the same time, to be somewhere else. And alone on that small plane as it headed northward, I had a feeling I was on my way.

At the bottom of the jetway, I was ejected into a red-carpeted area of San Francisco Airport with its distant ceiling and cavernous spaces. A herd of fellow travelers was clumping near my arrival gate. They were untidy and un–Van Dale looking—wore beards, muttonchops, Afros, ethnic fabrics, shawls, beads, and bright colors. The smell of BO was everywhere, and people were pressing up against each other for incredibly long hugs and gazing into each other's eyes. I kept wondered if these ragtag figures were hippies who hated the war and went to love-ins and were still consoling each other about the Kennedys or Martin Luther King Jr., like all those crying people I'd seen on TV.

I scanned the horizon of heads. Where was he? Then I heard a gentle voice that didn't seem much older than my own.

"Inez?"

A girl bent down before me. She smelled like vanilla and cinnamon, like a bakery. Her straight, dark hair was parted in the middle and her face was flat like an Indian's. When she smiled, her large mouth revealed two wide front teeth and a gap between them.

"Inez," the girl said again. Her teeth were like a rabbit's. The lashes of her brown eyes were coated in mascara. I stared at them for what seemed a long time, in silence, and then I realized there was a blue dot under each eye. A dot of blue eye paint. Almost like a clown.

Cookies, I thought. *The girl smells like cookies, like vanilla wafers.*

"I'm Cary," she said, pausing for a moment. "I'm your father's friend. He's waiting downstairs. How was your trip?"

"Okay."

"Did you sit at the window?"

I nodded.

"I love the window," she cooed. "Did you look down and see all the tiny swimming pools? Were the farms like squares of a checkerboard?"

I nodded again, marveling at the girl's face. The blue dots. The gap in her teeth. Her nose was so tiny.

"That's so far out." Cary took an inhalation of breath, as though she were captivated completely by the thought of my amazing journey through space. I looked at her mouth. She had an overbite, but there was something else about the angles, the curve of her tongue, and something about her lips that seemed familiar.

"Did you fly through puffy clouds and watch the wings of the plane disappear and then reappear, clear and shiny?"

I nodded again.

"Your cheeks are so pink, Inez," Cary said, reaching to touch my face with the tip of a finger. "And you look so much like your father. He said you were very beautiful."

I must have blushed, because Cary paused again. "Hey. I have something for you," she said.

She pushed away the fringe of a beige macramé shawl and reached into the front pocket of her jeans to pull out small envelopes of white paper, each about two inches square. There were five or six of them, all labeled diagonally in tiny red letters: KER JACK CRACKER JACK CRACKER JACK CRACKER JACK CRACKER JACK CRACKER JA

"Prizes," I said, a flood of excitement in my voice.

"*Prizes*," Cary repeated in a voice so gentle that it was almost a whisper. "I've been collecting them all week. Prizes that I didn't open. They're all for you."

TWO

Telegraph Hill

He always did this embarrassing thing at the airport. It was one of his routines. "Inez!" he'd cry out theatrically, as though I were an old flame from whom he'd been separated at great emotional cost.

"Inez!"

His head shook in torment. His hands slapped down on his chest and throbbed above his heart. And then, when he wouldn't stop the bad dramatics, I conjured a look that had taken me a couple of years to master: abject disapproval. It was a game we played. He overdid. I downplayed. I just stared at him—deadpan—and tightened my lips until they became a knife edge across my face. He advanced, seemingly oblivious, a complete fool, his arms stretched out wide for a hug. Oh, no. That's when my lack of enthusiasm wasn't feigned. My father didn't bend down—he never bent, due to a bad back or possibly just something else inflexible about him—but threw his arms around the top of my head. My face pressed into his heavy belt buckle and just a couple inches above the crotch of his low-cut jeans.

After what seemed an eternity, he pulled away.

"What's this outrageous bag?" he asked, pointing down at the large pink suitcase. "Jesus, what a color!"

"The zipper broke on the one you—"

"All you need is a duffel," he interrupted. He'd given me a camping duffel and inflatable lifeboat from Abercrombie & Fitch the summer before, hoping to encourage a sense of rugged self-reliance. "It looks like a bottle of Pepto-Bismol, Inez. Or like something you'd take on a charter-bus trip of the Hawaiian Islands."

I forced a smile.

Cary shrugged. "Gee, Paul. I think it's really neat." She tried to catch my father's eye. "Where'd you get that groovy bag, Inez?"

"Is it neat?" He faltered, temporarily at a loss. "Perhaps so. Gee, what do I know, right? I'm so out of it. Hey, Inez, you're looking swell. *Swell.*"

I didn't say anything for a while, just watched him lift the suitcase to the hatch of the small car and felt an old dread returning. He acted so glad to see me but at the same time seemed sorry I'd ever been born.

"Let's go!" he called out. And in one fluid motion, he jackknifed his long, lean body and dropped into the driver's seat of the MG. Cary waited beside her open door so I could climb in the backseat. Except it wasn't a backseat, really, just a narrow ledge. When he'd first gotten the car, the year before, I was able to crawl right in. But now some gymnastics were required. I stepped backward through the door and positioned my bottom on the ledge before squeezing the rest of my body inside. As we rode along, my head bent down to avoid painful contact with the roof, my clodhoppers were wedged up against the back of the front seats and one elbow was positioned on the ledge to steady me during my father's great bursts of speed and frequent lane changes. Once, the year before, during a particularly exciting stretch of road, he swiveled his head all the way around to tell me that sometimes he wished he'd become a race-car driver, but now it was too late.

Cary smiled at me sympathetically. "How's it going back there?"

She seemed a little younger than Marisa, as far as I could tell. Or maybe just softer and more vibrantly sweet, if that was possible. But, just like Marisa, she generated an atmosphere of intelligent passivity, of being a good-natured passenger in a Paul and Inez Ruin Weekend. The only other noticeable pattern as far as I could tell was that both women had dark hair, large eyes, small noses, and an overbite. But then, my mother had all those things, too.

"How is *Mrs. Craig?*" my father asked. "Any goose-stepping in the classroom?"

"Mrs. Craig"—he turned to Cary—"is really uptight. Right, Inez?"

"Yeah."

"She's an angry John Bircher who's got Inez in her grips for third grade. She hobbles around on a wooden leg like Captain Ahab and has one of those bird's-nest hairdos. And according to Inez she's made the class memorize the names of Richard Nixon's cabinet."

"Oh, God!" Cary shrieked. "You're kidding!"

My father watched me in the rearview mirror. "Inez, who is the secretary of health, education and welfare?"

"Robert Finch."

"Hey!"

"Secretary of state?"

"Henry Kissinger."

"*Herr Doctor Strangelove,* you mean."

Cary giggled.

"Mrs. Craig is totally paranoid and always raving on about the commies. Right, Inez? Completely hysterical. Just like my mother. I don't get it," he went on. "It's hard for me to get that worked up. Who needs more labels? Right, Inez? To me, hawks and doves are all birds, and politics is just a lot of wing flapping."

My neck wasn't in a position to nod, but I tried—strangely enthralled by his charm, almost hypnotized. My chin moved up and down a bit, and I hoped that he could see it in the mirror.

"Don't vote," he said. "*It only encourages them.* Right, Inez?" Then he lowered his voice to paternal tones. "Memorizing isn't such a bad thing anyway. It's how we learn stuff—"

Behind the MG an explosive rumbling quieted all conversation. From the slanted hatch window, I saw a dark cluster of motorcycles getting bigger, enveloping our car on all sides. There was a group of eight or ten men in denim and leather and World War II helmets spray-painted black.

"Harleys," my father said.

"Far out!" said Cary. "The Hells Angels."

At the very end of the pack, a skinny girl was wearing a crocheted halter top and black leather pants. She was sitting on the back of a bike, slightly elevated, hugging a guy with a skull on the back of his jacket. My father traced her with his eyes, then sped up—seeming to want a closer look.

"She must be freezing," he said.

"Wow." Cary squinted. "That bike is so beautiful. *So are they.*" My father kept his eyes on the girl. In the middle of her back, a thin ridge of spine disappeared under the halter band and strings, then rose out again.

"What do you think, Inez?"

A Harley was a kind of motorcycle. I'd guessed that much. The girl on the back must be the angel. But where was hell?

I opened my eyes. The light was bright and sharp and fell in blazing shapes around me. My father's studio apartment on Telegraph Hill was an airy white room, decorated sparely and simply. There was a brown corduroy sofa where I always slept, a couple of low white tables, a flamenco poster, and two guitars leaning against a redbrick wall. Another wall, floor-to-ceiling windows, looked out over San Francisco Bay and the island of Alcatraz. Bisecting the room was a deep red folding screen, and behind that, the vast expanse of Dad's king-size bed.

Unlike Abuelita's house in Van Dale, which was a forest of artifacts and souvenirs and yellowing snapshots collected over the years and never pared down, my father's place was devoid of sentiment. No clutter. No framed pictures of family members. No treasured remains of boyhood or school days. No signs of his former life as a suburban dad or evidence of me or my mysterious half brother, Whitman, who lived in England. It took a little getting used to—the sterility of my father's surroundings. While Abuelita kept things forever, as if, like a magic lamp, they might contain a genie of good feeling inside them, my father's things carried no such hope. Objects were set out to be admired for beauty and contemplation: a single lily in a glass cylinder, a Japanese Go board, an ancient bird carved from marble. But when I looked at them, I felt sort of empty.

"Inez, you're awake!" He loomed over me with a smile. His hair was drier and looser than when I had seen him three months before on Christmas Day at my Grandmother Ruin's house. And rather than the strained expression and three-piece suit he had worn for the holiday in San Benito, he was in jeans and a collarless white shirt and seemed in a cheery mood.

"Great music last night, wasn't it?"

We'd gone to Alegrías, a flamenco club in North Beach. He went there every Friday night, whether I was visiting or not.

"Antonio is amazing. A real *manitas de plata.*" He mimicked playing the guitar, hunched over.

"Silver hands?"

"Yes! But if you say somebody's a *manitas de plata,* it means he's a terrible show-off. Like, '*Antonio, you egomaniac!*' What a cat. He's just amazing. Hey, listen, if I could play like that, I'd be a show-off, too."

My father did play, but not like that. He'd lived in Spain after college and again when he was in the air force. He'd been stationed there and stayed—studying guitar in some dusty town called Morón de la Frontera that he still talked about. He'd been an outsider in a dark world that he never quite returned from. Flamenco captured his attention completely, struck him in a place the rest of us couldn't reach.

"Pancakes?" he asked. "Or what about waffles? I have a cool new waffle iron. It's German and makes these perfect waffles—crunchy on the edges and top, a bit softer inside. What are you in the mood for?"

During my previous visit, Marisa had spent the night and disappeared behind the folding screen in the living room, turning up the next morning in a white robe and wet hair. But this morning I saw no sign of Cary. She'd come to El Bodega for paella, the three of us waiting forever for our big bowls of saffron rice baked with clams and spicy sausage and chicken. It must have been ten-thirty—way beyond my Van Dale bedtime—when we left the restaurant and ambled into the bizarre nighttime world of North Beach. In my purple windbreaker and knee socks, I passed men wearing baggy velvet caps, women in witch's coats, panhandlers, winos, an array of beckoning shops selling army surplus, candles, posters, and incense. (Van Dale offered nothing like this.) One place had a storefront window featuring an enormous stuffed tiger with a cigar coming out of its mouth. An old amusement-park ride was displayed in another storefront—a large clown face with a deranged smile. "Hey, Cary, look!" my father called out, pointing to the black-light posters and long glass cases. "A new head shop. Check it out!"

At the corner of Grant and Green, we'd turned uphill and soon arrived at Alegrías, hidden behind a plain factory façade—no advertisement, no sign indicating it was an establishment of any kind. A man in a priest's long jacket and white collar was standing out front.

"Richard!" my father called out. The two men talked for a minute or so, exchanging observations and jokes about Chairman Mao that I didn't understand. My father handed him some folded-over bills, and we went inside.

Down a flight of stairs and around a dozen or more crowded café tables, we arrived at a corner table in the back where my father always sat. As my eyes adjusted to the darkness, I noticed that the room had been painted red since my last visit in the fall—walls, ceiling, stage, chairs, tables, floor. A waitress appeared instantly, greeting us with husky good humor, almost excitement, as if she'd been waiting all night to come and get my father's drink order.

"There's a table of women over there"—she nodded in one direction near the stairs—"who asked me if you were Gregory Peck."

"A poor man's Peck," my father said, looking up at the table of women with a smile. One of the women raised her hand—the way Indians do in old westerns. *How.* Another bent her head coyly toward her straw.

Cary squinted in their direction and produced a contented smile.

A few moments later, all the chairs onstage were removed but one. A man carrying a yellow guitar came on. He was young, not quite twenty. He wore a white shirt and black pants and walked to the chair with a casual, untheatrical manner, as if he were arriving at a doctor's waiting room.

"Antonio!" a male voice yelled out.

"Ay-ay-ay!" cried another man, with expectancy.

"Hombre!" my father called out, half serious, then laughing.

The guitarist didn't acknowledge the calls—no bow or even eye contact. His pale face looked only at the floor. His hair was long and thick, swept back from his forehead. He rested the bottom of the guitar on his thigh so the instrument stood up from his lap. A few seconds later, he shifted the position of the instrument so it sat more diagonally against him, then hugged it closer, almost squeezing, and began to play.

The tune was slow, hesitant, mournful. It was called a *soleares*. The mother chant. The song of loneliness. My father had played them for years, as far back as I could remember. He'd sit for hours in our Menlo Park house on a black bentwood chair in the middle of our living room. A guitar was in his lap. His eyes were distant, almost as though he were in a trance. Sometimes, when he seemed less miserable and wasn't playing guitar, he'd take me on the back of his motorcycle if I promised not to tell my mother. I must have been five or six, clinging to him like a little ape. We'd drive to the water, to a harbor of some kind, and get off the bike and walk around. He'd point out different boats with different rigging and teach me how to tell them apart. A ketch, a yawl, a ketch-rigged yawl, a sloop. He explained where wind came from or how gravity held things to the earth, or how an airplane overhead could fly.

I remembered him sitting on the floor of the Menlo house playing with puzzles. He loved any kind of puzzle—dots and boxes, hex, rolling balls that dropped into holes, knots that needed unknotting, and iron chains that fit together perfectly into shapes that, once separated, seemed impossible to form again. In the mornings I'd sit in his lap while he read the newspaper aloud to me—Lee Harvey Oswald, Vietnam body counts, the Buddhist monk who poured gasoline all over himself and burst into flames. My father whispered and ran his fingers along the lines of the sentences until, one day, the letters on the page began to repeat in patterns that I could recognize.

He did card tricks for me, magic tricks that he'd been practicing since he was a boy, making aces materialize and disappear. Then one fall afternoon—it was late in the day and the sun was streaming in the window behind him—he was sitting on the carpet in my bedroom and wiping his face. He was trying to explain why he wasn't coming to Abuelita's with us and trying to explain something else, but he drifted off into words that I didn't understand, patterns I couldn't follow, and then no words at all. After that, he wore his wraparound sunglasses in the house, and the next morning, like a pair of aces, my mother and I disappeared.

I must have fallen asleep at Alegrías—and been carried home— because I had no memory beyond Antonio's first song. The next thing I heard was the terrible whine of my father's coffee-bean grinder. Why couldn't he buy cans of ground coffee like everybody else?

"Hey, I've got some plans for the morning," he said, handing me a mug of coffee and hot milk, a tradition begun the previous year. As far as his plans, I could have guessed what they were. Friday nights we went to Alegrías. Saturday always began with pancakes and a few errands—the grocery store, the laundry, sometimes Design Research or a new jeans store on Leavenworth called the Gap. Later on we might walk into Chinatown for dinner. Squeezed into the day—or Sunday morning—we went to Fort Point. We drove along the Marina and into the foresty Presidio, an old naval base, and parked at a crumbling nineteenth-century stronghold underneath the Golden Gate Bridge. We walked around the old fort, which was cool and dark and smelled of mold, and then we walked to the rocks and felt the sea spray on our faces and looked up at the orange-red bridge rising dramatically before us.

But this Saturday was different. After the usual errands, my father didn't descend into the Presidio. He turned right and took the car over the Golden Gate Bridge, across the bay, and into a long tunnel on the other side. We left Highway 101 for a street that weaved through hills with grass so new it looked wet with green paint. I had never been in the Marin Headlands before, and it was jarring, after so much commotion and traffic, to find myself in a wild, uninhabited place. We bumped up and down on a rutted dirt road, nearly got stuck twice. My father pulled the car over and put on a denim jacket.

He walked ahead, leading me to the crest of a rolling hill with slopes of purple lupines. Beyond that, I could see an empty beach. The sand was brown, the color of honey. The ocean stretched before us, gray and turbulent. Clouds were gathering overhead.

"Moody day," he said. "Isn't it great?"

I'd never seen a beach like that—so inhospitable, so cold. Why were we there? My father was still looking at me, waiting for some enthusiasm.

"Great," I ventured, a little hesitantly. "Really great."

"Isn't it?"

The sand grew harder as we got closer to the water. The curving, elegant tide line had left seaweed—little pods of air that I picked up and popped between my fingers. I drew a pod to my mouth, wanting to bite it.

"Inez?"

It was about the pod, I thought. He didn't want me to eat it. But then he smiled. "Hey. Do you know what those little seaweed balloons are for?"

"Floating?"

"Right! For thousands of miles. Across the sea."

He took the little pod from my hand—and drew it to his mouth. His front teeth crunched into the seaweed like biting a dill pickle. He made a face and spit out the flesh. "Blecch." He chuckled, patted my back. He walked ahead. After a minute or two, he turned to me again.

"Hey, Inez. I was wondering something."

"What?"

"Do you know what I do?"

"I'm not sure." I was suddenly nervous. World population, statistics, predictions about the future. I should have known, yet whenever he tried to talk about his work, I tried to follow along but the words got ahead of me, out of sight. "I just think for a living," he'd once told me, but I knew he used a big computer—the size of a garage—so who did the thinking, my father or the machine?

"I guess what I meant to ask," he said, "is whether you feel like you know me."

"Yes."

He waited a moment but seemed disappointed by my brevity. "I'm glad that you feel you do," he said. "Because it's very hard not to feel known—or understood. I never thought your mother understood me. So it was sometimes hard. Do you know what I'm talking about?"

"Yes," I lied.

He paused again. "Have you ever felt misunderstood and lonely—or not appreciated? Do you know that feeling?"

I was preparing what I might say when he continued, "If you were feeling that way now, would you tell me?"

"I guess so," I said, "but I don't."

"Are you sure?"

"Yes."

He looked at me with a mix of sympathy and disbelief. "It's not so much fun to be a kid," he said. "I remember what it's like. I really do. Sometimes I look at you, and even though you're very quiet, I can guess how you are. Do you think I can?"

"I don't know," I said. As we walked closer to the surf, it suddenly seemed too rough, the water going in too many directions.

He bent down to pick up a stick from the ground, a piece of driftwood that had been smoothed by years of water and sand and turbulence. I stopped with him. "You're smart," he said. "You notice things, don't you? And you're careful what you say. Those are good qualities to have. There's nothing wrong with keeping your feelings to yourself if you want to. Or keeping your thoughts to yourself, if something inside is telling you to keep quiet. Do you have that sometimes?"

"I know what you mean," I said.

"I think you have all kinds of thoughts about things that are really interesting," he said. "But you aren't sharing them with me. That's okay. It really is. But someday I hope you will."

"I have something to ask," I said after a while.

"What?" He smiled.

"How do you know what you want to do when you get big?"

"You don't," he said, seeming thrilled to tackle a question. "You never really do. Maybe your mother did. But most people don't. It's like musical chairs, really. At some point the music stops and you have to sit down. You know that game? The music stops and it's time to settle on something to do with your life. Mostly it's a big accident. Some people—your mother—it's different for them. They have a kind of genius or talent for something. It drives them toward things and to a certain kind of life. But most people, the rest of us, probably you and me, just end up with more choices. Maybe that's what your mother didn't like. She felt she never had a choice. She was born to dance, that's all. Everything else was secondary. But don't worry about that. Don't worry about your future. Are you worried?"

I shook my head.

"Well, don't be. Just find something you love doing—and then do it as well as you can. That way it will never feel like working."

"Okay."

I looked down at my clodhoppers—and the little holes on the surface of them, the decoration that formed a swooping band across the middle, were filling up with grains of sand. And my socks, which were too small, had begun to disappear inside the heels of my shoes like they were being eaten. I looked up at my father. His brows were knit, and his face was achingly handsome.

"I don't mean to heavy you out. Am I, Inez?" He reached for my hand, and I took his. We walked while the clouds gathered and the mist accumulated, until it became a thick fog. By the time we headed back, I could barely see the hills.

At the top of the crest, he stopped and turned around.

"What a beautiful spot."

I nodded.

"Isn't this a beautiful place?" There was something fragile in his eyes, almost afraid.

I nodded again.

"Wouldn't it be great to build a house here? Right here. Right on this spot?"

"Yeah."

"God, I'd really dig that. Maybe I could. Or maybe we could. And you'd come live with me. How'd you like that?"

"Oh," I said, startled. "That'd be great." But I didn't think so, not really.

THREE

Thanksgiving

During the lull between his calls and letters, it's not that my father was dead in my mind, exactly. He was kept on hold, cinematic freeze frame—the pause button not released until I picked up the phone or stepped off the plane. Maybe it was painful to think of him, or maybe his unpredictability and aloof nature made it impossible to project him into material existence. He lived so separately from me, and in such different circumstances and climate and culture—except for our mutual devotion to *Laugh-In*—that thinking about him was like trying to ponder what a character in a movie might be doing long after the movie ended.

Over the spring we'd seen each other twice. Over the summer only once. Cary greeted me at the airport gate each time with her foggy sweetness and vanilla-wafer smell and hung around all weekend. She taught me how to dog-whistle—and how to make loud shrieking sounds by blowing on a grass blade. She took me to the university where she studied music and played Bach's *Goldberg Variations* for me on a huge black piano. She always told me how beautiful I was and how much fun I was. My father was working on a research project at a computer lab in Berkeley and was busier than usual in those days. He talked about "microchips" and "mainframes." His work was "uncertain and new," as he cryptically put it in a letter, "and therefore exciting to me." This only created an additional layer of haze around him and his life.

I was caught up in Van Dale and its various offerings that summer anyway. There were piano lessons with Mrs. Zacutti, pottery classes at Logo Park, and day camp at Verdugo Hills Recreational Center, where Robbie and I liked to dive for sunken Band-Aids at the bottom of a vast swimming pool. A family with three boys, all older—Alan, Steven, and J.P.—had moved into the house next door and invited me to play war with them or, to be more precise, to play a nurse who tended their battle wounds. More often there were long afternoons in Robbie's backyard, where she and I played badminton and tetherball or just rolled on the grass and looked up at clouds. By the end of July, my feet were hardened by shoelessness and my body was tan and lean from swimming.

He sent two letters a month. These were typewritten perfectly on blinding-white paper with a discreet but painstakingly considered letterhead, PAUL N. RUIN, that was always engraved, never printed. There was one for my mother with a child-support check and another for me with ten dollars. There was always a note, with a vaguely conspiratorial air.

> *Darling Inez,*
>
> *Money has a funny power on people. The ones who really care about it, and devote their lives to making lots of it, have always seemed like crazy, misguided people to me. Somebody once said to me (a bit meanly), "If you're so smart, how come you aren't rich?" But intelligence has nothing to do with making money. You just have to care a lot about money. (Which requires, actually, a kind of stupidity.) I've never cared about money. In fact, I care so little that it borders on shameful disregard.*
>
> *I'm saying all this because I want to give you an allowance. (You see, I can't wait to give some of my money away!) You can spend the*

allowance or save it, whatever you choose. But it comes without the
need to do chores and duties, etc. It will be a way for you to practice
having money. Your mother does not agree with my methods. But I
trust that you will do the chores she asks of you whether money is your
reward or not. (Otherwise you'll make me look bad, okay?)
    Love,
    Daddy

He called every week or so—asked about my classes and friends and made suggestions that I tended to ignore. "When you're playing war, why don't you ask the boys for your own gun, Inez?" he said. "Forget being a nurse." He didn't mention building a house in the headlands again—or me coming to live with him. Dreading the latter prospect, I never raised it.

I asked about Cary instead. He always chirped up. "Oh, she's great," he'd say. "She misses you! And always asks how you're doing. She was in Italy for a few weeks—in Tuscany. And now she's busy working on a dissertation. It's very interesting. It's about how music travels among cultures the way language does, and follows the same rhythmic tendencies. Do you know what a dissertation is?"

"No," I asked. "What?"

I'd become more confident, more outgoing. I asked more questions. I laughed more easily and smiled with my mouth open. A certain formality was dissolving. When I looked back on my life at six or seven, it was as though I had been only half awake, or slumbering in a coma. Now a veil had been lifted, a Halloween costume pulled off my head, and the colors of the world seemed greater in number and more subtle, and sounds more complex and mysterious. In late August, when I turned nine and threw a slumber party with the few girls who weren't away on trips, I felt so alive, so awake, and so happy that my mother's pleas for us to "get some sleep" seemed an awful prospect—the death of a consciousness that I'd only just discovered. The world seemed new and in need of reconsideration.

Birthday packages arrived, as they always did, but this year they seemed larger and grander than ever. My grandmother in San Benito, Marguerite Ruin, sent a tiny convertible sports car driven by a Barbie doll with a dark ponytail. She sent a copy of *Anne of Green Gables*, a book that I wouldn't read until years later, and a wooden keepsake box that spelled out INEZ on the lid with inlaid mother-of-pearl shadowed by bits of ebony. Two packages came from San Francisco, a small one from Cary Knowles— "Who's that?" my mother asked—with a set of blue-and-green beaded coin purses of varying sizes, each bulging with rings and unopened Cracker Jack prizes and tiny bottles of frosted nail polish. In a larger box, my father had sent a ball-shaped white transistor radio, an envelope with a birthday check for ninety dollars (for turning nine, he said), and, underneath, two sleeveless dresses in bright colors with bold swirling patterns and jagged stripes. The label said MARIMEKKO, FINLAND.

I lifted the dresses out of their tissue wrapping, grimaced, then quickly shoved them back inside.

"Maybe you'll change your mind," my mother said, a little cheerily. "They look big."

"Colors are nice," said Abuelita. "Your father must have picked them out just for you."

"Or maybe somebody else did," said my mother.

I looked down at the box—the way he wrote *"Inez Ruin"* so precisely, and the round pink San Francisco postmark—and my vision began to blur. The check felt very thin in my hand, nothing but paper. Not like a present. And suddenly, as I stood there, my mother circling nervously and Abuelita with her grim consolatory expression, I felt very far away from him. He didn't know me anymore. He didn't understand. Otherwise why would he have sent something so wrong?

"I guess I blew it," he said later, when he called with birthday wishes. "Your mother says you really hated the dresses. Is that so? Cary thought you'd look great in them. Do they fit at least?"

"No," I said, "there're way too big."

"Well, maybe there's still time."

But school began, and the dresses hung in the back of my closet, forgotten and stiff above a pile of clodhoppers that I had started refusing to wear. With the neighbor boys at a Catholic school across town and involved in sports all afternoon—a cease-fire declared and my nursing efforts no longer needed—I was happy to start fourth grade with Miss Roth, a young waif with a short Twiggy hairdo who married around Halloween and announced that her name was now Mrs. Shockley.

Quietly, from my desk in class, I contemplated my teacher's sudden shift in status. I looked for outward signs of unhappiness and deterioration. I searched the surface of her sallow face for wrinkles and her eyes for tiredness and stress. Was she still pretty? In a blast of warm weather in early November, when Mrs. Shockley came to school wearing a sleeveless dress, I focused on her armpit stubble and felt it to be, among other things, the dire sign of neglect and fading youth. And I wondered when, having exhausted her supply of good cheer and energy, Mrs. Shockley might leave her husband forever.

One sunny morning in November, my mother gave me a long bath and shampooed my hair. She put me on a stool in the kitchen and cut my bangs. A white dress with pink smocking—one that Abuelita had made for me—was pulled out of the closet, along with a pair of white tights and party shoes, and I was carefully dressed, put in the car, and driven out of Van Dale. The blue Mustang traveled along the ridge of the mountain into the foothills of Eagle Rock, where the houses were perched on stilts and hillsides overgrown with ice plant.

Pasadena unfolded at first as a gulch, an *arroyo seco,* at the end of a long, elegantly arching bridge. My mother and I crossed the bridge, and soon enough Pasadena became a city—seedy and ramshackle in the bright light of day, lined with nightclubs and dingy shops. As we headed down Orange Grove Boulevard, the stores and seediness disappeared and the city became a place of enormous houses and wide streets lined with palms and lawns wet from sprinklers. The houses were bigger than anything in Van Dale. They were mansions, lumbering stucco palaces with dark overhangs and slanted roofs, set way back from the curb or mostly unseen behind tall black iron gates or walls of cement. On New Year's Day, when the Rose Parade seemed to spontaneously arise, Orange Grove was congested and alive, but the rest of the year it had the hushed serenity of a cemetery. My mother drove farther into what seemed a green wilderness of wealth and gigantic pointy-finned Cadillacs, until we entered a neighborhood with even wider streets, bigger houses, taller palms. The air seemed lighter and cleaner. There was a sense of peace and invisible perfection. San Benito had the manicured beauty of a movie backdrop and the calm of heaven.

The sunlight was strong and hot, but it was dark inside my Grandmother Ruin's house, and cool. The air smelled like roasting turkey and onions and pumpkin and spices, and the large rooms contained small clusters of people who were holding cigarettes and glasses with liquids. I could hear murmuring and the tumbling of ice as the water glasses on the dining table were filled. Years later, when I thought back on the day, I wouldn't remember greeting anybody. I remembered only the library and being lost in its darkness. Above the fireplace there was a portrait of a man who looked like my father, except he had wild hair and a long, gray beard. On other walls there were maps of Kentucky and Virginia, bookshelves with worn volumes of Shakespeare and Toynbee and Gibbon, nautical guides, travel journals, and two sets of encyclopedias. There was a mantel clock, chintz slipcovers on the love seat that felt slick and icy, and on top of a small desk in the corner, there was a black telephone and a silver cigarette box lined with thin, fragrant wood.

A bowl of pale pink roses sat on a low table by the window, along with a selection of news and political magazines that my mother and Abuelita never had at their house in Van Dale, full of opinions they didn't share. The *National Review. U.S. News & World Report. Human Events.* But I never wanted to talk about politics in San Benito, where the house was full of people who appeared to agree strongly about everything—the war, civil rights, and, most particularly, that communists and unshaven hippies and Negroes were taking over the country. Sometimes I looked at the portrait of the hairy man over the mantel, my great-great-grandfather, and wondered if he was a hippie. But I kept that to myself. I was just a girl on my own, in transit, a half Ruin, a traveler from the modest outpost of Van Dale.

From the darkness of the library, I watched my mother in the foyer. She was buoyant, and her hair looked almost blue-black against her pale forehead. Her wool shift was tight in the bust—all her dresses were too tight lately—and there were half-moons of wetness under her arms. My Grandmother Ruin seemed very cool and relaxed in a blue knit skirt and cardigan, three strands of pearls, a lit cigarette. She was trying to convince my mother to stay at least for a drink.

"Oh, come now, Consuela. You must say hello to Julia and Ann. I've no idea where Paul is. He drifted off, as usual. But please do stay. Please. You must. Oh, dear, you look so well. How is Adela? How are things? *How are things?*"

My grandmother circled my mother with warmth and enthusiasm, the kind of unabashed acceptance that, I later learned, she reserved for servants and very rich friends. Did my mother want to stay for dinner that day? Maybe so. But, alone in the library, I remember wishing that she were gone already—and just imagining her vanishing from San Benito released me from the tension of our drive from Van Dale. I relaxed in the coolness and smell of camphor and spices, the tinkling of ice in glasses. I became part of the large spaces, the thick carpets, the low-light sconces, the shadows of the mysterious library where my dead grandfather, N.C., was rumored to have hidden money behind secret panels. In San Benito there were no great sweeps of feeling, no hysteria, no loud sounds, no intrusions or surprises. I was simply a granddaughter in a house with a butler who carried a silver tray and asked me if I wanted a

Shirley Temple. I was in San Benito, a hamlet inside a hamlet, a place where I didn't even need to think or have opinions or do anything for myself, because everybody had already done it for me.

I stood at the window of the library and studied the patio and the weird light that a huge green awning cast on everything below it. Bougainvillea was draped over the awning and trees like garlands, like Mexican festival paper. There was a Spanish theme to most everything in the big Spanish house—wrought-iron tables, archways, terra-cotta tile floors—and a fountain spluttered into a clam shell on a mossy brick wall. My grandparents had raised three children there, my father and his two older sisters, indulged them with handmade clothes and music lessons and eggs Benedict brunches at the Vista del Arroyo Country Club, things my father came to reject and criticize. When he returned for holidays and illnesses, he wore a rumpled suit and black knit tie and agony on his face. For years I thought the agony was about Easter or Christmas or Thanksgiving—he hated all holidays—or maybe just about me.

The patio had a brick floor with a crisscrossing pattern that was hard to sweep, according to Jose, my grandmother's gardener and handyman who always prodded me to talk with him in Spanish. Green canvas chairs were set up in semicircles. There was a swinging sofa that was awkward to sit down on, teetering tables for drinks, and carved wooden boxes of more cigarettes. Beyond, a flat sweep of Kentucky bluegrass was kept dense and low for croquet. On the other side of a hedge and a massive California live oak, there was a rectangular-shaped swimming pool edged in Mexican tile, a pool house that smelled peppery with mold, and a brick barbecue that was never used.

From the window I noticed movement on the small pathway that led to the pool. One of my four cousins from Newport Beach, I assumed. I pressed close to the screen door, hoping for a better look. A boy was coming down the gravel path, behind a wall of shrubs and trees. I saw the top of his head bouncing above a hedge. I caught bits of his torso, his shoulders, covered in a brown corduroy jacket. I saw his legs—and jeans. He was picking up gravel from the pathway and throwing it ahead of him. He was somebody new.

I stepped outside. The air was warmer under the hot awning.

He was tall and lean—long arms and long, spindly legs. His hair was limp and dark, but lighter on the ends, as if he'd spent the summer in the sun. When he turned his head to the side, I saw his pale face and the edge of his profile—a nose that was already prominent, a high forehead, full lips above a long chin. He moved with an energetic grace, a kind of strange happiness that wasn't oblivious as much as expectant, as though every moment that bloomed before him were a surprise. He was radiant, so radiant, and I kept my eyes on him and then crossed the patio as loudly as I could.

He didn't seem to hear me. I stepped down to the pathway, scuffing my party shoes on the gravel. Then I kicked some gravel ahead.

He turned. "Hello."

"Hello."

"I just climbed into the neighbor's yard."

"You did?"

His eyes were almost black.

"I met an old woman," he said. "She was wearing a bathrobe and shower cap. She was watering camellias. Do you know Vivi?"

"Who?"

"Vivi. Mrs. Swigg. She lives next door. She said that her husband died a few years ago watching the Watts riots on television—he had a heart attack—and now she's alone. Have you met her?"

He was staring at me so intensely that it was almost as if his words were just things coming out of his mouth—something to pass the time while he was staring. "She showed me her garden," he said. "She gave two camellia trees to the Huntington Library last year, she said. *Camellia japonica*. Do you know the names of plants?"

I said nothing.

"I guess not. Do you know the names of trees?"

I shook my head.

"That's a carrotwood," he said, pointing to an old tree with deep glossy green leaves and a wide canopy. "That's a live oak." He pointed to the heavy tree by the pool.

"I know about that one," I said, looking at the old oak. "Grandmother told me."

"Who?"

"Grandmother."

"You mean Marguerite?"

I nodded.

"Why don't you call her Marguerite?" He smiled. "I do."

That was when I knew. The look on his face, his princely tone. When he stepped into the sharp sunlight, his eyes became golden like my father's, and not black. But he had an accent—was he British or something? Was he twelve or thirteen? He was so darkly beautiful and confident. He knew plants. He'd climbed over the wall. And there was something about his hair. . . . It fell almost to his shoulders, far longer than the hair of any boys in Van Dale. How did he come to have hair like that? He was so unlike the other Ruin cousins, or the second cousins, or the blond, tennis-playing Orange County contingent who were always comparing yacht clubs and not looking me in the eyes.

"But she's my grandmother," I said.

"Don't be so boring," he said with a chuckle.

"What?"

"She's my grandmother, too," he said, shaking his head. "Don't you know anything? You're Inez. Aren't you?"

I nodded.

"And your father is Paul Ruin."

It was the way he said it—the whole name, *Paul Ruin*—the weight of it bearing down on him, the shadows stretching out around it, that made me so glad, suddenly.

"Whitman?"

"I've been waiting all morning," he said. "Didn't they say anything?"

He brushed his bangs away from his eyes and then grabbed my chubby hand to shake it. He bowed, sort of mock-formally. Then he leaned toward me to kiss my cheek, leaving behind a small smudge of wetness where, a minute later, I could still feel the cool air.

Halfway between the house and the street, in the middle of the stone pathway, Marguerite was standing with my mother. The two women were gesturing at the trees and azaleas and perfectly tended grass with glides of hand. My mother looked fleshy and round, bursting with ripeness. Marguerite looked dry and prunish, her bony shoulders holding up her knit suit like a wire hanger. She was doing most of the talking. She seemed to be looking at her former daughter-in-law with both regard and wariness, or perhaps just regret. Where there had once been only affection, there was something else between them now—a distance, a kind of canyon over which all their goodwill could not cross. The fact that they were halfway to the street seemed odd to me, too, as though Marguerite were slowly, and unconsciously, urging my mother back to her car.

Whitman and I were standing at the open door—looking out. "Is that your mother?" he whispered over my shoulder.

"Yes," I whispered back. "Where is yours?"

"She won't come anymore."

"Why not?"

He shrugged.

We heard a voice in the hallway behind us. It was Aunt Medora, the ancient second cousin from Kentucky, creeping toward us on her swollen feet that rose out of her wide pumps like bread dough. Whitman seemed stricken, eyes darting. Suddenly, as if we'd been able to read each other's mind, we ran to the center-hall stairs as fast as we could. We went up, two steps at a time, passing the etchings of the Alhambra which ascended on the staircase wall. We passed the tolling grandfather clock on the landing, its chimes growing louder and louder as we approached. In my mind it had become a stand-in for the absent N.C. His clock face poised on us, its mouth tolling and tolling, as though saying, *LOOK, LOOK, INEZ AND WHITMAN! They're here! Coming up the stairs!*

On the second floor, we flew down a long corridor and into a bedroom, then closed the door behind us. The bedroom had once been Aunt Ann's. It was decorated in floral chintz, matching curtains, spreads, chaise.

"Think anybody saw us?" Whitman asked, out of breath.

"No."

"I felt like hiding," he said.

"Me, too."

"Every time I'm here, I feel like that."

"You do?"

He shrugged, looked around. "So does our dad, you know. He's hiding out somewhere, or gone for a walk. Marguerite's been looking for the last hour—before you came."

Whitman. I'd been hearing his name for so long. I'd seen his first-grade picture and another one, a year later, when his front teeth were missing. In my mind I'd sealed him there—no front teeth—and it hadn't occurred to me that he'd be older than I. He'd lived in England and then Boston. His mother was an artist of some kind, designed gardens or painted gardens. Marguerite's photo albums were pocked with missing pictures of her.

"Where do you live? Boston?" I wanted to show that I knew something.

"Not for long," he said.

"What?"

"We're moving."

"Where?"

"Here." He pointed to the ground.

"San Benito?"

"God, no." He made a face—a grimace. "California somewhere. Not here. Are you kidding?" He shrugged again. "You're Mexican, aren't you?"

Just like that. I'll never forget it.

"My mother's half," I said, "and half Peruvian." He stared at me. And I must have been staring back, a little hard.

He shrugged. "It's no big deal. You don't have to look at me like that. I was just curious, that's all. How long are you staying—overnight?"

"How long are you staying?" I asked.

"Until the end of the weekend."

"I'm just here for dinner."

"Your mom, too?"

I shook my head.

"Oh, that's too bad. Marguerite was hoping she might stay. Have you ever seen his old room? Dad's. It's not really a bedroom anymore."

I followed him down a long hallway to a smaller, much sunnier wing of the second floor. We walked past a small, utilitarian bathroom and a tiny maid's room. "That's where Fitzy used to live," Whitman said. "Have you heard about her yet?" I shook my head. "Dad fell in love with her. Miss FitzWilliam. Marguerite didn't want to fire her, so Dad was moved into a bedroom farther away. But here," he said, pushing open a door, "is the bedroom that used to be his."

We entered a large room that was decorated more like an upstairs library than a bedroom. The walls were lined with shelves of books. A small television with a V-shaped antenna sat in the corner. There was a twin bed covered in upholstery fabric and pushed against the wall like a sofa. Above the door there was a framed photograph of Albert Einstein.

"I can't believe Marguerite allows that to stay," Whitman said, pointing to the photograph.

Whitman's things were tossed all over—clothes, sneakers, copies of *Surfer* magazine. An open duffel sat on the floor. He walked into a closet and pulled open a drawer in a built-in chest. He wanted to show me something he'd found. A few old swimming medals skidded around, their gold tone peeling off. There was a pocketwatch with a smashed glass, a tarnished silver thimble, and a box of assorted campaign buttons, about half of which said AU H2O 64.

"These couldn't be Dad's," he said. Digging deeper into the box of buttons, Whitman picked out two more. One button said, NO MORE FIRESIDE CHATS. Another said, WE DON'T WANT ELEANOR EITHER.

"Who's Eleanor?" I asked.

"Eleanor Roosevelt. *You've never heard of her?* N.C. hated the Roosevelts so much that he used to collect Roosevelt dimes to keep them out of circulation. My mother told me that. The Ruins are all knee-jerk."

"What?"

He pulled out the drawer farther and reached deep into it, extracting a circle of small, dark, brassy keys and shaking them like a baby rattle. "Not Dad, though. You know what he says. 'Don't vote—'"

"'It only encourages them,'" I said. We both laughed.

"Look here," Whitman said, reaching down to the back of the closet. Some framed pictures were stacked and leaning against the wall—a few diplomas, an award of some kind. Behind these were two hand-tinted photographs of a nude girl. She was standing in a pond or lake, kind of hunched over. Her breasts were small, almost flat. The water was so blue. Her skin was so pink. "I discovered this last night," Whitman said.

"Who is it?"

"Nobody," Whitman said. "That's the whole point. She's a nude. Doesn't matter who she is. Isn't that funny?"

I wasn't sure why it was funny—and there was something familiar about the girl. Who was she? But after a long look, my eyes left the naked girl and traveled around the bedroom. I studied the soft brown carpet, the heavy wooden blinds, the dark, solid feeling. Until that moment, as I stood there with Whitman, it had never occurred to me that my father had been a boy once. He'd been a boy in this very place. But aside from the shelves of books about card tricks and magic, the picture of Einstein, the diplomas, a few swimming medals I wasn't even sure were his, and maybe the nude girl, there was no trace of that boy anymore. Only Whitman, and his scattered clothes, and his open, empty duffel.

"Do you know how your mother met him?" he asked.

"How?"

"Oh, I have no idea," Whitman said. "Just wondering."

"She was dancing in New York. He came backstage."

"Oh," he said with a strange distance, or insincerity, as if he didn't believe anything I said. "Marguerite says your mother doesn't dance anymore."

"She does," I said.

"She does?"

"She's teaching."

"That must be fun."

"I lied," I said, sinking down on a twin bed against the wall. "She tried teaching but didn't like it. She couldn't stand all the girls who weren't any good, who didn't have any talent. She hated that. Sometimes I think she hates my father—our father—too."

"She's still in love with him," Whitman said.

"Really?"

"Mine, too. She told me."

"Oh." He understood everything. I could see that.

"Have you met Cary?" I asked, wanting to change the subject to something easier. "She's neat."

Whitman said nothing.

"Don't you think she's neat?"

He sat down on the bed and threw a gangly arm around my shoulders. "I think you're neat, Little Mexican. I thought I wouldn't like having a sister. But maybe I do. Now, come on, let's go find everybody."

My mother was standing by her blue Mustang, poised to climb inside. A small crowd of us were gathered around her. We'd already said good-bye, wished her well—*Come again, come again,* like she was still part of the family. And suddenly he appeared out of nowhere, bounding up the sidewalk of El Molino Avenue in a blousy shirt and a pair of paisley bell-bottoms. "Connie! Connie!" my father cried out. His hair looked long and shaggy. His mouth was open in a big, cunning smile.

"Where have you been?" Marguerite called, not too loudly. Her party voice.

My mother winced and then managed a courageous smile. It was hard to tell whether it was completely artificial or something pulled out from the depths. It was hopeful, that smile, and crumbling into a tremor. My father put his hand on her bare arm. Would they kiss hello?

"How can you stand it?" Whitman whispered in my ear. He grabbed my hand and we tore off down the service driveway, pulling at each other's hands and yelling out, comically, "Good-bye, everybody! Good-bye, good-bye!"

"Good-bye!"

"Good-bye!"

There was a burst of laughter behind us, the Ruins all waving and shouting, a wild release of tension, almost uncontrollable hysteria, and our father's booming theatrical laugh. When we got to the garage, Whitman stopped—out of breath.

"Wow! Your mother," he said, gasping. "She's so much prettier than mine."

1972

FOUR

Seventh Grade

Dear Inez,

How are things in ol' Van Dale? Is it really the home of the American Nazi Party? (I read that somewhere.) I hear reports from your mother, the ever-popular Consuela Garcia, that you attended a father-daughter dinner on the arm of somebody else's dad. Was that okay? Did I blow it again? Please air any complaints, large or medium or small. I can handle it. I really can, my dear.

Is Robbie's dad nice? Just wondering. He couldn't be as wonderful and charming as I am. Please don't tell me. I'll be devastated. . . .

Enclosed please find a postcard of Richard Nixon's birthplace. Ha! See you soon! And then what larks we'll have!

Love,

Dad

Robbie lived at the end of a quiet cul-de-sac on Valley View Road. No matter how hard I pedaled my orange ten-speed, it was a seven-minute ride from Abuelita's—uphill all the way, near Van Dale's illustrious mountains, where the houses were glassy and quiet, except for the yowling of coyotes at night. The Morrison house wasn't one of those, though. It was a cookie-cutter ranch with folksy Dutch flourishes—shiny white Dutch door, scalloped trim, a funny gambrel roof that looked as if a barn had fallen out of the sky and landed on some pimply stucco walls. Out front, where the cement sidewalk curved into a semicircle, dichondra grass grew in islands surrounded by a sea of white stones, and small sculpted topiaries sprang up from nowhere. All this was the creation of Dr. Morrison, an unassuming chiropractor with big bones and a gentle comb-over, who spent his Saturdays tenderly pruning and edging and mowing his enormous rectangle of lush lawn out back.

All together, there were seven Morrisons who varied in small degrees of blondness and ruddiness and girth. Boo and Bradford Morrison had spawned two sleepy-eyed boys who couldn't run very fast and three cherubic girls who were destined to spend adolescence and adulthood swinging from one fad diet to the next. Brad Jr. was the oldest offspring at nineteen, a romantic figure to me, particularly as his mission neared and he spent the summer immersed in the study of Japanese. I wasn't really sure what that meant—"Brad's mission"—or what he was supposed to be doing in Hiroshima, but by the rules of the Mormon Church, he was allowed to call home only twice a year now, on Christmas and his mother's birthday. All other contact was by mail.

Next in line of Morrison offspring was Brenda, a lumbering strawberry blonde with a machine-gun laugh and so many freckles that if you stood far away from her, she almost looked tan. Like Brad Jr., at summer's end she had departed the house on Valley View Road—been packed up and driven across the deserts of California and Nevada to Brigham Young University in Utah, where she had begun college.

After Brenda there'd been a lull in fertility, a span of five or six years during which Dr. and Mrs. Morrison prayed a great deal, consulted a specialist, and were on the verge of adopting—they'd always wanted a big family—when they discovered that another baby was on the way. A miracle. A godsend. That story about Robbie, which was recounted many

times to me, always fit with the rest of her. She brought surprise and relief wherever she wandered. Not that Brad was sullen or Brenda dis-
agreeable. But in a family of seemingly good-natured and uncomplicated
pleasers, Robbie was, by far, the most exuberant. She shouted herself
hoarse at football games, had trouble staying seated during spelling bee,
and managed to avoid being mean to anybody but, at the same time,
never seemed fake. And if she'd been troubled by anything in her life—
her chubbiness, her paltry allowance, her wardrobe of clothes made from
McCall's and Butterick patterns, or her irritating younger brother and sister, whom she was forced to baby-sit weekday afternoons—no one but
God could have known. She was upbeat, almost pathologically so.

Mornings we walked to school together, Robbie descending into the
flats of Van Dale and ringing our doorbell. In the afternoons we were
shuttled home by her mother, who routinely pulled up to Eleanor J. Trup-
ple Junior High between twenty and thirty minutes late, a harried figure
behind the wheel of a dented gold Impala.

"Hola!" Mrs. Morrison shouted, the window of the Impala rolled down.
She and Dr. Morrison had met in Guadalajara, on a church trip, and they
continued to be great lovers of Mexico—and thrilled to inflict their bad
Spanish on me. *"Nos tienes arretos ahora! Dos o tres solamente."*

"Just a few stops today," I whispered to Robbie.

"Oh, *Mommmm,*" Robbie whined as she got into the car, but even her
adolescent moans had a joyful, half-serious sound. "Are we going to miss
our show?"

There were always stops. And there were always a few more than Mrs.
Morrison said there'd be. Pulling up to the no-parking zone of retail
shops and craft stores, she was always in need of posterboard, some colored yarn, or collage glue. She drove crazily and made dangerous U-turns.
She never seemed entirely in control of her destiny, as if some higher
power were guiding her. Sometimes Robbie and I were squeezed in the
back along with painted sets for an upcoming musical or cakes in wobbling Tupperware containers. Sometimes we were asked to pitch in—

otherwise we might not get home in time for *General Hospital,* our obsession since midsummer.

"Oh, it'll be just a few seconds, Robbie doll," Mrs. Morrison said. "Inny, you don't mind, do you?"

On this particular September day, there were quilting squares to pick up and plaster leaves for a "giving tree," whatever that was. On other days there were "it'll be just a second, Robbie doll" visits to convalescent homes, rehabilitation centers, the Y, and several other Mormon churches. Boo Morrison was always on the road in her dented Impala, spreading herself too thin and making deliveries—spaghetti and meatballs to somebody who'd been ill, lemon chews and chocolate chop suey cookies for a bake sale, hand-sewn costumes for a play. No religious organization put on more Broadway musicals than the Mormons in L.A. But while the rest of the world was belting out new tunes from *Hair* and *Jesus Christ Superstar,* Robbie's church was regaling Van Dale with reprises of *Seven Brides for Seven Brothers.*

Robbie and I disappeared quickly inside the Morrison house once the errands were done—tearing straight for the den, where Resa and Ron, the younger Morrisons, were already planted in front of the television. Wrenching them away and gaining control of the appliance was an ugly struggle that Robbie won on a regular basis, even though "the little guys," as they were always called, had dibs because they'd gotten home first.

"Our show is on," Robbie said.

"Who cares?" said one of the littles.

"Me, I care," said Robbie.

"We were here first."

"But I'm in charge, you little guys!"

"We were home first."

"But I'm in charge!" Robbie hollered. "*Mooooommm!* Aren't I in charge?"

With Brad and Brenda away and Mrs. Morrison constantly on the go, it sometimes seemed that Robbie was running the house. Or she and I were. I was a fixture on Valley View Road. Aside from the afternoons when Robbie and I had volleyball practice, almost every weekday afternoon, rain or shine, we'd linger inside the Morrison house until four-thirty, when *Dark Shadows* ended, and then wander into Boo Morrison's bathroom to experiment with her impressive selection of cosmetics and ash blond hairpieces.

I knew my way around Mrs. Morrison's closet. She favored turquoise and aqua dresses with short jackets, polka-dot blouses, peach-colored scarves. In her shower stall, there were pieces of white knit underwear draped over the curtain bars. These mysterious Mormon "garments," as they were called, looked frontierish, something a cowboy would wear under his jeans in *Bonanza* or *Gunsmoke*. As for the Morrison kitchen, I knew my way around that, too. The chocolate chips were kept in a cabinet over the electric cooktop. Peanut butter cookies, when they existed, were stashed in an aluminum canister with penguins on it. The jar was lined with white porcelain, like an ice bucket. It probably was an ice bucket, too. But since the Morrisons never drank alcohol or served cocktails, I'm not sure they'd have known.

Near the pass-through to the breakfast nook, there was a ledge or countertop piled with church directories, newsletters, *Ensign* magazines, book bags, keys, sunglasses, nail polish. The cleaning and straightening of the house was the responsibility of Robbie and her busy mother, and therefore the place was always in total disarray. On a juice can with the label peeled off, the word "tithing" had been written in black marker. Ten percent of all the Morrison kids' allowances, birthday cash, baby-sitting money, or any other income that they might bring in went into the can—and was sent to the church in monthly increments.

Most nights Dr. Morrison arrived home in time for a late dinner, sometimes eaten all by himself—reheated casseroles, hamburgers, tacos, never a production—and afterward, to relax, he played an electric organ in the Morrisons' sunken aqua-blue living room and fell asleep to his own music. Robbie and I would hear the organ throbbing on one chord for a very long time, then discover that Dr. Morrison had drifted off in the middle of "Fever" or "Look at Me."

After dinner that night, Robbie and I asked permission to go to 31 Flavors. It was a warm Friday, and the crickets were chirping, and the air on the Morrisons' cinder-block patio had a wonderful, free, end-of-summer feeling that seemed to call for an ice cream sundae. I remember that we kept it quiet—so the littles wouldn't beg to tag along. Dr. Morrison gave us a few dollars and told us to come home before dark.

Robbie and I headed off—down Valley View Road and our old route to elementary school. It seemed like another lifetime ago that we'd graduated from sixth grade. I half wondered if Mrs. Craig and Mrs. Shockley and all the rest of them were still alive. Robbie and I trooped along in our after-school duds—cutoffs with long denim strings hanging down and tickling our thighs, little T-shirts that sometimes revealed bits of tummy, and flip-flop sandals. We'd grown our hair out—it was long and unbrushed and fell down our backs like clumps of dead seaweed. We were always looking for cures for split ends, among other things.

"What's that stuff your cousin tried for greasy hair?" Robbie asked.

"Pissed," I said.

"That's right. Pssssssst," Robbie said. "Dry shampoo."

"It comes in a can. You spray it on. It's white, like that fake snow you spray on Christmas trees," I said. "Flocking. You get a blast of white foam on your head."

"Oh, gosh!" Robbie squealed.

"And then it dries clear, and you brush your hair, and it's not greasy anymore. Lisa says it really works. You know, like, in an emergency."

Nothing had come between Robbie and me for five years, since we'd been the two best readers in Mrs. Kinney's second-grade class. No boy had driven us apart. No other girlfriends—and we shared many—had threatened our bond either. For two summers in a row, we'd survived Camp Ka-u-la, a dilapidated campground near Frasier National Park with torn canvas tents and no flush toilets, run by the Camp Fire Girls.

More recently we'd spent two weeks in a stuffy cabin at Camp Fox, in a remote corner of Catalina Island with wild pigs, where Robbie and I had been urged to accept Jesus into our hearts during a secret hilltop ceremony next to a huge white cross, and we did. We were urged to read *Good News for Modern Man,* a tepid adaptation of the New Testament for young readers, and we did that, too.

Robbie and I never needed to pledge our devotion to each other, though. That was a given. We spoke in squeaky voices to each other, did impressions of Mr. Shroeder, our super tall French teacher, shared a four-year crush on Dr. Mark Toland of *One Life to Live* (played by Tommy Lee Jones), and indulged each other with reminiscences about dead pets. Robbie told the story, over and over, of finding her parrot Lolita dead at the bottom of her cage—how scary Lolita's eyes looked—but it took several years before she revealed that Dr. Morrison had backed over Ruffy, the old spaniel that predated me, in his Cadillac DeVille.

I never talked much about my father. He and Cary seemed a world away from Van Dale, and their lives indescribable. Robbie had never met my father. Would she have liked him? Would she have seen his charm or just his weirdness? He was busier than ever in those days—his computer project in Berkeley had become a full-blown company. He had a partner, Don Harrison, and an office near our old house in Menlo Park. He rarely ventured into Van Dale in any case. We met up in San Benito or at Marguerite's beach house in Laguna. As for his personal life, I wasn't sure that Robbie would understand that either.

My mother became a focus of fascination instead. The previous year she had begun dating Rod Weeger, the coach of the eighth-grade boys' basketball team at E. J. Truppel. It was funny how awkward my mother was about the whole thing at first. She could barely say his name out loud. They saw each other on weekends, but later on, as the romance endured, he came around on weekdays, too. Coach Weeger was a pleasant guy, and even-tempered. He was a bit taller than my mother, had light brown hair, a waistless athletic build, a perpetual tan, and pants that rode so high on his body that they seemed belted under his armpits. On weekends, when he wasn't playing golf or tennis or watching sports on TV, he'd arrive in his ancient VW wagon for dinner. It was always the same: a Spencer steak with A.1. steak sauce, a baked potato drowning in butter and sour cream, an iceberg lettuce salad splashed with Good Seasonings dressing that my mother made in a special "Good Seasonings" cruet. He and my mother drank Coors beer in tiny cans and sometimes daiquiris, which made my mother laugh really loud. When she did that—laughed so loud—Coach Weeger looked at her in a haze of love, like he couldn't believe his luck, and I always left the room.

Robbie acted as if the thing between my mother and Coach Weeger were as fantastic as something transpiring on *All My Children,* like when super aged Dr. Joe Martin fell in love with Ruth, the nurse with dentures on the seventh floor. It was interesting, as far as I was concerned, but not all that romantic. And when Robbie grew tired of asking me about it, she sometimes asked me about Whitman.

"How's your brother?" She asked nonchalantly as we walked to 31 Flavors, like it didn't matter. But I knew it did. "Have you heard from him?"

"Next weekend I'm seeing him. We're flying up to San Francisco together."

My brother loomed over our universe, mine and Robbie's, like a figure of fantasy who might float in from HippieWorld at any moment. He and his mother lived in Santa Barbara for a couple years, in the guest cottage on some estate, before moving to a communal farm in Ojala. Patricia kept to herself, never came to San Benito, but Whitman liked to describe how she was overhauling the grounds and gardens of the Theosophical Society and attending teachings by Krishnamurti, an Indian mystic who drew crowds of followers—but not anybody in Van Dale from what I could tell. Whitman liked to play the mystic, too, in those days. He was always making predictions, like when another earthquake was supposed to strike California and make it fall into the ocean. He'd grown taller and darker, and his hair fell in a great shaggy disarray about his shoulders. It went perfectly with his ratty clothes, Jesus sandals, vegetarian diet, and a feminine-seeming Guatemalan pouch worn across his chest that drove Marguerite totally nuts. But you had to love him. Everybody did. He was friendly and liked people. He'd stayed at our house twice—just came and happily hung out, calling Abuelita "Mrs. G," and my mother "Connie Mama." Everybody got a nickname. I was always "Little Mexican" and Robbie was "The Latter-Day Morrison."

Whitman brought something exciting into our lives—and made us feel, for a time anyway, like we were living in HippieWorld with him. One summer night, after he and Robbie and I had gone swimming up the street, at Christa Nixon's house, we came back to Abuelita's and turned off all the lights in the house. Whitman lit some incense. Then he brought my little portable stereo into the living room, put a Joni Mitchell album on the turntable, and made us listen to the songs in the dark.

Mostly, though, Whitman talked about surfing: the shape of waves, the direction of the wind, weather patterns, the creation of tropical storms, the pull of currents and riptides. I'm not sure why, but Robbie and I were enthralled. He laughed at our jokes, I guess, and told us we were cute. Despite what we must have looked like then—the acne flare-ups, the oily hair, and the unwanted budding of our breasts—whatever Whitman said, we believed.

"What are you getting?" Robbie asked when we were about a block away from the ice cream store. "Hot fudge sundae?"

"Hot fudge," I said, "with two scoops of chocolate mint."

Whitman had all kinds of surfboards—and equipment. Wax, wetsuits, racks for the car. He had stories about his surf heroes and famous surfing spots around the world. Over the summer I'd gotten a complete indoctrination to this world when we'd met up with our father for two weeks at Marguerite's shingled house on Moss Cove. The house was crowded with cousins and other relatives who had also chosen the second half of June for a sandy and somewhat alcoholic Ruin family holiday. There were rounds of gin and tonics. Rounds of cribbage and bridge. There were packs of cigarettes smoked. There were dozens of ruby red grapefruit halves consumed at breakfast and bowls and bowls of cereal consumed with table cream before bed at night.

Whitman vanished early in the morning to surf at Big Corona or Salt Creek or sometimes the Wedge in Newport and didn't reappear until late afternoon—the sleeves and top half of his wetsuit peeled off and curling below his skinny waist. My father spent his days philosophizing with an Irvine physics professor who lived nearby or locked in ugly debates about the war with his sister Ann, whose car was plastered with RE-ELECT NIXON bumper stickers. And I, who had long ago decided that my cousin Lisa was far better company than my gloomy and complicated father, spent mornings and afternoons with my body planted on the sand beside hers, greased up before the sun like a roasting chicken.

Each night I was torn away from Lisa and the family bridge game to attend the movies with my father and Whitman—made more bearable when a system for picking the films was established. We took turns choosing a movie, and no matter what it was, all three of us had to attend. For my father's first two turns, he'd taken us to see an incredibly bloody movie, *The French Connection,* which I wasn't allowed to tell Abuelita or my mother about, and three days later a documentary about Woodstock, which introduced me to full frontal nudity and frequent use of the word "balling." When Whitman's turns came, he picked a smattering of low-budget surf films—they looked like home movies and had no audio but for the dull strumming of a guitar. The soggy old cinema where they played was near the pier in Huntington Beach and had a distinct beach smell: mold, urine, and sour wine mingled with freshly lit marijuana.

When my nights came, I was excited to exercise my power. I took my father and Whitman to see *The Sound of Music,* a movie that rendered them speechless. (I assumed this was a positive sign.) Three nights later, during a hot spell, I chose a movie that I'd been longing to see: *Gone with the Wind.*

"Well?" my father said afterward in the car.

I was throbbing with feeling—and a strange ache, oddly enough, for the Civil War days. Those dresses! The dancing! And since the ending of the film, when Rhett Butler walks off—maybe the whole thing reminded me of my mom and how stupid she'd been, *how could Scarlett possibly let him go?*—I'd had to stifle a bout of open-mouthed sobbing.

"Awful," Whitman proclaimed. "The worst movie I've ever seen."

"*Really,* Whitman," my father said dryly. He seemed amused. "You don't think it's the greatest romance of all time?"

"It makes *Sound of Music* look like a masterpiece," Whitman said, speaking for the first time of my previous choice. "It was so artificial and racist—and disgusting. Plus, the whole thing takes place indoors. Oh, except maybe the burning of Atlanta—that was outside—and so phony. Inez, please *don't* say you really liked that?"

"Inez?" my father asked.

He looked in the rearview mirror at me. I was brushing my bangs away from my face, but later on I wondered if he thought I was wiping my eyes.

"I mean," Whitman continued, "what awful people, and that horrible bitch Scarlett O'—"

"*Okay! We get it!*" my father exploded. "You talk too much, Whitman! Do you know that? Just shut the hell up!"

My body was shaking—jangling, my heart pounding. The remainder of the ride back to Laguna was quiet, and the movie no longer seemed like a jewel of perfection that I was dying to see again with Robbie, but rather like something sick and wrong for having caused such a terrible rift.

My father parked the MG on the steep hillside next to Marguerite's, and both he and Whitman quickly evacuated the car. While I sat in my little cavelike space on the back ledge, I heard footsteps up the stairs to the bungalow. The beach-house door opened with a rusty squeak, closed, and then opened again. When I got out of the car, I heard waves breaking on the rocks at Moss Cove a block away. I looked up at the clear night sky over my head and into a field of stars.

My father liked to complain about the way Marguerite had furnished the beach house, grousing that it was absurdly formal, everything upholstered in damasks and striped satins—"she's from the East, where people still care about all that crap," he'd say—but as I entered its yellow light and walked beneath its low beamed ceiling that night, smelled the peppery mold in the shadows, and saw the figurines on the mantel, I remember feeling warm suddenly, and better about everything. It was a cozy house, and old-fashioned, and done in a woman's way—and that night I was tired of men.

I heard my father making a phone call from a tiny bedroom downstairs. Whitman was in the galley kitchen, pouring shredded wheat into a bowl. All the Ruins ate sugary cereal with cream before bed, and even Whitman had once said, "it's what killed off N.C." But there were no jokes out of Whitman that night. From the doorway I saw his fallen face and realized that he wasn't a boy anymore, exactly—broad shoulders, a beard growing on his cheeks and chin and upper lip.

"I don't care if you hated it," I said to him, under my breath. I pulled on the hem of my ragged cutoffs and smoothed my tank top. "You're entitled to your opinion."

Whitman watched me carefully—and the way I yanked at my clothes. His face was very still. He was holding the bowl of cereal in one large hand, a soup spoon hovering above it. "It's not that," he said.

I watched his mouth while he chewed, then caught his eyes, hard and lonely. He took a bite of cereal and looked like he was going to chew off the top of the spoon.

"What?" I asked. "What is it?"

"Nothing." And then he swallowed.

Cary arrived the next morning—a surprise—and was making pancakes before most of the house had come alive. One by one, as they straggled downstairs, she met our cousins, Newell and Amanda and Lisa and Lizzie. And she met Aunt Ann, when she returned from walking her dogs. After Whitman appeared, Cary asked him about Moss Cove and Barking Sands and other points of interest in Laguna, where she'd never been, and she found a way—as she usually did—to make things feel okay again. Effortlessly sunny and patient, a bit daffy, she had a presence that diluted the intensity of my father and made being with him bearable. Even Whitman returned to normal, as though he'd passed through the problems of the night, or beyond them, with a resiliency I wasn't sure that I myself possessed. And when my father insisted he wasn't interested in a trip to either Disneyland or the Sawdust Festival—"You'll have a terrible time, I'm sure of it"—Cary took us anyway.

It was a short drive along the coast highway and then into the rolling hills of Laguna Canyon to the Sawdust Festival, an annual craft fair. The summer traffic slowed us down, and the air grew warm as we drove inland. Looking for a parking space in a yellow field, Whitman rolled a joint and smoked it with Cary. I sat on my ledge in the back of the MG and pretended not to notice.

Arriving inside the gates of the festival, we found ourselves in another world. Most of the vendors and tourists were dressed in heavy Renaissance-style clothing—ladies in peasant blouses, bodices, long velvet gowns, and peaked hats. There were men in medieval court costumes and black leather. There were jugglers in harlequin patterns. There were mimes in whiteface and black knit caps. The smell of sweat was everywhere, and ripe body odor. Cary was wearing a calico granny dress and brown boots which had seemed a little out of place at the Ruin cottage—neither yacht-clubby nor sporty—but now I found myself wishing I'd worn something more medieval and fanciful than a pair of white bell-bottom jeans and a loud purple top.

Cary stopped at a booth. "Hey, Inez, why don't we have your cards read?"

"My cards?"

"Tarot cards." Whitman sighed wearily, looking over at the willowy blonde who was running the booth. "She's telling the future with them."

Cary got in line at the booth, behind a man with a reddish Afro and tiny glasses. His pants were baggy and gathered with a drawstring around his thin waist. I stepped closer and tried to see over the frizz of the man's hair. The willowy blonde had laid down six cards in the shape of a cross on the counter. Another four cards were arranged in a column down the right-hand side. Each card had an illustration and words below, in

French: *Le Magicien. L'Empress. Valet d'Epées.* I stared at one card with naked figures precariously positioned on a spinning wheel.

"*La Roue de Fortune,*" the reader said in a lilting, otherworldly accent to the man with the Afro. "The Wheel of Fortune." She pointed at the card with a thin finger weighed down with a huge ring. "The most recent sphere of action," she said. "This is what is happening now. Very intense. Are things intense?"

The man nodded.

"Way out," she said. "Inevitability. Fate. You are up against it, man. But it will also bring luck."

"Heavy," the man said.

"Yes," said the willowy girl, nodding slowly—as though each nod were bringing her closer to the realization of an eternal truth. "Get your mind around it."

I stepped up to the counter, and Cary pulled three dollars from a fabric pouch she was wearing over her shoulder. "Ask the cards a question," the reader said to me while handing over a thick pile of cards. "Ask and shuffle."

Wondering what to ask, I stopped for a moment and then shuffled the big cards clumsily. I handed them back, and the reader began to lay them down in the same cross configuration. When she was done, she pointed to a card on the left side. It was a queen who was standing with a long pole or staff in her hand. *Reine de Bâtons,* it said.

"Queen of Sticks," Cary said.

"Wands," the reader said, correcting her.

"Oh, right."

"You're going to encounter a powerful woman soon," the reader continued, looking only at me. "A kind woman. A good heart. A woman you can trust."

"That must be you!" I said to Cary.

"Yes!" Cary chirped merrily. "Don't you love her crown?"

"No," said the reader, her voice a bit grave. "I'm afraid it's a fair lady. Light-haired and pale. Like me."

Cary and I shared a look. Within seconds, Whitman appeared in a silly court jester's hat, and the strange moment dissolved. "Hey," he called out, "what's going to happen to you, Inez? That's the great mystery."

My father was waiting at home that night—with presents he'd bought during his day alone. He'd taken Whitman's van to the garage for an oil change. A bunch of peacock feathers had been found for Cary. He presented me with a paperback copy of *Great Expectations* that he'd gotten at a bookstore on the coast highway. We were alone in the beach house that night—the aunts and cousins at dinner or the movies or drinking at the neighbors'—and my father started reading my new book aloud. When his voice gave out, Whitman carried on, passing the book to Cary after a while.

As Cary read, my father and Whitman seemed okay with each other again—grievances repaired or forgotten. Tension gone. We were caught up in the book, the story of Pip, and we followed the boy from the windswept cemetery on the marsh to Miss Havisham's cobwebbed estate, from the heat of the forge to the mannered company of Estella. Sitting in the yellow light of Marguerite's living room, and on her taut damask chairs, listening to the sound of the waves and Cary's soft, careful voice, I felt suddenly, all at once, a great rush of feeling—as if I were part of something special and wonderful and very small, as though twine as thin and fragile as smoke surrounded the four of us—and was pulling us closer and closer.

"What larks!" my father said. "What larks, good chap, old Pip!"

In late August a package arrived for my birthday—a deck of tarot cards in a purple velvet pouch. There was a brief note.

Happy Birthday, Inez.
You are the neatest girl I've ever known. And may your future be full of great kindnesses and grand magic.
I love you.
Cary.

. . .

Robbie and I stalled at 31 Flavors, hung around by the drinking fountain and talking, digging into our sundae cups of ice cream, until we realized it was growing dark—if not dark already. We decided to take a shortcut home, even though it was forbidden. It went through a slightly less manicured part of town, and the streets were less traveled and not well lit. But we'd arrive home a few minutes sooner.

We walked almost in the middle of the road. The houses were dark, except for a few lights. When we heard a car, Robbie and I moved to the edge of the street. A white Corvair went by, driving slowly—almost as though the driver were looking at us. Was it Abuelita? I threw my hand up to wave at her, thinking we'd get a ride home. The car slowed again and might have stopped, I'm not sure. Then I noticed that it wasn't Abuelita's car at all. The black-and-yellow license plate was different, with different numbers and letters, and I quickly pulled my hand down to stop waving. I felt my heart thumping, a surge of embarrassment over a small mistake made.

"Who's that?" Robbie said.

"I thought it was Abuelita."

"They slowed down."

"I know."

"Probably because you waved."

"I know."

Robbie and I kept walking, engrossed in a discussion about split ends—we spent hours on this topic—and something my cousin Amanda had said. If you pulled on your hair in the shower, it grew out faster. That's what women in France did, Amanda said.

Up ahead I noticed a white Corvair parked on the street. *That's weird,* I remember thinking. *Another one.* As I drew closer, I looked at the license plate and realized it was same car that I'd seen a few minutes before, the one that had slowed down when I waved. My heart began beating quickly again. I was just about to grab Robbie's arm when the door of the car swung open. Falling out of the driver's seat and onto the street was a large, burly man wearing only a bra and a garter belt and stockings.

Robbie and I ran and ran, stumbling in our flip-flops. We went as fast as we could. We went as far as we could. I'm not sure if the Garter Belt Man, as we came to call him, even bothered to chase us. He seemed too fat for that—hadn't he groaned as he fell to the street? And there was something theatrical and pathetic about the way he'd burst out of the little Corvair, something that made us feel sorry for him. ("Poor misfit," Robbie said the next day.) For years afterward, in my dreams and nightmares, he'd turn up during times of anxiety and disquiet and change. Sometimes he chased me, this half-man/half-woman—this transforming person—but eventually I'd had the dream so many times that when he made an appearance, I'd laugh in my sleep. He seemed harmless, cartoonish. And he'd never really chased us, or appeared again. I'm not sure if the Van Dale police caught him or if he just moved on. But the night we finally saw him, Robbie and I ran all the way home, and just before arriving there, we made a pact we wouldn't tell a soul. I'm not sure why.

FIVE

Justine

The baby fat had vanished, and my body was as shapeless as my stork legs: I was a long tube of a girl. And I was always pulling on my bangs, to make them grow faster. And if you massaged olive oil and mayonnaise into your scalp, your hair really grew fast. That's what Amanda said anyway.

How does a girl grow up? Does she imagine herself a woman—and simply direct herself there? I nurtured opposing selves in those days, as though I were two people, or three, each of them incubating in separate honeycombs. One girl—the visible one—was settled innocently in Van Dale with Robbie and our shared collection of Nancy Drew mysteries. Another girl made trips to San Francisco in her knee socks and jumpers and saw *The Godfather* and *Bullitt* and sat in North Beach cafés drinking dark espresso with three packets of sugar. But there was a third girl, a nymph secluded in the deepest interior of me—in the same place where I prayed, made wishes on pennies, yearned for a boyfriend, and fantasized that I was living in a high-rise apartment with mirrored walls and track lighting and silver trays of decanted liquor. In that part of me, I resembled Emma Peel in *The Avengers* and was often a secret agent on a vague mission to save the country. Usually I was in the company of a male colleague, a fellow spy who looked like one of the men on *The Man from U.N.C.L.E.* I was frequently forced to spend the night in the same hotel room with this male colleague and share a bed—on a mission we pretended to be married, for the good of the country—where we would comically argue and fight for the sheets and then wind up rubbing up against each other and kissing. I was always clever and amusing. I wore catsuits or low-cut dresses and sometimes even had breasts. (The importance of them was just beginning to dawn on me.) If I happened to find myself alone in the afternoon, not at Robbie's, and I wasn't in the mood for breaking the house rules and watching *Dark Shadows* (it gave me nightmares), I sometimes crept into my mother's bedroom and tried on her gigantic bras. I stuffed them with knee socks and tights, three or four pairs in each cup. Then I gravitated to the back of her closet, where the flamenco dresses were stiff from neglect and the dance shoes were stacked in dust-covered boxes. I tried them on, too.

I prepared—as though for a long journey. I had grown tired of dolls and tea parties with my stuffed animals. I often forgot to bring Coco into my bed at night or felt too lazy to reach down and find the spot where the blanket had fallen on the floor. I contemplated dropping out of Camp Fire Girls. The uniform was so dorky I'd stopped wearing it to school on meeting days.

The mirror beckoned. And the open closet door. I was always standing slack-jawed in front of the closet in those days. Rays of sunlight came in from a tiny window, and I'd watch the dust motes settling on all the things that I didn't want to wear anymore. My hair was long and center-parted. My teeth were cinched by metal bands and wires. In my baggy cotton underwear, I looked into the void. What could I wear? Who would I be?

A large suitcase was sitting open on my bed. It was orange and made of soft rubbery pleather. It was creased to look like real leather, but it was stretchy and pliant and took the shape of the contents of the bag.

I'd packed a pair of white corduroy bell-bottoms, a clingy striped top with a long, pointy collar and the two Marimekko dresses from my father, which I now loved—even though they were a little tight and short and beat up, because I'd been in them all summer. I was still deciding about a navy blue polyester double-knit pea coat with gold buttons and matching miniskirt that were lying on the bed.

It was only October, but it would be freezing in San Francisco. It always was. San Francisco had the coldest, windiest, most inhospitable climate that I could imagine. (I visited in July once, and from Fort Point my father and I watched a yacht sail under the bridge. Everybody on deck was wearing a ski mask.) Inside a waterproof side compartment of the orange suitcase, I had packed all the toiletries and cosmetics that I would require for a weekend: a clear green Oral-B toothbrush, a small tube of new mint-flavored Crest, a tube of Blistex.

In a zippered compartment in the ceiling of the bag, I'd carefully stuffed Coco, a pack of tarot cards and a paperback copy of *Great Expectations* that I'd been reading for so long, since June, that the edges were worn and fuzzy.

Merlin was sitting on the bed next to the suitcase. He was gray and longhaired, with vibrant golden eyes. He was an outdoor cat—he had a penchant for catching lizards in the backyard, blue jays in the front—but I liked to sneak him into my pink bedroom at night and hide him under the bedsheets until he fell asleep. I liked the feeling of his soft fur on my newly shaven legs. I liked the vibration of his purring against my stomach. And even though Merlin was only slightly more domesticated than my old pet, Dr. Guinea Pig, who was buried in a shoe box under the avocado tree in the side yard, when I looked at Merlin, I felt an almost human connection with him. He was the first cat I'd ever known, really. He'd arrived, a stray, yowling out by the street. When Abuelita and I rushed out to the curb of Ardmore Road to investigate, Merlin was just standing there, imperious, and staring at us with hypnotic eyes.

The walls of my room were covered in striped pink wallpaper—the same paper that my mother had put up during our first summer in Van Dale—but it was pocked by stickers, ripped off in places, particularly near the twin bed where I slept. Posters had been tacked up: a large black-and-white image of Robert Redford in mustache and black cowboy hat from *Butch Cassidy and the Sundance Kid,* a picture of James Taylor in a blue work shirt from the album cover of *Sweet Baby James,* and a very tall and narrow poster of Wilt Chamberlain holding a basketball. Coach Weeger had given that poster to me—and made me into an L.A. Lakers fan.

On the desk where I did my homework and sometimes pretended to be a secretary working in a Manhattan office building was a pink Princess phone, three copies of *Mad* magazine with the sticker pages torn out, my copy of *Good News for Modern Man,* and buried below all that rubble, a photograph of Barnabas Collins, the lead vampire in *Dark Shadows,* torn from an old *TV Guide.* I had a slight thing for him.

The Princess phone rang. I jumped and shrieked. I didn't have time for a phone call—and I was always overreacting to things in those days, constantly edgy and spasmodic and shrieking at things that didn't need to be shrieked at.

"Pronto," I said, assuming it was my father on the line. He loved the gag greeting, the "I. P. Freely" and "County Morgue" stuff.

"Hey."

"Whitman?" I shrieked again.

"God, don't have a cow."

"What's up?" I asked. "Have you packed yet? You better be packed by now."

"Not quite. I still have to put my board inside a sleeping bag and then duct-tape it really tight," he said. "It'll look like a big silver mummy."

"You're bringing your surfboard?"

"Yup. I'm going to surf Rippers."

"Rippers?"

"Down by Half Moon Bay. A spot called Ripper Lane."

"Tomorrow?"

"That's why I'm calling," he said. "Looks like I'm not flying up until Saturday morning. The waves are too good here."

"Hey, no fair," I said, and then produced a loud moan. "No fair. No fair. I'll have to go to Alegrías without you."

"You'll live."

I huffed.

"Dad say anything to you about Justine?"

"Who?"

"His neighbor."

"Does she work at Harrison-Ruin?" I was confused—and feeling distracted, hurried. I was always frantic and distracted in those days, and thrown off. A terrible listener, too.

"No," Whitman said impatiently. "Forget it. I'll see you when I see you."

I walked through the stuffy airplane and into the cold air of the tubular jetway and emerged into the soaring spaces of the San Francisco International Airport. Beyond a rope and stanchion, I saw my father. What was he doing there? He never met me at the gate—ever.

His hand was up. It wasn't a tired wave exactly, but slower and much less theatrical than usual. A moody wave, a laid-back, philosophical wave, his right arm drifting ambivalently over his head.

Our eyes met, and he mouthed my name.

"What are you doing here?" I called out. I hadn't yet noticed his air of restraint, the mellow thing. He wasn't offering our oft-rehearsed greeting—the hands over the heart, the lovesick facial expression. He was just there, himself. In those days it was called "being real."

His hair was longer than the last time I'd seen him, and it covered his ears and was pushed back off his face by a pair of large aviator sunglasses on top of his head. He was wearing a collarless linen shirt starched very smooth, almost stiff—not tucked into his jeans but hanging straight down. Over that there was a long, black motorcycle jacket. We hugged for a while, and my cheek felt the crunch of hair under his partially unbuttoned shirt. When I rose on my tiptoes to kiss him, I smelled something very fresh—clean and herbal and powdery. I turned my face toward the regal figure nearby, a very tall woman with perfect posture and a taut, full-lipped smile. Her creamy linen dress was only a bit darker than her skin, which was so pale it looked almost blue. Her blond hair was twisted into a topknot that stood straight up from her skull.

"Inez," my father said, "I want you to meet my friend Justine."

She gave me a formal greeting while holding her smile—"How do you do?" in a gentle but halting voice. She didn't crouch or stoop when she talked to me. It was more of a bow. After she said hello, she said nothing—just searched my eyes as if waiting for a connection to form, or perhaps simply hoping to glimpse the real me, the unguarded me. After a few moments of failure, she stood erect again and stared into the depths of the airport lounge.

"Hi," I said finally. Usually when I met somebody new, it didn't take much to relax me. A joke. A shrug. A shared sense of something. But this seemed to be the kind of gesture Justine didn't know how to accomplish. She looked across the vast spaces as though hoping to find an exit door.

"Come on," my father said anxiously. He led the way to an escalator, and I followed up in the rear. I found myself staring at Justine's back—studying the weave of linen, the nape of slender neck, her absurd hairdo. My father became a blur in the background, a nonevent compared to the compelling mystery of this new person who was so fey and fragile and otherworldly. Stepping off the escalator and following my father to the grungy baggage-claim area, where the conveyor belt of bags was already streaming by, she moved with a bizarre combination of grace and stiffness, like a tragic queen.

She spoke to me again. This time trying a new approach—informal, almost countrified.

"You're only twelve and, gosh, so tall! You're a weed! You'll be tall as me someday. Pretty soon."

I smiled but kept my mouth closed to hide the braces, which probably made my smile as awkward as hers.

"You're both so tall—you and your brother," she said. "He was here a couple weeks ago. We had a great time. He's incredible, isn't he?"

I nodded, felt a twinge—a new feeling burbling up. Whitman had been trying to tell me about Justine, hadn't he? Staring at the black rubber baggage belt, I was hit by a sudden bolt of terror.

"He's coming, isn't he?" I said. "He's still coming tomorrow, isn't he?"

Justine paused, waiting for my father to answer that question, but when it was obvious that he'd been too far away to hear it, she spoke up. "Tomorrow. He's coming in the morning. And he's bringing his surfboard. Can you believe—"

"His surfboard?" I played dumb.

"There's a swell or a storm," Justine said. "The waves are supposed to be great all weekend. He didn't want to miss out. So we told him to bring his board and we'd all take him. Isn't that cool? It's so great that he digs surfing so much." She paused. "I can't wait to watch him—can you? Paul tells me you guys get along like gangbusters."

I mumbled some acknowledgment of this that Justine couldn't make out and that I didn't bother to repeat. Over the loudspeaker the baggage-claim number was announced in a startlingly loud and indistinct voice, and Justine jumped at the sound of it. She was skittish, even more skittish than I was. And she was shy, and a bit awkward. There was something wounded about her pale blue eyes. I smiled at her, finally, and wished more than ever that Whitman were arriving now with all his good cheer and asides and funny nicknames. His enormous surfboard would amuse and dominate and somehow put everybody at ease. Who was Justine anyway? Where was Cary?

"Hey, Dad! That's mine," I yelled out. The orange pleather bag was at the top of the conveyor belt, just about to drop down. I'd been planning this moment in my head all week. Obsessed with luggage and good taste, he'd hate the bag—really hate it—but then he'd laugh. Wouldn't he? It would be a great joke between us. We'd be laughing about it for years, I imagined. But just as the ugly orange case descended the belt, Justine swept her hand up, apparently to wipe a hair from her eyes—it seemed involuntary, like the shooing away of a fly or moth—and when her hand came down, it caught a string of grayish beads she was wearing around her neck. With another sweep of her hand, beads began dropping to the floor, scattering over the linoleum and rolling under the baggage claim and next to people's shoes.

"Oh, no!" she cried out, but only in a half whisper, as though she weren't capable of anything more forceful. *"My beads."* She bent over and faced the scuffed linoleum floor, picking up the tiny balls with long, slender fingers. But they kept rolling and scattering beyond her grasp. "Oh, I need to . . . Please . . . Could somebody help? The beads. They're Peruvian. *Pre-Columbian . . .* " She was on all fours, her thin arms reaching in every direction. As the passengers from the PSA flight gathered to collect their luggage, a crowd began to form around her. People bent over, people on their knees—people who previously, at the arrival gate and on the escalator, had been gaping at her in a kind of baffled amazement, as though she weren't quite real. Now, with a chance to help her or speak to her, men and women and children dropped to the floor—just as Justine herself rose—and they were searching the surface of the linoleum, the thin channels between tiles and the space under the conveyor belt of luggage, which was now moving, for any sight of her dull gray beads, which were, unfortunately, the very shade of the airport floor.

Justine stared down at all the people, and the dirty linoleum, and the beads, and held out her hands. She cupped them as though she were feeding pigeons, but instead of birdseed flying out of them, the strangers in the airport were dropping beads in.

My father took up a collection of them, withdrawing a large white pocket handkerchief from his motorcycle jacket—a perfectly laundered and pressed square of the thinnest linen imaginable—and unfolded it. He made a pouch with his fingers and then carefully poured in the beads. When he had finished gathering up all the rest, taken them from me and Justine and from the crowd of good citizens who were still discovering them in tiny cracks and crevices, he twisted the pouch into a ball and meticulously tied a knot to keep the beads from falling out.

Without one word of complaint about my hideous new suitcase, which had now circled the belt twice—or grousing that I continued to check my luggage instead of traveling with a small carry-on, as he had long advised—he led Justine and me out to the airport garage. There the tan MG was parked beside another sport scar, a very long, silver, bullet-shaped Lotus Elan. Justine's slender hand pulled out a key.

"Your father claims you don't mind being squashed into the back of his car," she said to me. "But, Inez, how can you possibly fit? You've got to stop being such a good sport."

She opened the thin door of the Lotus, and a cloud of powdery patchouli wafted out. "I was hoping you might drive back to the city with me."

I'd have preferred sitting with my father—no question—or even being scrunched into the back of the MG. But it seemed impossible to turn down Justine's offer when, suddenly, so much seemed to depend on our getting acquainted. Inside, the Lotus had a glossy wooden dashboard and an alluring array of dials. It was even lower to the ground than the MG, if that were possible. I stretched out my legs, now dotted in goose bumps, and pulled down on my navy blue polyester double-knit pea coat and skirt.

Justine positioned herself in front of the small steering wheel and drew a soft black leather driving glove over one hand. With the other she pulled out a hard red pack of cigarettes from the tiny glove box, removed one skinny brown cigarette, and twisted it into an ivory holder, which she held in her bare hand. "Do you mind?" she asked.

I shook my head.

"I probably shouldn't," Justine said. "I only wanted one because I guess I was feeling nervous to meet you."

I looked over at the MG, where my father was putting on a pair of black driving gloves, too. And then, together, the cars growled and drove off, first in single file—my father ahead—and then parallel in adjoining lanes of Highway 101. Once we were under way, my father began to run through his various driving gags and got us laughing. They were reliable, and funny—even after he'd done them dozens of times. He accelerated quickly, so the engine would explode with sound. He pretended to be having a heart attack—something he did almost every time I rode in the car with him—and fell over into the passenger seat as though dead. After resuming a normal driving position for a few minutes, he tried another tireless routine: He sank so low in his seat that his eyes were barely able to see over the dashboard, and it looked, to anyone else on the road, as if a child or, better still, a dwarf were driving the car.

"We're neighbors, your father and I," said Justine in a soft voice. "That's how we met."

"Oh."

I watched her hands on the wheel. There was something about her wrists, her long hands and fingers, and the way she moved—graceful, almost floating—that reminded me of my father. And of Marguerite, too.

"He really sort of rescued me," she continued. "I was having a very sad time. I was sort of sad and shut in. My marriage was falling apart, and I was so unhappy, crying all the time."

Her eyes stayed on the road. I wondered why on earth anybody would tell a story like that.

"I kept seeing your father coming up the hill on the Triumph—his motorcycle—and pulling into my turnaround. The driveway. And I kept thinking, *Who is that incredible-looking man? He's so handsome!* The more I looked at him, the more handsome he seemed." She stopped for a second. "You must know how handsome your father is."

"Yes." I nodded and pulled my pea coat tighter.

"And so when I saw him down there cleaning his bike one afternoon, I just opened the window of my apartment and shouted out, '*Hey, Triumph!* When do I get a ride?'"

We pulled in to the city, after a few long silences, drove up the steep hill into North Beach, and then veered into the driveway of my father's building, next to a space where two motorcycles were sitting. One had a purple gas tank; the other tank was orange.

My father got out of the MG, didn't say anything to Justine or me, just pointed at the bikes.

"Oh," she said with a little sound of surprise.

"Later?"

"Sure," she answered. "Do you want to come by after you get settled?" This unfathomable exchange ended, and Justine glided up to an iron gate next to my father's building and opened it with a key. She walked through a small courtyard and opened a glass door on the other side, and then she vanished.

"She's my neighbor," my father said as he stood with me in the lobby of his apartment building waiting for the small elevator. "That's her town house next door—has its own entrance. I used to see her come and go with her husband, Ricardo Monti. He's a race-car driver, sort of well known. And one day she was looking out her window and yelled, "Hey, Triumph!" And I yelled back, "Hey, Neighbor Girl!" And that was it. We've seen each other every day since. We've been hit pretty hard. Do you know what that means?"

I shuffled around and found a way to say yes that might hint, in an unsubtle teenage way, that I would be very relieved for this conversation to end. But, squeezed into the tiny elevator, my father continued, unabated, seeming not to sense any hesitation in me, or discomfort, as though his enthusiasm for the subject at hand were blinding.

"Isn't she spectacular?" When I said nothing, he kept on, excitedly.

"You'll see. She's very special. So kind and gentle. She's lived all over and speaks four or five languages. Her family used to own most of downtown. You know Polk Street, where all the queens are? Her father's a Polk. Anyway, she grew up here. Her mother lives in London—very proper, has a title. God, do I sound overly impressed? You know what I mean. It's all very interesting, and it makes her interesting in some ways. She's a Buddhist. Did she tell you that? Anyway, we get along like gangbusters, as they say. You know that expression, 'as they say'?" He chuckled. "Please be nice to her, Inez. Will you? She's very delicate—and been through a lot lately. She needs a friend."

He neglected to mention what happened to the famed Richardo Monti—but, more important, he had neglected to mention someone else. An hour later I made inquiries while he was grilling cheese sandwiches.

"Where's Cary?" I asked.

"Cary," he said. He flipped the sandwiches in the skillet and then pressed down on them with the back of the spatula. "Wonderful woman."

"What happened to her?"

"What do you mean, 'what happened?'"

"Did she die?"

"Of course not." His voice had an edge—and when he turned around, there were beads of sweat on his forehead. "Listen, if you aren't going to be reasonable, I won't either."

I left the kitchen for my familiar spot on the brown corduroy sofa, which, like the leather ledge in the back of the MG, I felt was mine. The sofa was where I slept, looked at the cartoons in the *New Yorker* and the nudes in *Playboy,* and where I watched TV. After a minute or so, my father came into the room and sat down on the arm of the sofa. He looked at me for a few moments—it seemed like an endless period of time— while I stared at the table.

"We're still friends," he said. "We're in touch. We talk. Cary finished her dissertation—that's all—and she went back to Italy for a while. She likes it there. Her mother lives there. And she has friends there. And there was no reason for her to stay in California." His eyes seemed hurt, and weary from having to explain himself. I wondered if by "friends" in Italy, he meant that Cary had other boyfriends.

"I'm not interested in getting married again," he went on. There was a long pause, during which he held my eyes, and then he added, "In fact, I'm really not into marriage. Period. I've done quite a lot of thinking about it and decided that it doesn't work."

"It doesn't?"

"It's a bad deal for everybody—particularly women, I'm afraid."

He was looking at the floor, just staring, almost like how he looked when he played flamenco. "Even more than my not wanting to be married again," he said, "I don't want any more children."

I nodded as though I understood perfectly. But I noticed that my father said the word "children" with the same slightly bitter tone that my mother used when she said "bar" and "bus" and "Las Vegas." A kind of angry sound.

"So?" I used a neutral voice that hid, I was certain, the hurt feelings I wasn't sure I had, but if I did, I really didn't want to discuss.

"*So?*" He seemed a little deflated, like he knew I was about to corner him.

"Why not?" I asked. "Why wouldn't you want more children?"

He didn't say anything for a while. Just looked at me. "Well," he said finally, "I wouldn't do that to you and Whitman."

I wasn't sure what Whitman and I had to do with any of this—or my father's plans for the future. Nor, frankly, at this moment did I feel like an enormous piece of my father's life.

"You guys are very important to me. Do you understand?"

I looked down at my fingers. They were fidgeting and beginning to peel off an oval of frosted nail polish I'd applied the week before. God, what was he talking about?

SIX

The White Tent

Justine's town house was very spare, even emptier than my father's apartment. It seemed quite odd to me—a large empty space punctuated with things I'd never seen anywhere, ever.

In the past my father's girlfriends entered our world and I never saw theirs. Marisa had come and gone without my knowing whether she lived in a house or an apartment. I'd never seen where Cary dwelled when she wasn't with us—it had never occurred to me that she might live somewhere on her own. So gaining entrance into the private world of Justine was a revelation of sorts and carried a certain thrill, a peek behind a forbidden curtain. But there was something troubling about it, too, for it made her seem excruciatingly real and, even worse, permanent.

Outside, we walked up to her iron gate. My father pulled out a key and unlocked a glass door that led to a flight of polished steps. As we ascended, the by-now-signature smell of Justine grew stronger—patchouli and cigarettes, a waft of lavender incense. At the top of the landing, a child's tricycle was parked on the wooden floor. It shocked me. Bikes belonged in driveways, or garages, or under the roofs of carports next to the family garbage cans. What was a bike doing inside? Was it ridden inside or out? And where was the child?

My father disappeared down a wide center hallway to find Justine—I heard a "Hello, darling" followed by a pause and then the sound of a kiss. I wandered into the stark living room. The windows looked out on the bay and Alcatraz—the same view my father had—but inside this cavernous space with its tall ceiling, I felt on the edge of the world gazing out. Dusk was settling, and the headlights of cars crossing the Bay Bridge were flickering on.

An enormous white leather sofa was pushed up against one wall. A carved wooden table held a bronze Buddha and a collection of smoking paraphernalia—a little urn filled with cigarettes, a silver cup of wooden matches, an abalone-shell ashtray, a small clay pipe, and a scattering of ivory cigarette holders. Aside from this corner of activity, which fascinated me, there was nothing else except a large white tent.

It stood square in the middle of the room. It was made of a very fine silk, or parachute nylon, and pulled taut with ropes and thin white rods. The ceiling of the tent formed a whimsical peak at the top.

"Cool, isn't it?" my father asked me, when he reentered the room alone.

A big white tent. Right in the middle of the room. "Yeah," I said, trying to seem underwhelmed. "Neat."

Justine appeared. She had changed into something else fluid and exotic, and she carried tasseled silk cushions for the floor. "Hello," she said to me with another uncomfortable smile, then went away, returning with a silver lantern. There was a lit candle inside it. She hooked the lantern high on the center pole of the tent so its walls became almost translucent and its peak a spire of light. "I'll make some tea," she said, then swept out of the room.

My father looked at me, and pointed at the glowing tent again. He nodded. I nodded back. Speechlessness seemed the appropriate reaction.

"Cool, isn't it?" he said, nodding again. "Or, as you always say, 'neat.'"

It *was* neat, as well as beautiful and playful and beckoning, if I'd had all those words at my disposal. But, for me, "neat" was meant to capture it all. The apartment was neat. The Lotus was neat. And watching those pre-Columbian beads scattering all over baggage claim had been kind of neat. What I really didn't love was Justine.

She was carrying a large kettle away from the stove when I came into the kitchen. There were hooks on the ceiling where copper pots and pans and bowls of all sizes were hanging. I had never seen a copper pan before. I had never seen pots hanging from a ceiling before either. And just as I was about to ask if she needed any help with preparations—as my mother and Abuelita had taught me to do—Justine turned to me.

"Chamomile or ginseng?" A tendril of hair fell away from her topknot.

"What?" I watched as she tried to pat the tendril in place, but it kept falling down.

"Which would you like?"

I wasn't sure what she meant.

"Chamomile helps you quiet down. Ginseng gives energy. Yin and yang." She was looking at me, still waiting for something.

My father popped his head in. "She's asking what kind of tea you'd like, Inez."

"Oh."

"Chamomile or ginseng," he said. "They are both kind of herbally tasting, except I guess the ginseng is a bit spicy. Yin and yang are male and female energy. I bet you've seen that yin/yang symbol—the circle with the black and white teardrops that fit together? It's sort of a hippie icon." He drew it on a little notepad to show me. "An ancient Chinese concept, but the hippies have taken it over as their own." He laughed and turned to Justine, "Hey, Neighbor Girl, that smells marvelous."

"Your favorite."

"I thought my new favorite was lops suchuan."

"Gunka nijing oolong."

They both laughed.

"Oh, *thaaaat's* right," he said merrily. "But let's not forget the effects of the red hibiscus. Wow. Wasn't it red?"

It was hard to burst in. Were they still talking about tea? "I'll have ginseng," I said finally.

"Ginseng?" Justine said, seeming startled, as though she'd forgotten I was in the room.

"Good choice!" my father said, shaking himself out of reverie. "You'll love this chamomile Justine's got. I'll have some, too."

Dinner at El Bodega remained largely the same long ritual. The restaurant was small—only big enough for six or eight tables—and the ceiling was low, creating a cozy space where Hector played guitar, served dinner after an endless wait, and his bony wife with armpit hair danced in the middle of the room while the clients ate paella. Justine seemed familiar with the drill, as though she'd been going there all her life.

"Pablo!"

Hector always called out my father's name, as if he hadn't just seen him the week before.

"Hola cabrón!" my father responded to his friend. "We'll have three paellas. And whatever questionable flamenco you're prepared to provide."

There were laughs and a few more harmless jabs. Then, once we'd settled into a booth, the men discussed a new classical guitar album by Julian Bream and an appearance in town over the week by flamenco guitarist Paco Peña. "Aside from that den of inequity, Alegrías, there's not much happening in town, flamenco-wise," Hector said. He leaned his heavy hands on the edge of our table. He was a burly guy with a thick head of hair and furry arms. "And I can't take Ernesto's dancing anymore. I mean, why doesn't he just put on a dress?"

"I know, I know," my father laughed. "That red sash! Antonio's good, though."

"Oh, sure. That cat plays better than anybody else around," Hector answered. "It's good for the scene that he stays in San Francisco. Although I'm not sure why he does."

Antonio was always discussed—and after a handful of Friday nights I'd spent watching the guitarist through the cigarette smoke at Alegrías, he seemed to me, and apparently to everyone, a fantastically attractive figure. *Manitas de plata.* He was still young—not much older than Whitman— and had the same dark looks as Whitman, and romantic hair that fell tragically in his eyes.

"Played a powerful *taranta* last week," my father said.

"I heard, I heard," said Hector. "He can bring it on, in spite of the jones. He's got a real—"

"I know." My father cut in.

"It's gotten so bad that—" Hector looked over at me and didn't continue. I was surprised, because I was usually invisible to him. We all were—the children or girlfriends of my father, probably because we had nothing intelligent to say about flamenco. So it was even more shocking when, in the next moment, Hector looked into my eyes.

"How's your mother?"

I froze, momentarily shaken.

"I was thinking about her this week," Hector continued, looking over at my father. "So gorgeous. Really added something to a production. Paco Peña was good, you know. But the troop is pretty bland. Didn't you think so, Pablo? Cotton legs and no passion. They don't have a Consuela Garcia."

"Well, who does?" my father said, chucking uncomfortably. He was hoping this subject would be dropped soon.

"Oh, well, that's true." Hector was studying me, as though searching my face for something he'd lost. "Where's she dancing these days?"

I felt myself growing hot—and I looked down at the table, almost involuntarily, when I realized that I was the only person at the table who knew the answer to Hector's question. My father never asked me about my mother. And now, coming from Hector—how did he know my mother?—the conversation felt so personal, particularly after all the years that he'd treated me like I didn't exist.

"She's taking time off," I said.

"Time off?" Hector looked over at my father, who shrugged. "What's she taking time off for?" Hector continued. "I mean, if she's not dancing what's she doing?"

Not wanting to launch into a long description or reveal too much, suddenly feeling protective about Mom—Hector couldn't possibly understand her or why she was dancing or not dancing—I came up with something as innocuous as possible. "Tennis," I said. "She's gotten into tennis." This was suitably bland information, and the focus of attention might turn elsewhere.

"*Tango?*" Hector asked.

My father perked up. "She's gotten into—"

"Tennis," I corrected.

The men shared a look and then returned their gaze to me, as if to demand elaboration. I felt a funny rush of power. I hadn't realized that my mother generated this kind of interest—now or at any time. I looked over at Justine and wondered if it was okay to keep going, but I did anyway.

"She's really good—a natural," I said with a swelling of pride, parroting a line that I'd heard Coach Weeger say. "She's dating the basketball coach at my school, and she's already better than him."

"Dating . . ." Hector had a twisted look on his face.

"*The basketball coach,*" my father finished.

There was another long silence.

Hector shook his head. "Playing tennis. Jesus God."

"I know," my father agreed.

"Can you imagine?"

"No."

"I'm so sorry," Justine leaned over with a solemn whisper, as though there'd been a death in my family—the cause of which had been the most gruesome accident imaginable. "Everybody says your mother was one of the great *flamencas* of her generation."

She was?

W hitman arrived at the airport the next morning. We waited for him at the gate—our new tradition—and he emerged with a sleepy face and bloodshot eyes. He was wearing a pair of army fatigues, a long-sleeved T-shirt that said JACKS SURFBOARDS, HUNTINGTON BEACH PIER, a necklace of brown beads, and a beige fisherman's sweater tied around his waist. His hair was below his shoulders and sun-bleached to copper on its wispy ends.

He walked up to Justine first—gave her a kiss on the cheek and greeted her in a startlingly loud voice, as though trying to yell her awkwardness away. (It seemed to work.) Then he bent down, gave me a kiss that turned into a hug. He whispered in my ear, "Hey. Looking good."

My father threw his arm around Whitman's shoulder, and they walked ahead, their voices rising in humor. Something about Whitman's bloodshot eyes. "Are you stoned?" I heard my father say. And then he and Whitman both smiled and broke into laughter. Whitman said something about "buds," and they laughed again. "Hope you saved some for me." Watching them from behind, I noticed that Whitman was as tall as my father now, but his body was stockier than my father's and seemed stronger. His arms were muscular, and his neck had thickened. As they turned their heads toward each other, I noticed a slightly changed feeling between them, a kind of distance or wariness or mutual respect—it was hard for me to know which. The fraternizing of equals, perhaps. In the old days, when Whitman first moved to California with Patricia, my father seemed to dote on him, encouraged his interests and eccentricities—and I'd always suspected that he favored my brother in some quiet, subtle way. They had male things in common, an interest in cars and motorcycles, natural history and physics, and they were always recounting some story about an explorer or military hero, Sir Edmund Hillary or Admiral Nelson. But now, since the summer, I guess, my father seemed to study Whitman with a judgmental eye. He was a man, and, I supposed, more was expected. My father seemed quick to criticize—or instruct. At the same time, I began to notice that my father was more lenient with me, still coddled me with flattery and indulgences. He doted on me and greeted almost every remark with an outburst of amusement and applause.

To Justine, though, my brother was like a young god—and capable of unleashing her most unguarded, enthusiastic self. At the baggage claim, when a handler emerged from a back room with Whitman's surfboard encased in the sleeping bag and wrapped in duct tape, Justine rushed over to the sleeping bag, threw her thin arms in the air, and exclaimed, "Far out!"

"It looks like a mummy!" I called out, excited.

"*Whitman,*" my father said, a little sourly. "What's with all that duct tape? Don't you think you might have overdone it? How are we going to get the board unpacked?"

We walked to the airport parking lot, where the two sports cars were parked together again. The men discussed wind resistance and aerodynamics—then attached four Styrofoam blocks to the roof of the MG. The mummy was carefully laid to rest on top and strapped on.

Justine and I rode in the Lotus—and I watched my father and Whitman talking in the MG as it moved along in traffic, a lane away. They seemed cheerful and buoyant. After a few minutes, a lit joint was passing between them.

Ripper Lane was a forbidding surf spot, called "Ripper Jacks" or simply "Rippers" by locals, and even then with an intonation of awe and wonder. There was no sand, no beach—only rocks, and most of them very pointy. The nonpointy ones were dotted here and there with sea lions that snarled and snapped at the air, when they woke up. Fog or morning haze hung over the spot, and waves seemed to loom out of nowhere and crash on the base of a low cliff. The kelp beds were so thick—an unusual variety with large pods the size of cannonballs—that when the waves rolled in, the pods rose up, too, and the surface of the swells looked like a seething tangle of snakes.

Aside from our pilgrimages to Fort Point—or the day my father took me across the bridge to the Marin Headlands—I had never been to the beach in Northern California. It was always too cold, too windy, and nothing like the beaches of the south, where the sand was toasty and the ocean warm enough for bathing in the spring and summer and sometimes into October. In the south, getting in the water didn't require much courage or planning. In the north it seemed to require both.

It was freezing at Rippers and damp inside the shadows of a eucalyptus grove where my father and Justine parked the MG and the Lotus. The eucalyptus trees smelled like mint, but a bitter mint, so strong that it almost burned your eyes. How did Whitman stand the cold? This ran through my mind as he stood by the side of the MG and unfastened the mummy from its blocks on top of the car. He unzipped the top of the sleeping bag and easily slipped the glistening green-and-blue board out of its casing, like a smooth bug emerging from a chrysalis, and leaned the board against a tree. He pulled off his army fatigues and wool sweater and slowly stretched into his long wetsuit.

Justine stood off by herself—not wanting to see Whitman changing, I suppose. She was wearing a black leather jacket, blue jeans, and a pair of high-heeled black boots. Her bracelets were heavy and abundant. Her hair was up in the topknot—but lots of tendrils were cascading down in the wind. To keep warm, my father wore a turtleneck under a heavy shearling jacket, and I'd put on three layers of clothes—all the tops that I'd brought for the weekend. When Justine saw me shivering, she opened the hatch of the Lotus and pulled out an enormous fur coat. "You better wear this," she said. Her face was pink from the cold, and her eyes were very blue and insistent.

"Chinchilla," Justine said, holding open the thick coat. It seemed like a huge dead animal with all its bones removed, and I stepped into the coat as if I were entering an entire room of fur. As soon as I got inside, I felt enveloped in warmth and the scent of patchouli.

The sky was gray and murky overhead—the color of the coat—and Whitman led us beyond the grove toward the open sky and where a narrow pathway ran along an edge of a cliff. There was something wild in the air, a kind of electricity and freshness from the sea spray and wind, and suddenly we were giddy, almost jubilant. We were all surfers now, as if Whitman had taken us into a new world and transformed us at the same time.

"Whitman, this is so exciting!" Justine cried out.

"Way out!" my father shouted. I'd never seen him look so happy to be anywhere—or so expectant of a good time.

As we drew closer to the water, the wind got stronger and whistled in my ears. I saw the gray ocean water far off. I heard Whitman say, "*Whoa,*" but it wasn't until we arrived at the bluff that I saw what he meant. There were huge waves, coming one after another and breaking onto the rocky cliff. There was only one other surfer in the water, as far as I could tell—neither male nor female, old or young. Just a dark speck, way out, with a long white board.

"Maybe this isn't a good idea," my father said to nobody in particular. Whitman was silent.

"Whaddya think?" my father said. He was treading lightly, I could tell—not wanting to spoil things.

Whitman was undeterred. He walked past us with his shiny board under his arm, the leash dangling on the ground behind him.

I looked for a comfortable place on the cliff to sit down and watch—but at the same time I worried about the borrowed coat. Justine and my father remained standing, so I did, too. Whitman climbed down a pathway in the cliff that led to the rocks below and disappeared for a minute below us, and then reappeared as he made his way across the rocks. He moved slowly, gingerly. By the time he reached the water, he was a small figure in the distance. He strode through five yards of shore break, then carefully lowered himself to the board and paddled out.

This seemed to take forever. He was on his belly. He paddled and paddled. When he arrived at the place in the water where the waves first rose to break, he stopped paddling and repositioned himself on the board. Then, after another long wait, he swerved his board around to face the shore and began paddling quickly, sometimes looking back at the wave forming over his shoulder. He stretched out, flattened himself against the board, paddled harder and faster, and tried to catch the wave as it began to curl. The wave was thick and moved slowly at first, then more and more quickly, and finally, as it collapsed, Whitman disappeared inside a cascade of white water and foam.

I waited to see his brown head bounce up to the top of the water again, but it didn't. I looked for shadows, for the darkness of his wetsuit.

"Jesus, where'd he go?" my father called out. The wind was strong, and it was hard to hear him.

"I don't—"

"Do you see . . . ?"

"I don't—"

My father looked at me kind of funny. He was trying not to get worked up. "Goddamn it, where is he?"

Down the beach we saw a dark head in the water. Whitman raised his arm over his head. We waved back.

Whitman tried to catch a few more waves, but his timing was off. Opportunities rose up, then were somehow never seized. Bored, I began to make circles in the dirt with my tennis shoes and practiced curling my tongue into a long tube and whistling through it. I pulled on my hair and wondered where we'd go for dinner and what movie we'd see, as I watched the gulls swooping down near the shoreline, felt the buffeting of wind on my numb face, and then became almost mesmerized, as though, surrendering to boredom, I had fallen into a kind of walking coma.

Whitman tried another wave—the quick turnaround, the rapid paddling, his body flattening down on the board. But in the glare of the morning sunlight, I lost sight of him. No sign of a head or dark wetsuit. My father must have lost sight, too, because he began pacing, back and forth, very close to the edge of the cliff. After another second or two—how much time, I don't know—he began to scramble down the bluff to the rocks.

"Paul!" Justine called out. Was she trying to stop him? The wild sage scratched my father's face and his zip-up boots were sliding on the dirt. He disappeared for a minute under the cliff face and then reappeared on the rocks below us. He stopped momentarily and studied the horizon, covering his brows with his hands and looking for Whitman. And then he began to wade into cold ocean water in his jeans and big brown jacket with a kind of unsteady panic that I had never seen, in him or anybody else. His head was swiveling back and forth, almost crazily, scanning the water's surface. His feet slipped on rocks. Why didn't he take his boots off? By the time he was nearly up to his waist, the thick waves were breaking on him and the shearling coat looked heavy, so heavy, so cumbersome, that it seemed impossible he could swim.

Just then I heard a voice far away. It's possible that I didn't really hear anything. But I had a feeling of something—I knew something—and I turned to look down the beach and saw Whitman's silhouette on a jetty. The glare was shimmering, almost blinding, but he was motionless—just standing and looking at the sea. The wind must have changed direction suddenly, for I thought I could hear him calling out, "Paul! Paul! Dad! Dad!"

"It's Whitman!" I yelled, kind of hysterically, and I began scrambling down the cliff. The fur coat kept catching on things and dragging on the ground, slowing me. I couldn't bear to look over my shoulder at Justine—just imagining her horror. "He's gone in!" I screamed in Whitman's direction, as if he would be able to hear me. "Dad's gone in!"

Whitman couldn't have heard me but must have seen me crawling down the cliff. He bent to set his board on the jetty, and then he ran toward the water again, yelling—sounds that barely registered against the surges of wind and falling waves. All I could see was his mouth opening, again and again, as he called my father's name, just as Paul was probably calling his.

My father was waist deep in the sea when there must have been another momentary ceasing of wind, a miraculous few seconds of quiet when he heard Whitman. He turned around suddenly, twisting to look back. Then his shoulders sank—an instant of relief, perhaps. A shrug. Then he threw his hands up in the air. Disbelief? Exasperation? Which was it? I remember studying every breath, every gesture and expression intently. He seemed to be acting as if a joke had been played on him, a cruel joke, on purpose.

The waves were breaking against his back as he approached the shore and fell to his knees a few times. He looked down at the water with disgust, as though he were angry at it, hating it. And he was still looking down at the ground of rocks when he reached Whitman and me on the jetty. He just kept going. He trudged, almost an overstated trudging. Like one of his gag walks.

"Wasn't that weird?" I called out as he passed by. But he didn't look up, just kept going—making his way up the cliff. And when he got to the top, he disappeared.

"He must be really mad," I said.

Whitman shook his head. "Asshole."

"Hey, it was really scary. He thought you were drowning, Whitman. He totally lost it."

I imagined that my father had stopped at the top of the cliff—that he'd gone to Justine. But when Whitman and I reached the bluff, she was standing alone, too. "Where'd he go?" Whitman said.

Justine had a defeated look on her face, and pointed to the eucalyptus grove, making no sound except for an exhalation of breath. He'd gone to the car. I remember wanting to run to him—to see how he was—but I hesitated, not wanting to face him either.

"What do we do now?" I said.

"This is ridiculous," said Whitman. "He's stoned. And he's acting like a child."

Justine had a look of disagreement on her face, but instead of saying anything, she began walking toward the grove. Whitman and I waited a few moments, then followed. About halfway, we heard Justine's shriek and quickened our pace. She was bent over next to the car—at first I thought she was screaming, or swooning, or hysterical. But it wasn't that. We drew closer and saw my father sitting in the driver's seat of the MG. He was smoking one of Justine's brown cigarettes in a long ivory holder. And he was completely nude, but for a road map over his lap.

"Hey, Whitman," he said, with a witheringly dry delivery, "nice bit of surfing."

Later on, after hot showers and lunch—and a special trip to Perignon Laundry to see if my father's shearling coat could be saved—we all sat through a matinee of *Lawrence of Arabia* at the Bay Theatre on Stockton and ate so much popcorn we decided to skip dinner. By sunset Whitman and I were left alone in the apartment. My father had slipped next door to spend the night.

"So what do you think?" Whitman said, sitting down on the arm of the brown corduroy sofa.

"Of what?"

"How the weekend's going so far."

We both laughed.

"Complete disaster," I said.

Whitman said nothing.

"Don't you think?"

He shrugged. The goal in those days—or maybe it was just a California thing—was not to make a big deal out of anything.

"What is that supposed to mean?" I asked.

"It is what it is."

"It is what it isn't," I said.

"You sound like a Zen monk."

"You're the hippie, not me."

"I'm a hippie? Who says?"

"Dad."

"Shit, *he's* wearing the love beads, not me."

I pulled at Whitman's necklace.

"These are rhino horn," he said, "for sexual power."

"You went to that war protest," I said, uneasy with the rhino-horn idea. "And you live on a commune."

"I live on a commune?" he said, a little mockingly. "I guess you're right, then. You're always right, Mexicali Rose. *I'm a hippie.* Just don't tell Marguerite." He picked up an issue of *Playboy* magazine that was sitting on the low white table and began flipping the pages. He looked at a cartoon, chuckled, then flipped the pages again. He found the centerfold and turned the magazine on end.

"So how do you like Justine?" he asked, his eyes not looking away from the page. "She seems to have a big effect on him."

"Yeah," I said. "Like, what's with the driving gloves?"

"Oh, God," he groaned, closing the magazine. "I know. And *Lawrence of Arabia* again. Do you think every time he gets a new girlfriend he'll make us watch it with her? I suppose it could be worse."

"What happened to Cary?" I asked.

"That's what I'm talking about. *Cary.*" Whitman rubbed his face, then sighed in a bored way. "Good riddance."

I thought of Cary's voice as she read aloud to us over the summer, or her smile, or the tarot cards in my suitcase that I'd brought for her to read in her kooky, amateurish way. Whitman had never liked her, I could see that now. But he and Justine—they had something. Hard to say what.

"Justine's so old," I said finally. "So grown up. So serious."

"It's about time," Whitman said.

My father and Justine did seem like a pair—their lanky frames and handsomeness, their strange, unearthly elegance. They had the same pervasive feeling of gloom, the same silliness. Their motorcycles. Their ultraspare taste in décor. Even their cars were about the same size. And even though Justine had tried to be kind to me, and open, she made me uncomfortable. Instead of bringing me closer to my father, as Cary had done, she made me feel like a suburban rube with cheap clothes and a weird best friend. ("She's really a Mormon?" Justine had asked in a breathy, incredulous voice. "Like ten wives sort of thing?") Since meeting her, I'd felt further and further away from my father, as if he had drifted to sea and become an island that I couldn't swim to anymore.

"Hey, don't get glum," Whitman said to me. "He's really in love. I've never seen him like this before."

Somehow I knew that—felt that—and it made everything worse.

"And anyway," he went on, "she's so rich, you know, and that might be fun."

"Money isn't fun," I said.

"No?" he said. "Well, you're wrong."

1973

SEVEN

Laguna Beach

This is my prevailing memory of Abuelita in my childhood: She made hot cereal in the morning and would leave the top of a double boiler full of congealing Roman Meal or Cream of Wheat for me when she left for work. I was supposed to have a bowl before school—no exceptions. Abuelita wasn't that fussy about anything else. She made few demands, had very few edges. I made jokes about "cold gruel" and "mush," but I ate it. Her belief in cooked cereal was something like my mother's belief in Jack La Lanne or, later, Werner Erhard. Cooked cereal was a way of life, like exercise or awareness, that would fortify me for the perils ahead. I never really questioned this, the same way that I didn't really think about who Abuelita was. Her existence seemed humdrum and practical to me, about working and saving money. I knew Abuelita—the smell of her hair, the smoothness of her hands, her round belly underneath her slick rayon dresses, the sound of her soft, muddled English—but my real knowledge of her, aside from her role as my caretaker and all the Roman Meal she cooked over the years, was profoundly incomplete.

Was she happy? Had life met her expectations—or not? I didn't wonder about such things until years later, when I began asking those questions of myself. Unlike the Ruins, who were complicated and self-indulgent and begged for your attention and analysis, Abuelita was modest and understated. She wasn't larger than life; she never tried to be. She was just Adela Traba Garcia—rarely sick, never late, utterly without drama, and her energy was unflagging. She was disciplined and methodical. She knew how to strive but didn't like to waste too much time on dreams. The Ruins were romantics—always finding ways to feel special about themselves and better than other people. Abuelita had a way of reducing everything to duty. She never mythologized or tried to beef up family ties with sentiment. She just left cooked cereal in the double boiler for me—and sometimes bacon rolled in a paper towel. She did my laundry, too, and cleaned the house, and picked avocados from the tree in the side yard and cut them into salads with a homemade lemony dressing. She did the household sewing—all hems and popped buttons. She made most of our meals, except when Coach Weeger came over and my mother wanted to demonstrate her abilities.

Aside from a few loved ones—and that would include her employer, who was like a god to her—people who lacked energy or discipline could come in for criticism from Abuelita. She was lenient and forgiving until an invisible line had been crossed. After that, people were expunged from her life. Her sister Rosa had been expunged. Her aunt and two cousins, who arrived in Van Dale and complained about America and then overstayed their welcome to the point of freeloading, not to mention ruining two green towels with bleach spots, were expunged. And then, in a previously unexplored category of expungement, there was Carlos "Charles" Garcia.

I was thirteen when I finally heard—from two chatty cousins visiting from Peru—how Abuelita had come to be alone. A reference to "La Habra" was blurted out, followed by cries of disbelief over my ignorance. A long story ensued, which was sprinkled with colorful distortions. Even if only half the story were true, Abuelita was still made more alive to me. Not that she wasn't real before, just mostly a composite person of my own creation—a pair of brown hands, a crusty double boiler of cereal, a pitcher of lemony salad dressing. Now she became something else: The story about her aloneness made her as big as the universe. If there was one story like this about Adela Traba Garcia, there must be others.

According to Ana and Alexita, my grandmother's cousins from Trujillo who drank too much coffee one morning and became enormously talkative, Charles Garcia was a tall and rather suave Mexican—he knew classical music, could play the piano. (They raved about this ability, as if a monkey had been miraculously taught to play Chopin.) Abuelita met this incredible man in the backyard of Mr. Feinman's house, where Charles was cleaning out a swimming-pool filter. He was dashing. He wore beautiful shirts. And he wiped his hands with a clean white handkerchief before he reached out to introduce himself. They were married several months later, during a brief window when Abuelita was susceptible to romance. My mother was born to great fanfare and excitement but soon became a source of concern and emotional distraction. Little Consuela never smiled—who heard of a baby that never smiled?—and my grandmother spent her days fixated on trying to make her daughter happy. When Consuela was five and started school, Charles began frequenting a Mexican social club in La Habra, often in the company of women who were not Abuelita. He was a flirt, an incorrigible playboy, and a fatally unserious person, according to the cousins. He lived to dance and drink—working was the lowest priority. Abuelita, who was consumed by productivity and breadwinning, let it go on, at first too busy to notice and later too proud to make demands. And then, about the time she took driving lessons and purchased her first car, a green Studebaker, Abuelita came to assemble in her mind a very pleasant future for herself without Charles Garcia. Not long after this vision felt complete, according to her two cousins, Abuelita prayed for her husband at Our Lady of Assumption Catholic Church on Kenneth Road, neatly packed his clothes in shopping bags, wrapping his shoes carefully in tissue—the way she'd been taught to pack for Mr. Feinman—and drove down to the pool-service company where he worked and placed the bags across the seat of his truck. She returned home just in time to greet the locksmith who was changing the locks and to double-check that the phone company had disconnected the line.

I never saw Abuelita naked. She dressed and undressed quietly in her room, which was bigger than mine or my mother's. Her clothes were practical and old-fashioned, all dresses in dark rayons and cottons. She did not care for the beach or pool. She did not own a bathing suit. She did not have a T-shirt or shorts or even a pair of pants. She had no "play clothes" to speak of, or casual things. She did not play. Working was her main thing, and making deposits in her savings account. Aside from driving—she loved her car—her only hobbies were knitting and some occasional crocheting. That's how she passed the idle hours at Mr. Feinman's, when the house was clean and all the meals were cooked. She killed time with knitting. Her hands moved like a machine—a blur of motion, needles clacking, and the sleeve of a sweater would begin accumulating in her lap. When I was little, I liked Abuelita's sweaters. I felt almost invincible in them. As I grew older, they filled me with shame and guilt, because I never wanted to wear them. They bore no resemblance to things in stores or things on TV.

My mother understood—one of the bonds we shared. Her relationship with Abuelita was fraught with similar strains of guilt and shame. Nobody in our lives would ever be as hardworking or selfless, or as innocuous, and this would prove to be achingly difficult to live with, which might explain why my mother and I never talked too much about Abuelita. There didn't seem a point. And that's why I waited until the gossipy cousins left for another part of California—for another relative's house where they could colorize family secrets—before I asked my mother about Charles Garcia. I was nervous and thought it would be a big deal. But my mother had a blasé look on her face as she confirmed most of the story and denied a few other parts (that I've left out here) and then casually changed the subject.

"Did anybody call for me this afternoon?" she asked.

My mother was mainly interested—feverishly—in two subjects in those days: tennis and real estate. Mornings, she took clients around Van Dale and Burbank and La Crescenta in a lumbering white Lincoln Continental Mark III coupe that swung into the hills where the glassy houses were and down into the flatlands with their cheap bungalows. Afternoons, she headed to the Van Dale Community Center courts to play tennis, quite often with the clients she'd previously been driving from stucco house to stucco house. My mother's discipline and athletic ability, which had been lying dormant for years, had finally found an outlet. The phone in our house was always ringing, and a notepad in our kitchen kept lists—court times, tournaments approaching, escrow news, closings. She registered for each Van Dale Community Center tennis tournament as soon as the clipboard went up—and quickly rose from solid C player to the top of the B's in the round-robin pyramid.

On the subject of my father, she had relaxed. Maybe Coach Weeger had something to do with it. Or maybe my descriptions of Justine had detonated like a canister of nerve gas over all my mother's remaining hopes and indecision. Now that my father was deemed unattainable, she didn't need to worry about whether she was supposed to be with him or wonder if a terrible mistake had been made. Released from a kind of mental prison, she had become energized—and overflowing with drive and ambition. She acquired new listings with ease. She paid off the Lincoln early. She opened a stock account at Morgan Stanley and upgraded her tennis wardrobe to beautiful knife-pleated skirts and monogrammed sleeveless polos. The bottom of her closet was a clumpy landscape of white Tretorns in various states of newness. As for evenings, she spent most of them on Ardmore Road returning phone calls. Weekends, after the tournaments and open houses, she reserved time for Coach, who, like me, found himself playing second or third fiddle to my mother's roaring new passion: her old self.

Not that I noticed too much. The love that I was angling for in those days came in the form of Patrick McClarty or Doug Daley or Kenny Frank, boys who lingered in my shady driveway after school or turned up at Robbie's to play tetherball. They didn't really talk to me. They didn't explain what they were doing in my driveway or at Robbie's. They showed up like stray dogs—and punched each other repeatedly on the upper arm or back, gave each other head noogies with their knuckles, and sometimes wrestled one another to the grass. When offered a basketball—or any kind of ball—they drifted to the middle of Ardmore Road, where they tossed and dribbled, passed and faked, and continued to not talk to me. It was a performance, mostly, to be watched with aloof but patient eyes from the front steps of my house. I was beginning to realize the quiet reserves of power that I could release with the tossing back of my long dark hair or the smoldering (I thought) of my closed-mouth smile. And as much as I might be silently aching and unable to sleep due to my throbbing love for Patrick McClarty or Doug Daley or Kenny Frank, I certainly didn't want that to show.

Even so, there were embarrassments and humiliations, like the time Patrick said my bangs looked "shaggy" and I cried in the shower so hard afterward that I bumped my head on the tile and bruised my forehead. A little dark egg appeared the next morning on my brow, surrounded by a sore spot, and Brenda Ross turned around in class and said, "Oh God, you've got the biggest zit coming."

On another level of humiliation, many degrees worse to the point of being catastrophic, was the summer day that my period started and some of it, mixed with seawater, seeped out of the crotch of my bathing suit and dribbled down the insides of my thighs.

My father was at the beach that day. He liked to tan and had laid down two enormous towels into a cross, anointed his skin with Sea & Ski

Dark Tanning Oil, and stretched his arms out like Jesus on the cross. When I emerged from the water and felt something warm on my thighs, I saw him lift his head. His wraparound sunglasses hid where his eyes were looking. Had he seen the mess on my thighs or not? It was hard to imagine that he hadn't seen something. Then his head lowered again.

In general, my father seemed to enjoy making intrusions on my privacy. For a man who had loved many women and was canny about human nature, he was completely dumb to the delicate aspects of mine—either because he didn't understand the sensitivities of a thirteen-year-old girl or because he simply found my mysteries too compelling to resist. He grilled me about my ice cream and candy consumption—and linked it to my intermittent acne. He'd been quick to notice the growth of hair under my arms and inquired about my methods of shaving. One morning in the beach-house kitchen, he said in a loud voice, "Is that a bra you're wearing, Inez? Good God, *are you really wearing a bra?*"

When I cringed, he said, "Don't you know that women all over the world are burning theirs?"

"The body is beautiful," he persisted, whenever he had the chance. He disapproved of modesty and always zeroed in on signs of it, as if shyness and hesitancy could be drummed out of me. "It's not healthy to breathe too much steam produced by tap water," he said when I insisted on closing the bathroom door while I showered. He took to mentioning a nude bathing spot in La Jolla—it was called "Black's Beach"—at dinner. He was thinking of driving us all down there to check it out. "What? You wouldn't go to a nude beach, Inez? There's no need to be so *uptight.*"

As if to demonstrate his own belief in the body beautiful, he paraded around the beach house after showering with only a white towel wrapped around his waist, sometimes for hours.

"The Ruins aren't into modesty," Whitman explained coolly when I made a passing observation that Dad was a "perv." But Whitman was onto something. Aunt Julia was seen Windexing dog slobber off the sliding glass door one morning while wearing only a pair of yellow rubber gloves. Aunt Ann had no problem sitting on the toilet with the bathroom door wide open. Marguerite never seemed the least bit modest either—happy to air her elephant skin and old bones at Moss Cove and jumble up her skinny legs into all kinds of unfeminine sitting positions in order to play a round of honeymoon bridge on the sand. The cups of her white bathing suit always kept their shape, I had noticed, despite the fact nothing except a pinch of wrinkled flesh seemed to be inside them.

The Ruins—as I began to see with time—weren't simply immodest. They were theatrical and outrageous and provocative. Strangers were often targets. Late one afternoon, following a long day of tanning, my father arrived at Moss Cove dressed as Lawrence of Arabia, his head and body draped in large beach towels. Another day he wrapped his face in Ace bandages, put on a suit, hat, gloves, sunglasses, and walked down to the beach as the Invisible Man. At the Jolly Roger, a coffee shop where the Ruin aunts and uncles and cousins went for breakfast in the summer—known to the family as "the JR"—my father insisted on a specific table in the back room. This table was waited on most mornings by a dark, fetching, and quite buxom young woman in a low-cut wench getup, like something from a pirate movie.

"Tell me, is the orange juice fresh this morning?" my father asked without fail.

"It's fresh-frozen," the wench would answer.

"But is it fresh or *frozen*?" my father would ask—in a tone that seemed both berating and flirtatious.

"Fresh-frozen," she would respond with a chuckle.

"How can it be both, Kathleen?" he'd say, reading the nameplate that rested just above her cleavage. "It must be fresh *or* it must be frozen."

Whitman and I were largely immune to our father's charm in those days. We were sick of him, I suppose. He was mountainous and over-shadowing—and his gags had become tedious. But that summer in Laguna, at the height of his awesome powers, he kept a breakfast table of teenagers—me and Whitman, three nieces, and one nephew—completely rapt. We gathered around him, laughed at all his jokes, even the old ones. He was dashing and gallant, and he wore jeans and cowboy boots around the beach town. He did deadly impressions of the milkman, the post-man, and any poor stranger who wandered into our lives. He bought us grown-up books like *Portnoy's Complaint* and *Slaughterhouse-Five* to read, brandished words like "twat" and "snatch" and "tit," took us to R-rated movies full of untold bloodshed and nudity, and gave motorcycle rides on an ancient bike that Uncle Drew had stashed in Marguerite's garage. At breakfast at the JR, he beguiled my Ruin cousins with his bachelor wis-dom and outrageous probing questions.

"How do we feel about breasts these days?" he tossed out one morn-ing while eyeing his fleshy waitress across the way. "Are you girls eager to have them—or not? Are they entirely out of fashion?"

"*Dad . . .*"

"I've already got them," chirped Amanda, a peppy cheerleader type who was Whitman's age. Like all of Aunt Ann and Uncle Drew's children, she had grown up in Newport Beach and knew little else. "How could they ever go out of fashion?"

"But, Amanda, my dear," my father said, "flat is in."

"You don't have breasts," said her younger brother, Newell, a towhead with a sunburn and peeling lips. "You're flat as a pancake."

"Newell—" my father interjected.

"Flatsy."

"Then I'm in," said Amanda with a huff.

"Nobody's got big boobs in our family, Uncle Paul," said Lizzie, who had dark hair and Marguerite's gray-blue eyes.

"No?"

"No."

"All Ruin women are flat-chested," Whitman observed. "Aunt Ann. Aunt Julia. Marguerite. Except, considering what Consuela's carrying around, Inez might wind up okay."

"You're so *lucky*, Inez," said Lisa.

"Yeah."

"I don't want them," I retorted. "They're always in the way."

"Sure," said Newell.

"You should see Mom play tennis," I said. "Her boobs stick out so much she has to swing around them."

"Inez, be kind," my father said.

"It's the truth."

"We're just talking hypothetically," my father continued in professorial tones, as if wanting to veer from the subject of my mother. "If you girls had them—*big ones*—would you wear a little blouse like our waitress's— and show them off?"

"Yes!" Amanda cried out.

"Yes!" Lizzie yelled.

I looked across the way at Kathleen and felt sorry for her. "No way," I said under my breath. "That's so gross."

"Someday you might feel different," my father said to me.

"But," Whitman replied, "she might not."

My brother was my defender—and did this without disturbing any of my many (and various) delicate boundaries. When personal subjects were discussed, he displayed an overriding gentility and discretion that my father, and indeed most of the Ruin family, seemed to lack. He was capable of a diatribe against leg shaving, which he found bourgeois. He might remark that in England, where he had been partly raised, "people weren't as hung up about their bodies." But he would never have asked me, as my father did that summer afternoon when the brownish stains on my bathing suit didn't come out, if I "needed anything at the Laguna pharmacy, like Kotex." And Whitman would never have attempted to pry and poke his way into what could have been the most delicate territory of all, as my father did on the night the three of us went to *La Dolce Vita* at the Lido Theatre and I announced afterward (from my increasingly awkward perch in the back of the MG) that Marcello Mastroianni wasn't my "type."

"Did I hear that right?" my father asked with a weird tightness in his throat. "Mastroianni is not *your type?*" He chuckled and tried to make the discussion jolly, but I could tell that my revelation had struck him personally. Until then I hadn't realized how much he looked like the Italian actor, or at least must have thought so.

"No."

"Really? *Mastroianni?*"

"Really, really," I said. "He's gross."

"Oh, Inez. You think everything's gross."

"No I don't."

"You don't think Marcello Mastroianni is good-looking? Good God, Inez." He turned the MG onto Pacific Coast Highway and headed south for Laguna. I said nothing, realizing that it was time to lie low.

"I can see why," Whitman offered from the front passenger seat. "He's almost *too* good-looking. And he's really a weenie in *La Dolce Vita*. I mean, that's the whole point. Isn't it? He's a shallow weenie, and so is everybody else in the movie."

I tried to stifle a chuckle.

"I'm just interested in getting to know Inez better," my father continued, now serious and unemotional, as if he removed all personal investment in this debate and had only a clinical fascination with the subject. "It's interesting that she says somebody isn't her type. It means she has a type, that's all. And I'm only curious what that type would be."

"Not him," I said.

"'*Not him*,'" my father repeated. He smiled and shook his head. "And how do you feel about Steve McQueen? James Coburn? Charles Bronson?" *I* shook *my* head. "Eastwood?" Then he turned and faced Whitman but seemed still to be talking to me.

"You know, Inez. It's completely okay if you're not into men."

A funny sound, like a gurgle, came out of Whitman's throat.

"That would be perfectly okay. I mean," my father continued, "if I were a woman, I'd be into women. Without a doubt. They're so much more interesting and evolved."

"And if I were a man," I answered. "I'd be a homo."

Whitman laughed with an explosion of air, managing to spray gobs of spit on the dashboard. My father shot him a look. "Homo isn't exactly the way— Inez, don't say 'homo.'"

"What's wrong with 'homo'?" I said. "You're always talking about the queens on Polk Street."

"I just wanted you to know it would be okay," he said. "I was trying to be serious—and say something important. I wanted you to know that there's nothing wrong with being a—"

"I know," I said.

"But you should feel fine about—"

"I get it," I said.

"I just—"

"*I get it*, Dad."

"You—"

"She gets it, Dad," said Whitman.

"Okay," my father said with a sigh. "She gets it. She gets it. We all get it."

In Laguna he missed Justine, and that may have accounted for his occasional irritability during our days there. Love made him foggier and nicer at home in North Beach, but during absences from Justine in the summer and over the Christmas holidays, he seemed restless sometimes. After tanning and swimming, he'd go off by himself in the beach-house apartment and call Justine on the phone.

"You've never been to Laguna?" I overheard him say one day. "It's got lots of fake artsy charm—shingled cottages, surf shops. Ice cream cones, frozen bananas. Corn dogs. That kind of thing." He paused. "*You've never heard of a corn dog?* It's a hot dog coated in an inch of cornmeal and deep-fried. I know. Gag. *Wretch*. The name 'corn dog' says everything you need to know, really. The whole scene is very Middle America—and geared for perpetual youth and bad taste."

He paused again, for a longer time. "I know it has that reputation. The beaches are lovely, kind of like the Amalfi coast. There are some nice houses in the hills, I suppose. Mother's isn't one of those. She's got this big bungalow that's depressingly overdecorated. Terrible French stuff. One of the bedrooms is done in pink and gray. Sort of a bubble-gum pink meets battleship. Looks like she's expecting Mamie Eisenhower to turn up any second."

Over the year Justine had made an impact on his life in many small but noticeable ways—the driving gloves he wore, a heavy cashmere throw at the foot of his bed, a black-faced Rolex Oyster Perpetual watch on his wrist, an Egon Schiele lithograph of a nude with her legs akimbo on his bedroom wall. He'd given up his modern stainless-steel flatware for every day and was using a set of heavy sterling that Marguerite had parted with. His laundry was now picked up and returned by Perignon—he'd stopped bothering to shuttle it around himself. And his wardrobe, which had previously consisted of corduroys and turtleneck sweaters, jeans and the occasional black knit tie—the epitome of hip academic understatement—had become more eccentric. He was wearing collarless shirts in very fine linen, left open to the middle of his chest. At night he'd taken to wearing a black sealskin fedora around North Beach. This was joined by a black turtleneck and, later, a black wool cape that he'd gotten made in London. "It's my new look," he said to me a few times, as if amused by his own nerve. "Whaddya think?" I always smiled and said, "Neat," but in my mind I was wondering why a man so good-looking would want to dress like Vincent Price in *The House of Wax.*

With Justine he'd grown more social, too. They went out a great deal—dinner parties, film screenings, museum openings, Haight-Ashbury happenings. Justine sat on the boards of a Zen center and an art school, which required a certain amount of boho entertaining. As though wanting to keep up his end of things, my father organized a flamenco festival at Alegrías and began to throw *juergas,* or flamenco parties, of his own—inspiring the local dancers and musicians with good wine that they otherwise couldn't afford, and good dope. Spending most nights with Justine—and her angelic, yellow-haired daughter, Lara, whom he seemed to tolerate with calibrated affection—his apartment next door on Telegraph Hill Boulevard became mostly an office.

His company, Harrison-Ruin Computing, was doing well in the race to develop and manufacture semiconductor parts but required more managing and travel and attention than my father seemed interested in. He rarely mentioned his partner, Don Harrison—as if a gulf had grown between them. In fact, he rarely discussed Harrison-Ruin, almost as if he were embarrassed to have to be working at all. (When people asked him what he did for a living, he had three different stock replies: "I'm in the trades," or "As little as possible," or sometimes, if he was feeling a bit hostile, "I used to be a doctor but decided people weren't worth saving.") Aside from puzzles and problems that he enjoyed solving, like riddles, or talking with colleagues about burgeoning technologies, my father didn't seem interested in business or making money. Rather, he just craved independence and freedom—and more time to play. The more successful he became, the more he talked about wanting to travel or moving across the bay or designing his own house, but those dreams didn't seem any more serious than his periodic threat to sell the MG and buy an old Bugatti.

I still thought of Cary from time to time. There were no pictures or lingering signs of her at my father's office-apartment on Telegraph Hill, but she hovered like a ghost in the air around my bedroom in Van Dale, where the tarot cards were kept in good order in their velvet pouch, as if they could still communicate her advice and sweetness. As the days passed and months unfolded and brought more occasions with Justine, and more time for me to see how unusual she was, and vulnerable, and extravagant—there was a garageful of motorcycles, a closetful of fur coats—and how crazy my father was about her, it was clear that reminiscing about Cary, or even missing her so much, was both pointless and painful. The childlike intensity and easy warmth that Cary had brought to every visit to San Francisco began to seem something to outgrow, like my baby blanket. But more and more, without much to draw me in, I didn't really care for my weekends in San Francisco—and began to resist going at all.

"Marguerite thinks you're at a crossroads," Whitman said to me on the phone. "That's what she told Dad. You're at a crossroads, and she thinks it's time for her to step in."

"That's so stupid," I said. But I suppose she was right. If at eight I had been drawn to pairs and even numbers and symmetry—to sorting the world around me into collaborations and harmony—now that I was thirteen, my mind made studies of discord and asymmetry. I noticed the odd thing, what was off kilter. I was acutely aware of what didn't seem to fit and what was out of place. And when I was with my father and Justine, visiting their foggy universe of beautiful people and rich hippies, I felt out of place. My clothes were wrong, and I never knew what to say. My father didn't fit into my world, and I didn't fit into his. Where did I belong?

EIGHT

Tea with Marguerite

Most of my memories in San Benito are of watching Marguerite in her own house. I followed her around, room to room, while she explained things to me, showing me how to wind the mantel clock or telling me the story of some ashtray or figurine. She loved her things. And she was always straightening, or fixing, or perfecting something that she felt had gone to seed. I watched her make the beds in Aunt Ann's room before my first sleepover there. She rejected several smooth sheets for being wrinkled and improperly laundered, then spent a great deal of time demonstrating how a bed should be made with hospital corners. She had me practice hospital corners, finally shouting out, "Good girl! That's it!" and went on to show me, in detail, what constituted a fine wool blanket and which blanket covers—they were seersucker—were "the good ones" to buy.

The afternoon we had "proper tea," agonizing care was taken with each chicken salad sandwich—the perfect cubing of a chicken breast, the measuring of five level teaspoonfuls of mayonnaise, the chopping of equal-size celery bits, the slow sprinkling of celery salt. She laid out the slices of Northridge white sandwich bread on a wooden cutting board and carefully buttered each slice from edge to edge, leaving no surface area dry, before she spooned the chicken salad onto it. Every so often she wiped her hands on a white apron that was tied over her navy blue dotted dress.

It was warm, and I could barely stand anywhere without leaning on something or slouching, as though my body were feeling its weight intensely. I watched Marguerite from behind. Her body was slender—jutting collarbones, a big rib cage, toothpick legs. Her arms were a bit too long and disproportionately thin, the way a snowman looks when you use sticks for arms. I used to stare at the bumpy blue veins in her hands and drift off into a foggy state of mind. Was it adolescence? Was it something else? I always lacked energy in those days, or what Marguerite called "gumption." At home in Van Dale, I would have hopped onto the kitchen counter and watched the cooking. Or I would have slumped to the linoleum in my low-rider jeans and Mexican top with a drawstring neckline. Without even asking, I knew this wasn't an option in San Benito, where a certain formality was maintained.

"Lettuce, Inez?"

"Huh?"

Marguerite turned around and shot me a look. Everywhere lately, people were shooting me looks like that. My mother, Abuelita, teachers in school. "Lettuce on your sandwich?"

"Yeah—I mean, yes, *please.*"

The kitchen in San Benito seemed a vast space to me—and usually accommodated two or three cooks with room to spare during the holidays or when Marguerite threw parties. Unlike our tiny kitchen at Abuelita's, where the shelves and window ledges were cluttered with gummy teapots, framed postcards pictures of Peru, a plastic hula girl that Mr. Feinman had brought back from Hawaii, Marguerite's kitchen didn't look homey at all. Marguerite felt that a decorated kitchen was tacky. She preferred an impersonal, institutional look. The walls and cabinets were white. There were no patterned curtains or wallpaper. The countertops were dark wood, and glossy, and held a large white porcelain sink that I had a faint memory of sitting in as a baby.

"Inez, do you drink— *Inez?*" Marguerite was cutting off the crusts of the sandwiches.

"Yes?"

"You drink tea, don't you?"

"I drink coffee with hot milk sometimes at Dad's," I said through a yawn, not really answering the question. "But not at home. Mom won't let me."

"I suspect," said Marguerite, "that you do all kinds of things with your father that you don't do at home. Am I right?"

Marguerite was arranging the sandwiches on top of a paper doily. When she moved over by the window, the bright sunlight came through her thin white hair, and I could see the outlines of her scalp and the shape of her small head. It had never occurred to me that my grandmother had a scalp—or a head, really. Marguerite was one of those old women—San Benito seemed populated with them—whose appearance was entirely about her straight white hair and her tan, and maybe the gold rope she wore with her cashmere sweaters.

"I had ginseng tea once," I blurted, still hopelessly out of sync, "and couldn't sleep that night. Whitman and I can stay up as late as we want at Dad's."

"Well, why not?" Marguerite chuckled and made a few slurping sounds with her mouth. "It's fun to stay up late, isn't it?"

"Yeah," I said.

"Your father was always a night owl. Me, too. N.C. was the only one who liked the morning. As far as I'm concerned, I could do entirely without it."

I'd stayed over at Marguerite's—and endured the nighttime tolling of the grandfather clock—when Lisa was visiting from Newport. We carried our small suitcases into Aunt Ann's old room and quickly scattered our things everywhere, then tried on each other's bras. We pretended that we were spies for a while, Nancy Drew or the Girls from U.N.C.L.E., and went outdoors to hide by the brick barbecue that nobody used, or in the pool house, which really had a wicked smell. We looked for secret notes—sometimes Whitman left them around. We tried to find secret panels and hidden money in the library. And we liked to raid the pantry, off the kitchen, where Marguerite kept ancient fruitcakes and all kinds of sweets and boxes of expensive chocolates. At night Marguerite made us root beer floats, and we watched the ten o'clock news with George Putnam in my father's old bedroom—and later the beginnings of the Carson show. Then we'd say good night to Marguerite, and the rest of the night was a blur. Lisa and I closed the door to Aunt Ann's room and stayed up, talking about boys at school, swapping stories about our friends, analyzing family members, and musing about Whitman's love life. As in, did he have one?

When we woke in the morning, around nine or ten, Marguerite's bedroom door was still closed. It would stay closed until around ten-thirty or eleven, when it opened a crack. That meant my grandmother was taking breakfast in her room—black coffee, half a grapefruit, a bowl of cereal on a tray—and would see visitors. We'd peek around the door, and there she'd be, looking shockingly pale against huge pillows on her pink canopy bed, like an uncooked turkey. Her thin white hair was messy and vaguely Medusa-ish or, once, pressed down by a strange hairnet that didn't match the color of her hair. She wore a satin bed jacket over the top of her sheer nightgown—Lisa and I could see peeps of Marguerite's nipples and protruding belly. But all that was too horrible to focus on. Her gray-blue eyes were the main thing, and they shone with outrage in the morning, as though she were barely able to contain an urge to kill something.

"Inez." Marguerite turned around in the kitchen and was staring at me with a look of disbelief. *"Inez."*

"What?"

"I was asking about where you'd like to sit. Since we're having a *proper tea,* I thought we'd take it in the living room. Shall we?"

She carried a large silver tray out of the kitchen. Numbly, I followed her. It felt like a long distance, like crossing the desert to Aqaba. Halfway to the living room, I realized that I was meant to bring a tray with me, too, and not just follow my grandmother like a mindless gosling. So as Marguerite wobbled her way across the obstacle course of Oriental and Native American carpets, each of varying thicknesses which her pencil-thin legs must have memorized, I doubled back to the kitchen, slid another silver tray off the counter, and hurried to find that Marguerite was already setting up on a tiered table next to the piano.

"Can you manage?" she asked. "Can you? Good girl. Fine. Yes, just rest it there."

She immediately left the room, heading to the kitchen once more for cookies and cakes, and I watched her—*what a lot of work this all was*—vaguely wondering if I was supposed to follow again, and help.

Exhausted, I collapsed into a striped chair instead.

In the low light of the wall sconces, N.C.'s face looked down at me from a portrait. He seemed flat and unreal. In the background of the painting, there was a tiny rendering of Lawton Dam that was done in great detail, whereas my grandfather looked about as out of focus as a face on Mount Rushmore. He'd built a lot of dams in California—and, according to Whitman, destroyed forests and wildlife and exploited untold hordes of Mexican laborers. I had no idea why Lawton was special. Marguerite might have told me once, during one of her long monologues about N.C. and how brilliant and perfect he was and how he rescued her from a sad childhood and brought her west and made a fortune as an engineer. But aside from passing references to dams, N.C.'s career was a mystery to me, the way everybody's career was something of a mystery to me—and a very dull mystery, too. Anyway, engineering feats weren't really what the Ruins talked about when they talked about N.C. In the twelve years since his death, he'd been reduced to just three attributes: He loved the horse races. He loved to sail. And he loved reading about the rise and fall of the Roman Empire, sometimes in other languages.

The dams that he built were just his job, and in California, as everybody knows, it only matters what you do on weekends.

At some point or another, Marguerite had attached a poignant little story to most of the objects in the room. She had walked me around and rather laboriously explained the provenance of every piece of furniture, every porcelain figurine. It was a pretty dreary mélange of stuff. There were cumbersome chairs, sconces dripping with cut crystal, and ornate decorative objects—combined to create a kind of somber clutter that seemed at great odds with the simple California sunlight and mild climate outside the heavy curtains. In the corners curio cabinets were filled with small porcelain shoes, Battersea boxes, carved bottles, and netsukes from Japan. In front of the fireplace was a large paper fan— why?—and above the mantel a haunting portrait of a very young girl, a New England ancestor with a sour expression and a determined little grip on the arm of an Empire chair. Marguerite had lots of sour-faced New England ancestors but not many family heirlooms—her father had gambled and lost everything well before the Depression. Yet somehow she'd wound up with a portrait of her great-aunt, Nettie Snow. I didn't seem to know much about Nettie, however, except that she was dead.

I leaned over a nearby table and opened a candy dish. There were always surprises in these covered dishes—gum, soft mints, Marlboro cigarettes that I sometimes took into the powder room and pretended to smoke—but inside this one was a piece of paper. Unfolding it, I saw Whitman's printing: RONALD REAGAN FOR PRESIDENT, it said. I giggled.

"What's that?" Marguerite asked imperiously while setting down the cookie tray.

I folded the note and stuck it in my palm. (My father, who had begun to teach me his card tricks, would have described this move as "palming it.") Marguerite took an endless amount of time getting situated and finally sank into a mushy love seat by the fireplace.

"It's a note from Whitman," I said, squeezing my fist tighter.

"It is?" She didn't sound surprised. "About what? Whitman was just here—last week or two."

"Nothing," I whispered. "It's just a silly note. He's being funny."

"Is he? What does he say?"

I felt my pulse quicken—the note seemed sacrilegious to me. God only knew what Marguerite might do. "It's just a joke," I said. "That's all. Nothing. He left it for me."

She stared at my hand. Her eyes were intense, like a sharp stick poking me. "Whitman is rather devilish, isn't he? He's going to give Paul a run for his money. Ha!"

I scooted the note into my fingers and then, in one quick gesture, slipped it into a front pocket of my jeans.

Marguerite looked over at the tiered table. "Let's start with tea," she said, her voice becoming instructional. "Black for me. A little sugar." I reached for a cup and saucer with one hand, then picked up the teapot. The previous Easter I'd spilled a demitasse of coffee all over my dress and had gotten an unforgettable stare of displeasure.

"I hear he's been coming to your house a good deal—has even stayed the night," Marguerite continued, watching the pot as the tea poured out. "He never stays overnight here. I hope Whitman's not a great burden to Mrs. Garcia in any case. I do hope not. Is he, Inez?"

I shook my head.

"Perhaps if I installed a slide for the swimming pool, my grandchildren would visit more."

I stirred a small spoonful of sugar into her cup and handed it to her.

"You forgot my napkin," she said. "That's it. Good girl. Now serve yourself and sit down. The only thing that interests Whitman these days is surfing. Am I right? He has that wonderful red surfing car—"

"Van."

"Oh, yes, it's a *van*. And all those special racks and boards and wetsuits. He came by last week and showed me the whole thing. Plunged into the pool wearing his complete getup. He looked so dashing! So tall—and those nice Ruin shoulders. I must say, Whitman might wind up being better-looking than Paul. Don't you think? Have you seen him in that black wetsuit? Oh, of course you have. Men look so terrific encased in black, don't they? Nothing like seeing a man in white tie."

White tie. What was she talking about? It was, no doubt, another by-gone detail from Marguerite's dying world. I sat down with my trembling cup of tea.

"How are your mother and grandmother?"

"Okay."

"Connie's still at tennis?"

I nodded, took another sip.

"And you say she's awfully good? She's gotten so sporty. Ready for the sandwiches? Excellent. Me, too."

That was my cue to serve. Everything was a cue—and it was exhausting trying to catch all of them. "Take one of the clean, small plates," Marguerite commanded from her pillowy throne. "That's it. Those are dessert plates. How do you like them? They're Limoges, from France. Isn't that a lovely pattern? It's a very old one. That's it. I'll take one chicken salad and one cucumber sandwich. No, no. Not the cookies. *Not yet.* Do you ever take tea at home? Oh, that's right. You said you weren't allowed. Mrs. Garcia must have some nice china. Mexican patterns—or Peruvian?"

I shook my head vaguely, still not entirely sure what a pattern was. Abuelita had a few things from Peru, but they were never used. Sometimes, on a really busy weekend, we used paper plates for all the meals. We used paper napkins, too, not even the good kind.

"May I have a bit more, please?" Marguerite held out her cup and saucer to me. "Your mother has a boyfriend, Paul reports."

I nodded and focused on pouring more tea and handing back Marguerite's cup without spilling anything and getting the knife eyes. I put four sandwiches on my plate and took a bite of one before sitting down.

"Rod Weeger," I said.

"Rod what? Never mind, finish chewing. And he's nice? *Finish chewing, Inez.* I can see traces of your sandwich in your mouth."

I nodded and swallowed, but it seemed to take a long time. "He's a PE teacher at my school, and—"

Marguerite turned her head away and looked at the tiered table of sandwiches again.

"Can I get you more?" I asked.

"Please. If you could. One of each. And how does school go?" Marguerite didn't want to hear too much about Coach Weeger.

"Fine."

"Straight A's?"

"Close."

"Your father always got straight A's."

"My mother, too."

"Did she? She's so pretty I guess it's easy to forget how smart she is."

Marguerite made more slurping sounds with her lips that I gathered she couldn't hear. She rested the cup and saucer on the table and picked up a sandwich. "Your father went to cotillion when he was thirteen. Do you know what that is?"

I shook my head.

"*Cotillion.* I think you'd like it. You learn to dance and things like that—the waltz, the fox-trot. Things you'll need to know when you make your debut. And later on, in college, and forever. Invaluable. The Arroyo puts together a very nice coming-out party."

"Coming out of what?"

Marguerite chuckled. "Inez, you're so amusing."

I stood up. A box of chocolate miniatures from Jurgenson's had found its way to the tiered table as well. I was just about to reach for some cookies and cake, and maybe a piece of chocolate, when I caught myself.

"Would you care for some chocolates or cookies, Marguerite?"

"Lovely. Very lovely. A small assortment," she responded. "And do you know which ones are the coconut crèmes? You know, there's a code. Each kind of chocolate has a different swirl on the top. The circle is a raspberry crème. The triangle swirl is a coconut. Yes. Good girl. I'll have one of those. A cookie, too."

I walked to the love seat and handed her the plate.

"They use the old ballroom at the Arroyo for their cotillion—it's very nice," she said.

Back at the box of chocolates again, I picked one with a little wave on the top. "What's this?" I asked, not wanting to discuss learning to dance or anything at that club of Marguerite's.

"Bring it closer," she said. "Oh, that's a very yummy one! Chocolate crème!"

I held the small chocolate crème between my fingers and studied all its sides.

"Try it!" Marguerite blurted out. She watched me excitedly as I popped it into my mouth, seeming to hang on every chew that I made. "Can you believe how creamy?" she said with a slurpy voice. "Like velvet."

She picked a cigarette from a white marble urn. After she lit it up, pursing her lips together and sucking like her life depended on it, I could smell the menthol. It was such a sharp smell it almost made me flinch. She blew out a giant gust of smoke that seemed much bigger than her body. She looked at my jeans and then down at my feet.

"Well, I say. Those are interesting shoes."

"Earth Shoes."

"What are they called?"

"*Earth Shoes.* It's a new thing. The heel is lower than the toe." I tipped up my shoe to show the heavy rubber sole and the way it was slanted. "It's supposed to be a more healthy way to walk. Supposed to be good for you. Natural."

"Really."

"It's supposed to be like walking in the sand. The heel goes lower."

"Amazing. And your top looks authentic. Straight from Mexico. You and Whitman are really full of new trends. Some of them, of course, I really don't care for. The miniskirts are awful, to my eyes, and the— But, say, *how do you like Justine Polk?* She came down to go to the races at Santa Anita with your father a few weeks ago. You can't imagine the flowing robes that girl had on, and the biggest fur coat I've ever seen."

Justine? Had he mentioned coming to San Benito with her?

"She rides, you know. A beautiful rider."

Marguerite kept some horses at the Arroyo Club, a part of her life that had always intrigued me. Why would my father and Justine come to San Benito—just to go to the races? It didn't make sense. Had I known that Justine was an equestrian? I thought about the ponies in Griffith Park, the acrid smell of the stable, the little circle the ponies rode in, attached to metal arms like spokes of a wheel. Those were the only horses I'd ever ridden.

"It seems serious," Marguerite was saying. "I suppose they might marry. Such a handsome couple. Don't you think so, Inez?"

"Huh?"

"Paul and Justine Polk. They might marry."

"No they won't," I said—probably with too much certainty.

"No?"

I shook my head. "He doesn't believe in marriage."

"Your father?"

"He doesn't believe in it. He says it doesn't work." I smiled a little wickedly.

"Ha!" Marguerite cried out. "What a madman! Marriage doesn't work *for him,* is more like it!" Her eyebrows lifted—and she suddenly looked a great deal younger. "Justine Polk is so lovely. Those blue eyes! And from a family that's very . . . Well, how do you like her, Inez? She's quite beautiful, isn't she? Whitman seems completely enthralled."

I shrugged.

"What?"

"She's okay."

Marguerite stifled a smile. "Just okay?"

"No, not really."

"No?" Marguerite began to laugh really loudly—a deep, smoky cackling. It startled me, mostly because I had caused it. There's no way to describe how rewarding this was, how suddenly happy I felt in my grandmother's company as I watched her collapse into indescribable glee. She was still a girl, I could see that suddenly, and not much past my age.

"I'm just being honest," I said.

"Of course you are!" Marguerite reached out—indicating she wanted help from her downy prison on the love seat. "Tell me more! Tell me more! But let's walk in the garden, shall we? My legs have fallen asleep."

We covered most of the pathways of the garden, Marguerite explaining what was blooming and what was about to bloom, a parade of Latin names that I forgot instantly. When we rounded the bend and arrived at the pool house, we came upon the figure of an older man in pressed khakis, a handsome white shirt, and a straw hat, skimming the surface of the pool.

"Who's that?" I whispered to Marguerite.

"My new pool man, Carlos. Very nice."

He looked up for a minute, tipped his head—a confident, Old World nod—and continued to skim red bottlebrush needles from the water. Across the way, in a shaded area of the garden, I could see Jose kneeling and spreading white powder under the azaleas. "Bonemeal," Marguerite said. "Doesn't it smell just awful?" She stopped for a second, almost as though disoriented, then swung around quickly and faced me.

"What does he do?" she asked, grabbing my arm.

"Carlos?"

"No. *Your ridiculous father.* What does he do for a living? He seems to be making money, but I can't for the life of me figure out how."

I shrugged, shook my head, and turned down the corners of my mouth into an expression of abject disapproval. Marguerite let out a little whoop and laughed. Then she patted my hand—the softest, gentlest, most reassuring gesture. She was the only person in my life who ever did that.

"Impeach Nixon," she said.

"What?"

"Ronald Reagan for president."

"What?"

"I always check that dish."

"You do?"

1975

Wolfback

What surprised me most—stunned me—was how my father could consider living someplace other than Telegraph Hill. His life there, particularly in the small neighborhood where he had lived since separating from my mother, seemed irrevocable and permanent. He was a fixture in North Beach, almost a part of its steep slopes and narrow alleyways, spaghetti restaurants and pizzerias. I couldn't imagine him away from all the smells—the espresso, the incense, the sour wine (as if poured into the gutters), the mustiness of Alegrías, and the saffron and clams in El Bodega.

But he complained about traffic and noise—the huffing and grinding of the great tourist buses when they reached the top of Telegraph Hill. He hated the parking hassles and delays, the fireworks in neighboring Chinatown ("New Year never ends," he'd sigh). He groused that North Beach, once an authentic ghetto of Italians and Beat Generation poets, had become commercial and touristy and expensive. "It's an Italian theme park," he said, "owned by the Chinese."

He was just building a case—convincing himself it was okay to leave the city—but, in truth, abandoning North Beach never seemed the real goal. He was drawn, almost irrationally, to building a house. Inside the Marin Headlands, and between two state parks, he'd found a little slice of land not far from where we had walked that gloomy day six years before. He'd imagined it perfectly: a simple cottage of glass set snugly on a cliff overlooking the beach.

At first he talked constantly about the house—how it would look, where it would sit on the hillside, the way the teak would age with time. Later he grew quieter, ruminative, as if it were a secret mistress he wanted all to himself. Even when he called or wrote, wanting to discuss other things, it never seemed far from his mind.

> Dear Inez,
>
> I hope you aren't worrying about high school—and what unexpected changes it might bring. Perhaps, like me, you will find yourself generally untroubled by change. There will always be uncertainties in the future. In fact, they start being fun! When there aren't enough uncertainties, I always feel a little nervous.
>
> I'm happiest when improvising. Of course, this could be seen as a major fault. Since birth I've possessed many gifts, traceable to Marguerite and N.C.—certainly not the result of any particular effort on my part—and these talents have offered me the option of improvisation when my plans were either incomplete or lacking—which is to say most, if not all, of the time. (You've probably noticed this, right?) I've always had a weird aversion to planning and no fear of drifting in my life, because of my ability to respond quickly to immediate events— a major resource. But sometimes I worry that my energies have been spent trying to respond and land on my feet, rather than building anything important. That's how I seem to like things: slightly unsettled. Lately, though, I sense it might be time to settle down.
>
> Ten Four,
> Daddy-O

He didn't appear to care much about Harrison-Ruin anymore. The company was involved in developing a microprocessor, but this achievement left my father restless and bored, almost disdainful of his colleagues and partner, who talked only about stifling the competition—the handful of larger companies who might dominate the market with inferior products. "It's a waste of time even thinking about IBM," my father liked to say. "If you spend time and energy checking out who's in the race with you," he said, "you've already lost." He preferred experimentation and being on the edge—ideas, not implementation. Rather than worrying about Harrison-Ruin, he focused his time and creativity on a slice of land and a house of glass. It was an irrational, almost crazy pursuit. He was forty-seven. Is that why? Or maybe the explanation was more fundamental: He'd finally made enough money to finance it.

After the land deal closed, and well before the permits were obtained—that took a year—he began interviewing architects and finally settled on a modernist named Ooee Lungo, a stocky South African with a symphony conductor's wild head of hair and flinging arm gestures. Before long, Ooee had swept into our lives, always seeming to arrive with expensive bottles of wine and handfuls of fresh herbs. He loved to cook and drink, always with gusto and impatience. Like my father, he was single— a playboy, I suppose—and he showed up for any event where some pretty women might be present: flamenco parties or *juergas,* art openings, El Bodega for dinner, the weekly "talent show" (as my father had started to call it) at Alegrías. He was gregarious and fun-loving, a devilish charmer who managed to fit into any scene. He arrived at Marguerite's beach house for two nights and took over, cooking an enormous rack of lamb, playing cards, offering skim-boarding lessons to various assembled teens— he'd grown up at the beach—and then soaked in the bathtub until noon the next day, smoking cigars and reading the *International Herald Tribune,* which he'd gotten Aunt Julia to fetch in town.

My father called him by his first name—OH-ee—but to my cousins, who embraced him as a long-lost uncle, he was "Lungo" or "Lungs." Food and wine and women (when Justine wasn't around) were all he and my father talked about, when they weren't discussing The House in pompous tones, using words like "breakthrough" and "statement." They fought about the design details and loved making up by agreeing. They were competitive, particularly about their engineering skills. Since I was little, I'd watched my father take things apart—a clock, a television, a transistor radio—and put the pieces back together. He liked fixing things, reordering things, and toying with machines. When my parents were still together, he'd built a record turntable and stereo receiver out of parts he ordered from a German catalog, and then seemed determined to tell me all about it—how the needle read the grooves in the black disk, how the sound traveled into the speakers, how the music came alive. And later, whenever he took the MG to a garage for repairs, he spent a great deal of time talking to the mechanics about the problems and possible solutions. (He burned through quite a lot of mechanics.) When workmen came to fix something in his apartment, he watched over their shoulders and asked questions until, pretty soon, he'd made it clear that he knew more about wiring or plumbing than they did.

Building a house was a way to employ all this knowledge, but not only that. He seemed to be searching for a chance to express himself, and his taste, and his ideas about the world. It wasn't just a house but a series of daring experiments—and both he and Ooee enjoyed how impossible it would be to pull off. They were like boys planning to build a fort or a tree house. They'd formed a club of two and seemed to speak in their own language. The structure would be "both transparent and hidden," they said. Even the stone steps to the beach would be camouflaged by trees and shrubs. But they weren't just stone steps. They were "a transition" and "a conduit of energy" and "an invisible passageway to nature." And the stone steps had to be just right.

Around Ooee my father was unguarded and passionate. But when old friends and colleagues—or, most of all, Marguerite—asked how the house was coming along (so much easier than inquiring about a computer), my father made the project sound effortless and routine. A simple thing. Just a little house across the bridge. "A cottage on the beach," I heard him say to Aunt Julia, "almost Japanese and *very small*." He was conspicuously modest and vague about his plans until he began trying to obtain licenses and permits to build next to state parkland, and then he became frustrated and irritable. "Who knows!" he'd say angrily if anybody asked how it was going, or "I'm pressing on! There's nothing else to do."

I visited North Beach just once that winter. I was always batting away his offers and invitations in those days. I had lots of reasons—school events, parties, football games, and reports—but mostly, when I thought about heading to San Francisco for another weekend of wailing flamenco singers and being squeezed between the wilting Justine and the booming Ooee Lungo, I felt like dying.

It was always more fun, and more relaxed, to meet up in Laguna. And in that familiar setting—breakfast at the Jolly Roger ("But is it fresh or *frozen?*"), tidal-pool explorations, walking to town, sailing around Newport Harbor in Uncle Drew's old wooden boat, a movie at night and bitter arguments about the movie (now a family tradition), the late bedtime, the sleeping in, getting up for the JR breakfast again—the differences between my father's life and mine seemed smaller. I had room to be myself. And, although inquisitive as ever ("Lizzie," he asked my seventeen-year-old cousin one morning at the JR, "are you really still a virgin?"), my father was pleasantly muted at the beach. Even his rhapsodies about Justine, which were tediously frequent in the early days of their love affair, were dwindling in number. Now he rarely spoke of her.

So that one visit to North Beach, on a cold weekend in February, I was treated like a visiting dignitary. Aside from a trip to the headlands—so he could proudly show me his vacant lot of land—the entire weekend unfolded like a production designed to please me. There were trips to Cost Plus and hippie shops to buy incense, candles, and an old army jacket. I was taken to the Gap for cords, Tower Records for the new Boz Scaggs album, and even indulged in my wish to see *Barry Lyndon* for a third time. Justine materialized with gifts: a string of pounded gold chain from Morocco, a bottle of scented bath water from Floris in London, a Buddhist *mala* of wooden prayer beads. In the past I'd always been just along for the ride, wedged into a social calendar and lifestyle that she and my father kept. Or wedged into Whitman's ambitions. But Whitman was traveling that year, and away, and I wasn't wedged into anything—not even the back of the MG. My father borrowed Ooee's blue Saab to drive us around.

On the second afternoon, when my father had "some work to do," Justine asked if I'd like to come see her. She'd make me lunch, she said, and we'd have some tea. I rang the bell several times, and she finally appeared in the courtyard in a pair of baggy pants and an open linen shirt. Her blond hair was down, falling well past her shoulders.

"Aren't we about the same height?" she said in a gentle voice. Her blue eyes looked at me for a few seconds, then skidded away.

She led me down the hall to her bedroom, where a king-size bed sat on a white platform. A wall of square windows on the other side of the room allowed some dusky sunlight to filter in. There was a round white table next to the bed—exactly the same table that my father had in his apartment. There was only one painting hanging on the wall, a rectangle of blue brushstrokes of water or sky.

"I'm cleaning out my closet," she said. "And before my sister picks over everything, you might want to take a look. There are some nice sweaters. A few wonderful coats. All kinds of things."

Justine pulled on a silver knob and opened a door. A gust of patchouli blew out. A light flickered on inside, automatically. "Isn't that light great? Your father's idea."

Her closet, like the rest of her town house, was orderly—sleeves fell in rows, the silks and linens so fine they seemed almost poignant. Toward the front there were blouses and some scarves folded on hangers. Toward the back there were coats and long sweaters, shawls and ponchos. Everything was soft or long or gauzy, like something Ophelia would have worn while she floated down the river and drowned.

Why did I feel so nervous suddenly? Standing in Justine's open closet, while seeming on the surface an easy thing to do, was intensely personal, as though I'd wandered into the woman's most private unseen realm. "Take your time," Justine said, backing away. I moved a few hangers along the sleek wooden pole, casually, as if I were in a department store and browsing the racks. Way in the back, I came upon some Moroccan robes and smocks and caftans, things she'd bought when she'd lived in Tangier.

"That's a djellaba," Justine said, pointing to one long robe in pinky beige silk. "And that's really more of a *machzania*." She touched a creamy blue garment with a large hood. "It's a robe that you wear on the outside, like a coat. The hood protects you from sandstorms and the sun."

Sandstorms? The sun?

"See anything you might like?" Justine asked quietly.

A brown cashmere poncho jumped into view. Just as I was about to reach for it, doubts filled my mind. *Where would I wear such a thing?* And why would I want Justine's clothes anyway? Except . . . who knows, there might be a remote chance that I would become someday the sort of person—uh, woman—who could wear things like that. It was implausible, almost laughable. And seemed totally *outrageous*. But as I stared at the heartbreaking array of delicate and exotic clothes in the closet, I suddenly wanted to believe that it might be so. Desperately.

"See anything you might want?" Justine asked again.

"Oh," I mumbled, embarrassed. I felt a surge of feeling that I couldn't quite fathom or express. I suppose it was desire, followed by greed or possibly jealousy—under a shroud of confusion. I wanted everything, every single thing, very badly. Not just the clothes. I wanted to have long, pale hair like Justine's, and a gentle refined voice. I wanted to ride motorcycles and smoke brown Sherman cigarettes in long ivory holders. Why had it taken me so long to see that? "It's all so neat," I said, my head cluttered with new thoughts. "I can't decide."

She stepped away, as if sensing that I needed "some space," as people said then. I heard a faucet in the bathroom turn on.

I tried to picture my life ahead—and what clothes I might need some-day. I felt a kind of panic, a sense that I might never have this chance again or be offered an array of free clothes as beautiful. What would I need in the future? The problem was, I couldn't project myself into the future—see beyond my immediate circumstances. Graduation from ju-nior high loomed. And over the summer I'd be riding my bike everywhere. In a caftan? I'd be swimming at the Verdugo pool. In a djellaba? I'd be away at horseback-riding camp—sort of a girls' dude ranch in Colorado that Marguerite was paying for—but for that I'd probably need a flannel shirt and my paddock boots. But what about the fall? Van Dale Senior High would be starting. Maybe then I'd need some grown-up things.

Just a few weeks before, a girl in art class had made a crack about my platform saddle shoes. "What are those?" she'd said in tones of ridicule. She was a new girl who had arrived midyear from another part of Los An-geles, and I guess she'd never seen platform saddle shoes before. But Shelley Strelow—that was her name—was onto to something. She had style, knew how to tie a scarf. She had wavy, brown, shoulder-length hair that she kept off her face with a pair of sunglasses on top of her head. She wasn't California-girl cute, but more exotic than that—giant eyes and a prominent nose, and she wore makeup like she knew what she was doing. And gold hoop earrings. Coming to a new school in the middle of ninth grade couldn't have been easy. But she already seemed bored.

"See anything?" Justine said.

The brown cashmere poncho was short, above the knees. Would Shelley Strelow wear something like that? I stepped farther into the closet and pulled the poncho out. It was so thick and soft. The hood ru-ined it in about ten ways, but I had to take something. Marguerite had drilled this into me: Always take one thing. Don't turn offers down; it's rude. *Always try one.* And, once in my arms, the poncho felt like it be-longed to me already.

"That's all you want?" Justine said. She hesitated for a moment, then walked back into the closet and picked out a sweater, then another and another—an armload of sweaters—things in browns, autumn colors and earth tones. She threw them on her bed. "There!" she said, holding a long chocolate V-neck in the air. "See how great this looks against your skin?" She turned me around so I faced a mirror on the inside of the closet door. "See how it works with your eyes?"

I nodded and kept nodding. "Take all of these," she said, pointing to the pile on the bed. "I have too much. And they look better on you! I insist." She went back inside the closet and was studying a section of blouses—and then began lifting hangers of them and collecting them in her hand. I was flushed, excited, made anxious by her generosity. "But how am I going to get everything home?" I asked.

Justine walked to another door and opened it, reemerging from this second closet with a large leather suitcase. "Here we go," she said. "But first let's see if we can fill it up!"

I bought a notebook and started a journal that year—the word "journal" seemed so much more mature and important than "diary"—and into those fresh, clean notebook pages I jotted musings about life, fluctuating philosophies, and what seemed like crucial observations. It was written self-consciously, a little blandly, too carefully, as though Abuelita or my mother, or even God might be reading over my shoulder. I never wrote much about my parents, either of them. What they did—or neglected to do—didn't seem worth recording. Maybe I wasn't conscious enough, or sensitive. But when my father wouldn't come to my graduation from E. J. Truppel because he didn't want to spend two hours standing next to my mother and Coach Weeger, the journal contains no mention of it. When I walked in on Coach Weeger crying—my mother had refused to marry him—no mention. How I really felt about Abuelita, or Robbie, or Marguerite: nothing. Most of the notebook is taken up with accounts and descriptions of boys that I knew but barely remember now. Pat McClarty plays a central role during the first half of that year. I had learned that he was moving to the Midwest, and I poured out my anguish in poems about the sea, and ships lost, and people drowning. And then, on June 17 when school got out, Pat vanishes like one of the ships. Another name appears: Antonio. The notebook pages begin to steam.

It was warm, oddly warm, that June. My father and Justine met me at the airport in Ooee's Saab, and we drove through town, then over the Golden Gate Bridge, then into a tunnel. We followed a wide, twisting street, then bumped on a small dirt road, coming to the ridge of land in the Marin Headlands where my father's house was being built. A foundation had been poured, and there were cement blocks, and white pipes, and holes where a sink would go, or a toilet. It was just a pit of cement, really, with green-wire rebar springing up like hairs. We stood around for a long time while my father described his plans. I remember that he seemed ridiculous and pretentious to me. He had a hushed voice when he talked, as though he were building a shrine. We stood where the living room would someday be, and waited for the sunset. At about eight-thirty, the sun dropped behind a row of lavender clouds that looked like bubbles, and nobody said a word.

That night my father and Justine threw a party. It was an informal affair, mostly flamencos and a few gringos like Ooee Lungo and some of my father's computer-world buddies that he'd dragged into the flamenco scene. It was the same party that I had been to a few times before—with varying degrees of interest.

I was standing in the kitchen of my father's apartment when Antonio entered the room—coming by the refrigerator for a beer. He was wearing a pair of tight jeans and a black shirt that was open to his bare chest. It was strange to see him out of the traditional stage getup. *Manitas de plata.* He seemed undressed. Too real. Too close. He stopped for a moment to speak with me. In the past I'd gone unnoticed, an invisible person.

"Your father," the young guitarist said, "is a good guy." He leaned back against the frame of the kitchen door.

"Yes," I said, nodding. I thought he was talking about my father's loyalty over the years to Alegrías and the ragtag group of guitarists and singers and dancers. But Antonio was looking at me as if there were a question in his mind, something unfinished. "Wait," I said, "you mean his playing? It's really good?"

He laughed. The door of the refrigerator opened again, and I watched the light change on Antonio's face. He bent his head to the flame of a match, and the light changed again. His skin was tawny. His nails were filed perfectly, the way my father kept his. Everything he did seemed in slow motion—the way he moved his hands to the match, the way he talked or shook his head. His shaggy black hair seemed weighted with something extra, dark and serious, a sleepy magic. "His playing? Your father . . . he's okay for a—" He stopped himself. "But he looks like a *gitano*, no?"

"Do you think so? He'd love to hear that, I'm sure," I said, feeling glamorous with a cigarette and a brown beer bottle in my hand. "He'd love to not be a—"

"And you—*mexicana*?"

"Uh-huh." I nodded, hesitant, suddenly worried he might want to speak Spanish, which I couldn't do very well. "And my grandmother is from Peru."

Antonio didn't seem to be listening to what I was saying. He just stared. "Peru," he said. He pulled away from the doorframe and leaned his face closer to mine. "You like him. Yes?"

"Like him?"

"You *are* like him," he corrected himself, and then gently ran his hand up and down my bare arm, from the edge of my T-shirt sleeve to my wrist. I remember struggling to breathe, and I felt a sensation, a buzzing of nerves, all the way into my feet. The *flamencos* were always touching each other, I told myself. It didn't mean anything.

"Ay!"

It was Ooee. When he walked into the kitchen, Antonio drew his hand away from my arm and slipped it quickly, or the tips of his fingers at least, into the small front pocket of his jeans. Ooee hovered, crowded next to me. He patted my shoulder, almost stroked it. "You saw the house today, I heard. What did you think of—"

"Inez!" my father called out, squeezing into the small kitchen. He stood between Ooee and Antonio. "Inez!" he said again, now in a Castilian accent, Ee-NETH.

I smiled a little sheepishly and kept my cigarette and my beer low, almost behind me. He was looking at me—studying me.

"*Hija,*" he said finally. He saw the beer, for sure. I watched his eyes for a flicker of disapproval. No sign.

"*Hija,*" Antonio repeated with a chuckle. He looked over at my father, then back to me. Ooee was looking at me, too, and suddenly I felt a flutter of excitement in my chest, almost like a wave of sensation—embarrassment mixed with thrill. My father and Antonio and Ooee smiled, all big grins, wide and open, like they were waiting for me to say something, or do something, but at the same time it didn't seem to matter what I did. Nothing was needed, except for me to stand still. Smile back. Just let them look. Something had changed—their eyes had changed. They were looking at me in a new way. And there was something about them, these three men, a kind of silly shagginess, but underneath, a darkness, a nighttime intensity that seemed dangerous and undefined.

My father ran his hand along Antonio's black shirtsleeve. His hand stopped near the crook of the guitarist's arm and stayed there for a while. He was about to say something when a cloud of patchouli blew into the kitchen.

"Hey!" Justine was wearing a blue-gray sheath that looked almost Grecian. In a small gold clip in her hands, she held a joint—as skinny and round as a white birthday candle. "Cambodian," she said, offering it to Antonio.

"Ah," Antonio said, smiling so that creases radiated from his eyes, warm creases, almost like rays of sunshine. My father was smiling, too—and studying me.

"Inez?"

"What?"

"Why don't you put that beer in a glass, instead of drinking out of the bottle?"

Ooee laughed.

"Okay." I said.

"And one more thing."

"What?"

"Are you up for a little dope?"

Later on, in Van Dale, I tried but couldn't find a way to tell Robbie about the grass—or much else of what happened that night. She wouldn't have understood or approved or anything close to that. Maybe if Whitman had been around, instead of halfway across the world, I might have told him. "I can't believe you waited so long to get stoned," he'd have said. "What did you think would happen—you'd lose your mind and jump out a window?"

I suppose I wanted to join the party, become part of the fun—and dwell in the grown-up world of Justine and my father and Ooee. It seemed new and sophisticated and brought me a few inches closer to being a girl who could wear a brown cashmere poncho. But when I thought about Robbie, I hated the mounting list of secrets that I was keeping from my best friend. The three beers I drank with Antonio, then another two with Ooee, and the glass of incredibly good wine he'd insisted that I try. And what about the grad-night party at Kim LaVelle's house? Right after Tad Brown told me that I had beautiful feet and that he loved me, Kenny Frank threw me into the swimming pool and ran his hands along my thighs and underneath my stretchy bra cup. He was a baseball player—and oh, my, his calluses felt good. I hadn't told Robbie about that either.

Mostly that summer Robbie and I talked about drill team at Van Dale Senior High School and whether we were going to try out. Drill team girls wore purple uniforms and silver cowboy boots and paraded around the Van Dale field, almost militarily, during the halftime of football games. While the marching band played, they danced in rows, like a big cornfield of girls. During tryouts you were given some kind of routine to learn in a couple hours and then perform. Everybody from my Camp Fire Girls group was trying out—as well as almost every other girl I could think of. But something felt funny about it to me. Just thinking about being on the grounds of Van Dale High made me skittish, for one thing. Terra incognita. But thinking about memorizing some kind of prance and arm waving, or attempting a cartwheel on the football field, filled me with panic beyond measure. The tryouts were approaching, and I just couldn't decide.

"Drill team?" my father asked on the phone. "What's that? Sounds like a dental procedure."

"Come on," I said. "You know what a drill team is. They do routines at halftime, like a spirit squad. And you can't be a cheerleader if you aren't on the drill team."

"You can't?"

"No."

There was a long pause.

"You mean," he said, "you wouldn't get to be like your cousin Lizzie at Newport High, doing all those kicks and arm gestures—and *the splits*? Shouting out, 'Go, team, go! We're going to win! Win-win-win! Kill! Kill!'"

"Nobody says, 'Kill! Kill!'"

"And you wouldn't have to practice those routines all summer?"

"No, I wouldn't."

Another pause. Then: "What a shame."

"I knew you were going to say that."

"Why bother asking, then?"

"Because—"

"Kill! Kill!"

"*Dad.*"

"What?"

"So you think it sounds really lame?"

"Jesus, don't you?"

TEN

The Ojala Valley

I thought it was funny that Whitman didn't want to go to college—and that nobody made a stink about it. He went off on a yearlong adventure instead. I'd gotten a couple postcards from Baja, where he was surfing down the coast. From Hawaii he sent a whole green coconut with my address burned into the skin—and a stamp affixed—but after that, nothing came. He was in Fiji and Tahiti, we heard, then Sydney for the winter and New Zealand for the spring. My mother and Abuelita were flabbergasted that he'd been allowed to just wander like that. Marguerite was furious. Did Whitman have a plan? But my father believed that nobody should be "made to go to college," as he put it—and, indeed, he felt forcing Whitman to do much of anything was unwise.

"He's got to come to all big decisions on his own," my father said. "Or else he'll just blame me, or blame his mother, or, worse, he'll never learn how to make a big decision at all."

My father railed against any talk of the future—his future or ours—that seemed too practical or conventional. Whitman and I were supposed to have freer and more creative young lives than he'd been allowed. Independence and honesty were emphasized, not "selling out" and follow-ing the herd. Hard work was admirable, along with accomplishment, but only if unencumbered by mindless ambition. Success was overrated, my father preached, and of dubious long-term importance. Success stole one's freedom and required too much compromise—and too much con-cern for the whims of the masses. I suppose this philosophy, which he tried hard to instill in us, communicated a sense of futility and, perhaps, my father's own regrets. He had employed his brains and energy to build a company that now only made encroachments on him. Why should Whitman and I bother trying too hard? Where would it get us? Besides, what was more of a turnoff than somebody who tried too hard? In Cali-fornia the point was to *not try*.

If there was a center of the not-trying universe, it would have been the Ojala Valley. I'd never been here—only heard stories and gotten whiffs of the valley's zeitgeist from Whitman. He made it sound like a Shangri-la of experimental thinking, sophistication, and phenomenal creative en-ergy. According to Marguerite, Ojala was only a few slippery steps away from Sodom and Gomorrah. People ran wild and took acid in Ojala, even had orgies. Nobody had a real job—they grew their own vegetables or bartered or lived off trust funds or food stamps. To make matters worse, there was a long tradition of mysticism in the valley. The Theosophical Society had a center in Ojala, and Whitman had told us all about its nineteenth-century founder, a con artist and visionary named Madam Blavatsky, who talked to the dead. Whitman had stories about Krishna-murti, too, an Indian lord who gave lectures about the meaning of life and drew crowds of thousands of people. Whitman was my only contact with this intriguing world, and whenever he arrived at Van Dale and San Benito, he smelled a little like incense and fruity massage oils and carried around lots of new and faintly reckless ideas in his head. I'd missed see-ing him over the year—missed all his bulletins from the counterculture frontier. So when he finally returned from his mysterious travels among the coconuts and natives and invited me to visit him at home that summer, I was excited almost beyond words. And I was even more thrilled when my mother and Abuelita deemed that I was old enough, at nearly fifteen, to go. It felt like I'd been trying to get to Ojala for years.

Whitman pulled up our driveway in his old van with its spray-painted Rust-Oleum spots and faded bumper stickers supporting Shirley Chisholm for president and a ban on green grapes. The sky is usually blue and the weather predictably good in Los Angeles by July. But this year the June clouds were still with us—overcast, gloomy days that didn't turn sunny until just before dinner. I remember the rush of excitement that afternoon and the sense of adventure as I waited for the fog to clear and for Whitman to arrive. My mother and I watched from the living room windows and saw him hop out of his van.

He'd been gone nine or ten months. It had been that long since I'd seen him anyway. Not that he'd visibly changed. He seemed more or less the same old Whitman, wearing the same old wrinkled work shirt and army fatigues. He was a little thinner and stringier, and very tan—almost muddy—the color you get when you've been in the sun year-round. He walked with a slight trudge, although maybe that's hindsight. But I remember sensing something a bit tired and world-weary about him. He was smiling and in good cheer, but somehow diminished in his general level of enthusiasm. He wore a pair of small gold wire-rimmed glasses, which gave him a studious, introverted look.

We waved him inside, and he gravitated to Abuelita's dining room table. He was wearing sandals, and I noticed as he crossed the room that his feet looked banged up. He had acquired a number of small bluish wounds and cuts that had healed but turned dark. One of his big toenails had come off—and was just growing back, a flaky stump of hardened skin. Sitting down at the table, he picked out small oranges from a ceramic bowl, juggled three of them for us, and then peeled and ate one piece of fruit after another with his long, tan fingers. It was always jarring to see Whitman at Abuelita's house. His colorful stories—and bigness—made the rooms seem small and the old upholstery dingy. I saw the house through his eyes—or tried to—and imagined what he might be noticing. Rather than books in the bookcases, there were odds and ends, magazines and junk and useless clutter. There was an old brown TV console in the corner of the living room, something that would have horrified Marguerite. And the dining room table wasn't off by itself, secluded in its own separate room, but in the middle of the floor plan, at the intersection of all activity. Sliding glass doors opened to a view of an unremarkable shady garden and a cement patio where I used to skip rope as a girl but that went neglected now.

It's not that I worried, really, what Whitman would think. He was a hippie—that's how I thought of him—and not judgmental, or not supposed to be. But somehow I couldn't help being conscious that somewhere, surely, there was a place where he made note of these things. He was my father's son, after all, and Marguerite's grandson.

"Where's Mrs. G?" he asked.

"Feinman's," I said.

Whitman clucked sounds of disappointment.

"She never stops," I said.

"Feinman had bypass surgery," my mother offered.

"Well," Whitman said with a smile, "tell Mrs. G that I was asking for her—and give her my love."

Only my mother and I had flexible days that summer. In fact, since school had gotten out and I'd been to San Francisco, there'd been nothing but a long, free, and too-flexible stretch of weeks that I'd filled up with television, lots of television, and by playing a Paco Peña record over and over and daydreaming about marrying Antonio, except when I played Boz Scaggs and daydreamed of marrying him. In the afternoon sometimes, I went to Robbie's. When she wasn't busy with drill-team practice or doing Mormon stuff.

"So, Connie Mama, are you ready for the weekend before you?" Whitman asked.

My mother laughed her loud, panicky laugh—and changed the subject. While I was in Ojala with Whitman, she and Coach Weeger had arranged to take a four-day seminar at a hotel in Westwood. I wasn't sure what "sensitivity training" was supposed to do for them, but my mother had become very loud again and super laughy. She seemed to be dreading this thing called "est" like it was a treatment for cancer.

The drive north to Ojala required traveling on old highways with two lanes of cracked cement. We passed farms with yellow fields. We passed strange small towns with dusty streets lined with palms, and people living on the outskirts in trailers. It grew dustier and dustier, and very hot, until we entered a shady, narrow pass between rolling hills. On the other end was a lush, green valley.

Ojala was an old spa town—with hot springs and a few big rancheros and fat farms—that had become, in the last ten or twenty years, a magnet for artists and bohemians. From all I'd heard, I wasn't sure that I was going to like Ojala or feel comfortable there. I was apprehensive—but excited to be alone with Whitman. Wherever he was, I knew I'd be okay.

He was considering what to do next, whether he'd go to college or get a job, but he never talked about it. And after regaling me with a few stories of his travels—a school of hammerhead sharks in Fiji, a wipeout on the barrier reef where he lost his surfboard, taking mushrooms on a beach in New Zealand—it was hard to imagine him doing much else except more travel. He was still living with his mother in those days. I'd never met Patricia, or even seen a photograph. Marguerite had removed all images of her (and my mother) from the family albums that sat on top of the piano in her living room. But I'd heard a few things from my aunts. Patricia had grown up in Boston, the daughter of a surgeon. She'd studied art at a fancy private school—the East seemed full of those—then lived in Paris and worked as a sculptor's assistant. After marrying my father, she'd become interested in gardens and gardening—Marguerite was an influence, apparently—and then, after her divorce, she'd worked on the grounds of an old estate in England as an apprentice until becoming a landscape designer and master gardener in her own right. Whitman had told me she'd been involved with an English architect while living abroad, and when things fell apart, she'd moved to California to get over him. In Ojala there'd been a brief flirtation with a lute player and a longer romance with a street mime called "Nado," but she was now alone, or seemed to be. Whitman hadn't mentioned anybody in a while.

"She's very beautiful," Aunt Ann said, "and *intellectual*," as if that might be a little questionable. My mother had always been vague on the subject of Patricia, as though my father's first marriage hadn't really counted. "He complained that she was difficult," she'd once told me. "Impossible to get along with." Those shards of information, combined with the fact that Patricia had never made an appearance in San Benito since moving to California five years before, helped to form an impression in my mind: She was brooding and strange—as well as antisocial.

I was surprised, then, to be greeted by a tall, blond, heavyset woman at the door of an elegant farmhouse. This woman who called herself "Pat" wasn't at all the severe, difficult bohemian that I had pictured, but bright and cheerful. She wore a shift with a tropical print, big gold earrings, and a pair of white slip-on sandals. Her light, chin-length hair was tied back in a small, neat ponytail. Her handshake was firm, a huge squeeze.

"I'm so thrilled to finally meet you! My gosh, you look like Whitman!" she said in a robust, throaty voice. She seemed to have Whitman's exuberance and outgoing spirit—but along with warmth there was a polite distance. Something about her blue eyes and freckles and white-blond hair reminded me of Doris Day.

The farmhouse was cozy but not small, by any means. It was cleaner and more traditionally decorated than I'd expected. White cotton sofas and chairs were placed about the living room along with round tables with batik cloths over them and glass tops. Lamps dotted the room, spreading circles of yellow light upon collections of things arranged beneath them—beach shells, driftwood, the corpses of a few beautiful moths and butterflies. Around the large fireplace, there was a design of blue-and-white Dutch tiles. And on the mantel, and scattered throughout the room, there were framed pictures of dogs and people—none of whom I recognized, except Whitman. Tall bookcases stretched to the ceiling, loaded with hundreds of oversize picture books, art books, gardening books, and essays on photography. On the walls there were more photographs—Whitman pointed out a few by Edward Weston and some nude torsos by Edward Steichen. I couldn't remember if I'd ever seen photographs like that before, except in a museum. I'd never really been in a house like Patricia's before either. In her kitchen there was a deep bain-marie on the stove and another pot of boiling potatoes. "I hope you like vichyssoise," she said. I nodded enthusiastically. Whatever vichyssoise was, I was going to like it.

Whitman took me to the guest room. Rather than a bunk in some barn or on a moldy futon on the floor—I can't stress how dingy I'd always imagined Whitman's and Patricia's daily lives must have been—he led me to a spacious room with a bright, handmade quilt thrown over the bed, pressed linens, a high ceiling, and its own airy bathroom. There was a bouquet of lavender next to the sink and, on a chest of drawers, a vase of pink flowers with sunny yellow centers. "Those are cosmos," Whitman said, setting down my duffel on a bamboo luggage rack. I marveled over the flowers—was it the room, or the ceiling, or the sunlight, or my low expectations that suddenly made everything look so perfect?

Cheered by my enthusiasm, Whitman insisted I see the garden. The house was set on what appeared to be a large piece of property. It seemed like a park to me—with no apparent fencing or walls, except for an outdoor eating area with a brick-and-stucco fireplace. Farther back, a large vegetable garden spanned thirty or forty square feet. Had I ever thought about how vegetables were grown or what the plants looked like before the fruit was picked?

Patricia grew everything in raised mounds of earth, more than a foot across and separated by channels where the garden could be watered easily. Whitman explained that there were sections in the garden for different types of plants, which were rotated from year to year to keep the soil healthy. There was an area for melons and squashes and pumpkins, another for beans. There were potato vines and onion stalks. There were shiny purple eggplants and furry okra. The row of tomato plants went on and on. I'm sure I'd never seen a tomato plant before that afternoon. The only edible things that Abuelita grew were avocados. And Marguerite, besides her arbor of sour grapes, had only trees: kumquats and grapefruit and Meyer lemons.

Whitman began collecting ripe tomatoes in a wicker hamper that had been left hanging on a post. Patricia's plants were almost as tall as he was, over six feet high, and when I touched a leaf, it was sticky and damp and left an intoxicating smell on my fingers. He filled up half of the basket with tomatoes, some yellow, some red, and then stopped to pluck a handful of tiny round ones. "Sweet One Hundreds," he said, popping one into my mouth. The marble-size tomato exploded between my teeth—warm, sweet—and seemed like eating sunshine itself.

He straddled a raised bed of lettuce and other things—*what was rocket?*—clipping some leaves for a salad. Then he walked across the garden to a composting area where piles of brownish leaves and yard cuttings and citrus peels were stacked between hay bales. Whitman placed my hand near the bottom of the pile to feel how warm it was. "The organic matter breaks down," he said, "and when it's rotting and decomposing, the chemical changes cause it to give off heat."

"Is this the fertilizer for the farm?" I asked.

"What farm?"

"Your commune."

"What commune?"

"This. Aren't we . . . isn't this a commune?"

"This is our house. My mom's house."

"But I—"

"We only lived on a farm co-op when we first moved to Ojala. Mom was just getting the lay of the land and learning about California gardens, western varieties and all that. You know it's a completely different climate from the East Coast or England. Different plants and an entirely different growing season. It's really two springs, two falls, a long, dry summer—"

"I thought—"

He went on, a bit defensively, "She bought this house four years ago. It was a working ranch at the turn of the century—and, of course, modernized at some point. Then it was a second home for a propmaster at Paramount Studios. He lived here between pictures. He planted most of the stone-fruit orchards and liked doing all these wild horticultural experiments, grafting a branch of an apricot onto a peach tree."

Whitman's eyes were flashing. "Mom's got—I don't know—almost twenty acres. We sell only a small amount from the orange groves and the avocados. That goes to independent farm markets to offset the costs of running everything else. But she doesn't live off the proceeds of the farm—or break even." He turned away, with his back to me.

"And beyond that barn," he said, pointing to a brown wooden structure in the distance, "which is mostly empty except for a couple old tractors that don't work, is Ocotillo Creek. It's a ways down, and there's a great swimming hole, if you don't mind leeches."

By dinnertime we were all laughing about the impression I'd had—and how wrong it had been. We sat down at a small wooden farm table in the kitchen, the three of us, and ate a simple meal of cold leek and potato soup with cream, crusty bread, and a salad from the garden tossed in a fresh mustard and garlic vinaigrette that I'd watched Patricia make, her tan hands holding the small white bowl and a whisk.

"Now I know what they are saying about me in San Benito," she said. "That I'm a dangerous hippie."

"It's not that," I said, feeling sorry I'd been so candid. Was Patricia hurt or not? I couldn't tell. "Marguerite only talks about Ojala, never you. She doesn't say that much about my mother either. I don't think she likes talking about the past too much."

"Except she talks about N.C. all the time," said Whitman.

"And Paul—he never mentions me?" Patricia's eyes were piercing and strong.

"Not to me," I said. "Never."

"Oh, that's so interesting," she said. "Maybe I should be relieved. God only knows what he'd say."

"He talks about you to me, Mum," Whitman broke in. "Always asks how you're doing. But I don't think he really likes to analyze the past or revisit it. He's too shallow and self-centered for that."

I was surprised by his assessment—and that Whitman was allowed to openly air such a harsh view. Abuelita and my mother would never have let me say anything disrespectful about my father. But at the same time, it was a thrill to be in a place where brutal honesty was allowed.

"I don't think that's it at all," Patricia said to Whitman, as if reading my mind. "Your father's much deeper and more complicated than you want to make out. Although I can't exactly say that I haven't been tempted, from time to time, to draw similar conclusions."

Whitman smiled. Patricia chuckled. "He doesn't say much about his marriages," she went on, "because it's the only thing in life that he's been a total failure at." She leaned over her bitter greens and looked at me with a quizzical expression. "I mean, don't you think that's got to be it, Inez? He hates his failures. It's certainly not that unusual—lots of people can't seem to stay married—but I think he was ashamed in a peculiar way, not because of N.C. and Marguerite or any embarrassment he might have caused them. He never cared what they thought. He enjoyed torturing them, in fact. But there was something about our divorce that injured his pride and sense of infallibility. Honestly, I don't think it occurred to him that I was devastated. I remember a telephone conversation we had one night, after his marriage to Consuela had fallen apart. He seemed so sad, so disappointed in himself. It was as if he were ashamed he didn't know himself any better—that he'd fooled himself twice, or been fooled by his heart, before figuring things out."

My mother never had any words to describe my father, aside from the occasional dig that slipped out when she wasn't careful. A few years earlier, she had decided that she didn't approve of him anymore—his ritzy boho lifestyle, the cape-and-fedora thing. She'd lumped all his failings into class failings, I suppose. He was spoiled. He was careless. Everything had been too easy. She'd made up her mind about him and didn't want to know anything more. Sometimes she played dumb when his name was mentioned, as if surprised to learn that he was still alive.

"What didn't he figure out?" I asked.

Patricia picked up the bottle of wine and poured herself another glass.

"You said that he married twice, made the same mistake twice," I went on, "before he'd figured something out. What?"

"Oh," Patricia said, taking a sip. "Monogamy isn't the problem so much. It's really about sustaining it. Over time one woman isn't enough—that's all. I think at first he thought it was me. That I wasn't enough. So it was my fault. I'd let him down. And I think he hated me for that. And when he met your mother—my God, he was so in love with her—he figured she would be enough. I mean, just look at her. How could *that* not be enough? She looks like Sophia Loren, for God's sake. And she was probably a lot nicer to him than I was. And when she got pregnant with you—everything was so different in those days, of course. If you were pregnant, you got married. Maybe Paul knew by then, I don't know, but eventually Consuela wasn't enough either. He needed somebody *new*. He needed to be in love—and have somebody wonderful in love with him."

When I didn't speak up right away, she said, "What does your mother say, Inez?"

"She doesn't talk about him too much."

"No?" Whitman seemed disbelieving.

"Not really."

"Consuela's very private," Patricia said, smiling a little crookedly at her son, as if only part of her wanted to smile. "That's all."

"She had trouble making up her mind," I ventured. "I know that. When I was little, when we left—when she left him. She seemed sorry she had. And then it was like she was waiting for him to come back. But he didn't."

"No," Patricia said. "He's brilliant at making it look like it's all your idea. As if you're the one leaving, not him. But he'd already found somebody else—right off. There was a graduate student, wasn't there?" Patricia and Whitman were both looking at me, but my mind was miles away, and my heart pounding. All these things—a revelation. I'd never known people could talk like this.

"What was her name?" Patricia asked me.

"You mean Marisa?" I answered.

Patricia nodded.

"Oh, right," said Whitman. "We were still in England then."

"She was his math student," I said. "Beautiful blue eyes—like yours, Patricia. And giant boobs like Mom."

Patricia laughed.

"Actually," I said, "she was really sweet."

"Of course she was," Patricia said.

Then I had to say it—the words were on my tongue, pushing against my lips. "I didn't know they *had* to get married," I said. "Nobody ever told me that."

Patricia looked up, casually, almost as if she'd been waiting for it. Almost as if the whole thing had been planned—and it probably was. "Oh, but, Inez—it's not what you think. *Really.* I didn't want any more children—one was enough for me. I thought I'd hit the jackpot with Whitman. And it did seem as if your father was excited to have another."

The next morning there was no wind or clouds, and Ojala seemed suddenly like a very dry and hot place. When I woke up and looked out my sunny bedroom window, I saw Patricia moving a hose around the vegetable garden, watering. She and Whitman were talking quietly in the kitchen when I arrived there. After breakfast it was decided somehow that Whitman and I should take a swim. Curious to see the swimming hole, and trying not to worry about the leeches, I put on a small bikini, some shorts, and a heavy pair of hiking boots that I'd borrowed from Patricia, who was cooking up something for a group of people who were coming by for lunch.

We took a short hike through the woods, and Whitman led me to a sunny area beyond the trees where he had a forest of marijuana plants growing. He walked me around his tall grove of contraband, pulling off leaves and smelling them, examining tops. His mother knew about it, he said—and didn't disapprove. He pulled a small metal pipe from a pocket of his shorts, pressed some dry buds from another pocket into the snout, and held it out.

"No thanks."

"Ah, come on," he said. "They're very mellow buds."

"I don't want to."

"I thought you were into it."

"Just once."

"Once? But nothing happens the first time," he said. "Didn't you know that? Come on. Might as well try it again. Nothing will happen this time either."

When he lit up the pipe, the smoke smelled musky and sweet, and clouds of it came and went as we walked into the shady woods. I took a few careful puffs, and Whitman called out the names of the trees as we passed them—the old live oaks and white pines and dried-out cedars. But as the minutes passed, he grew quiet. That was the bad thing. I'd noticed it before, that day at Ripper Jacks and other times. When Whitman was stoned, he retreated, went inside himself. He grew silent and seemed almost sullen. Where had he gone? And when would he return? I hated how much he seemed to desire that separation from the world, and distance from me. I was lonely suddenly, even more than if I'd been walking in the woods by myself.

We came to the edge of Ocotillo Creek and walked uphill to a wide spot in the stream where the clear water had pooled in the sun and shadows and formed a swimming hole. The air smelled fresh and green and wet— almost a faint metallic smell. Huge gray boulders stood at the edge of the water, dappled with sunlight and spots of pale lichen. I was looking at a beautiful, smooth boulder, the swirling green water that grew brown at the muddy bank, and worrying again about leeches, when I heard a sound.

Two naked bodies—horizontal blurs of pink-white flesh—were sunning themselves on a large rock across the way.

Whitman yelled out. "Hey-ya, Ross!"

"Hey, man."

"Nice hot day."

"Yeah," Ross said. He twisted his head around and saw me. "Who dat?"

"My sister."

"You got a sister?"

Both heads lifted off the rock. They belonged to two guys—and one of them, Ross, looked as if he might swim over. Sure enough, he sat up, slid off his boulder, and hit the surface with a splash. Underwater, his body looked long and pale—yellowish, not pink—and his hair was much shorter than Whitman's, a honey color and full to his ears. With each stroke of his short journey, my dread grew. I became intensely aware of my shorts, my T-shirt and bathing suit, my socks and clunky hiking boots. How was I to greet a nude man? Would he stand up, full frontal, and shake my hand?

Whitman, completely oblivious to my distress, was quickly removing his shoes and socks—then inching his shorts and underwear over his buttocks. Within seconds he was naked, and without the slightest hesitation he scrambled up a large boulder next to us and took a leaping jump into the air.

Meanwhile Ross had made his way to the shore and rose from the swimming hole like Poseidon. "Hey," he said, smoothing his hair with his wet hands and wiping the water from his eyes. "Didn't know Whitman had a sister." He hugged himself to keep warm.

"I'm Inez," I replied with great nonchalance. Years of practicing a blasé expression were serving me well. But it was awfully hard to keep my eyes from drifting to Ross's taut waist, and below.

"The water's unreal," he said.

"Can't wait," I said, as if I swam with naked men every day. I unzipped my cutoffs, then fumbled with my hiking boots—the laces seemed to have been knotted three times—and when I'd finally gotten them off, Ross was back in. His big nude body wasn't visible anymore, except for his head on the surface of the green water, next to Whitman's, as they watched me.

I suppose that I could have swum in my bathing suit. But to keep it on—when everybody else was naked—seemed to me prudish and awkward. While removing the suit seemed unimaginable, and nightmarishly scary, the kind of exposure I'd spent my whole life avoiding, it also became, in my mind, the better choice. It was the progressive choice. It was the confident choice. After all, I wanted to be the sort of person who could tear off her clothes and plunge naked into swimming holes. And at some point I'd have to start. Later on, in my fantasies of what happened that day, I threw my bathing suit and shorts into the branches of a nearby tree, climbed the tallest boulder, stretched my arms high up over my head, and did an elegant dive into the water with a great hollering of naked exhilaration. That would be my mother's way—the shy panic and laughter. It would have been my father's way, too—the detachment and theatricality. But in reality I unsheathed myself as nimbly and quietly as I could, like a little mouse, stepped onto a flat rock at the water's edge, and slipped in without fanfare or shouts of exhilaration. As I submerged into the cool water, I felt a great groaning weight lifted from my being.

My mother didn't have close friends, really—aside from Coach Weeger. She had tennis partners, old classmates from Van Dale High, and clients she'd found or sold houses for. Their conversations were about practical matters and daily life—which dry cleaner did the best job, which butcher had the best steaks. Mostly they talked about tennis. It was a complete universe and language and religion in those days. You didn't need friends or ideology. You just had to know what players you liked. Pancho Gonzales, Arthur Ashe, Björn Borg. Those were the gods of Van Dale, and my mother's gods. Below them in Olympus, there were only lesser mortals and demons. There was a young man with funny bangs and knee socks named Jimmy Connors. My mother and her Van Dale friends weren't sure they liked him. A young girl named Chrissie Evert was always winning, but like Connors, she seemed dogged and square and had no personality beyond her amazing tennis playing. For my mother she was like a dancer who knew all the steps and performed technically well but had no style.

In North Beach my father and Justine had a small circle of intimate friends. They never talked about sports—or seemed aware of the World Series or the Super Bowl or when the U.S. Open was being played. They never talked much about the news either. They rarely gossiped or even exchanged much information. Rather they shared a wavelength, an attitude, a sensibility. And, like my father and Ooee, they were members of some undefined worldwide bohemian movement. They weren't sellouts. That was the main thing. They had their own ideas about things—and none of them particularly practical or grown up. One of my father's oldest friends was a filmmaker who had worked for six years on a short documentary about fog. Another was a painter of all-white paintings and then, a few years later, of all-black paintings. And aside from the artists and *flamencos*, who were loyal to the music but little else, my father's other friends were mostly academics—engineers and mathematicians, none of whom I was able to communicate with. They were friendly enough and I admired them, but I never knew what they were talking about.

At Patricia's that day, I was introduced to an entirely different tribe of characters. She said she was having some people "over for lunch," and they began to pour into the house, one by one, two by two, and in clumps. Eventually the house grew so crowded with people that it was hard to move from room to room. Patricia swirled around in a bright blue tent of a dress, almost a caftan, and a heavy gold necklace that she said had been a gift from Marguerite years ago. People kept arriving and arriving—neighbors and more friends—and there was lots of food and wine—lots of wine—and Patricia's friends knew labels, vineyards, grapes, and they compared various vintages of Chablis and Zinfandel with epicurean relish. There was a garden designer named Mickey with a loose red Afro to his shoulders. A tall, Norse-looking woman named Gertruda had a huge straw hat that she didn't take off all day. A British writer named Sebastian came with a Turkish woman named Sebnam, who wore a gold lamé bikini top and tight white capris. There was a pair of men who stood next to each other from room to room and talked like an old married couple. Were they?

"How'd you like the creek?" a young man with blond hair asked me. He was wearing jeans and a pink button-down with the sleeves rolled up. It took me a few seconds before I realized it was Ross, all covered up and dry and barely recognizable.

"Perfect temperature."

"Not too cold?"

Ross looked awfully good in clothes—would the boys in Van Dale have dared to wear pink? I tried not to think about how, just a couple hours ago, he'd seen me naked.

"Was it colder than usual today?" I asked.

"It seemed that way—although I'm not sure the actual temperature really changes that much. I was at the hot springs earlier in the morning, and maybe by comparison the creek seemed frigid to me." Ross stood really close when he talked to me. In fact, most of Patricia's friends did that.

"No leeches, though," I said.

"They're harmless, if you don't let them hang on too long."

"Whitman promised that I'd see one."

"There's always tomorrow," Ross said with a smile, "or later tonight."

I nodded, trying to contain an explosion of feeling that I was having in that moment, a mix of joy and dread and excitement—the thought of nighttime, and water, in combination with Ross. He had none of the jitters of the adolescent boys in Van Dale who stood next to me in their bathing suits at swim parties or on the grass at the Verdugo Community Center, all bottled up and clammy, barely containing their secret plans for touches and feels and grabs. But Ross, when we'd finished swimming and were standing around naked, hadn't jittered. He didn't even stare— or not stare. He'd just gotten out of the water and moved to the warmest boulder and lain down in the sunshine. I stole glances at his penis, watched it loosen and grow longer. I couldn't believe how unscary it was. How relaxed, how quiet, and how lovely his body looked, so smooth and tan.

Patricia glided from room to room at lunch, made people laugh and then, just as quickly, disappeared. The burden of entertaining wasn't a burden but a release. She grew lighter and easier in a crowd. Not many of her friends seemed to be native Californians. They were from the East or Midwest, parts of Europe or Israel. It was an odd assortment—farmers and artists and writers and people who just worked in Ojala, in cheese shops or coffee shops or waiting tables. It was hard to tell what anybody did, exactly, because none of them talked about their work. They talked about their gardens, or a recent day at the beach, or a hike in the hills, or a meal they'd eaten. They talked about books they were reading, foreign movies they'd just seen, and things they wanted to do in life—dreams they had, trips they wanted to make. They were all enormously supportive of Whitman. They loved how adventurous and resourceful he was. They asked where he was going next. And they seemed excited for me, too, just for being a girl with my future in front of me and Whitman for a brother. The lunch—I realized later—had been thrown in my honor, or for my amusement. But Patricia had handled this so quietly, with the gentlest touch, that I never felt the strain of being an honoree.

She wasn't from California—that was why, I felt sure. She wasn't descended from frontier robber barons like Justine, who'd been raised with so much room and money that she didn't know how to be around regular people. Patricia wasn't a first-generation assimilation test case like my mother, who, besides being stunningly beautiful, just wanted to fit in. And, unlike Marguerite, a traditionalist who looked at the world and felt it was going down the tubes—the quality of everything was deteriorating— Patricia was excited by anything new, anything she didn't know about. Every tomato she tasted was the best, every friend she introduced to me was the most amazing of all. I'd never met anybody so easy and enthusiastic, and more than once I wished she were my mother—not just Whitman's. But at the same time, it was impossible to imagine that my father had ever been in love with somebody so fat or so old.

A few days later, when I got home to Van Dale, Patricia's lust for all things in life hadn't traveled with me. Abuelita's house looked darker than ever, the upholstery shabbier. The streets seemed so regular, too uniform and straight, all the houses so close together. The sidewalks bugged me, and the tall, brushed-aluminum lampposts that hung over the street. The Verdugo pool was so antiseptic and chlorinated. I looked at the kids in their nose plugs and goggles and neon-colored bathing suits, and I felt sorry for them. I missed the swimming hole and the large, smooth boulders. Where was the dappled sunlight and shade of the woods? And why weren't there any boys in Van Dale like Ross or Whitman, who swam with me and just let me swim—no grabby hands—all of us enjoying the water, the nighttime, and the glimpses of the full moon behind the branches of the oaks? I hadn't been gone that long, but sometimes just a couple days in a strange new paradise can change the way you see things forever.

ELEVEN

Shelley Strelow

Whitman left that fall for South Africa, where it had been arranged he'd live with Ooee Lungo's sister in Cape Town. She was married to the head of an airline and offered Whitman a guest cottage on the grounds of her house. I don't remember when he left, really—or how I said good-bye. I was starting Van Dale High and feeling barraged by low-level anxieties. I wondered how strange and overwhelming my new school might be, how hard the classes would be, and whether Justine's elegant castoffs were the right clothes for such a place. And then, as soon as the school year started, I had to deal with my mother. She was suddenly trying to connect with me, grasping at me as if I were slipping through her fingers. She cocked her head when she looked at me, as though I weren't the same person anymore, as though I'd mutated, become possessed, or a stranger had taken over the body of Inez Ruin. But believe me, after est, she was the one who'd turned weird.

One morning I caught her looking down at a notepad by the phone where I had doodled

SHELLEY STRELOW
SHELLEY STRELOW
SHELLEY STRELOW

"Who's that?" my mother said.

"My friend Shelley," I said. "You remember. We went hiking?"

She knew full well who Shelley was. (Maybe she just wanted to forget.) Before they'd met face-to-face, I said that my new friend liked to hike. My mother got the impression that Shelley was an outdoorsy type, like an older Camp Fire girl—or maybe a kid who had grown up doing all kinds of outdoorsy things with her family, like scuba diving or sailing. Los Angeles was full of those families. They camped on weekends, or went diving, or took overnight sailing trips to Catalina Island. They drove to Mammoth and skied for the holidays. That seemed healthy to my mother. She'd gone to high school with kids like that and always felt left out.

"She looks like Joan Crawford," my mother said after meeting Shelley for the first time. "The young Joan Crawford. *Her eyes.*" They weren't innocent eyes, she was saying. They were cynical and worldly eyes. Over the summer Shelley had gotten a different nose—it had been cut down into a bob, a classic California nose like Cheryl Tiegs's or Christie Brinkley's—and this made her eyes seem almost too big and bulgy. Her eyes were intense and angling for something. She'd had sex already. Definitely. You knew that. It was in her eyes and walk and the way she held herself, and in her incredibly short cutoffs with the white denim strings that hung down her thighs and looked like Tampax pull cords, and in all her opinions that she shared with such magnificent confidence. She had moved to Van Dale from Los Feliz Hills, where David Feinman lived and all those movie people with spoiled brats who had nannies like Abuelita. Shelley was more of a city kid, and not docile and trusting and sweet like Robbie. She used the word "dick" in conversation. What more did you need to know? She had no sweetness. She'd been a Sears catalog model as a girl, and I guess that impressed me, too.

Mom liked the hiking—and she hung on to that for a while. Some things in life had to be introduced early on: camping, skiing, scuba diving, horseback riding. It was programming. That's why she was so high on me going off with Marguerite on the weekends, to ride. *Everything was programming, and people were just machines,* like Werner Erhard said. My mother was full of Werner talk in those days. He was the mysterious figure behind est and all the est philosophy, and he had pretty much replaced Arthur Ashe and Björn Borg. And after taking the est training, she'd become talkative and almost strident. She was openly reflective, too, but she was bad at it. Introspection was so new to her. She exploded with revelations—some of them totally stupid—and being around her felt like a demolition derby. I kept my head down, went about my business. No way was I going to ask her about being pregnant when she married my dad. All that would come out anyway, since she was reviewing her whole life like a movie she'd never seen before.

She danced because she needed love, she said. She danced because her father liked dancers. That was obvious, she said. Abuelita was a hard worker. Charles Garcia was a dancer. And so my mother, needing something she called "confirmation," became a hardworking dancer. All other aspects of life that might interest an adolescent—clothes shopping, boyfriends, crushes on pop singers—were approached with a psychic frugality that bordered on masochism. She excelled at tap—both buck-and-wing and soft shoe—by ten. She began ballet at eleven and ascended quickly, her body deemed perfect for classical dance: small head; large eyes; broad back and shoulders; long, shapely arms and legs; a high instep. Her teachers urged her to continue. But her breasts grew, and grew and by fourteen, after two years on pointe, my mother despaired at her own lack of *ballon*—she couldn't seem to linger in the air. Eventually she wandered away to study flamenco with Cinco Sais, a well-known instructor with a small dance studio in Verdugo Hills.

"Cinco Sais. I used to think that was an accident," she said one night after dinner when I was trying to do my history homework. "But it was a choice. Cinco was a choice, and flamenco was a choice." And then she grew quiet.

Life was a bunch of choices—one of the many helpful things est taught. You weren't a powerless victim if you interpreted your life that way. You chose your parents. You chose your husbands. And if you chose to take an airplane to New York and it crashed and you died, you needed to see how it had been a choice. When you got on a plane, you took responsibility for the possibility that it might crash. If you didn't want to die in a plane crash, then you shouldn't get on a plane. It was really that simple. You were in control. And with this new approach in mind, my mother started to look back on everything and began to take responsibility for lots of iffy decisions. Did she really care about dancing at all? Was it really in her blood—or was it just neediness and programming?

At Cinco's studio, for hours each day, she worked on learning the varying rhythms, or *campas,* of the flamenco songs—hammering out the complex beats with her feet. Her back arched. Her arms floated over her head. Her hands took the shape of doves in flight. She learned to make her face proud, almost haughty—and, at other times, fierce. There were so many *palos* in flamenco, so many rhythms and moods. She mastered the mournful *taranta,* the sensual tango, the exuberant *alegría,* the raucous *bulerías.* The music released something deep and wild and unexpected within her—extremes of feeling, the sorrow, the joy, the delirium that Abuelita had never allowed inside her orderly house. Flamenco took hold of her, pulled and stretched her. It freed her.

"It was all I wanted in life—meant more to me than school or my friends," she said in a rare moment of poetic feeling. "Flamenco called to me, and I followed. But then something else came along."

She was touring with the José Greco Dance Company in New York City and coming out of the cramped dressing room at the Marcus Aurelius Theater on Forty-seventh Street, expecting to meet up with an old friend from high school, when she looked across the hallway and saw a tall, dark-haired man leaning against a backstage wall and staring at her. Who was he?

"Connie!" she heard a voice call out behind her. It was Steve Huth, her old friend from Van Dale High. Steve was a gregarious guy—valedictorian and former student-body president—who had been trying to date my mother for so long that it had become a joke between them. He rushed over to her side, full of praise for her performance. My mother smiled. She was feeling particularly good that evening, wearing a new red coat and her cheeks flushed from performing, and she couldn't help continuing to notice the tall man against the wall. He was so handsome and his face so tight, almost severe. He wore a long blue-black wool overcoat that matched the color of his hair.

Steve was saying something about a friend of his—he'd brought along a fellow mathematician from Caltech, a friend who played flamenco guitar.

"Really?" my mother asked, looking over the top of Steve's head. A mathematician? Ugh. She had never cared for guitarists either. Her mind was still at the wall. "You have a friend who plays flamenco?"

"Paul!" Steve yelled out into the crowd. Then he turned toward the hallway wall and yelled again. "Paul! Come on! This is my famous friend Connie I've told you so much about."

My father straightened himself, parted with the surface of the wall, and as he walked toward her, my mother watched a wide smile appear on his face. She'd never seen such a smile, she said. It was like a current of energy that made her giddy and short of breath. And suddenly she felt alone with that smile, as if all the stagehands and crew, *flamencos* and their families and their equipment—their chairs, guitar cases, heavy shoes, trunks of clothing, boxes of thin wooden matches and blue-and-white packs of Ducados cigarettes, their clouds of smoke and clanking bottles of beer, as well as poor Steve Huth—had become a blur of flesh-pale motion, a soft fluttering of sound and dim light. The smile grew larger and more powerful as it came closer, and to my mother it seemed to generate the effect of an immeasurably vast theater crowded with people who were all jumping to their feet and applauding.

"And I remember feeling," my mother said, "that maybe the only reason I'd danced at all was so I could meet *him*."

Shelley and I started hiking in late September, after Whitman had taken off for Cape Town. The first day of class, we'd discovered each other in Ceramics 101, and something clicked right away. Shelley was irreverent and funny—made terrible fun of people—and I'd never really had a friend like that. A few weeks into school, we decided to get together on the weekend, and Shelley suggested hiking. I bounced out of the house that morning in shorts and tennis shoes, sweatshirt and bandanna, carrying a little knapsack on my back that held a thermos of water and some Wheat Thins. That seemed pretty wonderful to my mother. How healthy. And, like horseback riding, it made me outdoorsy, and she was glad about that.

The next week Shelley came over to the house after school one day. She was sixteen already and had a car—a blood-red Volkswagen Karmann Ghia convertible that didn't appear particularly safe—and my mother looked at Shelley, and she looked at that Karmann Ghia, and it was as if she were waking up from a long sleep. Her head cocked to the side. And suddenly she was paying attention to me in a whole new way. I'd always been a good kid, responsible, like a cactus that didn't need much watering. I didn't go overboard or have huge, overwrought passions. I had a head on my shoulders, my mother thought. But then she saw Shelley and the Karmann Ghia, and my mother started to act like maybe the head on my shoulders had fallen off.

Fresh from est, she tried out her new head-shrinking techniques on me. She would sit me down on the sofa, or on her bed, for long heart-to-hearts. She wanted honesty, she said. She wanted real feelings. She kept the analysis going while we shopped for new underwear or went to the grocery store. She always dragged the conversation to the subject of Shelley. "You don't need to go along with the crowd," my mother said. "What crowd?" I asked, in resistant and adversarial tones.

My mother suggested that maybe I was full of fear, the way she'd always been full of fear. She'd danced out of fear, she told me. She'd played tennis out of fear. She'd sold houses out of fear. "In est I got clear about that," she said. "I really *got it*." Looking back, she knew she'd made mistakes. She wanted to make sure that I didn't make the same ones.

I was desperate to stop her from squeezing est thinking into my head. In the past she'd worried about me in spurts, like when the Garter Belt Man was running around town exposing himself and kept eluding the Van Dale police. But in general, over the years, I'd tried to give her little to worry about. She'd never found out about my crush on Antonio—or how Ooee, drunk, had sucked my earlobe after the flamenco party and said he was waiting for me. I never told her about how great Kenny Frank's callused hands felt as they rubbed my breasts, and my stories about Ojala had contained no mention of Ross or skinny-dipping or Whitman's grove of marijuana. Mostly I'd talked about how fantastic Patricia was—and I hadn't guessed that that would drive her craziest of all.

Oh, there'd been a few times when I was making the transition to junior high and asked to pierce my ears or wanted to wear pantyhose—but that hadn't been difficult for my mother to squash. It was normal girl stuff, and not troubling to her. She'd been a little concerned about a pile of D. H. Lawrence books in my bedroom—*Women in Love* and *Men in Love*—and then, later in the summer, Dostoyevsky's *Notes from Underground*. She had a strange worry that I was bookish—"reading too much"—and not outdoorsy. But now, when she compared me to Shelley, all those books seemed healthy. TV seemed healthy. For God's sake, ten hours a day of TV was better than Shelley Strelow.

Robbie Morrison, I began to realize, was a human shield that had protected me against my mother—and all her fears. Whatever I did, wherever I went, it was okay because I spent all my time in the company of Robbie. I had lots of other friends from Camp Fire Girls and saw my cousins in Laguna, but if you drew concentric circles around me, arranging other people like planets around my sun, it was really only Robbie who was orbiting nearby. Whitman was a faint Pluto. As long as I was best friends with Robbie, my mother never had to worry. I got A's in school. I participated in team sports, returned my library books on time, usually made my bed in the morning. All along, my mother assumed that I did those things and didn't get into trouble because I was "square" in a good way, the way people used the word when my mother was a girl. But after Shelley turned up, my mother began to suspect that maybe it was Robbie Morrison who was a good kid and a square—her most outrageous act of rebellion was joining a Presbyterian youth group on Wednesday nights instead of doing something Mormon.

I guess, before Shelley Strelow, the only thing my mother had to worry about was whether I was becoming a Jesus freak or born again. My mother wasn't too wild about that youth group, or with my spiritual conversion to Jesus at camp. She seemed in a chilly mood when she had to drive Robbie and me to Van Dale Pres at night with our New Testament Bibles under our arms. Looking back, she should have been incredibly thankful, instead of mortified, when those church elders came to pray with me in the living room one night after dinner. It happened when I was fourteen. They just showed up. Out of the blue.

"What is it, Mom?" I asked from the floor of the den.

"Some church people are here," she said. She was wearing a very short white tennis skirt and a super-tight top that made her breasts look like missiles about to launch. "Did you invite anybody over?"

"What?" I was still embarrassed by everything in those pre-Ojala days. "I didn't invite them!" I blurted, almost hysterically, then lowered my voice. "I just filled out this card a few Sundays ago when Robbie and I went to the service."

"What card?"

The card was white and had said ARE YOU A VISITOR? at the top. It looked a little like one of those scorecards at a miniature-golf course. And next to the card—in the wooden pocket of the pew where the hymnals were kept—was a small brown pencil, just like those miniature-golf pencils. The combination was irresistible. So I filled out my name: Inez Ruin, 314 Ardmore Road, Van Dale, Calif. 91202.

A few weeks later, three somber-looking people were standing in the yellow no-bug light of Abuelita's porch.

"Inez? Inez Ruin?"

My mother shook her head. They'd said my name "EYE-nez," which meant they didn't know me too well.

"We're from the ministry of Van Dale Presbyterian Church," said one lean woman with plain gray hair and a cardigan sweater.

"Oh."

"We've come at Inez's request," said a man with a square jaw and a crew cut. "We hope you don't mind."

"Just a moment," my mother said, closing the front door partway and heading down the hall to extract me from *Beacon Hill*, a new show about Irish maids and butlers working in a mansion in Boston.

I was wearing school clothes, a skirt and V-neck sweater that was dotted with lint from the green-and-yellow shag carpeting in our den. I tried to compose myself and not laugh nervously. My heart was pounding as I wandered fake-sleepily toward the front door.

"Hello, Inez. I'm Mrs. Potter," the tall woman said, "and this is Mr. Edwards and Miss Ryan. We're from the ministry of Van Dale Presbyterian and just stopped by to pay a call. May we come in?"

The theme song of *M*A*S*H* was starting up in the den. How I longed to be back there. Instead the churchwomen had surrounded me on the sofa and everybody's head was bowed. "We ask for your guidance, dear Lord, and your mercy. . . ."

Their eyes were closed. Everybody's eyes were closed. And heads lowered. My hair was hanging in my face like a waterfall of darkness and limp reeds.

"Inez has asked Jesus into her heart. . . ."

I was dying inside, or wishing to be dead—I wasn't sure which. Down the hallway I could hear my mother in the den chuckling. Knowing the pain and humiliation I was going through, she must have found that episode of *M*A*S*H* hilarious.

After about twenty or thirty minutes of prayer—an eternity—I walked the church elders to the front door with a promise that I'd be seeing them at the fellowship hall after the service on Sunday, a complete lie.

"Oh, God," I said. *"Mom."*

"What?"

"Oh-God," I went on. "Oh-God-oh-God. Ohhhhhhh."

"Who were they, honey?"

"I don't want to talk about it," I said. "Please. *Really.*" Seeing the clock on the wall, I made a groan of despair. "I practically missed the whole show."

W as she slipping into my bedroom to spy? I'd started wondering about that. The wallpaper was peeling off in one corner of the room, and there were marks next to the bed, slashes in blue ink, where I was counting something. By Christmas, just three months after Shelley Strelow appeared in my life, there were three dozen slashes on the wall. Did my mother see them? Did she assume they were some kind of accident with a ballpoint pen?

My mother was suddenly picking up clothes from the floor of my bedroom, too—unprecedented. It felt like years since she'd been in there, years since she'd really noticed me or wanted my complete and utter attention. Oh, she'd put me to bed when I was younger. Or she'd arrive with a new blotter for my desk, or a wastepaper can, or a new pair of tights. But, for the most part, I picked up after myself, and Abuelita did the rest. Abuelita ran the house, really. So it was odd when I walked in and found my mother neatly arranging my underwear and sweater drawers. Was she checking for cigarette smoke?

She talked about "taking responsibility" for everything in her life now—so I guessed she'd be taking responsibility for my cigarette smoke, too, and everything else about me. Since est she had sorted her memories and experiences into a pyramid of moments that were entirely her responsibility. Something she had "created." (She'd created me, hadn't she?) The other new development in those days was her reliance on the word "asshole" when explaining her new philosophical approach to life. She talked about needing to assume responsibility and quit being a victim and "an asshole." In est everybody who didn't "get it" was an asshole. It was a word that my mother had never liked—and Abuelita was completely scandalized by it. But, as my mother had explained to me, whatever you didn't like about a word, any word, it was just a quality that you had assigned to the word—and nothing more. If your experience of the word "asshole" was a negative one, that was just your experience and nothing more.

"As Werner says, 'Everything you experience doesn't exist unless you experience it,'" my mother said during one of the mini–est seminars she tried to give me at home. (She'd offered to pay me a hundred dollars to attend a real seminar, but I'd refused.) So whatever was ugly and disgusting and vulgar about the word "asshole" was only something ugly and disgusting and vulgar that was lodged in your mind. I got that. I really did. I got that we were all carrying ugly, disgusting stuff around with us, like bad luggage, and that word "a-s-s-h-o-l-e" was just a word like any other. As Charlene, the est trainer in my mother's first basic training, had said to her, "'Asshole' is just seven letters assembled in a particular way, and you've assigned vulgar thoughts to them. It's just seven letters, or, to be exact, it's six letters, which are really quite beautiful, if you look at it another way. You are creating what it is. Consuela, do you get that?"

"I get it!" my mother said she said. The roomful of 249 other basic trainees broke out into wild applause.

Applause. Maybe she still liked that. Mom went on to take the advanced training, a special course on "commitments," another on "clarity," an all-nighter called "As Werner Says," and she'd redone basic three times. She'd been transformed by est, changed the way she did everything. She saw her life in a new way and saw all the things she needed to take responsibility for. She had a daughter, a mother, and a relationship

with Coach Weeger that she needed to take responsibility for. And my father—how to explain that? He was smart, handsome, charming. But
mostly she had married her father, the way all women marry their fathers,
hadn't she? That's what Charlene had said. I kept wondering if it was
really all that simple.

And she'd driven my father away, she said, exactly as Abuelita had
driven away Charles Garcia. "I really got that," my mother said. She
didn't seem sad about it. Just certain—with an edge. She talked about
wanting to wake up to her life and see how she was creating all her mis-
givings and her doubts, too. She helped other people buy houses but
couldn't decide whether to buy one of her own. She saw other people in
happy marriages but couldn't make a decision about Coach. She was
stuck there, too. The reason she didn't want to marry him, as she carefully explained to me—in great, tedious detail one afternoon—was the
marrying-her-father thing. Coach Weeger was a nice, decent guy and not
a ladies' man (or "wandering eye," as Abuelita used to say). He was a
steady, true-blue type, but he bored my mother to death, because he
wasn't enough like my father or her father. He was such a nice guy! And
that was the problem.

My mother didn't know where she stood with a really nice guy, she
said. It was almost as if there wasn't enough to react against, nothing to
play ball with. No wall or backdrop. It was like dancing without a partner.
When she was with a man like my father or her father, whom she remembered as a long, lean, dark man with rigid tastes in everything, particularly music, and a kind of meticulous silence that he brought home
with him every night like a twisted, knotted rope—a kind of angry
misery—she knew who she was every second. "I knew who I was and
where I stood," she explained one night while we were doing the dishes,
"because he was so angry. It was like an energy force. You really knew he
was in the room. And because of that, I knew who I was and where I
stood. His anger centered me. Cinco Sais. Same thing. My old dancing
teacher—wait, isn't it funny that I used to call him my dancing *coach*?—
he put his hand down my pants when I was fifteen. Did I ever tell you

that? He molested me! But he was so angry, and I felt centered around him. I was just a passive receptacle of that energy." The way she described it, being a "passive receptacle," made it sound like she was just a sponge that absorbed anger. And then eventually, if you squeezed her, she'd produce tears.

Coach didn't present an energy force that my mother could feel, she said. He produced lots of kindness and love—he was the nicest guy you'd ever want to meet, but lacking something, which, after est, she suspected was just misery and anger. Coach wasn't an angry person. He was actually pretty happy and settled in his life and not all that complicated. The only thing that made him unhappy, or angry, was the fact that he wanted to be married to my mother and live with her—and she couldn't decide. That was the one spark of excitement in his eyes, the spark of passion and anger which reminded her of her father, but if she married him, that would go, too.

She talked about Coach a great deal in those days—much more than about Dad. That puzzled me, because as far as I could see, what had happened to all of us, our family, was worth a lot of talk and confusion. Why did she leave him? Was he already seeing Marisa or not? But she skipped over that. She acted like he didn't exist anymore. He wasn't Paul Ruin. He was just a surrogate. A shadow. A stand-in for her dad.

Where was Charles Garcia anyway? A few months into her est phase, we were watching *The Merv Griffin Show* one afternoon, and my mother said, "I wonder where he is."

"Who?"

"My dad."

She needed to take responsibility for not being in touch with him. In the past she'd felt numb when she thought about him, she said. He hadn't written or called in thirty years. The real "picture" that my mother "needed to look at" was how she'd allowed him to do that for thirty years—and never tracked him down. If she wanted a father, he was probably still out there somewhere. So it was her decision not to have a father. Right?

TWELVE

Neeplus Erectus

I t was weird winter weather, day after day of streaming sunshine, nights so cold everybody needed a down jacket at the last high school football game. Not that I went to the game or had any signs of school spirit. I couldn't have cared less. Besides, it was embarrassing, almost painful, to watch Robbie shouting and jumping around in front of the huddled stadium crowd in her little kick-pleat skirt and purple sweater with a big silver VD in the middle of her chest. I stayed home and watched *Serpico,* flipping over to *The Rockford Files, Chico and the Man, Sanford & Son,* and for laughs, *Donny and Marie.*

I slept late the next morning and was still in bed when our doorbell started ding-donging. Through the open curtains of my bedroom windows, I could see Shelley Strelow standing on our front porch. She was wearing a pair of cutoffs and a T-shirt with studs and rhinestones circling the neckline. Shelley's mother had gotten the T-shirt in Westwood, where a glitzy old Hollywood look was resurfacing. I guess it was only a matter of time—after five years of brown beads and billowy Gypsy dresses—that tailored jackets and satin and rhinestones would come back.

"Ready for a hike?" Shelley asked as soon as I opened the door. Our hair was the same reddish brown color since we'd mixed powdered henna and water into a stinky vegetal mud and plastered it on each other's head. We wore it shoulder length, and Shelley had badgered me into getting feathered bangs. After that, she'd pierced my ears. She put a cold apple behind my lobes and just jammed a sewing needle in. I heard the layers of skin popping, and Shelley didn't even flinch. Not even a little gasp.

"Where is everybody?" Shelley looked around the dark ranch house.

"Out."

"Out?" She smiled. "Really? For a while?"

"Come on back to my room," I said. "I've gotta change." On the way I pulled my tank top over my head, wadded it into a ball, and then, arriving in my room, tossed the top in the direction of the hamper but missed. It fell onto a pile of other clothes that hadn't made it into the hamper either. "Oops."

Shelley dropped onto one of the twin beds. "The curtain's open," she said. "You're putting on a great show."

"Oh, yeah!" I yelled out, scooting my pajama bottoms down. "Hey, I'm flashing the street."

"Look! Isn't that Kenny Frank—"

"Ha. Ha. Very funny."

I closed the curtains, and the room grew dark. I yanked my bottoms to the floor, grabbed them with my toes, and flung them in the direction of the hamper. "Oops."

"You have the best nipples," Shelley said.

"No I don't," I said, looking down. "They stick out."

"That's a good thing, *you fool,*" Shelley said with her trademark acidity. "Mine are so flat. Look." She lifted up her T-shirt and pinched her thumbs and index fingers together, tweaking her nipples. "This is the only way I get EN—or is it called NE? Unless it's super cold outside."

"What are you talking about?"

"*Nipple erectus,*" she said. "It's Latin."

"No it's not."

"How would you know?"

"I know, that's all." Sometimes when I was with Shelley, I started talking like her—my voice became lower and dripped with sarcasm. "The Latin word for nipple is something like 'aorta' or 'oriole.'"

"It's neeplus. *Neeplus erectus.*"

We both laughed, repeated our new word, "nee-plus," half a dozen times. Then Shelley stopped laughing. "I brought some," she said.

I was searching through my underwear drawer for a pair of purple bikini bottoms that were grown up enough for Shelley to see. She always made fun of my white cotton ones, calling them "Baggies."

"What?" I said.

"Reefer," Shelley said. "Do you wanna?"

"Oooooh, I can't," I said with a sinking feeling. Sometimes if you disappointed Shelley, the fun was really over. "I'm spending the day with Marguerite."

"Hey, I want to meet her," Shelley said. "And I'm dying to see that house. Is her driver coming for you?"

"He's not a *driver.*"

"He drives, doesn't he?"

"He's a gardener. A handyman guy. He runs errands."

I turned my attention to the other leg hole of my underwear. Shelley sort of scared me—the way she encroached on my life. My days with Robbie had been centered entirely on Van Dale, aside from summer camp and overnights in Frazier Park with the Camp Fire Girls. I'd never imagined bringing Robbie to Marguerite's house in San Benito, or even introducing them. But Shelley was exploratory, adventurous—and demanding. She had this attitude that everything about me was open for business, like I was a giant supermarket she could peruse. At first she was curious about Whitman—when I said that I had an older brother who was cute and surfed and was living in a hut on the beach in Madagascar. Then she wanted to know all about Justine. I'd told her about Justine's clothes and apartment and car. When I came back from a trip to San Francisco, she wanted precise details—and descriptions of every meal. Lately she'd developed a thing for my grandmother.

"Let me come today," she said in a taunting tone.

"Not today," I said, opening my closet door. "We're just meeting up at the Arroyo and riding. Sorry."

"You're a poop. A big party poop—"

"And I'm not getting stoned. No way."

There were marks on the wall next to my bed where I counted all the times I'd gotten stoned with Shelley so far. I had a compulsion to count things; I'm not sure why. If I'd been having sex with one of the many guys that I dreamed about having sex with—but I wasn't—I'd probably be counting that, too. With Shelley, I had once smoked ten dark brown Sherman cigarettes in a night. I had once consumed five screwdrivers—we mixed the vodka and OJ in an old mayonnaise jar at her mother's house. And on eleven Sunday afternoons, after hiking to our dope-smoking spot in the Van Dale hills, we sat down on the grass at Logo Park and watched all the guys gravitate to us like sad, hungry dogs.

"Why are you just standing there?"

"I can't decide what to wear," I said.

"Don't you lay stuff out?"

"Lay out what?"

Shelley pulled herself off the bed and stood next to me. We were about the same height, but our bodies were different, in terms of proportion and general maturity. She was all breasts and hips—and seemed older, more cooked, like a loaf of bread that had finished baking.

"Don't you decide what you're going to wear the night before?" she asked.

"No way," I said. "I never think about that. Do you?"

"Every night," Shelley said, reaching into the closet and starting to move the hangers around. "I pick out my entire outfit for the day. Even if I have several changes, I think about all the things I'm doing and all the places I'm going, and I come up with outfits for them. That way, when I wake up in a bad mood, like I always do, it's all done."

"I never do that," I said. "And besides, I always wake up in a good mood."

"Oh, right."

"I do. I wake up singing. Ever since I was little."

"You do not."

"How would you know?"

"Let me pick out something," Shelley said. She found a short, white wraparound skirt with navy piping. It was purchased, excitedly, during the tennis-lesson phase that Robbie and I had gone through. "Oh, God, what is *this*? Please don't tell me these are culottes."

"That's old. Leave it. " I slapped her hand away and took the hanger.

"Let me pick out something really nice for you to wear to Granny's house," she said, chuckling. "Hey, where are your boots?"

"In the back."

My riding boots had a special hold on her. Right from the beginning, when I had mentioned in ceramics class that I rode horses on weekends, she took a kind of predatory interest in me. "English?" she had asked. And it seemed to matter that it wasn't western. "Do you have those pants, those jodhpur things or whatever they're called?"

She was on her knees and found the black boots behind pairs of old Earth Shoes, Indian moccasins, and Stan Smiths. She grabbed a Dr. Scholl's sandal and lifted it with a pinched look on her face. "My mom says that only peasants wear these in Europe." Then she found my black riding boots. "God, they're so heavy and huge. What size foot do you have?"

"Nine."

"Right. Same as me." She rose up, her face red from squatting, and hauled the boots over to the twin bed. "What are these wood things?"

I pulled out the boot trees for her. Marguerite had ordered them, along with the boots, from a riding-apparel shop in New York City. Shelley yanked off her white Adidas and was trying to slide her bare foot into the boot. "It's not going to work that way," I said. "You need socks. And you need boot pulls."

"What?"

"Boot pulls. Oh, forget it," I said, walking away. "I need breakfast. I'm dying." I snapped on a stretchy bra, then got into a green crewneck

T-shirt and a pair of waist-high jeans, zipping them with a certain amount of effort and strain until the thin denim became a second skin. I couldn't imagine lying in bed at night and thinking about what I'd wear the next day—couldn't imagine anybody doing that.

Shelley was staring at me. "Forget the bra," she said. "I can't believe you're wearing a bra. You're better off without one."

"But what about my *Neeplus erectus?*"

"You think that bra hides it?" She laughed. "I can see your NE right now." She reached up and tried to pinch my boob. "Tweak!"

"Get your hands off me!"

"Hey, when's your mom coming home?"

"No idea," I said. "And it doesn't matter. We're not getting stoned. It's only nine o'clock in the morning."

Marguerite wore a pair of canary yellow breeches when she rode. They were immaculate and puffed out at the hips, came in tight at her bony knees, and descended, with a patch of golden suede, along the inside of her skinny calves. Her legs looked impossibly thin—like little twigs—and she was standing at the door to the lower barn and waving at me. I hunched over and gave her a hug. She seemed so small, just bones and fabric. As always, she wore a powder blue Lacoste shirt tucked inside her breeches. On her hands was a pair of soft kidskin gloves, a pale yellow that matched her pants. When we first started riding together, she bought me a pair of the gloves, too, along with jodhpurs and paddock boots. Last year I'd graduated to field boots.

"Your eyes are bloodshot," Marguerite said, picking some lint out of my ponytail. The sunlight was intense, and my eyes felt very small, like pin dots. And dry. "You must have hay fever," she said.

"Hay fever?" I smiled foggily, grateful for the alibi. "Maybe I do. Doesn't that make your nose run?"

"Well, sure it does," Marguerite said, turning toward the barn.

I sniffed as if my nose were running, which it wasn't, and rubbed my nose as if it were itchy. And maybe it was. Just thinking about hay fever had made me feel itchy suddenly. It hadn't hit me—how totally high I was—until I'd gotten in the car with Carlos. I'd waved good-bye to Shelley as she stood in the driveway with that smirk on her face that said, *Ha, ha, go see Grandma now,* and I was hit by a sense of dislocation. Where was I? Where was Jose? He usually picked me up. By the time Carlos rounded the corner of Ardmore and passed Casa Adobe, an old historic hacienda with stucco walls, I began to fret that he might want to make small talk. And I wasn't sure I could.

Carlos was the pool man at Marguerite's. I didn't know him well, had just seen him around, a tall, angular guy with a crisp white shirt. After pulling into the driveway of Abuelita's, he didn't get out of the car or come to the door. He just waited for me. He seemed freaked out, actually, but maybe that was just me. When I got inside the car, there were beads of sweat all over his forehead.

The drive took forever. Carlos went on surface streets instead of using the new highway that linked Van Dale and Eagle Rock and a few other nondescript suburban towns to Pasadena—and Marguerite's 1963 brown Oldsmobile made its way slowly, passing the bald hills and new housing developments. My mind kept jumping to paranoid thoughts about how Carlos might be kidnapping me or wanting to rape me. He spooked me out because his eyes were always lingering on me in a Boris Karloff kind of way. But then I saw Suicide Bridge in the distance and San Benito, where the grand Vista del Arroyo Club hung over the dry gulch like some kind of temple.

The Arroyo was a resort hotel in the twenties when Marguerite and N.C. lived there, before buying land on El Molino and building the house. The hotel was full of easterners and midwesterners in those days, transplants, rich people, entrepreneurs, tuberculosis patients and asthmatics, as well as anybody else who needed sunshine and dry air and wanted to spend winter days playing golf and tennis or betting on the horses at Santa Anita Racetrack. During World War II, the hotel became an army hospital and after that a training center for the U.S. Cavalry—when the stables were built—until 1949, when a consortium of investors, including N.C., purchased the building and grounds for a private club. The name stayed the same—the Vista del Arroyo—but over time it was also known as the Arroyo Hunt, or simply the Arroyo. When somebody mentioned having been to "the Vista," you knew they didn't belong.

Carlos took the ancient car through the club gates and along a driveway that was lined with art nouveau lampposts with globes. He drove behind the main building, a Mission-style fortress with a red tile roof, and then along a smaller drive that led downhill to the lower club, where the riding rings and barns were. Marguerite kept two horses there, Picasso and Chameleon. As the car descended the hill, I cranked the window down for air. The palms of my hands were sweating, and I was overcome by a wave of regret. I was sorry I'd gone along with Shelley. It was just supposed to be a few drags—just to make the afternoon more interesting.

We'd stood in the backyard, in the shadow of a ripped awning, and watched the alley for signs of my mother's car.

"Hey, be on the lookout," Shelley kept saying, "for Connie's low-rider."

Shelley seemed to have an edge in her voice whenever she talked about my mother, a mocking tone. She struck a wooden match, bent her head down, and took a long hit. She passed the joint to me.

"Hey, that's Thai stick. You're going feel it," Shelley said. But it was too late. I already felt lighter, kind of airy—giddy. Wow, it made me laugh. Shelley returned to her cracks about my mother's Lincoln.

"It's not a low-rider," I said. "What are you talking about?"

"You're right," Shelley laughed. "It's a Jew canoe. Nobody drives those big cars anymore but Jews."

Did I know any Jews? There weren't any in Van Dale or San Benito, as far as I knew. They all lived in Beverly Hills and Brentwood—in West Los Angeles, where the movie people were, and the New Yorkers. I wasn't sure what that meant anyway—being Jewish. David Feinman seemed mostly old and single and artsy—he lived in a modern house with a view of the whole city and ethnic tapestries hanging on the walls and Indian pottery on the shelves, and he had lots of black friends, musicians who took over the piano. We'd gone to a few parties at the house—I got the feeling that Mr. Feinman liked throwing parties—and my mother was always fawned over and told that she looked like Gina Lollobrigida and Sophia Loren. I also got the impression that Jews and blacks all worked in the music business and hung out together. Did Jews really drive Cadillacs and Lincolns? David Feinman had a giant black Mercedes-Benz—he'd loaned it to Abuelita when she forgot to set the emergency brake on her new Nova and it fell into the canyon next to his house. Anyway, I never thought about people's cars. People drove whatever cars they wanted. Didn't they? A car was a car. But to Shelley a Cadillac was a Jew canoe and any Chevy was a low-rider.

"You're reminding me of somebody from San Benito," I had said to Shelley. "One of those cotillion people."

My performance at the Arroyo Cotillion was always a source of amusement and ridicule to Shelley, but this time she didn't laugh. She was staring down at my riding boots with great intensity. "God," I said to her. "I'm so stoned. Are you?"

She shrugged, raised the joint to her mouth, but the cinder was dead. "My mom can't believe you're a beaner," she said pulling out the matches again and firing up the joint with a suck of her lips. She held the smoke in. "She's definitely got a *thing* about it. She says you don't look like a beaner at all. Want another toke?"

"I'm half."

"I know. You're half. I told her. But she claims that beaner genes are dominant. They take over whatever they're mixed with. You do have dark eyes and dark hair."

"So does my father," I said quickly, holding in a toke and trying to talk without letting any smoke escape.

Shelley was still staring down at my riding boots, which seemed very shiny suddenly. Marguerite had spent an afternoon showing me how to polish them.

I handed Shelley the joint.

"You look Venezuelan, my mom said."

"Oh, thanks." I was light-headed, almost dizzy. Venezuelan. Was that a compliment or not? Shelley's mother was even harsher and more critical than Shelley. Her husband had gone out for a carton of cigarettes one morning and never came back, the sort of story that made more sense the longer you knew her. And then she'd gotten a nose job and something else, Shelley said, and her whole face looked strained and tight.

"What does a beaner look like anyway?" I asked Shelley. "My mom doesn't look like a beaner."

"Your mom is definitely *something*," Shelley said.

"Everybody's something." It just slipped out of my mouth. "We're all *something*, aren't we?"

Shelley and I both laughed. Then we had trouble stopping.

"What's your mom's story anyway?" Her voice had that edge again.

"I told you."

"She's so into est. It's her whole life."

"She goes whole hog, that's all."

"Then loses interest. Like tennis and her flamingo."

"Flamenco."

"Uh-oh," Shelley said, watching the Lincoln Continental float into the open garage. "Here comes Mamacita. Think she saw us?"

I looked inside the dark barn and saw Picasso's head sticking out of his stall—and was filled with dread. I had groomed and tacked him dozens of times, could do it in my sleep, but not like this, with my mind noticing every single second as it ticked by.

I walked down to his stall and said hello to the old bay. I patted the side of his head and stroked his soft nose. Then I opened the wooden door to the stall and put a blue lead line around the horse's neck and took him out to the center of the barn. I put a halter around his head and attached it to the crossties on the wall—to keep him from going anywhere. Usually I didn't bother with crossties. But today I thought I should play it safe.

Marguerite was walking Chameleon, an eight-year-old palomino, out of his stall at the far side of the barn. He was younger and not beat up like Picasso, who was one stumble from being retired completely. Chameleon's coat was lighter and finer than Picasso's, a golden honey color, and his mane and tail were pale blond. Marguerite had gotten him just the year before, thinking that I would ride him, but he had a few quirks—he spooked easily—so Marguerite was working with him. For now I rode him only in the ring, not out on the trail.

"Sure you don't want to try Chameleon?" Marguerite said in a loud voice. She always offered the finer horse but seemed glad that I had some sense.

"I'm sure," I called out. My voice seemed loud to me, and it seemed like another lifetime ago that I'd been standing with Shelley in the backyard and watching my mother get out of the white Lincoln in her navy blue warm-up suit. She was carrying an armload of open-house materials and looked at us with a dead face. She didn't really greet Shelley or even smile.

"Inez," she had said in a certain tone. "Aren't you riding with your grandmother this morning?"

I carried a basket of grooming stuff and set it down by the barn wall. I took out the hoof pick, a small, pointed tool to pick mud and hay from the bottom of the horse's feet. When I was done, I ran the curry over Picasso's coat to loosen up the baked mud. Then I got two long, hard-bristle dandy brushes from the basket and went over Picasso's whole body, from head to tail, from the depression of his spine and then down each of this legs to the hoof. When I was done, I put a clean saddle pad on him—shifting it several times to make sure that it wasn't too far back—then returned to the tack room for the cross-country saddle that

Marguerite had given me a few months earlier for my fifteenth birthday. I lifted the saddle high, brought it down on the center of Picasso's back, and then I took the girth, a leather-and-elastic belt that wrapped underneath the horse just behind his front legs, and buckled it to keep the saddle tight around his chest.

"Land sakes." Marguerite was waiting by the back door, already up on Chameleon. "He must have been coated in mud. Was he? It's taken you forever."

"I'm done," I called out, slipping on the bridle and fastening the throat latch. I walked around Picasso, pulled each stirrup down into position, and then returned to his left side to mount him. I put my left foot in the dangling stirrup, hopped up and down several times, and threw my weight skyward and my right leg over him.

The trail went down into the arroyo, a gulch of open land below Suicide Bridge. Marguerite trotted ahead on Chameleon and kicked up a fine golden brown dust that seemed to fly against gravity, as though drawn to the sun. I smelled the sage in the warm sunlight, and in the shadows there was a rich, heavier scent, not quite mold, not quite earth, as if the darkness contained teeming worlds of life, secret and unavailable.

I felt the presence of something. What? A kind of energy—almost buzzing and alive—as if every tree and shrub and every cloud, all parts of the visible landscape, were expanding at the same time, getting bigger reaching up, and if I were able to become calm and quiet enough, I would see things getting bigger and eventually growing so big that they connected and touched. I noticed patterns of sunlight and shade, the shapes of leaves, the way that Chameleon's hooves left upside-down U's in the path before me— ∩ ∩ ∩ ∩ —as he went along. As a mental exercise, I tried to remember the whole day, chronologically, hour by hour, as though it were a long mathematical equation that I challenged myself to review in my mind. If I could do that, a treasure of self-knowledge and understanding would be unleashed. I'd seen on a Zen calendar the saying, "The way you do one thing is the way you do everything." And I remember feeling very strongly that this day was important—this one day—and how I lived it was going to reveal a small but essential detail that would be the key to everything.

I went back to the beginning. I woke up and began a pleasant daydream about Antonio. Shelley knocked on the door in her cutoffs and T-shirt. Then she lounged on my bed as if she owned it. She was always probing—asking rude questions. She asked me once if I masturbated, like it was a perfectly ordinary question. She asked if my mother was going to marry Bob Lasso, the dentist she'd met at an est event, or was she going to "string him along like she did Weeger." Was I going to inherit Marguerite's money someday? Shelley wanted to know that, too. "My father told me to expect nothing," I had answered. "Why?" Shelley snapped. "Is he planning to spend it all on himself?"

Shelley was too curious—gobbling up everything in life like a pig. Since moving to Van Dale, it hadn't taken long before she was having sex with Gary Kloss, a jock at Van Dale High who never talked to her during the day, just called her at night. She went out to see him, met him places or climbed in his bedroom window. She told me everything, all the details, as if it weren't humiliating to be on call for sex—just arriving inside a guy's bedroom window like that, like popping out of a cake. Shelley acted as though the whole thing with Gary Kloss were a huge adventure. He wasn't using her. She was using him.

The horses crossed a dry creek bed. Farther along there was a meadow where the ground was soft and even. The year before, Marguerite had brought me to the meadow to practice cantering on an open flat, the kind of unrestricted space that can sometimes excite a horse to race or come undone. But Picasso never lost control or raced. He was steady and predictable, an old horse who rarely got excited. After that, I always cantered in the meadow. Marguerite sat on Chameleon in the shade, by a small grove of eucalyptus trees.

"Don't let your legs grip him!" she called out. "Get your weight down into the stirrups! Get him collected! That's it. That's it. Good girl."

After eight or ten laps, I brought Picasso down to a trot, then a walk. And I joined Marguerite by the trees. "You're looking good today," she said. But she looked pale, tired, and one of her eyes kept filling up with tears. "Shall we head for the woods?" she asked. "Are you up for some jumping?" Her enthusiasm seemed forced, the way a kindergarten teacher sounds at the end of the day.

Marguerite led us to a path in the woods where we always jumped over fallen trees. It was shadowy and dark, and the smell of earth and secret worlds rose up again from the ground. A feeling of fullness. The world seemed cozy and full and perfect. The horses broke into a trot, as they always did in the woods, and, seeing a jump ahead, Marguerite brought Chameleon into a canter. I watched the horse sink down and change to a three-beat gait, then easily take a small jump over a log. Marguerite seemed to have lost her balance, though, and slid to one side, almost as if her girth weren't tight enough and the saddle was loose. I began to yell out—then I remembered how much Marguerite hated yelling, hated being shouted at—and I hesitated just long enough to lose my chance to be heard.

But then she must have felt herself listing and off balance, because she steadied herself with a firm push of her boots, dropping her weight into her stirrups and sinking into the saddle as if she were settling into one of those overstuffed down sofas in front of her fireplace.

I made a clucking sound with my tongue and got Picasso to canter, then made the small jump. When his nose was behind Chameleon's tail, I got a chance to say, "I think your girth might need adjusting, Marguerite. It looks loose from behind."

Marguerite said nothing. When she turned around, her face was shockingly white, almost yellow. And her eyes looked dizzy.

"Your girth—" I began to repeat. But my voice was drowned out by a sharp cracking sound overhead, a huge branch breaking off a tree. Was it a real sound? At first I wasn't sure.

"Marguerite!" I shouted in a kind of hysteria. Chameleon swerved to the right and then reared. By the time he bolted and Marguerite had flown off him, I realized that her boot was caught in the stirrup. He dragged her for fifteen feet or so. When she slammed into a tree stump and came loose, suddenly it was so quiet.

Sometimes in the past when I was riding with Marguerite, we'd come upon other equestrians. Marguerite would greet club members with a nod of her helmet, and sometimes, if she was in the mood, linger and chat. I had learned to nod my helmet when I was greeting a new person. It wasn't something Marguerite had taught me specifically, but more of a response to the notion, as Marguerite had presented it, that a greeting required some kind of physical acknowledgment. You didn't have to bow, exactly. You didn't have to shake hands. But you just needed to do something. A nod of the helmet. A smile. A lingering of eye contact. If you were in a chair, you stood.

I tried to keep myself alert to these things, particularly at the club. It was partly to please Marguerite—and also to erase certain impressions, and memories. . . . like the time I was sent to the Arroyo Cotillion.

The dress I wore that night was my first mistake. Lacking any direction, except that I needed to wear "a long gown," I arrived in a purple cotton-knit dress with thin straps—not realizing that cotton knit was a daytime fabric and too informal. I was thinking of the trend for old Hollywood-style glamour when I bought a small boa at a thrift store to wear over my shoulders. It wasn't a big, fluffy boa—I couldn't afford one of those—but what it lacked in fullness, it made up for in length. And I was thinking of my father and his cotillion days when I imagined that the young male members of the Arroyo would be rich sophisticates who'd appreciate my urbanity and my cotton dress, even though it kept gathering in a strange way under my armpits. Along with the boa, I carried a beaded bag, borrowed from my mother and smelling powdery and rancid, like old makeup. And, after great indecision and hand-wringing, I had decided to wear a pair of real dancer's shoes, with a high, heavy sole and ankle straps. They weren't flamenco shoes exactly, but like something you might see on the stage of a Broadway musical. Along with the boa, they were white.

I wasn't aware of my unusual appearance until, in the ballroom of the Arroyo, I noticed three boys staring at me.

"Man," one of them said. "Get a load of—"

"Va-va-va-voom."

"What's she got on her feet?"

"Beaner boats."

"Mexican jumping shoes."

I didn't realize that it might be intimidating to boys that I was several inches taller than any of them or that the absence of a bra might cause unrest. I didn't realize that the other cotillion participants, all from the staid towns of San Benito and South Pasadena, might know each other— and be dressed according to the customs of those places, not in an eclectic mix of Van Dale and Telegraph Hill.

Embarrassed but not defeated, I made small talk with a girl standing nearby in a romantic dress with a high Victorian neck. She had limp brown hair and large glasses and instantly began discussing the boys in the room—where they lived, how rich their families were, and what kinds of cars their older brothers drove.

"Hanson's got a Porsche. Can you imagine? That's really too much for an eighteen-year-old boy. It's so Marina del Rey, if you know what I mean. San Benito isn't flashy like that. Even the richest people here drive old station wagons."

I saw no contribution that I could make to this conversation, and I gazed out at the other cotillion kids, none of whom seemed particularly happy to be there.

"What about you?" the girl asked.

"What do you mean?"

"What kind of car are you getting?"

Mrs. Musio, the cotillion directress, had strawberry hair that was swept and sprayed into a meringue. She greeted each young woman and man by name and with a nod of the head. She introduced "Inez Ruin, a new participant," and then began searching for a suitably tall partner for me to dance with—a humiliatingly public effort. She finally located Donny Martin, a gangly blond youth with Germanic lips and crust in his eyelashes. He was the tallest boy in the ballroom. Even so, with my high heels, I looked out over the top of Donny's pale hair and could see his glistening scalp. He had terrible flop sweats. And later, when we began dancing, I got a blast of sour earwax smell by the side of his face.

The lesson for the day was the fox-trot. I could feel Donny's hot, damp hand on my back.

"One-two-three-four," Mrs. Musio was saying. "One-two. Make a box with your feet. That's it. That's it. Donny Martin and Inez Ruin, please step to the edge!"

My partner and I stopped dancing and walked to an X that had been created on the floor of the ballroom with beige masking tape. The music continued, another bouncy fox-trot. The other kids gathered along the wall.

"Mr. Martin, please ask Miss Ruin for a dance!"

He turned to me, pretending that we hadn't just been dancing. And then he froze.

"Speak, Marteen!" a boy called out.

"Ask her, buddy."

Donny grimaced, and I looked at the ground. When I looked at his face again, his mouth was open but no words were coming out. Overcome with compassion, I smiled as hugely as I could, hoping it might give him confidence.

"Go, Mar-ti-ni!" a boy shouted from the back of the ballroom. Mrs. Musio seemed not to care about the kibitzing, and when the boys realized this, their cries escalated.

"Martini!"

"Martini!"

I kept smiling and nodding my head to provide more encouragement. Donny opened his fleshy lips. "Miss Ruin—"

"Ask the Mexican jumping bean to dance, will ya?"

A huge laugh broke out. Mrs. Musio was finally provoked into scowling, which seemed to make the outburst so much funnier. She walked over to me and Donny. "I'm awfully sorry," she said. "I guess everybody's impatient. Now let's see if we can't try a little dancing. Can you manage, Mr. Martin?"

Donny nodded.

"Miss Ruin?"

"Yes."

Who knows what Marguerite was told, how it was described to her, but I came to believe that she knew everything—the white shoes, the purple dress, the droopy boa, the way I towered over poor Donny Martin and smelled his earwax but felt so much pity for him that it was almost like love. The ballroom broke into chants. The lonely fox-trot played with sour notes and false charm, and Donny and I clung to each other like shipwreck survivors, our limbs loose and gangly, drowning in shame. Marguerite never once mentioned it, never uttered the word "cotillion" again or talked about the importance of learning to dance or pouring tea or writing thank-you notes, except to say, once, after she'd seen me talking with Jose at the barn, a few weeks before our last ride together, "You know what, Inez? You have the best manners anybody can have. Because they aren't manners—that's why. It's just who you are."

THIRTEEN

If a Tree Fell

I woke up when the grandfather clock tolled once. *Saturday Night Live* had ended. My father turned off the television and left the room, and I opened my eyes and saw him wander out into the dark hallway and vanish. A few minutes later, I followed after him. A dim light was coming from Aunt Julia's room, and the door was ajar. I went in—he'd set up camp in there, since he had no bedroom of his own anymore—but her room was empty, somehow emptier than it had ever been.

Tomorrow everybody would turn up—Aunt Ann, Uncle Drew, Lisa and Lizzie and Amanda and Newell. Aunt Julia would stay for weeks and weeks, looking after the house, hiring and firing appraisers, attorneys, and real estate brokers. But the night of the accident, it was just me and my father. He'd flown down late that afternoon in his three-piece San Benito suit. It was too heavy for Southern California, and the vest gave it a Gold Rush feeling. The doctors spoke to my father with an alert but casual feeling—he'd gone to high school with the surgeon—almost as if they were talking to another doctor. There was an impersonal familiarity between them, a levity that lacked any emotion. And afterward my father seemed relaxed, almost jolly. He flirted with a hospital nurse, Renee, by grilling her. He made a joke about how it was the first time he'd seen his mother in public without gloves. He disappeared down a corridor and returned in a wheelchair with a blanket over his lap, pretending to be an invalid. The nurses loved that one. He stood by Marguerite's bedside and talked to her, like he'd just dropped in for tea. Of course her eyes never opened, or even fluttered. I can't remember what he said, really. He was mostly being reassuring to her. *Don't worry, Mother.* That kind of thing. *I'm here. I'm here, and Inez is still here.* I think he said, "We love you, and we're looking after you," but his voice never cracked, didn't carry one hint of sadness or stress. Then we took his boxy rental car to dinner at the Pie 'n Burger on California Boulevard.

Back at the San Benito house, I showered and found a pair of old flannel pajamas to change into. ("Hey," my father said, "I think those used to be mine.") I called my mother and Abuelita, both of them overwrought and reaching out, like they wanted to hug me and be emotional, but it was so unlike the tone that my father had established that I did my best to freeze them out. No Trespassing. That kind of freeze-out. Then my father called Whitman in Madagascar, where it was half a day later—and morning, or close—but got no answer. We settled into a night of TV watching upstairs, in my father's old bedroom.

"What's this show about?" he asked when I put on *The Jeffersons*. "All these people do is yell." We watched *Mary Tyler Moore*. "I've always had a crush on her," he whispered. He seemed largely unfamiliar with the shows and what was popular, except a new program that somebody, a new friend, had told him about. It was called *Saturday Night Live*. "Gretchen says it's great," my father enthused. Obviously, it was live— and that seemed hard to fathom at first. Improvisational. Seat of the pants. My father was in heaven. An actor named Chevy Chase opened with a fireside chat from the Ford White House. John Belushi skated in Rockefeller Center dressed as a huge bee. Gilda Radner talked about how she'd overeaten the previous Christmas. ("Isn't she incredible?" my father said.) The Stylistics performed, and I fell asleep—until the grand-father clock began to toll.

I stood in Aunt Julia's mirrored dressing room and looked at my father's stuff. His black leather dop kit was opened: a small red can of shaving cream, a silver razor that opened with a twist of the handle, a white styp-tic pencil, a nail file, a tiny bottle of Listerine, a clear green GUM tooth-brush. Everything so ordinary and yet imbued with a special kind of magic because they were his. I picked up his black address book and flipped around the pages. The names were written in tiny, perfect hand-writing, mostly names I didn't know. I looked at myself in the mirror. My eyes weren't bloodshot anymore, not really. But I still felt groggy and a lit-tle hesitant, as if each moment were so fascinating that I didn't want to leave it for the next.

That Marguerite might not come back—unimaginable. The house without her felt pointless. Aunt Julia's room seemed like a storage area now, like a big faux-Chippendale set piece. The desk with its ink blotter and crystal inkwell and cabinet full of leather-bound books that were too small and precious to read. And the curtains—just the right heaviness of chintz, the right transparency of sheers, venetian blinds underneath. Marguerite had made every decision—the length of the bed skirts, the width of piping on the coverlets, exactly where to hang the *Godey's Lady's Book* prints. She'd worked to get everything *just so*. When she was a girl in New Bedford, she'd watched the contents of her family house being carried out and put onto carts—she'd seen her bedroom furniture taken away, and her mother's dining room table and chairs. All sold, all gone. A family left destitute, taken in by relatives. She'd learned to do housework. She'd gotten jobs, later on, in New York. And once she'd married N.C., she spent the next fifty years accumulating things back, putting her house in order again, surrounding herself with all the things she'd lost. But in that moment, as I stood in Aunt Julia's pristine bedroom, all Mar-guerite's care and her meticulousness seemed absurd to me. What had she accomplished? What had it mattered?

She lingered in Crocker Hospital with her smashed body. She didn't really "linger," I guess. It was just a matter of one night. There was brief talk about the possible removal of her leg and how it had been "ground to powder," which had made me think of cigarette ash and body talc and Marguerite's powdery world. A trauma specialist with a beard offered a theory as to why an expert equestrian would fall from her horse—not the falling branch, the bolting horse, or that her granddaughter was too stoned to say anything when she noticed the loose girth and slipping saddle. Perhaps Marguerite had had a stroke. Not uncommon, he said. Quite possible, really. Tests were being done—although they'd eventually yield inconclusive results. It was only uncertainty that lingered and, I guess, guilt and questions, all of which I kept to myself.

I drifted into the back hallway, where the sconces on the wall were unlit, just chains of crystals dripping without purpose, and into the old nursery and maids' rooms, which had been left institutional on purpose. Marguerite had thought it all out. The maids would come and go. The daughters-in-law would come and go, too, wouldn't they? I imagined my mother—young, shining, still dancing, and happy to be a part of a fancy house and new world—bending over my crib or drawing my bath. And then I went down the back staircase, hoping to avoid the grandfather clock, which would be tolling on the half hour soon.

The dark kitchen was cold—a window had been left open—and I heard crickets in the garden and smelled fresh cigarette smoke. It was coming from the veranda. My father was sitting there in an old heavy coat of N.C.'s that he must have found in the front hall closet. Everybody had always wondered when Marguerite was going to get rid of it.

"What's going on?" he said.

He looked a little bizarre in the coat, like a Depression-era hobo. His face was drawn. "God, it's freezing," I said, slipping back into the house, finding a lined Burberry raincoat of Marguerite's, and squeezing my arms through the narrow sleeves until my forearms stuck out.

On the veranda my father was lighting up another cigarette. There was a wooden box on the table, a carved cigarette box that was usually in the library. Marguerite was smoking Dorals now, a low-tar and -nicotine brand with a weird plastic filter that her regular GP had encouraged her to try when she refused to quit.

I sat down in a squeaky wicker chair.

"Hell-o," my father said. He was cheerful in a strange way. It seemed fake. There was something going on. I could almost hear it, like background noise, and it made me wary.

"Hello."

"I talked to Whitman," he said. "Tried him again—and got him."

"Oh. How was he?"

"He seemed fine. His usual laid-back self. Happy but, you know, exhibiting that surfed-out response toward life. The waves are lousy in Madagascar, apparently, so I can't really figure out what he's doing there. But it's summer there now, and he has that summery sound. You know what I mean? Beyond that, I can't really tell how he's doing.

"Um."

"Marguerite thought he should have gone to college. That I blew it. Do you think I blew it?"

I shrugged.

"I wonder myself. Quite a lot."

He studied me while we talked, as though he were thinking about me in the future, imagining what he'd say when I didn't want to go to college either. But Abuelita and my mother would make me, wouldn't they?

"What did he say about Marguerite?" I asked. "He must have been worried."

"Oh, yes. Sad, sorry. All that. But he seemed more worried about you."

"He did?"

"He asked lots of questions. Many of them I couldn't answer."

"Um."

"He thought it must have been hard for you. A tough day. Was it?"

"I guess it was. Is he coming home?"

"For this? No."

"He's not?" I remember feeling shocked—or maybe just awfully sad, almost sick in my stomach. When people were ill, Marguerite was always getting on trains to see them. When people got married or died, she bought presents, wrote notes, sent flowers, called, made an appearance.

"Twenty hours on a plane?" my father said. "He didn't want to come. And I don't really see the point."

"But didn't the doctor say—"

"Thirty hours of traveling so he can come to a funeral?"

"You said twenty."

I couldn't believe he'd said the word "funeral"—snapped it out, killing her off already. Like he didn't care. He'd never cared about her, or anything she stood for, had he? His life had been a carefully planned rejection. When N.C. died, she'd made my father come back from Morón de la Frontera, where he'd been studying guitar and God-only-knows-what. She made everybody come to the funeral. She'd been proud of that. You were supposed to do that when somebody you loved died, weren't you? You came home.

"Do you want to talk about it?" he asked.

"What?"

"Today. What happened."

"Oh . . ." I said, sort of startled.

"Whitman had questions. I guess she just fell, and that's all. No more. I suppose that Drew and Ann will arrive at dawn and be asking questions, too."

"Yeah. It was pretty awful."

"Tell me."

"Scary. Hard to know what to do—" I stopped, realizing that I needed to begin all over again. "We were riding in that meadow below the club. I was cantering, and Marguerite was telling me what I was doing wrong."

He nodded. "Ah, yes. How very like her."

I shook my head—it wasn't like *that*. Why did he always have to turn everything into *that*? "Well, no," I said. "I mean, she was just giving me a lesson. That's what we always do. I ride in the meadow, and she makes suggestions. It's not bad. I like it."

"I see. She was helping you."

"Yes. And then we trotted into the woods, where we take jumps over fallen trees. It's not a big deal. I mean"—I gestured a distance of two to three feet with my hands—"trees that have fallen over. Just a few feet at the most. Nothing, really. It's not like we were jumping over fences and hedges."

"The woods beyond the meadow?" he asked. "I know that place. We used to set off cherry bombs there, so nobody could see us. When it was still a hotel. The old Arroyo. You set up jumps?"

"No. We jump over whatever's there."

He nodded. I looked at the carved wooden box on the table. The cigarettes were sitting inside, all lined up, cool and dry. I longed to open the box just to smell the sharp, unsmoked tobacco.

"And then?" he asked. "A tree fell?"

"No, it was a branch. Just a limb. I don't know. And, really, I never saw it fall. We just heard a loud cracking sound over our heads, way, way up, and then a branch started to fall—and hit other branches—but I never saw it land. It might have gotten stuck in the tree. I'm not sure. But there was a loud snapping sound, and Chameleon bolted."

"And Mother was thrown. Did you see that?"

"I think the girth was loose."

"You said that at the hospital."

"Did I?" I was looking down at the iron tabletop with its swirling pattern of leaves. The carved box had a different swirling-leaf pattern. My hand reached forward. "I'm going to have a cigarette now," I said. "Okay?"

"Really? A cigarette?"

"Yes."

"Are you sure that's what you want to do?"

I nodded and began talking again, partly as a distraction. "It was really so scary." I lifted the lid off the box and set it down on the table.

"What was so scary?" my father asked. "Do you want me to light that?"

I nodded and bent my head with a cigarette in my lips as he struck a match. "She was just lying there next to a tree stump," I said. It was eas- ier to tell the story now—but I wasn't sure why. "Chameleon dragged her, not that long, really. Her boot was stuck in the stirrup. And then she got slammed into this stump, and— All of a sudden it was so quiet. Every- thing was so quiet. And I could hear Chameleon galloping and galloping and getting farther away. And I looked down, and Marguerite was just a crumpled pile on the ground. She looked so tiny, just like a little girl. Ex- cept for her white hair. I could see her white hair against the dark earth."

"Against the dark earth."

I nodded.

"You thought she was dead."

"Did I?" I blew out smoke. It was weird that I didn't feel like crying. I didn't really feel sad either. I felt almost nothing. "I don't know what I thought. I guess I did. None of it seemed real."

"Like a dream."

"I don't know. I guess so."

"And you went for help."

"Not right away."

He raised his eyebrows. "No?"

"I wasn't sure it was a good idea to leave. I mean, we were a mile from the club, or half a mile—I have no idea. I don't have a good sense about distances and things like that. And I can get lost really easily. So I was afraid to leave. She looked so helpless and small. Leaving her seemed like a bad idea. All alone. What if she woke up? Chameleon was out there, gallop- ing around. For all I knew, he was going to come back and trample her."

"Unlikely."

"Unlikely." I nodded. "I finally decided that."

He was still studying me. "You're doing that all the time now?"

"What?"

"You hold that cigarette like a pro."

I didn't smile—or react. At first I thought he was trying to be funny, but then I could tell he wasn't. "I'm not inhaling."

"What are you doing with the smoke?"

"I'm afraid to inhale. I tried once, and I coughed and felt weird. Plus, it's better for me, right? It's not going in my lungs."

"You're just keeping the smoke in your mouth?"

I nodded.

"So you stayed with Mother for a while, hoping somebody might come along," he said. "Sort of a passive stance. The Prince Charming scenario. By the way, I'm not sure that's any healthier—keeping the smoke in your mouth and blowing it out. The nicotine is still being absorbed on a cellular level."

I shrugged, waiting to tell the story. I wanted to get through it. "I dismounted, tied Picasso to a tree, and sat on the ground next to Marguerite. I don't know how long. She was out cold. But I told myself that it was normal. Of course she'd be unconscious. She'd hit her head. I just needed to wait for her to wake up. No blood or anything. She was so still. I could feel her pulse on her wrist. I kept saying her name, and then I kind of touched her face—slapped it lightly, like they do in the movies—but she didn't move. Then I stood up and called for help a few times. Kind of circled the area around us, keeping an eye on Marguerite and yelling out for help. But I could tell that nobody was around. It was so quiet, except for the bugs. I kept hearing the flies or bees buzzing and birds flying off. Then I decided that I needed to ride back to the club and get help."

"You doped it out."

"What? Right. Yes." He knew. He seemed to know. *Doped it out.* I felt my heart race a little. Maybe he smelled the Thai smoke in my hair when he hugged me. Maybe he could tell by the way I was acting. "So I rode to the barn and got Mrs. Lemon and Paco. Chameleon was already there—he'd come back with Marguerite's saddle slipped all the way down, under his belly, so they knew there'd been an accident."

"Uh-huh."

"They were weirded out," I said, "like, right off Mrs. Lemon made a comment about how old Marguerite was—*'too old to be riding,'* something like that. 'I knew this would happen' kind of thing. Like they wanted to go right into blaming her—"

He nodded, still quiet.

"—and they called an ambulance, but I don't think they'd really thought it out very carefully. They were sort of panicked. How were they planning to get an ambulance into the woods?"

"Doesn't the club have rescue people on horses who . . . ?"

I shook my head. "They tried to drive part of the way, until the ambulance got stuck. Then they carried a stretcher. Anyhow, I wasn't there for any of that. I rode ahead with Mrs. Lemon, and we were with Marguerite. We kept waiting for her to wake up any minute, but she didn't."

I had prayed, actually. Quietly, to myself. I looked up at the trees and sky and tried to feel that feeling again, of being with the woods and the earth and the clouds and everything moving together, very slowly, everything breathing and growing at the same time, and I went to the place inside me where I felt a part of that, and I asked God to make Marguerite wake up. But I could tell that nobody was listening. I knew—I could feel that it wasn't going to happen. I was knocking on the door of an empty room. My request would be denied. That's how it felt. But I wasn't going to tell my father any of that. He was sitting there in that hobo coat looking a little crazy, like he was about to explode.

"I could tell there was something wrong with her leg," I said. "It was lying in a funny position, kind of an unnatural angle. Like it wasn't attached to her body anymore. You know what I mean? Like it was rubber."

He was very quiet, looking down at the table, almost in a daze, almost the way he looked when he played flamenco. A trance of some kind.

"You know what's funny?"

"What?" he said without looking up.

"I had this really bad feeling when we started out. There was something about her that didn't seem right. She was so tired and looked so pale and old. When I met her at the barn, I was kind of startled."

"Very important," he said, still in his trance and gazing down. "Important to pay attention to those things. Whispers. The whispers inside your head. Can't ignore them. Always a mistake. You'll know that next time."

His eyes began to brim up a little. I kept quiet, didn't want to interrupt him. He'd never been that way about Marguerite before. Usually he made an aside or irritated complaint. But the strain was gone. I looked away, at the tabletop, then at the crisscrossing bricks on the veranda floor. Marguerite might die—still impossible to absorb. She might have had a stroke, and that was why she fell, not the girth, and her leg had been crushed to powder, and her head. My father wiped his face with his fingers.

Maybe things could have ended differently. I could have yelled louder and not been so hesitant, or I could have paid attention to the whispers and not ridden at all—instead of going along with the plan. When you were stoned, it always seemed like your mind was making important discoveries about the world, poignant important discoveries, but they were temporary and not important in the end, and only the surface of the world was glittering and seducing you, the sunlight and patterns and colors, as distracting as a big circus show. My father would understand that if I told him.

"Dad—"

"You'll need," he interrupted, his voice distant again, "to call Justine sometime tomorrow. In the morning, if you can." He raised his eyebrows.

"Justine?"

"To tell her how you're doing, how everything is. She was asking about you—" And then he stopped abruptly. "She—" His eyes searched the dark garden as if looking for a few words or ideas to hang on to. "She and I have come to a decision."

"About what?"

"Well, it's time to move on. I know you'll want to say good-bye. You're old enough to appreciate that, right?"

. . .

He didn't want too much from his mother's house. He asked me to make a list of things that I might like later on, saying he'd keep them for me. It wasn't easy. Almost like trying to pick clothes from Justine's closet—it required a kind of foresight and imagination that I lacked. What sort of life would I be having? What would I need? When I said that I wanted Marguerite's canopy bed, he convinced me that it was ugly and old-fashioned and that I would be sorry that I'd taken it. ("You'll be dragging that awful thing around for the rest of your life.") When I said that I liked the portrait of the Ruin guy over the mantel in the library, he laughed out loud. I settled on some silver, some riding things, an etching of the Alhambra, and a clock. Not the grandfather clock. We all knew that Uncle Drew had his eye on that.

My father was in San Benito quite often in those days—attending to things, meeting with attorneys, meeting with his sisters. I figured out a lot then. I heard things, overheard things. I gained some wisdom and perspective. People seemed to have changed toward me, treated me differently, as if I weren't really Inez anymore. Maybe they just resented me for being with Marguerite when she fell. Or maybe they felt that she shouldn't have been riding at all—that she'd taken too big a risk in order to preside over my youth. She'd taken me in, made special arrangements to be with me. We'd had a bond. I saw that very clearly now. And this was hard for everybody else. When Shelley and I were stopped by San Benito police—they thought we were breaking into Marguerite's house one afternoon, when we were just hunting around for the hidden key—my relatives were oddly unsympathetic. Even good-natured Uncle Drew seemed to suspect me of something. That's how it felt anyway.

Whitman didn't come home from Madagascar for the funeral, or see Marguerite in her coffin as I did, with that awful coral-colored lipstick on her frozen face, or stand by her grave in the small churchyard in San Gabriel and throw handfuls of dirt and sing "Amazing Grace" while choked up, blubbering, as the rest of us did. Nobody seemed to miss Whitman either, but me. Nobody but me seemed to think it was wrong that he didn't come. Without him I felt more alone and more grown up. I felt more vulnerable and more noticeable. I felt different about my place in the family, and my father's place, uncertain about where we stood or who we were, as though a huge wave had crashed down and scattered and rearranged everything, and we were in flux, or floating, all drift-wood—moving forward and back on a new tide. Maybe everybody felt like that. Maybe we were all lost. Amanda complained that Whitman was listed as a secondary heir in Marguerite's will, "when he's already rich enough." There was a fight over a punch bowl—an ornate, heavy thing, sterling—how much it was worth, who had appraised it, and who was going to wind up with it, a fight that was never resolved. Aunt Julia and Aunt Ann stopped speaking. And everything became much harder after that. The grand house in San Benito sold instantly for an unimaginably modest price, because my father wanted the whole thing settled and the real estate market was at an all-time low. The house in Laguna was kept by Aunt Ann and Uncle Drew—and that only brought additional resentments. I wasn't sure how much money Marguerite had left, but my father insisted that the sum after taxes was negligible. Whatever the amount, he'd been dismissive. "Things weren't what they seemed," my father said. "I've ordered a bigger oven for the kitchen at Wolfback, and maybe I'll buy a new car." He was going to invest the rest of the money in a business that a couple of his former students had started, a company called Apple Computers. "Don't count on anything," he said to me. He repeated this line many times over the ensuing years, like a mantra. You shouldn't count on inheriting things, particularly money. "It's a bad idea," he always said, "and a bad way to live."

His house was finished early the next year. He and Ooee named it Wolfback after the ridge where it stood. By the time I saw it, my father had been living there for two months already. It was a clear, windy day in April, and huge white clouds hung dramatically over the Golden Gate as we crossed the bridge to Sausalito. He'd come alone to the airport, stood by my arrival gate looking gaunt and deflated before he saw me and then smiled so hugely when he did, blooming as though the sight of me had brought him back to life.

We entered the long, low tunnel underneath the Headlands. He turned off Highway 101 and took a winding road up into the green hills. I could see Rodeo Beach beyond, a line of waves breaking in the distance, and then the brown shoreline quickly disappeared as the car took several turns until we faced a dirt road with a heavy steel gate, almost agricultural-looking, like something for horses or cattle. The MG stopped.

"What's this?" I asked.

"My gate," my father said, reaching to open the car door. "Low-tech. I used a farm gate to fake people out."

He walked to the gate, unhooking a small chain in the back that was attached to a weight—and it swung open. He got back in the car, drove through, then stopped again to close the gate behind us.

"Kind of a hassle, isn't it?" I asked.

"It's subterfuge," he said. "It keeps people away. I don't want it to look like anybody's living behind here."

"Can't you get some kind of remote control? So you don't have to get out of the car?"

"Oh, Inez," he sighed. "You're so like Mother."

"It just seems like a pain," I carried on. He didn't intimidate me anymore. And being compared to Marguerite was a compliment, whether he thought so or not. He drove on, over a smooth dirt road that, once we turned a corner, was paved. "Getting in. Getting out. Getting in again. Having to move the gate yourself. It seems inconve—"

"It's what I want," he interrupted.

"Just a suggestion."

The car rounded another easy turn.

"It was just an idea I had. Sorry."

He pulled into a turnaround that was edged in flat paving stones.

Small plants were dotted behind the stones, sage and lavender and cat-mint. I could tell they'd been recently planted—there was a damp ring circling each small plant where it had just been watered.

"I'd really prefer if you said '*I'm* sorry—rather than just 'Sorry.' If you say 'Sorry' without putting 'I'm' in front, it's almost like you're kidding or being sarcastic. You know, like '*So-rry.*' It doesn't sound very nice. Do you know what I mean?"

I took a deep breath, trying not to exhale so loudly that it would sound like a huff, but it might have anyway.

"However, you have a point about the gate," he continued, sort of warming up again. "I could attach an electrical wire to the pulley, I guess. And there would have to be some kind of small motor. It would be neat, very neat. Maybe you're onto something, Inez. Maybe I was being too sensitive. I'm a little sensitive these days, particularly about the house, so you might be careful what you say."

"Okay," I said. Lately everybody was talking about sensitivity and be-ing sensitive, or oversensitive. But Whitman didn't have to come home from his surf hut for the funeral. He wasn't "into ceremony," he said, and he'd be with Marguerite "in spirit." Was he with me and my father in spirit? Did he care about us? What was the point of being sensitive if you couldn't bother with things like that?

My father led me to a small bridge over a dry creek of pebbles. We walked to a simple wooden door that opened onto a glassy atrium. There was a ceramic bowl of water there, with an orange goldfish swimming in it. There were some beautiful plants and river rocks, too, and from inside I could see various rooms of the house, almost like stage sets or boxes. In-side each glass box, the sun shone down from skylights and lit up the floor in long rectangles of light.

Across the atrium there was a bigger wooden door. With a gentle push, we entered the main foyer. I still remember the feeling, and the ex-citement, when it seemed to me that my father's efforts, and perhaps all the ruminating and gestating and secrecy, and all those shares of Harrison-Ruin Computing that he'd sold off, had been worth it. I had never been inside a house so magnificent. Every surface—from the sandstone fireplace that was shared by two rooms to the redwood paneling to the tall white walls and wooden ceiling—was simple and perfect. Long decks ran along the length of the living room and kitchen, giving the place the feeling of being part of the dry hillside, and protected by it, before one noticed that the house turned dramatically on one side to face the boisterous sea. Aside from a large round glass dining table and rattan-and-leather chairs, my father hadn't bought much new furniture either. He'd simply spread his small amount of stuff from the Telegraph Hill apartment into five times the amount of living space. The screens, the flamenco poster, the Egon Schiele nudes—there were now three of them—were all there, and welcomed me like old friends.

Having seen the first floor of the house—most of it taken up with a master bedroom suite with an enormous bath, dressing room, and office—we sat down in the kitchen to drink tea. I was curious to see the guest room—or my room and Whitman's—but my father had made some scones for my visit, the ones I liked, so we took a few minutes to eat them and watch a low layer of fog and mist sweep in from the hillside and overtake the beach. The house still seemed cheerful and open, surprisingly so, even though the hillside and beach were now encased in a gloomy wet mist. "Most people don't like the thick fog—which can last all day—but I do," he said, almost proudly. "I'm not sure why, but I think you're going to feel the same way. This side of the ridge has its own microclimate, really. Dense fog, mists—and then, just down the hill in Sausalito, there's blazing sunshine every day."

I felt like changing my clothes after the flight, maybe taking a shower. I walked back to the foyer of the house, grabbed my duffel bag, and looked around.

"Where's my room?" I asked. "Downstairs?"

"What do you mean, 'downstairs'? my father laughed. "There's no downstairs. This is it, Inez. And you're right here"—he pointed to the open living room—"on the ever-popular brown sofa. That's your favorite spot, isn't it?"

1977

FOURTEEN

Just Some Playboy

Behind the wheel of the MG, I was mobile and irresponsible. It was nighttime, always nighttime, and the world was waiting for me.

"Market Basket always sells to us," Shelley was saying. We needed some beer for a party—an event that we'd heard about via some strange party grapevine. I didn't know who was throwing the party or the exact address, but I assumed we'd find it, as Shelley and I always did, based on the din emanating from the kid's house or the twirling light on the policeman's car. Neighbors always complained, and the police always came.

I popped out my retainer, left it near the gearshift of the MG. I opened my wallet and pulled out my real ID—the one that revealed I was sixteen. And then I made sure my other ID was still there, the fake one that said my name was "Jade Dunaway" and I was twenty-one.

I didn't like smoking grass anymore—that was largely abandoned after Marguerite died—but what I missed in terms of giddy dislocation, I made up for with alcohol. Every weekend I drank in Shelley's backyard, in the backs of vans, in the balconies of movie theaters, and I drank at parties—at the houses of classmates that I'd never really talked to or knew. Sometimes I woke up in my bedroom at Abuelita's and smelled the cigarette smoke in my hair and tasted the sourness in my mouth and had no memory of coming home. How late was I out? How'd I wind up here? I'd open the curtains of my bedroom and see the MG sitting in the driveway, safe and clean and silent, keeping my secrets, awaiting another adventure. The nighttime called to me. The car called to me. Underneath the dark, starry canopy of the western sky, we drove to mixers and parties and discos, to gatherings of teenagers in vacant lots and Logo Park. We went to clubs on Sunset, concerts at the Greek and Shrine and Santa Monica Civic. The MG transported me, carried me along, protected me, lifted me, always waiting for me in parking lots and along roadsides to come back. I floated and laughed and drank and smoked, batted away the hands and mouths of boys—a tease, a public temptation—and then Shelley and the MG and I would drive to In-N-Out or Bob's Big Boy and have another beer on the way, a roadie, and for some reason—some bizarre, miraculous reason—I always found my way home.

At the parking lot of Market Basket, I looked at myself in the small rearview mirror. Did I look twenty-one? It seemed impossibly old, and mature, and glamorous, and so far away. I pursed my lips and sucked in my cheeks. But my eyes were still dewy and young—and maybe a little scared.

"You're doing that look again," Shelley said.

"What look?"

"That pathetic expression you always get when you're looking at yourself in the mirror but nowhere else."

Why were we still friends? Shelley indulged in heartlessness. She dispensed unbridled honesty. She ridiculed me for "being afraid of men" and said that I was insecure and had a complex. She was always talking about how Gary Kloss was "dying to do it" with me or how somebody else was "salivating" when he saw me. She loved dragging me into a room and watching guys' reactions. But I'd taken her for a pregnancy test at the We

Care Clinic in Torrance, where the nurses were chirpy and upbeat, and then I had to take her back a week later. While waiting for her "procedure" to be over, I read every pamphlet available about vaginitis, venereal disease, herpes simplex, and genital warts, about chlamydia and unwanted pregnancies. And then I'd seen her cry really hard—some kind of hormone deal—and writhe in pain. I wasn't going to be that stupid. I wasn't going to let that happen to me. Ever. Why were we still friends? Because she did the bold dumb things. And I'd thrown in my lot with her. Besides, she knew me inside and out. She got what I was up to. That counted for a lot. And we had a plan for our lives.

Instead of going to school on Wednesdays, we split up the week with a "field trip"—for mind expansion and sophistication and all the things we were missing by being stuck in the cultural desert of the suburbs. Sometimes we took the Van Dale Freeway into downtown Los Angeles and shopped. Sometimes, if we were dressed up, we went into Bullocks Wilshire and checked out the handbags or marveled at the hosiery and makeup. We never bought anything there, just gaped and fondled. It was on Melrose Avenue where we got most of our clothes—at crummy vintage shops full of musty racks and mannequins with missing limbs and deco posters under flickering lights. We searched for berets and old compacts, cigarette holders and cigarette cases and lighters—the ones with tired flints and cotton wicks that looked like clouds. We bought polka-dotted dresses with belted waists from the 1940s. We got into heavy coats with padded shoulders that it was never cold enough to wear, ever, along with boxy handbags that had small, tight handles and zippered compartments only big enough to slip a square mirror into.

When I wasn't in the mood for something previously worn—when I'd grown disgusted with my wardrobe of used clothes purchased with built-in BO that couldn't be eradicated, and maybe some light sweat stains—I wore a pair of lean Chemin de Fer jeans with an open-collared satin shirt. I was sleek and shiny, taut and long. My hair was dark brown again, and my perm had grown out and become a loose, shoulder-length hive of waves. I'd plucked my eyebrows down to a fine line that arched delicately over my eyes.

Sometimes we saw foreign movies at the NuArt or the Fox in Venice or the Tiffany on Sunset. *The Conformist. Rules of the Game. Jules et Jim.* We sat in the smoking section of the theater. Sometimes we drank wine. We put our Frye boots up on the backs of the seats in front of us—and took over an entire aisle with all our shopping bags and purses and coats that we never needed in L.A. but liked to carry around anyway.

We went to museums—to the Norton Simon, to LACMA, to the Getty that had just opened in Malibu. (So scary how the parking attendant checked my driver's license at the kiosk and said, "Okay, Miss Dunaway.") Shelley wanted to be a painter or a graphics designer—whatever that was—and I'd gotten into photography. For Christmas Dad had given me an enormous Nikon camera with a motor-drive and a 200-millimeter lens, and, like the MG, it was a little too much, and it overwhelmed me. I hadn't taken a photography course, but I read the manual, figured out the basics, and brought the camera everywhere with me: to Griffith Park Observatory, where Shelley and I went to see the laser light show; to Yamashiro's, a Japanese restaurant above Hillcrest, where I photographed the view of Hollywood and all the swimming pools. I drove the MG far up into the hills, along the ridge of Mulholland Drive where Marlon Brando and Jack Nicholson and Warren Beatty lived, but the road was surprisingly narrow and dusty, and the famous canyons and movie stars never came into view.

One midweek excursion we went south to Laguna Beach. It took a couple hours in those days, before all the highways were put in. Shelley had never been to Laguna—and I wanted to show her the village, and Crystal Cove, and Bluebird Canyon, and Main Beach, where all the aimless cute guys played basketball. I was dying for a banana-pineapple smoothie from the Orange Inn, and I wanted to have lunch at the JR for old times' sake. Shelley had never seen Marguerite's bungalow on Moss Cove either, or gone inside. But the closer we got to the old house, the more freaked I felt. Something unexpected happened—it was so weird. The house looked exactly the same, exactly, and this played some kind of trick on me, as if my body or some other part of me believed that it was the old days again. I couldn't shake that feeling. And my heart was pounding, because maybe Whitman would come out the screen door, and he'd wave. And maybe Marguerite was still alive inside there, and a bridge game was going, or cribbage, or everybody was having a bowl of cereal. It seemed impossible that I couldn't walk in the door and flop on a sofa or turn on the TV and watch *Gilligan's Island*. What made the whole thing even weirder was that my Aunt Ann and Uncle Drew lived in the house now. I hadn't seen them since the funeral. I hadn't seen Lizzie or Lisa or Amanda either, except at a Fourth of July thing at the Arroyo. I went just to be nice, and for old times' sake. But Lizzie and Lisa had gotten into the preppy thing so heavily—too heavily—and were covered in monograms and grosgrain and wore horrible khaki skirts that made their butts look huge. It was like they'd had memory loss, too, because suddenly they'd forgotten they'd ever burned incense or taken a macramé class or worn low-rider cords. Or smoked a joint. *What do you mean? We've always dressed this way.* They looked at me like I was from another planet, like some unpreppy lowlife who'd wandered into the club and was going to foul up their chances for junior membership. That's how it felt anyway. But they were the big embarrassment as far as I was concerned, not me. They were the ones who were lost and didn't know who they were anymore. Not me.

M y father taught me how to drive a stick. At Van Dale High, there was a driving class with driving simulators, and we'd sit in a dark theater and watch a big screen while we turned fake steering wheels and pretended to be driving—and not hitting that old lady or the child running after a ball. After that useless exercise, we were able to drive in a real car that was owned by the high school. It was an automatic, a huge American thing. One of those dinosaurs that nobody in California drove any-more, because of the gas lines. We were accompanied by an instructor, Mr. Luza, who was just another dim-bulb PE coach who smelled like sharp, stinky aftershave and used expressions like "golly gee." Mr. Luza encouraged us to practice driving with our parents, so I drove my mother's VW Rabbit diesel to the supermarket while she tried not to have a heart attack on the seat next to me. Then my father called one after-noon.

We were making plans for a visit. Summer was starting—the summer after Marguerite had died—and Picasso and Chameleon had been sold, and there was no beach house to go to and no riding camp in Colorado. But for some reason I wasn't feeling too sorry for myself. Turning sixteen seemed like an amazing thing in itself.

"I've been thinking about your birthday," my father said. "How about the MG?"

"What about it?"

"Would you want it?"

I must have misheard him. "What?"

"The MG. I was thinking of giving it to you."

I couldn't speak. I had died, really, and was completely surrounded in white light. *"The MG?"* I worried that if I uttered those two glamorous letters aloud, they might disappear. I'd never dared to imagine driving the car, much less owning something so fine and beautiful. My body came alive with desire, and excitement, and so much elation, that I wanted to hang up and call Shelley and, at the same time, race around the house shouting to Abuelita and my mother.

"I've got the Alfa Romeo now," he said very calmly. "And the MG—it's looking kind of lonely. Do you think you could take care of it?"

"You're kidding."

"I'm certainly not. What's the matter—do you have something else in mind, like a new Porsche?"

At first, after Marguerite—why did everything spin around her death date?—he showed up at the airport with Gretchen. She was an artist. She made paper, actually, which always seemed like a strange thing for somebody to make. She had red hair that fell in ringlets and googly green eyes and freckles. In her studio, off in some ratty part of San Francisco, she mixed vats of hot, starchy water with bits of fiber floating around in them. It looked exactly like swirling clumps of toilet paper in an overflowing bowl, and then she poured dye into the vats and then scooped out the colored tissue with a big slotted spoon and placed it onto a screen, almost like a window screen, but with bigger holes. When the water ran out and the clumps of tissue dried, it became "paper," and Gretchen framed the large sheets behind Plexiglas. They hung in hospital corridors and on the walls of banks. It was amazing to me that people really paid her for them. They all reminded me of toilet paper, or dried vomit. But Gretchen was nice, super nice. She was followed by a decisive blonde named Carol, who was an executive at I. Magnin, a department store—not really my father's usual type, not artsy enough and no overbite—and then by a few women whom he only mentioned on the phone ("I met the nicest ballet dancer!") but who didn't endure long enough for me to meet.

"Has he told you about Laurel yet?" Whitman asked me on the phone one night. He was back by then, finally, living in Ojala with Patricia—and helping her with a big landscaping project. Somehow I'd managed to keep Shelley from meeting him. It wasn't that hard, really. Whitman was around for only a couple months before he'd begun contemplating a visit to Hawaii and the winter waves.

"Who's Laurel?" I asked.

"A computer programmer," he said. "Not at Harrison-Ruin. Somewhere else. He seems really smitten. He went on and on about her the other night. She went to Radcliffe and has him reading Ovid."

"What happened to Carol?"

"Too into clothes, I think, and charity fund-raisers. She drove him into the arms of Laurel. She's into Catullus, too."

None of that meant anything to me. Ovid, Catullus, who were they? I imagined that Laurel looked like Ali MacGraw in *Love Story*, my only Radcliffe association, but she wound up leaning toward a semi–Bionic Woman type. Anyway, it was pointless to get caught up in my father's girl-friends or to follow their interests, because nobody lasted anymore. They came. They went. It was just a matter of weeks, or a few months. He made them cappuccinos in the morning with his new espresso machine. He made them salmon at night in his copper fish poacher—and poured glasses of Veuve Clicquot for them. They smoked very good dope and went to very good movies, and sometimes, if they were very special and it would be awkward otherwise, Whitman and I got to spend a day with them. We were treated like celebrities, visiting dignitaries. And I could tell, from the look on the new girlfriend's face, that my father had been bragging about us to her—making us sound like two geniuses, two beau-ties, the prince and princess of his permanent life.

The black driving gloves had disappeared, and the cape, and several other reminders of Justine. But a few of the things she'd brought to his daily life endured. He was eating off Marguerite's good china—and using his great-aunt's heavy silver. He had continued to collect Egon Schiele prints, and his laundry was still picked up and dropped off by Perignon. He'd gotten involved at the art institute where Justine had so much in-fluence and had become a guest lecturer there, giving slideshows on a mystifyingly broad range of topics: artificial intelligence, industrial de-sign, the psychological impact of typeface, the use of computers to verify the authenticity of Old Masters paintings. How he qualified as "an ex-pert" on any of these subjects eluded me but never seemed to trouble the beautiful young students who followed him home.

"I talked to Justine a few days ago," he'd say every so often. "She says hello and asked how you are. Boy, she sounds great."

She had moved out of the city and wound up in Big Sur. She'd re-vamped her life and downscaled—no grand house, no housekeeper, no Lotus, and her daughter, Lara, was going to public school. Whitman had visited them on a drive up the coast and reported back that Justine had given up meat, caffeine, and alcohol. She didn't seem to have a boyfriend, as far as he could tell, and spent most of her spare time at a Buddhist monastery in the hills.

"Maybe I shouldn't have let her drift away," my father had said, himself drifting into complete banality. There were a number of moments like that—when it seemed as if he hadn't been able to put Justine behind him. Maybe all of us felt that way. We missed her elegance and dignity, her shyness and honesty. We missed the stability and permanence she gave to our lives, even the sense of destiny. With Justine my father seemed part of something fated and special—as if he had unwittingly stumbled upon a soul mate.

"She just never felt comfortable with the terms," he said cryptically one night, in an effort to explain—soon after Whitman had seen her. What terms? "I couldn't promise there wouldn't be other people," he said, "but I promised I'd never lie to her. And I never did." *He couldn't promise there wouldn't be other people.* I was too young to comprehend the difficulties of that arrangement or to marvel how they'd stayed together as long as they did.

"She needed me too much," he said at another time, in a burst of candor. Her dependency made him "feel a way that I didn't want to feel," he said. She'd wanted to get married, too. "Which, of course, I couldn't do." The most surprising thing was how much my father seemed to enjoy feeling wistful about her. "She was so wonderful," he'd sigh, "wasn't she?"

After Laurel, a big mouth who brandished her college background with such frequency that it became a joke ("Let's count how many minutes it takes her to utter the word 'Radcliffe,'" Whitman said at the start of one weekend), my father fell in with Shanti, a quiet waif, an out-of-work programmer with a honey brown bob and a lisp.

Shanti wasn't her real name—there'd been a conversion to Hinduism at some point—and she'd met my father through the now-forgotten Marisa. ("She's a very *close friend* of Marisa's," my father kept saying, as if this connection added to Shanti's appeal.) Before long he'd helped her find a job at Harrison-Ruin, where my father still showed up occasionally for board meetings and consultations. Shanti seemed happy there, and happy with my father. She was smart and quick but relatively uncultured, which my father appeared to find fascinating, as if he'd discovered a pure savage to indoctrinate. To say she "blossomed" under his tutelage seems an understatement. She was around for the better part of a year, long enough to be queried on every personal subject under the sun, to read *Great Expectations* and *Portrait of a Lady* and *Even Cowgirls Get the Blues,* to be taken to *Lawrence of Arabia* and given a Rolex watch on her birthday. I'd even seen the inside of Shanti's apartment in the Marina one day. It was very small and drab—no light or style—and I was able to imagine, for once, how glamorous my father and his world must have seemed to her.

How old was Shanti? She wasn't up to code, that's all I know. My father and Ooee Lungo had worked out a simple math equation for what they believed was the perfect age difference between a man and a woman. The man's age was divided by two, and then seven years were added: $Y/2 + 7 = X$. Since my father was on the precipice of fifty, his ideal mate would have been thirty-two. But sweet, pliant Shanti couldn't have been much beyond twenty-five or -six, which is partly why, eventually, she was pushed out of the nest, encouraged to see other people, and then, when she consulted my father on her love life, urged to begin an affair with another young programmer at Harrison-Ruin, a guy named Bill Stein—who was brilliant, resourceful, and about a foot shorter than my father. Dad approved of Bill Stein enormously. And when Shanti would call my father and say she missed him and missed his company, he'd take her to dinner again and maybe sleep with her again, all the while counseling her on the myriad of ways she could improve and deepen her relationship with Bill.

After Shanti there was a stretch of *L* names, all short-termers: Lonnie, Louisa, Lauren. It was almost as though he were playing a game with himself. Lonnie was a ballet dancer. Louisa was a young architect in Ooee's firm whom I met only once—when she was still dating Ooee. I never knew too much about Lauren, an aspiring fashion designer, except she was also a friend of Marisa's and she'd gotten so stoned with my father once that she'd walked right into a glass door at Wolfback and smashed her tiny nose so thoroughly that she had to have an operation to make it bigger so she could breathe again.

Ooee wasn't around as much in those days. His architectural style had evolved—he'd added Palladian windows and Ionic columns to his bag of tricks—and he made a name for himself building museums and libraries in Atlanta and Houston. But he still kept a houseboat in Sausalito, just down the hill from Wolfback. And he was certainly around that September weekend after I turned sixteen, when Shelley and I flew up to San Francisco to collect the MG.

My father and Ooee were standing at our arrival gate when Shelley and I got off the plane from Hollywood-Burbank. Ooee's face looked very tan, and he was wearing a brown corduroy jacket and a blue oxford-cloth shirt. He'd gotten a new pair of horn-rim glasses in the Woody Allen fashion of the day, and these set off his fluffy white hair and brown eyes in a nice way. He looked adorable, like an enormous teddy bear. When he saw us approaching—Shelley and me—a look of wonder and thrill came onto his face that he couldn't possibly hide, or have faked, no matter how hard he tried. The gates of heaven had opened up. That's how he looked. We were two angels who'd come to deliver him to paradise.

"Oh, well!" Ooee called out, almost involuntarily. "Look at you two!"

My father was more restrained. His dark hair seemed severe next to Ooee's flyaway mane, and I noticed he was wearing a crisp new getup: a blue denim jacket over a thin white cotton shirt with the collar upturned. Rather than rumpled and approachable like Ooee, he looked almost too handsome to be real. And serious—so serious I worried that he might have changed his mind about the car. Was that it? Maybe my mother and Abuelita had finally gotten through to him. (They were both dubious about the car.) Then I realized it was about Shelley. My father hadn't met her.

"You're not at all how I imagined," he said to her right off. "I thought you'd be tall—at least taller than Inez."

"Nobody's taller than Inez," Shelley said without a smile. Her eyes were steady but gave off something else, a flicker of amusement.

"*I'm* taller than Inez," Ooee said, putting his arm around me.

"I mean girls," Shelley said.

"How tall are you?" my father asked, stepping closer to zero in on Shelley. He and Ooee were now circling her, moving in as if their noses were trying to catch a drift of her scent.

"Five-eight."

"That's pretty tall," said Ooee.

"I suppose," my father said.

Shelley shot me a look—an I'm-suffering-these-fools expression—and I wondered if she was okay, until we got to Ooee's Saab and I realized she'd been lying low and plotting her revenge.

"You're better-looking than I thought you'd be," she said to my father as he held the door for her.

"Am I?" he said.

"I thought you'd show up at the airport in pajamas and smoking a pipe like Hugh Hefner. Look at him. He's not very cute. I always figured that playboys weren't."

"Ouch," said Ooee, ducking into the driver's seat.

My father smiled and said nothing, just folded himself into the front passenger seat. Shelley and I were sitting in back. "Am I cute?" he asked after all the doors were closed. "I've never wanted to be cute. Paul McCartney is cute. John Denver is cute. My goal has always been *not* to be cute—just scary and delightful and take women where they've never gone before."

"*Dad.*"

Shelley laughed.

"You'd better be careful, Pablo," said Ooee. "She'll believe you."

"I'm serious," my father said.

"Yeah, right," I said.

Ooee shrugged with his mouth.

"Nobody believes me," my father said. "Nobody ever believes me." He threw his hands in the air. "Do *you* believe me, Shelley?"

"I do," she said. And she laughed again.

Shelley was given the full-length tour of Wolfback, with all the gushing and marveling that that required, and then she and I got settled in the living room. Sharing the brown corduroy sofa—recently expanded into a rather large sectional—we assumed our usual lazy positions. It's funny how easy it was to create a separate female space for ourselves, almost as if there were invisible walls around us. We filed our nails and applied new clear polish. We drank green tea and laughed at the cartoons in my father's *New Yorker* and *Playboy* magazines. We discussed what we might wear to Alegrías later that night. ("I'm getting so sick of that brown poncho," Shelley said.) Ooee and my father made phone calls and planned the afternoon. An hour or more passed by, and then it was finally decided that I should be taken out in the MG for my first stick-shifting lesson. But where?

"San Raphael?" said Ooee.

"Too far," said my father.

"The parking lot of Ralph's?"

"That hobo is there—shouting at the shrubs."

"The Marina? At least it's flat."

"The Presidio," my father said with great finality. But as soon as we'd crossed the bridge in the MG, he turned left toward the city, and not into the Presidio. He'd changed his mind. He had some coffee beans to pick up and wanted to "swing by" Walgreens pharmacy for some pills he needed.

In the parking lot of Walgreens, where I waited alone in the car, I looked at the dashboard—the gauges and switches, the black dials with white numbers and letters. "Hello," I whispered out loud. "*Hello, MG. Are you really coming home with me after all these years?*" I ran my hand along the black leather seats and white piping, then gripped the glossy wooden steering wheel.

"Why not drive it now?" my father asked, opening the door.

"But . . ." I stammered. "We're still in the city."

"It's not that congested," he said. "You can pull out into the street over there"—pointing to another entrance to the lot. "It's a dead end."

"Right now?"

"Once you get the hang of it, you'll see how simple it is," he said. "But let me take a few minutes to explain how the transmission of a car works and how the clutch operates. That'll make things easier for you."

He came by the side of the passenger door, waiting for me to switch places with him. I got out, walked around the small car, and sat down for the first time behind the wheel. How strange it felt, as if the world had gone lopsided.

"It's all very simple," my father said, oblivious to the momentousness of the occasion. And then, rather unsimply, he began to describe in agonizing detail the mechanical difference between an automatic and a manual shift and how an automobile clutch is designed to latch on to the various gears. "When you put your foot on the clutch pedal," he explained, "you are releasing the clutch from all gear options. When your foot is off the pedal, you are allowing the clutch to latch again." He cupped his hands and used his fingers to demonstrate a clutch that was "in gear" and "out of gear."

I followed his description and even found parts of it illuminating, but when it came time to find first gear and drive onto the dead-end street, the car lurched ahead horribly. "Release the clutch!" my father called out.

Quickly I took my foot off the pedal. As I did, the jerking and lurching only increased—accompanied by a loud thunking sound. "Release the clutch!" my father called out again.

"I have!"

The car died.

"But your foot is off the pedal!"

I put my foot back on the clutch, returned the gearshift to neutral, and started the car again.

"Don't hold the key on the starter!" he yelled. "You're— *Hear that?*"

I looked over. His face was red—the color of cooked lobster—and for some reason this gave me enormous satisfaction. "You mean," I said, holding the key on the starting position again, too long, until the screeching began, "*that* sound?"

"Stop it!" He reached over and tried to take the key. I grabbed it first. "Inez!" he exploded in a rage. "Have you been listening to me or not?"

"I heard every word."

"Okay," he said, taking a big breath. "Let's try again."

I turned the key gently until the car started and produced a wonderful low rumbling. It was a soothing sound, almost tranquilizing—and full of memories. I pressed down on the clutch pedal, put the car in first gear, and slowly began to lift my foot off the clutch. But again the car lurched forward in weird jumps and made a loud popping sound.

"Release the clutch!!" my father yelled.

"I have!"

"Release it!!"

"My foot is off the pedal!"

"YOU ARE ENGAGING THE CLUTCH, NOT RELEASING IT!"

Engaging the clutch? What was he talking about?

"Get out," I said.

"What?"

"Get out of the car."

I had troubled looking at him for the first few minutes. He seemed a forlorn figure in the middle of the parking lot—some kind of artsy drifter with nowhere to go. I hated the way that his shirt collar rose up against his cheek. And his legs looked too long. His hair, overly considered. What a fop. What an idiot. After a few turns around the lot, I went out to the street. I began to get the hang of the thing—the way you have to take your left foot off the clutch while you put your right foot slowly on the gas.

My father was standing perfectly still in the middle of the parking lot, like a great heron, and I noticed that he was nodding his head. The next time I looked over, he smiled and waved. The next time he'd thrown his hands in the air and was applauding.

He ran alongside the car and knocked on the window. "You did it, Inez! You did it! You doped it out on your own! Good for you!"

My father hadn't gone to El Bodega for a long time, it seemed. When we arrived for dinner, Hector looked stunned—not his usual fake surprise but something more honest. "Pablo, is it really you? I thought you'd died."

"No, just moved over the bridge," my father said stiffly. "But I'm back tonight."

"Good to see you. And the señoritas. And you, Señor Lungo."

But after all the buildup that I'd given Shelley, the paella didn't taste as delicious as I remembered—the clams were rubbery and cold. Alegrías seemed seedier than ever, too. The red walls were shiny in some places, dull in others, as though several kinds of paint had been used to patch things up. The wooden stage was banged up and in need of a broom. It smelled like mold, and wine, and maybe urine. When the dancers came out, they were bleary-eyed and off—or drunk. The sparse crowd consisted of no real flamenco aficionados, as far as I could tell. Aside from my father's old table in the back, it was mostly tourists and retirees. "They've made us a stop on a bus tour," Ricardo said dolefully at the break.

Shelley and I waited impatiently for Antonio to appear—I'd been telling her about him for two years already. As soon as the dancing started, we moved our chairs closer so we could talk. "Which one is he?" she asked. As each new guitarist emerged from behind the curtain and joined the ensemble of singers and dancers, I shook my head. "Not him either." Halfway through the show, when Antonio hadn't turned up, I finally leaned over to Ooee.

"What happened to Antonio?"

Ooee shrugged, then looked over at my father.

"Where is Antonio?" I said again.

My father shook his head. "Who? Forget about him," he said with a scowl. "He's into junk, not girls."

There was a disagreement about what to do on our last night. It was our family tradition to see a movie together, but Ooee objected. "*Network*?" he groaned. "Jesus, Paul. The girls can see a movie anywhere. I think we should go out on the town."

"Yeah," said Shelley. Her face was kind of open, along with her mouth. She looked up at my father with a funny self-consciousness, keeping her chin down as if trying to appear blasé, but she wasn't. "Come on, Paul. It'll be fun."

"Out on the town?" my father seemed incredulous. "What town?"

"Just a night out," Ooee said. "Play it by ear. Maybe hit some of those punk clubs by the modern art museum."

Shelley didn't say anything right away, just stepped closer to my father, as though trying to convince him with her body or smell or something. "Let's do it. Come on, *Paul.*"

He ignored her and spoke directly to Ooee. "No thank you. I'd rather see a movie. That's what Inez and I are going to do. Right, Inez?"

I nodded. Shelley looked kind of disappointed, or rattled, but not for long. After spending twenty minutes in the bathroom, she emerged in tight pants, very high heels, and a slather of heavy lip gloss, and she headed off with Ooee for the city. As soon as they were gone, my father and I studied the movie listings in the newspaper and tried to guess how long we'd have to wait in line. We'd stood for two hours to see *The Godfather, Part II* on its first weekend at the North Point and watched a joint being passed down the line until the roach got so small somebody ate it.

"Hey, the movie starts in ninety minutes," my father said, pointing at the paper. "We better get going."

A few minutes later, he was waiting for me in the driveway next to his Triumph and wearing a black leather jacket. He had a helmet under his arm. A smaller helmet was sitting on the seat of the motorcycle, along with a woman's black leather jacket.

"Whose are these?" I asked, picking up the helmet and the jacket.

"Nobody's. I just keep them around."

I was putting on the jacket when he pulled from his breast pocket a small silver pipe that Justine had given him. I could see he'd already loaded it with a small pinch of grass. "Want some?"

"No thanks," I said. "Don't do that anymore."

"No? Probably wise. I thought it would make the movie better and the wait a little more interesting. But you don't need it."

Just as he was tossing out that tepid approval, I extended my hand for the lit pipe and took a long drag, then passed it back. Then took another. After a third drag, he said, "That's enough," and put the pipe away.

He started up the bike with a few explosions of sound—so loud, unbearably loud—and we were off, down the paved driveway, onto the dirt road. I was on the back, hanging on to his waist, the seat rumbling under me and the sky hovering above. I began to notice the languid shapes of eucalyptus trees, the sound of the wind. The coolness on my neck and cheeks. When we got to the farm gate, my father pulled out his remote control. The gate lifted, and we sailed through.

Shelley and Ooee weren't around when we got home from the movie. And in the morning, when I woke up in the living room, the smooth sheets and wool blanket on Shelley's side of the sofa didn't look touched.

I stared at the ceiling for a few minutes, watched the bright sun coming in the windows. I heard the waves on the beach. And then I heard voices, some laughing.

I went to the window and stepped over to the glass door that led to the deck. Shelley was coming up the stone steps from the beach. She was wearing a sweatshirt and pair of short shorts. My father was behind her, but instead of noticing me at the door, his eyes had steadied themselves on Shelley's rear end.

"Are those hot pants?" I heard him ask.

"No!" she laughed, and turned around to him.

"What buns you have, my dear! What buns!"

He gave us a road map of California, with directions carefully highlighted in yellow marker. He went over all his instructions again, and the eccentricities of the car. On a cold morning, I needed to pull out the choke. Sometimes on the freeway, the car might seem to be out of gas, but it was just a finicky fuel pump—"and you can take this wrench and just give it a few whacks right here," he said, bending over the side of the MG, "and it'll work again." He explained how the fog lamps operated and how to use a tire-pressure gauge. He wrote in the operating manual the fine grade of motor oil that he preferred and gave me a folder of receipts—a record of the MG's every service call organized in chronological order. He handed me an AAA card and a gas card from Shell with INEZ GARCIA RUIN pressed into the plastic.

I started it up. The rumble of the engine was so deep and low that I could almost feel it in my blood. I waved and backed the car around, then looked over at him again. He was standing in the driveway waving—it was a Ruin family tradition to keep waving until the departing family member was out of sight. His hand was stopped in midair. And then I noticed his face. It was crumpling, his features squeezing into the middle and his eyes getting small. He was just beginning to cry.

I cranked down the window.

"What's the matter?" I yelled out.

"Nothing!" he shouted back, with his hand still lingering over his head. He walked closer and bent down. "I'm just sad, that's all. A beautiful kind of sadness. You look so damn wonderful in that car."

FIFTEEN

Ooee's Houseboat

I wasn't the only one who seemed skittish about sex. Whitman was twenty-one, and, as far as we knew, there'd never been a woman in his life. No talk of a woman. No signs of interest—aside from passing remarks and sometimes brutal criticisms about the girls my father brought home. They were "pathetic" or "way too young," and he seemed utterly bewildered by the attraction these women had for our father, although this was never a mystery to me. "Dad always finds these sweet, passive women," Whitman complained. "And then he trains them to become even sweeter and more passive. Don't let him do that to you, Inez."

Whitman hung out with other guys—surfers, mostly—who lived in ramshackle beach houses where the bedrooms were rented out weekly. From his descriptions of South Africa, and New Zealand before that, it seemed like a rugged but strangely romantic existence. They lived from storm to storm, drifted from surf spot to surf spot, eating mushrooms and smoking dope during the lulls. When they ran out of money, they took small jobs in town, or bought run-down cars and got them going and sold them for a small profit. Maybe they sold some dope, too. God only knows. But Whitman didn't work, as far as I could tell. Patricia's family had left him with a trust, the amount of which was never discussed in precise terms. "It's like Dad says," Whitman had once explained to me. "It's not enough to make my life and not enough to ruin it either."

In the middle of my junior year of high school, he'd moved permanently to Hawaii. He'd found a little house to buy in Haleiwa, on a narrow road of shacks and rentals where the surf pros lived during the winter competitions. It was on the beach, he told me, and as close as anybody could be to the heart of Oahu Island's famous North Shore. Waimea Bay was a short ride in one direction, Sunset and Pipeline in the other. It was emerging as a popular year-round resort and beginning to boom with new hotels and developments, and Whitman planned to set up a gardening business there.

"For all I know, he's a fag," my father joked a few times, but as soon as we'd laugh—because this couldn't possibly be true—we'd grow silent, because maybe it was.

"Maybe he's like me," I said one night at dinner during a visit. "Waiting for the right person."

"Is that what you're doing?" my father asked. "Waiting for the right person?"

I shrugged. That's how it felt anyway.

"That's so interesting," he said. This response, particularly his use of the word "interesting," meant that a lecture was about to come. "I hope you're not making the mistake of being too romantic, Inez," he said. "Sometimes it's not really like that. No right or wrong person. And hopefully, my dear, there will be lots of people—wrong and right and somewhere in between."

"I haven't met anybody yet," I said. "Not anybody I'd—"

"Not one? You mean you haven't—*at all*? There's been nobody?"

This flustered me. He seemed to want details and elaboration. But I wasn't about to discuss any of my Van Dale experiences, the dozen or so drunken episodes of slobbery kisses and clumsy juvenile groping. "It's not that I haven't done anything—*at all,* as you put it," I said. "I just haven't . . . done, uh, everything."

"Gone all the way, you mean." His face was dead serious.

I tried very hard not to blanch, although I doubt it's possible to control that sort of thing.

"Don't people still say that?" he went on. "'Going all the way'? Makes me laugh. Makes the whole thing sound like an obstacle course. First base, second base, third . . . home run. The old 'home run.' What's wrong with 'balling?'"

"Dad."

"What?"

"Nobody says that anymore. Nobody says 'balling.'"

"They don't?" He looked a little stricken—although this seemed like an act. "What do they say? 'Bedding down'?"

"'*Bedding down*'? That's like something from Shakespeare."

"Is it?"

"You say 'doing it' or 'sleeping with.'"

"What ever happened to 'making love'?"

"Gross. No way."

"What? Is that just hopelessly saccharine? There's a song on the radio, 'I Feel Like Making Love . . .'"

"Nobody likes that song."

"It's a huge hit."

"Anything like 'love' or 'lover' is bad news. You say, 'We're having sex.'"

"'*Having sex*'?"

I shrugged.

"Talk about lack of poetry. You might as well say 'laying pipe.'"

"What?" I laughed. "Laying what?"

"Pipe. That's an old expression. Laying pipe. It makes me laugh, too."

In those days my father seemed to be constantly slipping remarks about sex into our conversations as though it were a perfectly natural subject between a father and daughter. Maybe he was worried about

Whitman, who didn't appear to be staggering in his footsteps. To compensate, he began to work on me. He tried to be relaxed about it, and casual. But he brought up the joys of sex—its naturalness and beauty—every chance he got. It reminded me a little of the beach-house days, when he'd harp about my modesty and bra wearing and wanted to cure me with a trip to the nude beach in La Jolla. Now any opportunity to impart some of his philosophy about life and love and relationships with the opposite sex was leaped on with great glee.

"The most delicate little Chinese girl was working the register at the Nam Yun Palace tonight," my father said one evening over the winter when Ooee happened to be visiting. We were sitting at the kitchen table at Wolfback, eating takeout from the city.

"Young Oriental girls are so perfect," said Ooee, his chopsticks carrying a ball of white rice into his mouth. "Such a mystery."

"Young girls are wonderful—period," my father said. "Their hang-ups are so interesting."

Ooee gulped down the rice, excited to blurt out confirmation of this hard-won observation. "I know exactly what you mean!" he cried enthusiastically. "You always want to tell them not to worry so much—that in the long run all the stuff they think's so important doesn't matter."

"But they have to learn that for themselves," my father said.

"Learn what?" I asked.

Ooee and my father looked at each other—as though silently deciding who between them might do a better job of explaining all this. Finally Ooee returned to his chopsticks and the piles of food on his plate. My father spoke up. "They just have to get things straightened out," he said. "They have to sort through the fairy-tale indoctrination they get from their mothers and grandmothers—the ridiculous and shameful legacy of Cinderella and Sleeping Beauty. It's still alive in Middle America, I'm sure. And probably thriving in Van Dale. Girls are told that if they sleep with somebody, they need to marry them. That's the kind of dangerous information young girls are given. That's what Shanti's parents had told her. Can you imagine?"

Ooee nodded slowly, in complete agreement. "A Catholic education is the most difficult to overcome," he said. "The brainwashing is—"

"But," my father interrupted, "don't you think, Ooee, that once they break free of expectations or fears—I really think the Catholics work the fear side of the street and the protestants work the life-isn't-about-pleasure side—that most women are generally okay and much saner than men? This really seems so obvious to me. Once women are free of the indoctrination, they're really free of almost everything. Particularly if they never marry and never have children. Now, that's a recipe for a wonderful life."

Ooee was chewing and nodding but beginning to seem more into dinner than the conversation.

My father continued on his roll. "Men have a whole other load of baggage—and a terrible need to dominate and compete and be aggressive. There's always some poor rival in need of crushing. There's always some war to fight. And chest beating. It's so brutal and primitive—and behavior that's much more difficult to dismantle and haul away. Practically impossible."

"Although a big, healthy midlife crisis," Ooee said, "does wonders."

"Do you think so?" my father asked, as if he weren't so sure. "I don't remember you having a midlife crisis."

Ooee smiled with his mouth closed, then swallowed. "No," he laughed. "I bypassed one completely by never bothering to grow up."

Ooee and I both laughed. My father seemed irritated, though, as if our lightheartedness weren't in sync with some train of thought he was on. "I suppose I might have had one—once," he said finally, "when I left Consuela."

Ooee stopped laughing.

"I thought she left you," I said.

"Did she?" asked Ooee under his breath. "Still dying to meet her. I've heard she's so damn gorgeous."

"Well, I suppose you could say that," my father continued, looking only at me. "She did leave me at some point. She'd had enough—or something like that. I figured out a great deal during that period. It's not that difficult or complicated. You just have to decide to be honest with yourself—and then make your best attempt at it. You have to admit what you're after and where you want to go. How you want to wind up. And I suppose it helps to figure out what you're avoiding—what you're afraid might happen.

"You know, Inez, things usually aren't as black and white as we'd like. Whether your mother left me or I left her—"

"Takes two to tango," Ooee broke in. "Nobody is ever solely responsible for the end. Endings are inevitable. Everything ends. The better question to ask is—"

"What keeps it going?" my father laughed. "Right?"

"Right!" Ooee yelled out. After a little more laughter, he cracked open a fortune cookie and looked down at the slip of paper he'd extracted from the broken crumbs. At first I thought he was reading his fortune out loud, but then I realized he was just continuing the conversation. "Good sex," he said, "is the key to everything."

"True," my father said. "If the sex is good, things can't be that bad."

"A perfect barometer."

My father got up to clear the table. As he started to rinse off the dishes, I noticed that Ooee was looking at me.

His eyes were slightly beckoning. And, of course, it was hardly the first time. Years before, when he drank too much at one of my father's flamenco parties and kissed my ear, he'd whispered, "I'm waiting for you." *I'm waiting for you.* It was a phrase I found particularly haunting—and horrifying—and afterward Ooee's hovering quality really bugged me. I'd look away when his eyes rested on mine for too long. But so many years had passed, and he'd never sucked on my earlobe again, or talked to me like that, or even touched me in a suggestive way, so he'd stopped being a threat—or a predator—to me. He'd become a benign character in my mind, almost impotent. Until he and Shelley wound up together.

"Aren't you dying to know?" Shelley had asked me, almost as soon as we'd driven off in the MG together, my father still waving in front of the drive. "I mean, aren't you curious about what happened last night with

Ooee?" A full report would come, I knew, whether I encouraged it or not. That's how Shelley was.

"He's got kind of a big stomach," she said.

"Don't tell me anything else," I said. This remark would have the opposite effect, I knew.

"No, I mean it's kind of nice—having all that weight on top of you," she recounted. "He's so big and . . . I don't know. Male. All that hair on his chest and back, like an older guy has. And that loose, older-guy skin. You know, it feels so different from a young guy's skin. Softer. Not flabby, exactly, but . . . Anyway, he wasn't on the top the whole time. He's really into the oral stuff."

"He is?"

"Like, he just couldn't get enough of me down there."

"*Really*." My mind swirled—disgusted, delighted.

"God, it went on and on." Shelley laughed and then smiled quietly for a long time, as if she were reliving an incredibly pleasant memory and she wasn't going to speak again until it was over. "I don't think he wanted to go all the way, because he was worried I wasn't on the pill. 'You're not on the pill? *Everybody's on the pill.*'"

Ooee was newly empowered after that and, for a long time, a perpetually sexual presence in my mind. He wasn't simply more masculine, but almost a superhuman embodiment of potency and know-how. Having been pretested and certified by Shelley—who was already eighteen and enormously picky about men—I began to fantasize that someday, when I took the plunge, Ooee might be the right candidate. He was ancient and kind of fat, and maybe his skin *was* loose and soft. But he was safe and fatherly, adorable and a little silly. All those years ago, he said he was waiting for me. Was he still?

Sometime in the late spring, my father casually mentioned on the phone that Ooee was "back from Houston" and throwing a party on his houseboat the next weekend. I announced right away that I wanted to drive up in the MG and go. He got a kick out of that—the spontaneity, the desire to just show up and see him. In the past it had always been such a struggle to arrange dates for me to visit.

"Bring Shelley!" he said.

"She's busy," I said, lying.

"Oh, too bad."

It wasn't so much that I was jealous of Shelley, or jealous of my father's flirtations with her. Mostly I was afraid that she would interfere with my plans for Ooee. Time was passing, and I was suddenly in a great hurry. My junior year of high school was almost over, and not only was I ready to experience a good pipe laying but lagging behind—hopelessly behind. As Shelley had put it, "No girl who drives a car like that should be a virgin." Indeed, if anything, I owed it to the MG.

My father called the next day, insisting that I fly up—and not drive alone. He seemed buoyed tremendously by my imminent visit. And Ooee was "delighted" to learn that I'd be coming to his party, he reported. "He said to tell you that it was going to be a slightly dressy crowd—some of the museum board, I think—so you might want to bring an outfit."

An outfit. This seemed like an important sign, almost a directive. Ooee knew what I was coming for. Ooee *knew*. And he wanted me to be ready. I picked out a red dress that I'd gotten in a consignment shop in Burbank—a frock that didn't look old and secondhand as much as it looked like something Ava Gardner might wear, but not for long. How would I feel when Ooee unbuttoned it? My mind swirled with fantasies, so much so that I found it difficult to sleep. And then, very early the next morning, without a word to Shelley, or anyone, I drove to a pharmacy at the edge of town and bought a box of contraceptive suppositories that I'd seen advertised in a woman's magazine. They were encased in heavy silver foil and shaped like bullets.

Ooee's houseboat was so big it barely bobbed on Richardson Bay. The night was warm, and the moon rose in the sky, huge and luminous. People were spilling out of the main rooms of the boat and lingering outside on the decks. I didn't recognize too many of Ooee's friends. They were older and wore expensive clothes that—to my Van Dale eyes— seemed almost somber and funereal. And their voices were limber and confident and urbane. They made asides I didn't understand and jokes that sounded jaded. "So I finally get to see Ooee's Bachelor Barge," I heard one woman say, and then laugh wickedly.

Inside, Ooee was as charming and gregarious as ever, playing host to crowds of friends. He was behind the bar, recommending wines. He was passing around plates of food, urging people to try things that he'd made. And he was—no surprise—completely surrounded by a slew of women who all seemed prettier and more sophisticated than I. They were city women in their twenties and thirties, women with real jobs and real dresses and good, soft handbags—not stiff, thirdhand accessories from a consignment shop. Their hands held wineglasses at the stem like they'd had lots of wine, every kind of wine, and every kind of sex. "That dress is fantastic," my father gushed, and Ooee did, too, but their compliments seemed more about the big effort I'd made than anything else. Now it seemed silly to have made an effort at all. What had I been thinking?

Walking outside again, where I hoped to get some air—and put some distance between myself and all those glamorous women—I bumped into a guy with shaggy blond hair and almond eyes. He was younger than most of the other guests and seemed, like me, a little out of his element. Standing alone and looking at the bay, he wasn't drinking red wine, like everybody else, but holding a glass of water.

"Aren't you Paul Ruin's daughter?"

He explained that he had worked at Harrison-Ruin a few years ago, before going back to graduate school, and had seen me at a party once. "Really?" I asked, so overcome with flattery that I didn't realize it wasn't nice to openly not remember him.

"It was at your father's apartment on Telegraph Hill," he said. "I saw you across the room."

"The party for all the *flamencos*?" I asked. "A really long time ago?"

"Two years ago," he said, nodding. "On June seventeenth to be exact.

I have a good memory for dates, almost like a chronic brain malfunction. Somebody else at the party told me that you were only fourteen or fifteen, and I remember thinking, Oh, I can't talk to her. She's too young. I wanted to, though. I've always been a big fan of your father's. I guess I wondered what it would be like to be Paul's daughter. You guys look so much alike." Then he jerked out his right hand. "I'm David Yamato, by the way."

"I'm Inez."

He nodded and seemed to know that already.

"David!" I heard my father call out. "Inez!" He was standing across the deck of the houseboat, near the dock. "You found each other!" It relaxed me to see him, feeling sure that he'd come over and grease the wheels conversationally, help me feel less inept. But rather than walking over, he stood near the dock waving and smiling. Then I saw Shanti coming aboard. She was wearing a bright yellow sari.

"I'm in Pasadena now," David was saying, "at Caltech."

"Oh," I said. "My dad hated going there."

"I hate it, too," David said, nodding so vigorously that his bangs danced around his eyes. "But not the school, just L.A. Living there is a drag."

He'd grown up in Hawaii, he said. His family had a pearl business on the Big Island and spent holidays on Molokai—at a spot so remote they had to fly in on a small private plane. A place like that, I imagined, could make Los Angeles look pretty lousy to almost anybody. As David talked about Hawaii and his family, he seemed to grow more comfortable and outgoing, as if just thinking about home gave him strength. His mother was Swedish, he said. His father was Japanese. He had an older sister and two younger ones, and there was something in the way he talked about them, sort of proudly but without mention of any specific accomplishments, that made me feel certain they were very pretty. "When I lived in San Francisco, they loved to come visit me," he said. "But now they don't. They hate L.A., too."

I nodded, didn't say much. The superiority of Northern California—it was always there, like the cold summer. It was always there, a smugness and attitude. People in L.A. rarely said they hated San Francisco. It didn't work that way.

"My brother lives in Hawaii," I said.

"You have a brother?" David said with surprise. "Paul's never talked about him—not the way he does about you."

I described Whitman in gushing tones, as if to make up for my father's strange oversight. And as I told what I knew about Whitman's house in Haleiwa—a town that David seemed to know well—I realized that there was something nice and brotherly about David, too. He reminded me of Whitman a little, in fact. There was something about his jawline and the way his head and neck sat on his broad shoulders. He had the posture of an athlete, I suppose—a swimmer. And, like Whitman, David gave off the feeling of a guy who'd grown up at the beach—a deliberate cool, a relaxed reserve, like there wasn't too much to get excited about, except maybe a storm. "I don't surf too much anymore," he said. "I sailboard. Ever heard of that?"

The next week my father called me to say that David had asked for my phone number at home. Was that okay? "He's a lovely fellow," my father added in a collaborative, encouraging way. "Very bright. I think he finished an undergraduate degree at Stanford before he was nineteen. Impressive, huh? Anyway, I think he's just looking for a friend. He's apparently not too happy in L. A."

David's voice on the phone sounded young and sweet, almost like a girl's. "Hey, do you want to get together?" he asked. It didn't occur to me until later that he was twenty-five—almost ten years older. He raised the possibility of several things we could do together, all of them outdoorsy and athletic—tennis, hiking, or riding bikes to the beach. He talked a ton about sailboarding. He was so taken with the sport that he'd begun to shape his own fiberglass boards and experiment with various fins and sizes of sails. It wasn't quite sailing, he said, but not really surfing either. There were some good spots in Malibu for it, not far from Zuma Beach. Did I want a lesson? "How about this weekend?" he posed. "I have a spare wetsuit you could borrow."

We went hiking instead—accompanied by Shelley. I wasn't sure that I wanted to learn how to surf and sail at the same time. Or wear a borrowed wetsuit. And for some reason, still unclear to me, I hadn't wanted to be alone with David. Looking back, I guess I was a little scared, worried that he wasn't just a friend but had called for a date.

"He seems kind of faggy," Shelley said later.

"You think everybody's like that."

The following week we played tennis with my mother and Bob, her boyfriend. It wasn't a serious doubles game, just "batting around a few balls," as my mother would say. Bob was nicer than usual—impressed by David's Stanford/Caltech credentials—and David played tennis well, much better than I, and had a quiet sort of depth that seemed to make him fit into any group yet not become lost. He wasn't like Whitman at all, I remember thinking as I watched him play next to me. He wasn't chatty or buoyant or full of opinions. He was more methodical and studious. After an hour or two of playing and some banter, my mother and Bob left to see a new house that was coming on the market. David drove me back to Abuelita's in his blue Toyota Celica. He jumped out to open my car door, then quickly jumped back in and waved good-bye.

"He's a natural athlete," my mother said later, approvingly. In the last decade, her ideas about what made a man attractive had changed drastically. Athletic ability was now an essential ingredient, a reaction, as far as I could tell, to my father, who had no interest in sports and did nothing remotely physical besides having sex or riding his motorcycle.

"We're just friends," I insisted to Shelley—and to my mother, when she found the courage to ask me outright. And this felt entirely true until the end of May, when David casually mentioned that he'd be spending the summer in Hawaii, at his family's "retreat" on Molokai. He seemed so thrilled to be leaving and lavishly praised his family's property with its waterfall and "amazing swimming hole." He was packing up his sailboards and all his equipment, he said, and sending them ahead by freighter.

We were eating salads at Polly's Pies while David talked about his approaching summer. As I pictured him in the swimming hole and standing under its waterfall, I felt a sudden sense of loss and defeat—almost abandonment. How could he go without me? What would I do all summer? I found myself noticing how handsome he was. And I stared at his strong hands. By the time I got into bed that night, the transformation was complete. There was little else to think of but David, David, David. His hands. His shoulders. The nape of his neck. I thought back on our first meeting, the way he smiled at me on Ooee's barge. I wondered if his sisters had cute friends who might be in love with him. I wondered if he would be in contact with his old friend Gabby. He'd mentioned her in passing a few times. Did they ever date, or was that just my imagination? I even did the math—$Y/2 + 7 = X$—and was disheartened to discover that David was supposed to be with an older woman, a nineteen-year-old and not me.

By morning my feelings had mushroomed exponentially, as if a sheet had been pulled off David's head to expose the most wondrous boyfriend alive. With only a few days left before he'd leave for Hawaii, I kicked myself for not waking up to the obvious earlier.

As we made plans to have dinner on his last night in California, I had an idea—it just hit me suddenly—that it would be fun to eat at a restaurant in Burbank that Shelley and I had seen while hiking one afternoon. It was an old place, all wood and beams and decks, up in the hills. It overlooked residential Burbank and its downtown. It was called the Castaways. Come to think of it, the food was Polynesian.

"Hawaiian food?" David sounded dispirited. "That's what you want? Really?"

"Oh, please," I said in my sultriest voice. "I'm just *dying* to eat there.

I've wanted to go there *for years.*" I hoped that somehow, magically, the way I spoke these words would communicate exactly what I really meant. I was ready. And I wanted Hawaiian.

"Hi," my father said. His voice sounded contemplative—but a little curious, too.

"Hi."

"I've been trying to call all morning. What's the matter? Your voice sounds funny."

"I'm sick."

"Oh, dear," he said. "I'm sorry."

I said nothing.

"A head cold?"

"I'm not sure. I just feel awful. My head is killing me, and my chest feels tight. Like I can't breathe."

"Oh, I'm so sorry to hear that."

After a few minutes of discussion, during which I elaborated upon my various symptoms and he listened with great patience, he said, "David Yamato called me this morning."

"He did?"

"He's leaving for Hawaii, and . . . well, he said he was calling to say good-bye. He's such a lovely fellow, isn't he? But I think he was really calling to check up on you."

I said nothing.

"He's been trying to get a hold of you. He said that he was flying out later today and had promised to say good-bye before he did. I guess he went by the house, and you weren't there. And I guess he tried calling, as I did. Anyway, he's such a nice man. I hope you aren't playing head games, Inez. He sounded a little—I don't know—not himself. But I'm glad to find you at home."

"I'm sick."

"Oh, that's right." My father stretched out the vowels in those words for a long time, like he was thinking very carefully about how to play a hand of cards. "Inez?"

"Yes."

"What's going on?"

"Nothing."

He was quiet again for a moment. "Do you need my help with anything? Do you—"

"No."

"Really?"

"Yes, really," I said. "God, I feel so lousy."

"I'm very sorry about that." He was talking slowly, and so carefully, and so gently, he was beginning to remind me of Mr. Rogers. "Do you mind me asking when you last saw David?"

"Last night. We went to dinner."

"Oh."

"Maybe it was something I ate."

"Maybe," he said. "What did you eat?"

"Pork something. Cooked pineapples. It was Hawaiian food. Fake Hawaiian."

"Did you get sick right away?"

"No."

There was a pause. "So you finished dinner, and then what happened?"

"We had dessert and came back here—to Abuelita's. I knew David was leaving today."

It had started on the sofa in the living room. I suppose I'd hoped for it, and planned for it, because before the Castaways I had showered with incredible thoroughness, as though I were embarking on a long journey and might never have the chance to shower again. I'd shaved so carefully that not one tiny bit of stubble was poking up. I'd scrubbed my face with crushed apricot hulls and oatmeal. I'd Q-tipped my ears. I shampooed my hair three times with Pantene—and left the conditioner on a really long time. After I toweled off, I creamed my legs and arms, every single inch of my skin, with buttery lotion that smelled like lemons. If I were a goose, I'd have been ready for the oven.

David was all over me—I couldn't believe how loud his breathing was or how frantic his mouth was. It was like he was gasping and dying at the same time. And we rubbed up against each other and began pulling off our clothes like it was a race to nudity. We wound up in my bedroom with the door open—so we could hear if anybody was coming home—and we were writhing and lunging and pulsating and moving all over each other like two animals that were trying to burrow a home inside each other and stay for the winter. That's how it felt: I wanted to crawl inside David Yamato and live there forever.

And in the very early morning, after he put on his clothes and I heard the quiet motor of his Toyota Celica pulling away, I cried. A few hours later, when I woke up, I wanted to die.

A little before noon, he came back and rang the bell—I saw him through a crack in my window curtain. But I couldn't bear to answer the door. He rang the bell three times and stood there. And kept standing there. Like he couldn't believe I wasn't opening the door.

"Can I ask you a personal question, Inez?" my father asked on the phone.

"I don't know. Maybe."

"It's important," he said. "It's about something important—so I do really want to ask it."

"What?"

"Are you sleeping with him?"

I felt myself sort of warming up, kind of melting and getting liquidy. Almost as if my throat were filling up with water. Just the way my father said it—not like that old, creepy, prying, busybody way of his—but in a way that was different. Like he was trying really hard not to be upset, too.

"Just last night," I said. "We did."

"Oh."

He didn't say anything for a long time. I think he was stunned. And then, I don't know, it seemed like he was making a wild guess about something and was calculating the odds of being right. "Do you think you're in love with him? Because otherwise I can't—"

That's when I started to cry. There were too many things I'd never wanted to say, or think about, or feel. It felt suddenly as if all the things that I wanted in life—and hadn't even known I'd wanted—had gone. And all the people I loved. Marguerite was dead, Whitman was off. My mother was making sounds like she was going to marry Bob Lasso, the dentist. And now David would be just like that, too, wouldn't he? He'd joined a parade of people who were wandering away. He was going to be another person that I'd miss all the time, and feel sad about. When he'd rung the bell and I'd peeked outside my window and seen him, I hated him—hated to even look at him. And I never wanted to see him again. Now I realized it was worse than that. I never wanted him to go.

How come Shelley just yanked her underpants off and did it with Greg and Ooee and anybody else? How come everybody—Ooee and all those girlfriends, all those grown-ups on the houseboat—just slept with whomever they wanted, no big deal, like it was a gymnastics event?

"Inez?"

I made a crying sound that I knew he could hear.

"Oh, *Inez*," he said. His voice was breaking. "Oh, sweetie, I know just how you feel."

"You do?"

SIXTEEN

Dr. Lasso's Office, Please Hold

My father didn't continue his drumbeat for long about David's being "such a lovely man." In a matter of weeks after David's departure—maybe days—he'd grown weary of David and my endless need to talk about him. He became "a smart character," according to my father, and "a nice guy, I suppose." Then he finally descended to, "He's okay if you're into Asians. Are they really hairless, by the way?"

When I broached the possibility of a trip to the islands that summer—I was "dying to see Whitman" and "dying to see Hawaii" suddenly—Dad saw through my tactics and snapped, "My God, don't you have better things to do?"

"Not really."

This tropical dream died for other reasons, though. Whitman sounded uncertain when I floated the idea by him, as though he weren't quite ready to share paradise. David was perplexingly noncommittal on the subject, hedging with vague concerns about whether there was room for me at his parents' house on Molokai (wasn't it a compound?) until it was clear I couldn't come anyway.

Why wasn't I getting a job instead? My mother and Abuelita were insistent and almost immovable on the summer-job thing, as though it were an obligation to the universe that was long overdue. They pestered me and glared with Easter Island faces. What was with them? A job? *Work?* How had this awful development come about? And why now? Almost out of the blue, a new attitude toward me had emerged, accompanied by new expectations. It seemed so badly timed. I wanted all the fun accessories of adulthood—the car, the cigarettes, nighttime adventures, a sex life, things that had just come into my reach. But a job? My mother and Abuelita acted like I was on the precipice of needing to support myself. Filled with quiet hostility, I dodged the summer-employment issue until the end of June and then prevaricated until the Fourth of July had passed, only faking an interest in the help-wanted ads in the *Van Dale Star* while debating with Shelley (an unlikely "mother's helper" at three dollars an hour) about whether I could deliver pizza in the MG.

Then fate took over. A job fell on me. My mother's boyfriend announced that he could use some help in the front office of his dental practice in Montrose. One of his receptionists had undergone an emergency hysterectomy and would need the summer to recover. Bob was confident that I could handle record keeping, filing, and some "light typing," as he put it, and I didn't bother putting up a fight. Everything was stacked against me. My mother was elated. Abuelita was relieved. Even my father weighed in with, "A little work never hurt anybody," and chuckled sadistically. So I absentmindedly misfiled and answered the phone saying, "Dr. Lasso's office," as sullenly as I could, waiting for the long, hot summer to slump along to its end.

I should have been good at alphabetizing and filing—just the kind of rote organizing that I excelled at—but I was distracted by Bob's dental hygienist, an overweight bottle blonde with incredible stories about sex in the woods with drunken deer hunters and blow jobs in the backs of camper vans. In between tooth polishing and positioning the giant X-ray nozzle on patients' cheeks, Donna sat in a corner of the front office next to me, filing her long nails—hoping to achieve some kind of ideal equal length—while spinning her sexy recollections. She was always looking around to see if "Dr. Lasso" was in earshot. When he wasn't, she'd dig into a faux-leather tote for manicure tools and talk about the size of some guy's "schlong." She made me cry with laughter, and her raunchy stories made me ache. All I could think about that summer was David anyway. David nude. David on top of me. David in my bathroom, peeing in my toilet. Instead of keeping my mind on alphabetizing, I was in bed with him—and repeating our one night together again and again. I swooned over the open file drawers and sometimes nearly passed out.

"How's it going at Dr. Bob's?" my father would ask. He called too frequently, pretending he had a quick question. But he was checking up on me, fascinated by my painful descent into love. He'd track me down at work and try to humor me out of blue moods. "Whose mouth is Bob looking into right now?" he'd say with an edge in his voice. "Can you imagine the tedium of *that*?"

"No," I'd say. "I can't."

We were both anti-Bob, pretty much, and plotted against him for reasons that were never fully articulated. We were mean and unrelentingly petty. Bob's politics bugged us—he proselytized about the virtues of democracy like it was a religion. ("Why can't he leave the poor Soviets alone?" my father complained.) There was another matter, too: Furiously in love, Bob was proprietary about my mother, as if he were the first person to truly care about her. He had proposed and given her a huge diamond ring—something my father had never done. ("He didn't really give her a *diamond* ring, did he?" my father asked. "God, people are so uncreative.") How Bob won my mother's heart seems simple to me now. He did it with devotion, with honesty, with thoughtfulness, and with an aggressive campaign that made him seem forceful and manly. He wasn't charming or good-looking or anything like that—Bob was a wiry guy and not too tall, a suburban tennis player with a meatless track-and-field body, but there was something tough about him. It was a mental toughness, a clarity and determination. He had a certainty that made the rest of us look blurry and out of focus. Among the earliest graduates of est, he'd considered dropping dentistry to become a trainer. "How'd he luck out and land your mother?" my father asked with wistfulness in his voice.

"He's angry," I said. "She likes angry men."

"Does she?"

"That's what she told me."

"Really? Am *I* angry?"

"I'm not sure," I hedged, suddenly embarrassed. "I think the deal is . . . when she married you, she married her father."

"Oh, Christ, don't give me that mumbo jumbo."

I liked working in Bob's office, as it turned out. Bob was okay—a decent guy who'd never understand me, or probably never want to—and his office was a study in efficiency and good humor. He never tried to jolly up his patients but won them over, as he had Mom, with decency and attentiveness. I liked sitting behind the open window in the front office and studying people as they came and went, looking at their faces, and their clothes, and then peeking into their private files and gazing at the gaudy color photographs of their teeth and gums. "It's really kinda fun," I told my father after a couple weeks. "And the hygienist is hysterical."

"Donna?"

"Yes."

"The big blonde?"

Through a doorway I caught sight of Donna carefully clipping a paper bib around the neck of a reclining patient. Then she reached down and scratched her thigh, her long nails raking over her nude pantyhose and making a sound that I'll never forget. "She's not for you, Dad."

"No? She sounds like a riot. Hey, heard anything from dear old David?"

I said nothing.

"Inez?"

I said nothing.

"No?"

"Quit asking."

"I care. That's all."

"You're asking all the time. I told you, he's busy. He's working—he's designing a new sailboard. He might even go into business."

"You told me. All that Caltech know-how being dumped into sailboards."

"You're asking about him so much," I went on, "it's like you want me to notice he's not calling. Like he's ignoring me or something. But I *know* he's not calling me. Okay? *I'm* the one he's not calling, not *you*."

"That jerk!"

"*Dad.*"

"Time to find somebody else, Inez. Time to have some fun and play around. Don't get all tied up with one guy. Don't make that mistake. You've got the world on a string."

"No I don't."

"Are you kidding? Of course you do. *The world on a string*."

"It's more like dental floss."

Dad nagged me to visit—even tossing out mentions of Ooee like bait. "He's back in town after working on the fine-arts museum in Cleveland," he said. "And . . ."

Blah, blah, blah. I barely heard him. My old passion for Ooee seemed ludicrous to me now. Under the magic spell of David's young body and his wordlessness, and his not calling, and all those unwritten letters, Ooee's white hair and belly reminded me of Captain Kangaroo.

David. Thinking about him was like a methadone treatment program to help me ride out his absence. When I wasn't daydreaming about him that summer, I bored everybody with constant mentions of him, with musings and anecdotes pulled from a very limited supply—every topic made me think of him, or Caltech, or Hawaii, or sailboarding, or pearls— until I'd driven away everybody but Donna. "Does he have a nice schlong?" she asked. "*Oh, my God*," I'd whimper in love-drunk exhalations. Just thinking about David made me anxious and distracted. Just thinking about him made me feel miserable and wonderful at the same time. His lack of communication—only two letters all summer—fanned the flames in my heart and loins. He didn't write particularly well and demonstrated no originality. Nor did he come out and declare love for me. Yet every word seemed magical, every loopy *y* and dotted *i* inspired. Even his writing paper seemed imbued with his love and depth of feeling for me, if his words weren't. In my mind he wasn't maddeningly cryptic, he was bursting with desire! So in love he could barely speak! My imagination spun into the future, and I saw our life together perfectly: our wedding at the foot of a volcano, our little house on the edge of a Hawaiian beach, our gorgeous Mexican-Peruvian-Anglo-Japanese-Swedish babies. The only thing standing in the way of this tangible happiness was my graduation from high school ten months away. So far off it depressed me to think of it.

"Lovesickness is like seasickness," my father said whenever I sounded down or listless. "Everybody else thinks it's hilarious, and you think you're going to die. Is that how you feel, Inez?"

"Pretty much."

Toward the middle of August, when my mother and Bob went on a package tour to Europe—seeing Rome, Florence, Geneva, Zurich, Vienna, Paris, Brussels, Madrid, and London in thirteen days—I drove to Wolfback and remained there for two weeks, the longest stretch of uninterrupted time that my father and I had spent together since I was six. Dad made waffles in the morning, wearing his powder blue pajamas and green silk robe, and ran his noisy espresso machine. He did the dishes, chirpily asking a slew of personal questions—"Do you have bad menstrual cramps?"—and then he'd wander into his home office, still not dressed, and paid bills, logged on to his H-R computer that was hooked up to a mainframe in the Midwest somewhere, and made very long phone calls. I had no idea to whom, nor was I even curious. (When people talk about the curiosity of youth, I always laugh.) He seemed involved in something, or someone, with almost the same intensity as when he'd built his house, and this seemed to confine him inside all day, near the phone. He made BLTs for lunch, poached fish for dinner, and was uninterested in exercise of any kind, although he did have a reawakened passion for the piano. (He hadn't played since childhood.) All his inactivity made me restless, so after breakfast each morning, and a shower, I put on a pair of baggy painter's pants and a pair of hiking boots and left.

I went down the stone steps to the beach, then followed the shoreline until it ended. I climbed a steep hill of rocky chert to a pathway that wandered into to the dry red hills of the headlands and down into their middle parts and green valleys. I crushed eucalyptus leaves in my hands and stuffed the pods in my pockets. I saw hawks circling in the sky, a fox trotting off with a droopy mouse in its mouth. I heard a rattling snake and picked wild sage. It was so beautiful in the headlands and so empty—but rather than feeling liberated from incessant thoughts of David, I found ways to feel the whole of nature connecting me to him. The pale moon rose in the daytime sky, and I wondered if David had seen its face the night before. The wind buffeted my cheek, and I wondered where that air had been. David, David. Was I drawing a breath that had been in his lungs just days before?

Returning from my hike one day at noon, I saw my father outside the house in his green robe and stocking feet. His hair was still messy from bed, and his chin was peppered with stubble. He was standing in one spot, looking at a bare wall on the other side of the kitchen.

"Ooee and I were talking about a few small revisions," he explained, pointing to an edge of the garden where nothing had been planted. "Here's the corner where we could expand. See there? We could dig out a bit, add some foundation, and then build a separate apartment for you. Wouldn't that be nice? It wouldn't be very big," he said. "But I thought you might be coming up here for college next year, and you'd have a nice little dugout, with your own pathway and steps down to the beach."

He seemed alone that summer, kind of aimless and expectant. He was pushing Shanti into the arms of Bill Stein and had taken up with Louisa and Lauren, but they were off somewhere, both of them, and traveling with friends. During lulls like this, he usually looked up an old flame, picking up where he left off until somebody new appeared. But nobody was materializing.

Just when I began to worry that my father's supply of women had dried up, he took me out to lunch with Karen, a dark-haired lawyer and social activist who, at thirty-seven, seemed a bit older than his usual. Afterward, he and I drove over to Union Square and dropped in on Carol, a former girlfriend, the retail executive. She worked at Shreve's now and walked us around the jewelry store while Dad said he was looking for a birthday present for me.

"Where are you applying to college?" Carol asked in a matter-of-fact way.

I shrugged. I hadn't really thought about it yet, I said.

"Don't you have to apply in a few months?" She seemed troubled, almost stepmotherish.

"I guess so."

"Paul, haven't you taken her around to see some schools?"

"I was hoping," he said, "she'd want to go to Berkeley."

"Well, that's pretty hard to get into," Carol responded with a whiff of disapproval. "You'll have to broaden your— But didn't you teach there, Paul? Still, I don't think you can pull strings at a *state university*. I suppose you'd be close by, though," she said, turning to me again. "Wouldn't you?"

Was it a sign of parental neglect or healthy lack of pressure that we'd never discussed college? I assumed the wind would blow me someplace, the way it always had. Shelley was planning to go to art school in Rhode Island somewhere. But Berkeley? It was definitely too far away from David.

"Carol is so pushy," my father said once we were tucked inside his little Alfa Romeo and pulling away from Union Square. "Can you believe all that grilling about college? Hard to get in. *Give me a break!* She doesn't know how smart you are."

I nodded, but inside I was thinking, *A year from now, David and I will be married. And we'll be living on our own compound in Molokai.*

"I think you'd like Berkeley," my father continued. "I really do. Hey, that's an idea. Should we cruise over there now and check it out? Let's do it!"

But Berkeley seemed shabby and uninviting and even seedier than North Beach. The campus was empty, and the only people on the streets were winos and druggies and scowling Vietnam vets in wheelchairs. "Doesn't look like much in the summer," my father said. "Not too many kids around." Then we picked up a local paper, checked the movie listings, and trotted off to see *Apocalypse Now*. Afterward, inspired by the movie, we loaded up his pipe and took a few hits in the car. I held the smoke in my lungs for a long time, and he was watching me carefully, seemed to hesitate—but plunged in anyway.

"I hope you're not buying dope on the street, Inez." He was trying to seem casual when he said it, but I could tell he wasn't feeling that way. "Don't be that stupid, okay? There could be angel dust or God-only-knows-what-else in it. Pesticides and all kinds of poisonous stuff."

I shrugged, blew out the smoke, and said, "I've never bought anything, ever."

"Where does Shelley get her stash?"

"Some guy. I don't know. From her old school."

He sent me back to Van Dale a few days later with a plastic Baggie of sticky marijuana buds. "I'd feel a lot better if you smoked this and not Shelley's," he said with a vulnerable smile. A few weeks later, when school started, he asked me on the phone, "How's your supply? Do you and Shelley need any more?"

My birthday that year brought the usual greetings and celebration, trumped by a Rolex watch that my father sent, which—like the Nikon camera, and the MG before it, and perhaps the bag of dope—was way too much of a good thing for a young girl. The watch was nice, and a surprise, but most of my memories of the day are about waiting for a package to come from Hawaii—or a phone call, or something. With each minute that passed, from the moment I woke up in bed, I felt a growing dread. Each minute ticked by and seemed to steal something from me, a pint of blood, a piece of heart. A faith and hopefulness that I'd never regain. When a long cardboard box came with a bunch of waxy tropical flowers in reds and pinks with long yellow pistils, my heart raced with excitement until I read the little white card.

> *You are the sunshine of my life,*
> *Love,*
> *Whitman*

I'd never felt such piercing sorrow. How had I sunk into such unhappiness? Just months before, I'd been a carefree girl in a sports car, driving from party to party, a tease, a public temptation. I bounced out of bed, sang in the shower, merrily dressed in one of my thrift-shop outfits, passed notes to Shelley in class, snuck off to smoke a cigarette. I was always laughing, always having fun.

The race to love was sweet, but the arrival miserable. My feelings were fizzy and out of control—lifting and plummeting. Love had made me more sensitive and expressive and almost manic, but also pathetic and dramatic, narcissistic and so confused. Love didn't seem governed by laws that I was familiar with—or had encountered before—but ruled by magic and spells and wishes made on shooting stars. By the time the news came, I was almost ready for it.

David had decided to stay in Hawaii—and not return to Caltech. My father was the first person I called. "Dad," I whined, "he's not coming back this year."

"Oh."

"He's designed a board. He says it's called 'windsurfing' now, and his family gave him some money to make a bunch of boards and sell them."

"He's starting a business?"

"Yeah, with a big-name professional surfer and all that."

"Good for him," my father said. "Academia is overrated. And anyway, he'll be good at making money. He's got those Jap genes."

"*Dad.*"

"But you must be sad. Are you?"

"I am. I guess. But not as much as I thought I'd be." Just a summer of being in love with David and waiting for a letter, for a call, for anything, had exhausted me. The downsides of romance—and this new thing, sex—were hard to ignore. I'd spent an entire day waiting in the We Care Clinic for a doctor to give me a prescription for birth control pills. And after a few weeks of taking them, my face had broken out, I'd gained eight pounds, and I had no energy for anything, even getting out of bed.

"It's like having another job," I said, "this whole love thing."

"Oh, that's a funny observation," my father said. "You mean because it's so all-consuming? It does seem to absorb a great deal of time. But I like that part—all the hours spent thinking about the person, and daydreaming, and wishing, and aching to be together. And then imagining that they're thinking about you. The beginning of an affair is so wonderful."

"Not for me." The bladder infection I'd gotten after David left wasn't so wonderful, and how the bedsheets had been dotted with weird wet spots and gunk and scary blood, and then the constant stream of erotic thoughts that had bubbled up afterward, like lava after a volcanic eruption. "My whole summer was wasted thinking about him. Down the drain."

"Oh, don't say that! Not wasted. Think of all the things you know about now. And all the new feelings you've had. It gets easier—I promise. After the first few tries at love, you'll start to know what to expect. Then it will be more manageable and fun. And you learn so much! There's nothing like meeting somebody new and waking up parts of yourself that you'd forgotten were there—or never knew you had. The onslaught of new feelings and new experiences you can have when you're first in love . . . well, it's unlike anything else. Just a few more times and you'll get the hang of it. Really, love is like learning to drive. After a while you become accustomed to the new sensations and intense feelings, and they aren't so scary anymore. You know those nightmares you used to have about the Garter Belt Man? Well, it's like that. At first they seemed real, and you were afraid. Right? Well, after you had a few of them, you started to realize it was the same dream—another Garter Belt Man dream! And he wasn't really chasing you, and you weren't going to die or anything. Falling in love is kind of like that. The fear is only in your mind. You're afraid of being hurt, afraid of losing control. Afraid of change, newness, all the overwhelming sensations you're having. Right? But it's really nothing more than your own fears you're battling and getting used to. And after a while, after a few times, you can enjoy it, almost like an amusement-park ride, without much anxiety. The uncertainties that cause anxiety go away. Well, I guess they don't go away completely, all those feelings, but somehow you learn to enjoy having them."

"That's what I'd like. No anxiety."

"Well, I can't blame you. He forgot your birthday and all that. Not a great sign, in any case, that David deserves you. Even if the sex was great. But isn't it interesting how the heart repairs itself? How you could be so in love with David and now be okay that he's not coming back?"

"I didn't say I was okay—"

"Oh, you're great. You're fine! And there's really no reason you can't stay friends with him. Once you love somebody, there's no reason to turn him into a monster—just to help yourself get over it. I've always tried very hard to keep people in my life. It's the civilized thing to do."

But two months later, when my mother and Bob eloped, my father didn't sound so civilized after I broke the news.

"*Vegas?*" he asked. "You're kidding."

"No." I decided not to elaborate—or tell him that my mother and Bob had called from the Riviera Hotel, where they'd gotten a giant suite. Bob sounded like the same old Bob. No change. But my mother's voice was light and soft, not hysterical or loud or anything, just a little sad. Then again, maybe that was me.

"She hates Vegas," my father growled.

"They just wanted to get it over with," I said. "Isn't that funny?"

"No, I don't think it's funny," he said. "I can't imagine anybody being so stupid."

That was November. It wasn't until a couple months later, after the holidays, that anybody noticed my college applications were long overdue.

1978

SEVENTEEN

Haleiwa

The arrival of a camera in my life, one of many unasked-for gifts from my Dad, had preceded any passion for using it. But once I'd discovered that I was good at taking pictures—people said I was a born photographer the way they'd said my mother was a born dancer—it went everywhere with me, kept snug in a leather case that hung over my shoulder. If I left it behind, or had the wrong film, and came across something beautiful or haunting or strange—the flicker of a transient, one-of-a-kind image—I felt miserable and sad. Something rare and wondrous had slipped by, undocumented. An opportunity lost.

Taking pictures never felt like a defense against life or a nervous habit to distract me—something to do with my hands, or with myself, like smoking. It didn't lessen my exposure to life, only enhanced it. When I was among people who made me uncomfortable or in a landscape too unfamiliar, it was almost impossible for me to take a picture. The photographer in me was shy, I suppose, and liked to hide. But the beauty of the world beguiled me, pulled me out. It charmed and tantalized my hesitant side, and the lover of surface and texture. The camera encouraged me, drew me out. It taught me how to seize a moment. It banged against my ribs and reminded me to engage. Even so, my pictures were of buildings and signs in those days—things just beginning to decay—and sometimes of people looking away.

Hawaii seemed simple at first, and obvious, an oasis of clear blue water and yellow sand and salty breezes. On the tarmac of the Honolulu airport, the soft air surrounded me with a veil of sweetness, almost as if infused with syrup. Inside the airport there were refrigerated glass cases of bright plumeria leis to welcome bus charters, church groups, families on holiday, hordes of pale tourists in untropical clothes who seemed in dire need of transformation. By the time I reached baggage claim and found my two large duffel bags, so heavy I could barely lift them, I was dizzy and disoriented, intoxicated by the air and smells and colors and the sense of weightless removal from all cares of the world.

At a small terminal for private planes, I was met by a young pilot named Billy who had blond hair and an eastern accent—he was from Queens, it turned out. The Yamatos had hired him to bring me to the island of Molokai in a small four-seater Cessna. Billy was good-natured and smiled a lot, and he lifted my heavy duffel bags into the backseat of the plane without a groan or remark. I sat in front and watched him pull levers and flip switches and listen to incomprehensible airport chatter on the crackling radio. Our tiny plane ascended, rising beyond the blue sky and into a lingering mass of heavy gray clouds. It was raining below us and around us. The small plane continued on, weaving around the weather. I wasn't afraid. I rarely was in those days—youth's armor against a big horizon, I suppose. The flight seemed no more dangerous to me than a ride at Disneyland or speeding along Pacific Coast Highway in the MG.

At my father's urging, I had remained friends with David Yamato. A handful of letters had traveled back and forth between us over the year, and a few phone calls. Even though he'd invited me to visit the family compound on Molokai when he'd learned that I was coming to see Whitman, my conversations with David never dipped below surface cheer. He'd disappointed me, and I didn't want him to have that chance again. So we'd established a vague and undefined alliance of being not lovers and not quite just friends. We fell somewhere in the middle, a location that my father claimed was the very best spot for me and David and, in fact, for all future David Yamatos in my life.

"Nobody is ever just a friend," my father counseled, "and nobody is ever just a lover. It's best to refrain from making those sorts of crude distinctions."

During my senior year of high school, there had been lots of guys around—not quite friends, not quite boyfriends—but nobody who came to matter or brought me much joy. Whatever libertine ideas my father had desperately tried to instill in me hadn't stuck. David was the only one I'd slept with, and that, somehow, made a great difference.

There'd been talk of sending me to Van Dale Community College—a joke, I'm sure, meant to punish me. My father had mentioned art school, or at least some classes in photography. My mother suggested a year working full-time in Bob's office. I wasn't opposed to art school or Bob's office, as long as I could live in Hawaii for the summer. Three months, I said. I'd rent a room in Whitman's house. I'd take pictures, lots of them, and put a portfolio together. For this my mother extracted one solemn promise: that I would apply to college in the fall.

"Whitman didn't have to go," I complained to my father.

"You aren't Whitman," he said. "And you have a different mother—a mother who wants you, very much, to go to college."

"*She* didn't go to college."

"Perhaps that's why."

"But it doesn't seem fair. Whitman didn't have to."

"Whitman has resources," he said. "You don't."

"That doesn't seem fair either."

"It's fair," my father said after a pause. "And I wouldn't get in the habit of seeing things that way. Fair or unfair. It's an illusion—things only seem fair or unfair, but you can't know the truth. So you might as well assume that good fortune is yours and the world is looking out for you. And for God's sake, you know I am."

The remaining days of high school were agony. Each trip to my gray metal locker, each stinky gym class, each dreary drive home felt like sleeping in an old bed that needed to have its sheets changed. The world of Van Dale was tired, in need of a wash. I woke up every morning like an automaton and did as little as possible to get the decent grades I knew my mother expected. Shelley and I continued to take off Wednesdays but bickered more than ever. At the end of the year, we split up all the clothes we'd bought together, and the cigarette cases, lighters, compacts, and funny cocktail hats we'd never worn. And it was Shelley who drove me to LAX.

"Don't cry," she said.

"Why would I cry?" I felt my throat tightening.

"Because we're saying good-bye, you fool."

I was jolly at the prospect of seeing David again, and seeing a new place. From what David had said, I assumed that his family wouldn't be too different from mine—if my parents had stayed together. His father was a businessman. His mother was a weaver. Ethnically they were a mix—part this, part that—and, most likely, adaptable people who had learned to fit in anywhere. As the tiny Cessna dangled in the air above the Molokai hills and jungle, the small island looked like the greenest place in the world, and so welcoming. On the ground it wasn't quite the same.

There was no control tower, no landing crew to meet us. Only David, who pulled onto the small asphalt airstrip in an old red van. He was smiling and sunny, but lacking whatever it was—enthusiasm, nervousness, even irritation—that might indicate he had romantic feelings for me. After a short drive full of mindless pleasantries, we arrived at the Yamato family compound, a series of stucco cottages topped by angled ceilings lined with long trunks of sliced bamboo. The rooms were small and filled with rattan furniture and leather chairs that, in the intense humidity, smelled like rotting, uncured beef. There was an odd assortment of fabrics everywhere, patterns that didn't seem to harmonize, and in the middle of the living room there was an open rock pit where pigs were roasted whole.

Mr. and Mrs. Yamato were a comfortable couple—two people who had learned to fit together so well that, even though she had gray-yellow hair and blue eyes and he was dark, they'd come to resemble each other. Round faces. Chipmunk cheeks. Lazy, complacent smiles. They were friendly but humorless, and they seemed a little unclear about me—in particular, why I had come to see their son. They focused on my father, whom they seemed to know by reputation, as if David's old boss at Harrison-Ruin were our only real connection. Mr. Yamato was curious about my father. He'd heard things—or suspected things. I got the impression that they weren't positive. "Is he still a partner at H-R?" Mr. Yamato wanted to know.

"No." I shook my head foggily. "I don't think so anyway."

"You're not sure?"

I shrugged. "He might be a consultant now."

"What does that mean?"

Hardly a laid-back Hawaiian, Mr. Yamato was all business, a man who had built a pearl empire with offices in four cities and seemed unable to leave his competitive streak at work. My father's career choices and life seemed frivolous to him, almost wasted. Why had he given up his post at H-R, where he was, as Mr. Yamato put it, "a founding father"? Wasn't he interested in seeing his vision expand? Did he really not care about success?

"I'm not sure," I said. "He doesn't like running things. I think he'd rather just have fun."

"What kind of fun?"

I decided not to give a real answer and mumbled something about art and my father's guest lecturing at the institute. It really didn't matter what I said, though. All efforts to describe him to the Yamatos or articulate his strange approach to life only began to seem like romantic delusion or deliberate obfuscation for a darker, more troubling truth.

"He just walked away from success? From a business that he started?"

"Yep." I nodded, feeling both defensive and cavalier. "I guess he doesn't care about making money," I added stupidly.

"That's what all the people in tech industries say," Mr. Yamato replied.

I looked over at David, desperately hoping he'd help out, but he just smiled and nodded and added nothing to my account, as if unwilling to engage in any conflict. When Mr. Yamato was done grilling me, comfortable that his mysterious preconceptions about Paul N. Ruin had been confirmed, David got up to show me the room where I'd be staying for the night, a little den with a futon off the kitchen. "Sorry about Dad," he said, then gave me a soft peck on the cheek, the sort of kiss you'd give a sister. After he left, I looked around. My tiny room had a wet, depressing view of a green-corrugated fiberglass roof that was dripping rain on weedy gravel. Suddenly I was very glad to be staying only two days.

Nice pictures of the Yamato family were everywhere. The walls of almost every room of the compound were covered with them. Good shots, taken carefully, and the Yamatos were displayed in every state of pleasure and bliss and at every age, like a museum show of family happiness through time. There were old people with tan, dried-apple cheeks— probably grandparents. There were pictures from the sixties, when Mrs. Yamato was very blond and wore beads and had bangs in her eyes. Mr. Yamato playing golf, another of him sitting in the back of a speedboat. There were pictures of David and his three sisters when they were small, a collection of faces that seemed on a trajectory to becoming more Japanese with each child. In the background the sun was always shining. The sea was always blue, the sand yellow, the tropical flowers bright.

I couldn't help but think of gloomy Wolfback and how my father lived. There wasn't a picture of me or Whitman anywhere in the house. Aside from abstract paintings done by one of his friends—either all white or all black—the only images gracing the walls were a collection of Egon Schiele's prints, skinny women with armpit hair in various states of undress.

By dinnertime two of David's sisters appeared, and I found myself even quieter in the throng of Yamatos. Aside from a short discussion of David's new windsurfing company—he and his partner had created a line of boards and sails and were deciding on a logo—the family talked about neighbors and local developments with such insular passion that it didn't occur to them to provide me with background information so I might follow along. They mentioned Hawaiian things and a family trip to Sweden over Christmas—also subjects on which I had nothing to offer. They seemed clannish, almost cultish. They had nicknames and slang words for each other and everything else, and some of their jargon seemed to be in pidgin English, which wasn't considered a corrupt language of uneducated islanders but a much-admired way of talking. It meant you were Hawaiian. And I wasn't.

I wasn't Swedish either, a fact that Mrs. Yamato seemed to find unfortunate—almost sad. I wasn't Japanese, which seemed to make Mr. Yamato anxious. The family had decided that those two peoples ran the world and exceeded at all matters intellectual and artistic, even though, from what I could tell, David and his sisters weren't particularly either.

The sisters, Iris and Martika, were sleek and brown, their faces beautiful and exotic, but I had trouble reading their facial expressions—mostly because they didn't seem to have any. They were even more languid and self-satisfied than David. They didn't seem interested in the news, or movies, or things that anybody alive might have in common. More troubling, of course, they didn't seem interested in me.

"That's the definition of provincial," my father said when I complained on a transpacific call made from my den. "Sounds awful. I'm so sorry. That's why people go to college—so they don't wind up with nothing to say."

I counted the hours, the minutes, before Billy and the four-seater Cessna touched down on the tiny landing strip and took me away. I'd never been so happy to see anyone in my life. Billy smiled sphinxlike and put my heavy duffel bags in the backseat again. I gave David a dead kiss—purposefully lifeless, right on the mouth—and stepped away.

The tiny plane hauled itself into the sky, rose above the island, a green and brown lump of land with craggy mountains and dark sand beaches ringed in light blue. In a short time, we passed over the enormous crater of Diamond Head and the swirling streets of fancy houses set at the foot of the volcano like strands of gems, and we soon found ourselves hovering over the vast concrete intersections of the Honolulu airport.

Whitman was waiting at the gate with a huge smile and a hug and lots of questions for Billy—how long had he been flying, where was he from? What a relief. What an incredible relief. Before long we were inside Whitman's car, an ancient Plymouth Valiant that was so old and out of date it had a push-button transmission and holes in the floorboard.

It took a couple of highways to get to the North Shore of Oahu. We passed an exit for Pearl Harbor on the way, drove through pineapple fields and beside the arching spray of giant sprinklers that looked like starting gates at the horse races. Once on the coast, we passed Waimea Bay. In June there weren't waves to speak of, just a stretch of open sand and flat blue sea. There was a massive rock with clusters of tourists standing on top of it, like birds. About ten minutes beyond, Whitman pulled the car onto Ke Iki Road.

His house was a one-story ranch, not unlike Abuelita's, a box of yellow stucco and brown-painted trim that peeked out from behind trunks of palms and an overgrown garden. There were a couple of outbuildings—shacks, really—and off to the side of the house were three rusted cars with grass growing up around the fenders. "Whose are those?" I asked.

Whitman shrugged. "Came with the house."

Inside, there were three bedrooms on one side of the house: a room where Whitman slept, which was dark and unadorned; a room that was rented by a marine who came on weekends from the base in Wahiawa;

and a room for me, where a double mattress sat on the floor, a wetsuit and some old bowling shirts were hanging in the closet, and indoor plants sat on wooden crates near the window.

"Whose stuff?" I asked Whitman.

"The clothes belong to a guy who was staying here," he said. "He'll be back to clean it out."

Whitman seemed tall to me—and big—after my previous two days with David. And compared to David's subdued company, Whitman was lively and buoyant, sharing his thoughts and ideas easily. When we walked outside, to a long stretch of grass at the back of the house, he saw two neighbors sitting on the sundeck next door and pulled me over to meet them—John, a house painter with a constant slow-motion head-nodding gesture, and Jerry, a flirtatious pilot for Aloha Airlines, who insisted that I use his outdoor hot tub anytime.

"Doesn't she look like Sugar?" John said.

"Who?"

"Sugar," John said. "You could be her sister."

"A neighbor," said Whitman.

"She lives a few houses down," Jerry explained with a smile. "She's the heartbreaker of the neighborhood. Gorgeous lady. But now that you've moved in, we'll be falling in love with you instead." I must have looked a little stricken, because John started shaking his head. "Man," he said, "you're hitting on the poor girl already."

"I'm getting a head start," Jerry said.

"You're blowing it, man."

"Who says?"

There were more jokes like this—raunchy ribbing mixed with flattery that I wasn't accustomed to, since the guys in California showed interest by not showing it. Anybody who lavished praise or openly flirted was either super square or super old or both. But on the North Shore in those days, the ratio of men to women was seven to one. Competition was so intense that guys didn't have the luxury of subtleties.

"Inez, listen to me," Jerry said. "Everybody's going to try to snag you quick. Just take your time, darlin'. Make everybody take a number."

Whitman endured as much as he could and then, shaking his head, walked me to a bench at the rise of his backyard. That's when I saw the view: a dramatic stretch of reddish brown volcanic rock and the turquoise-blue sea beyond.

"Wow."

"I know." Whitman chuckled. "We're facing directly west, so the sunsets are really way too breathtaking."

Looking out over the ocean, across patterns of light green and dark blue, I felt as if I were standing not on the edge of the world but on the edge of time, too. The horizon was infinite, and so far away, so far from anything. Thinking about home was like looking into the sky and trying to imagine visiting another star. "Wow," I said again.

"I know," Whitman said. "But you'd be surprised how different Hawaii can seem after a year, or even a few months." Then he quickly changed the subject. "Hey, Dad said you had a lousy time on Molokai."

"Dad?"

"This morning. God, it wasn't even seven. He was so thrilled I don't think he could wait to call. He's spent the last year boring me with talk about your love life and what a dead soul your boyfriend is. He calls him Dead Soul, actually. And sometimes it's the Blond Japanese."

"He's not my boyfriend."

"Tell Dad that." Whitman laughed. "I've been praying you'd break up with that Yamato guy so I wouldn't have to hear about him anymore. And then, hey, go to college, would you? I'm tired of that screed, too."

Before I had time to protest, Whitman raised his hand to point where the rocks ended. "You can't really see it from here," he said, "but down there, beyond the rocks, is an incredible beach—just made for you. Perfect water, white sand. Great swimming. Not a surfing beach. Doesn't really break unless it's already huge in other, better places. But good bodysurfing—you'll see."

We had a dinner of white eel, barbecued—one of the local kids had caught it on the rocks and sold it to Whitman for three dollars—and after a few beers we smoked some Maui Wowie. It was sweet and smooth and so oily that the leaf resin melted into black tar at the butt, and, unable to inhale through it, we just let it burn and sniffed the smoke. Immediately afterward Whitman sank down in front of the television, his eyes heavy, and I remember thinking that maybe my arrival had tired him out. Or maybe he was just wasted. In those days you weren't just stoned, you were *wasted*. And that's how Whitman seemed to me: enervated, diminished, run out of gas. After all that Maui Wowie, I assumed I'd feel like that, too.

But I didn't. Surrounded by so many new things to look at, I felt very alive suddenly, and awake to the surface of the world that glittered so glamorously when I was stoned. The dark house seemed full of mysteries and the trade winds full of romance, and the wild lizards clinging to the walls in hopes of catching a mosquito mesmerized me. Getting undressed, I noticed an old scarf pinned in the middle of the ceiling to cover a bare lightbulb. The scarf very thin—made of fine silk—and old, something I knew from all my hours spent rummaging around thrift shops. The burnished colors were from the 1930s, browns and oranges and greens in a print of organic shapes—squiggles and snakes and cones. Who would think to pin a loose scarf over a lightbulb? The more I looked at it, the more beautiful the scarf seemed—the patterns it threw on the walls and ceiling, the way the shapes fell together, the warm colors and cool shapes. Who had found that scarf—and put it there?

The next morning I woke at dawn and pulled out my camera—funny, but I hadn't taken any pictures while visiting the Yamatos on Molokai—and focused the lens on the scarf. I turned the ceiling light on and off, watching the colors of the scarf change. I took pictures of the windows and the pale curtains blowing over them. Inside the closet golden sunlight had made its way onto the shoulders of a few old bowling shirts. A pair of orange high-top Converse sneakers were glowing in the same morning light. I barely moved anything—the compositions seemed to form perfectly without me.

The rest of the day, the rest of the week, everywhere Whitman took me, I pulled off the black leather casing of the Nikon and squinted into the viewfinder. I went through rolls and rolls of film, keeping them stashed in my duffel until I had enough money to process them. I photographed unpaved streets, missionary-built churches, the food markets with gorgeously packaged Asian products. I photographed the thick, oily hamburgers at Kua Hina, the clusters of flabby tourists on the big rock in Waimea Bay. A dripping ice cream cone. A pink truck selling Hawaiian shaved ice. At sunset, beyond Whitman's back door, I photographed the quiet ocean, ablaze in purple and yellow reflections, the moon rising in the tidal pools. The light wasn't as sharp and strong as San Francisco light. It was softer, freer, and looser. You could almost smell the gentle wind in it and feel parts of yourself lifting and blowing away.

Whitman spent every day with me that first week. When I asked about his gardening business and whether he was taking time from his work, I was met with vague nods and asides, as though I'd wandered into a zone of uncertainty. He had a contract to look after the gardens at a couple of restaurants on the North Shore and was watering the indoor plants at a hotel in Pupakea Heights, but otherwise, he eventually revealed, he was mostly hanging out and waiting for the surfing to get good. "The real waves don't come until the winter," he said, "with the storms." But it wasn't even the Fourth of July.

If I'd been paying closer attention—and not been so focused on myself—I would have guessed that my father had somebody new, somebody major, not just another Laurel or Shanti. Lots of little things would have given it away. He was looking at an old Cadillac limousine to restore. And he was talking about getting Hector from El Bodega to drive him around, since the restaurant was open only two nights a week now.

Before I'd left for Hawaii, he told me he'd decided to join the summer encampment of the Bohemian Club in hopes of eventually becoming a member, and the oddness of this eluded me for some time. He'd ordered new "evening clothes," as he called them—a tuxedo and a tailcoat—and when he told me the name of the men's store in the city where these suits were being made, J. Press, he seemed shocked that I'd never heard of it. ("Inez, where have you been? It's a preppy stronghold.") Sometimes he answered the phone with incredible urgency. And when he heard my voice, he sounded deflated and tried to hurry me off the line. Most tellingly, though, he hadn't asked me for "a list."

Since the beginning of high school, he'd gotten involved in the selection of my courses, insisting that I take precalculus and chemistry, among other electives. Mostly, though, he focused on my English classes. And at the beginning of each semester, he'd ask for a syllabus.

"A what?"

"A reading list."

"There's no list. Nothing like that," I'd say.

"There's always a list, Inez. A syllabus, for God's sake. What kind of school are you going to?" When a homework schedule was supplied, he began collecting the books and short stories on the list, pulling them from his shelves or buying them in bookstores. Then he lined up the volumes by his bed at Wolfback.

The Red Badge of Courage was the first book we read together, when I was in ninth grade. The next year, in tenth, he read *David Copperfield* with me, *The Scarlet Letter,* and *A Separate Peace.* The next semester we read *Huckleberry Finn, Vanity Fair,* and *To Kill a Mockingbird.* ("Too bad I'm not as serious as Atticus," he said, "You'd love that, wouldn't you?") When I was a junior, we read *The Sound and the Fury* ("exasperating"), *The Great Gatsby* ("perfection"), and so many Ernest Hemingway short stories that he began to complain. ("I've had an epiphany reading these stories again," he said one night. "Papa's an unbearable bore.") Toward the end of that year, after looking over the assigned pages of *Moby-Dick,* he huffed, "Forget this abridged nonsense! You can't just read a few pages here and there. You and I will be reading the whole book—ignore what the teacher says!"

"But there's so much about whaling," I whined.

"It's not about whaling!" he exploded. "For God's sake, Inez, can't you see that?"

My senior year came, though, and he never asked about my classes or mentioned "the list." I remember being pleased, to tell the truth. He was leaving me alone, finally. I could read less and skim more. I'd be free of his meddling—and difficult questions.

It wasn't until the spring, when I visited him for the last time before going to Hawaii, that things began to come together in my mind. There was a new smell wafting out of his bathroom, a formal fragrance with lots of high notes—more Parisian than herbal and hippie. He'd taken a shower, and I found him with a towel wrapped around his waist and trimming his hair with a pair of unusual scissors.

"They're made only for hair," he said in proud tones. "See the design? A friend gave them to me—brought them back from Finland."

"A new friend?"

He hesitated, and then his voice turned soft, almost a hush. "Well, yes. Somewhat new."

"Who?"

He looked at me in the mirror. "I can't say too much," he said, putting the scissors down. "I'm not trying to be evasive. It's just very new. We met a couple years ago but didn't really figure things out until pretty recently. Over the fall and winter. She's . . . well . . . she's sort of famous. So we have to deal with that. And she's been through so much—having such a hard time. At this point I'm just helping her out."

At the start of his relationship with Justine, he'd talked like that. No brash, sexist jokes like, "I mean, *what a body*," spoken in ironic tones. Instead he was "helping her out." So whoever this new person was, it was serious. *She's been through so much . . . having such a hard time.* That meant she was married—and her husband was still around.

"The funny thing is," he said, "she's very different from my—I don't know—my usual. She's very smart, of course, and accomplished. But she's shorter and rounder. And really not that beautiful. There's something a little coarse about her face. I'm serious. It's almost heartbreaking, the way she deals with it. There's something courageous about her— inspiring. I'm drawn —almost—to her lack of beauty. Can you understand that? She and I, we . . . we have something. There's *something there*. Very deep. I just don't know what."

At the end of my second week in Hawaii, Whitman took me to a party up in the mountains behind Haleiwa. "We missed last Saturday night because you'd just arrived," he said, "but every Saturday there's a party somewhere. And it's really sort of a mandatory night out. Everybody has to show." He drove the Valiant to an old wooden house with rotting trim and ceilings stained by leaks, where his friend Leftie lived. Funky Christmas lights were strung up in the backyard, and a collection of rusting cars was sitting on the grass—a time-honored North Shore tradition, I was beginning to figure out. New cars didn't belong. New cars meant you were new, too. And being new to the North Shore wasn't cool, unless you were either a really good surfer or a really cute girl. Then nobody minded at all.

The party was mostly outside, on a deck, where people were clustered around a bowl of Maui Chips and a cooler of beer. Some jays were being passed around. Whitman introduced me to a couple brothers from Brazil, Ray and Ricardo, and then sat in the corner of the garden with a surf buddy and talked waves. The next time I looked over, he'd wandered off.

Standing next to the potato chip bowl, I met a nurse named Kate. She was petite, and almost mousy, but had a strong feeling about her—a sense of terrific durability. "You've been here only two weeks, and you've already found your way to Leftie's?" she said. "You're way ahead." She'd been on the North Shore for three years, she said, had come for a holiday with two other nurses, fell in love with a guy who owned a T-shirt shop down in town, and after a few months "back home" in Nebraska, she re-turned to Hawaii to live with him. "We're not together anymore," she said. "Thank God. He's a real dick. But I'm sure glad we met. Otherwise I'd still be in Omaha."

She looked up, over my shoulder. I felt somebody tap me on the back. I turned around to face a guy with a head of dark, curly hair and a wel-coming smile. He had a gold hoop earring in one ear that made him look like a pirate. "Hi there," he said. "I know you."

"No you don't."

"Yes I do. From a photograph."

I must have looked puzzled.

"There's a picture of you in Whitman Ruin's room."

"There is?"

He nodded. "He must . . . Did you . . . ? I mean—"

"He's my brother," I said.

"Oh, God," he groaned. "All this time I thought he had a girlfriend."

Tomas was a garden designer who built patios and waterfalls. He'd once been a theatrical set designer in Florida, and, like half the North Shore, it seemed, he'd come to Hawaii in his late twenties for a visit and stayed. At thirty-two, after living all over Oahu, he had decided to build a house in the hills above Haleiwa. While his house was being finished, he'd lived at Whitman's—until recently.

"Are those your bowling shirts in the closet?" I asked.

"Are they in your way?"

"No," I said. "I've been photographing them! And your shoes, too!"

The scarf on the ceiling belonged to an old girlfriend—Sugar—who had tacked it there when she couldn't stand to look at the bare lightbulb any longer. "Oh, I've heard about Sugar," I said, but before I could won-der whether I really looked like her or not, Tomas began asking about my camera, and whether I used a flash, and what kind of lenses. Did I have a good telephoto and tripod? Was I staying around to photograph the big waves? Unlike Whitman's lascivious neighbors, Jerry and John—whom I was now habitually avoiding—Tomas presented himself as a friend, as another brother and kindred spirit. He didn't come on strong but rather flew under my radar. I remember watching him, as he described the light in Hawaii and the way the clouds threw shadows on the sea, and thinking, *Who is this incredible person? Where did he come from?* It sounds crazy to say that I fell in love with a guy because "he had an eye"—but it was something like that. Our eyes fell in love, our sense of design. Being with him wasn't an exchange as much as a confirmation of self. There was something about Tomas that reminded me of me.

"Have you been to old Honolulu?" he asked with a great swell of enthusiasm. "Oh, you've got to! And you've got to go there at sunset! You won't believe the old neon!"

The next night we drove into town together—to the old part of Honolulu, where the strip clubs and bars were, and the most beautiful ancient neon signs. Tomas had an unfailing eye for detail, for color, for light and mood, and for what exactly I was after in a photograph. He knew I needed fast film and no flash, and he seemed to have all the time in the world. He waited patiently for me to set up shots and never asked what I was planning to do with the pictures, just understood that I needed to take them. Over dinner in Chinatown, we quizzed each other about our favorite music and movies and books and food, and in the middle of the night, when we were still talking, I took a picture of Tomas looking right into my camera.

I'd promised my father that I'd take a class in photography in Hawaii. And I'd promised my mother that I'd live with Whitman for the summer— and let him look after me. She'd been very firm about that. But ten days after I arrived on the North Shore, I went to see Tomas's new house in a canyon, surrounded by open fields of conservation land, and I told myself that it was going to be just for a night or two. But it was hard to leave.

EIGHTEEN

Madam X

Dear Inez,

Experience is worthwhile if you know what to do with it. You'll probably see all kinds of new things in Hawaii and have lots of new experiences. But none of this will be valuable to you if you don't give yourself time to reflect on things you've seen, people you've met—and learn from them.

Meanwhile take lots of pictures! Amuse yourself! And let me know what you figure out.

Love,

Your Friendly Neighborhood Dad

p.s. I've always thought paradise overrated.

He sent five hundred dollars a month—and asked if that was enough. He never bothered me about getting a job or nagged me to take classes. But he called on the phone more frequently than ever before. I wondered, now that I wasn't living with my mother anymore, if he felt freer to call more often—or just more responsible. In a funny way, he'd taken over. My mother and Bob were so happy, and occupied with a house in La Cañada, a big clapboard Colonial that they'd bought and wanted to renovate. Since I hadn't seen their new house, it was hard to picture them or their new life together. In a strange way, this caused them to recede in my mind while my father loomed even larger. And while my mother rarely called, seeming almost embarrassed to intrude, my father rang up every night.

"Hey, Paul!" Tomas would say if he answered the phone. "How ya doing, man?" They'd talk about the weather or whatever I'd been photographing, and then Tomas always signed off with, "Come visit!" before passing the phone over to me.

"I'm never coming to visit," my father would say once he'd heard my voice on the line. "I hate the tropics."

"I know that."

"You promised you'd come back in the fall."

"Yeah, yeah," I laughed. "I said I'd apply to college in the fall—that's all."

It was weird how lonely Dad seemed, off-kilter and lost. He rarely mentioned his old girlfriends, old friends, or even Ooee. It was as if everything in his life had stopped. Night after night he called. Mostly after dinner. The time difference worked in his favor, making Whitman and me sitting targets long after anybody in the Bay Area had gone to sleep. Although I'm not sure Dad felt free to discuss Madam X—that's what he called her—with them anyway. In those early days, I'm pretty sure that Whitman and I were the only ones who knew about her.

She was difficult to reach, sometimes in seclusion, and still "having a hard time" and "going through a lot." But Dad seemed to be the one who was going through the most. When Madam X left for a spa in Baden-Baden, he came unglued, calling me at midnight with pointless observations about a tennis match he was watching on TV and then, after an hour of useless blather, finally inching his way into a discussion of love's latest wound. Madam X was finishing a book, he said, and much too busy to see him.

"What kind of book?"

"It's probably wise not to say," he said. "You might figure out who she is."

"Come on," I said. "I'm three thousand miles away. Who cares if I figure it out?"

"She writes romances," he said very quickly, as though this fact were something to face bravely and squarely, without dwelling. "Very, very popular romances."

"You're kidding."

"I'm not," he said. "Don't be like that. Don't be a snob."

"You're the biggest snob of all."

"I am not. I'm the very soul of democracy. Anyway, her books are quite good, I promise you."

"Romances? That's so sad."

"'Sad' is your new word," he said sharply. "When you were little, the whole world was 'neat.' Then everything was 'weird.' Or 'gross.' For a while everything was 'great.' Now everything's 'sad.' Since Marguerite, I think, everything's sad."

Uncharacteristically, he never asked too much about Tomas or our life together. At first I thought that he'd finally decided to give me a zone of privacy and a little room to breathe, until I began to suspect that he wasn't being generous or thoughtful at all. He just didn't want to hear about the fun I was having while he languished so drastically. The stream of beauties, each more accomplished than the last—who gave him hope, made him feel alive, and young, and desired—seemed to have dried up. He was down to one unattainable siren. And his need to possess her and prompt her to leave her husband overwhelmed him. He stewed. He reconsidered. He loved Madam X and then hated her. He wrote her letters, lots and lots of letters, he said. Good-bye notes that he never sent.

"Can you imagine?" he'd ask me. But I couldn't.

"What am I to do?" he wanted to know. But I had no idea.

We descended into long sessions of analysis. He called her Madam X, but the woman might as well have been Madam Y or Madame N. She was the unknown variable that constantly moved around an equal sign. He drew diagrams of her nature in a journal. He recorded the arc of their relationship with a formula. (He hoped to deduce when entropy would set in.) When he and I spoke on the phone, we became co-therapists. Madam X was our only patient. We considered the facts of her childhood of deprivation and trauma—her mother was kept by a gangster, her father unknown—and deduced that this had made her insecure but imaginative. She walked with a slight limp from some kind of foot deformity, and we analyzed how this had made her feel unlovable. "She's perfected how to walk so it's undetectable," Dad said. When he recounted again how unremarkable her appearance was, I tried to be reassuring. "That's okay, Dad," I said. "I was getting tired of all the drop-dead beauties."

But I had doubts about his new love. She was—as Dad finally revealed in a weak moment—a wildly successful romance novelist named Evie Valcour. She lived in a palatial house on Nob Hill that was filled with French furniture, mirrored bathrooms, antique wallpaper, and a personal staff of six. "It's really so gauche—the whole scene," Dad said, obviously hoping that a diatribe against her might make him feel better. "What does she need *all that* for?"

"I didn't realize that you'd been inside."

"Oh, I haven't. But I've heard from friends. And the house was featured in *Architectural Digest* last year, and I went to the library to look it up. The pictures weren't exactly perfectly clear on microfiche, but I saw enough. Believe me. She has a gold-leafed salon where she serves high tea."

"I can't hear any more."

"And gold flatware."

"*Stop.*"

"I know," he said. "It's all so disgusting and terrible. What am I going to do?"

Married for many years to a surgeon who abhorred society, Madam X made the rounds of the circuit alone. Sometimes Dad stole chances to see her by attending an opera ball or symphony auction, and she'd find a way to seat him at her table. At first I thought it was the game—the secrecy and plotting—that had engaged him so forcefully, but more and more, as I heard the confusion in his voice, and self-doubt, I worried that he'd finally fallen for a woman who was beating him at his own game. Madam X waffled about leaving her husband, whom she openly loved. When Dad had brought her to Wolfback, she hinted that it was small and a little too chilly. When they met up for a rendezvous in a city hotel suite, she sank into despair upon discovering that my father had stayed there many times with somebody else.

She was a devout Catholic, it turned out, with an austere streak. She wrote her gothic potboilers in a very small, very plain maid's room in the attic of her grand house. Dad seemed in love with the idea of Madam X toiling for hours on end with such discipline. And one night, when he was mentioning it for the seventh or eighth time, I suddenly remembered Marguerite's house—and Fitzy, the maid who had lived in the small room at the top of the kitchen stairs. Whitman had told me about her.

"Hey, wasn't Fitzy your first love?"

"Who?"

"Fitzy. Miss FitzWilliam or whatever her name was. Marguerite's maid in San Benito. Whitman told me you were in love with her. That's why Marguerite moved your bedroom. So she could keep her eye on you."

"Oh," he said. And after a long stretch of silence, "You're too smart."

We had lots of long pauses in our conversations by then, empty moments that he and I didn't try to fill with useless jabber. While he considered Fitzy in silence, I sat on the bed in Tomas's room and watched the green hills turn black and the sky turn orange.

"It doesn't seem right," I said finally, "that you're sitting around waiting for this woman to see you. My God, Dad, find somebody else to play with! That's what you used to tell me."

"Did I?"

"Last summer. During my David Yamato phase."

"How insensitive of me. What bad advice."

"No it wasn't."

"Love the one you're with and all that. Ugh. But you stayed abjectly loyal to David, even when he was boring beyond all measure, didn't write, forgot your birthday, and then didn't return to L.A."

"I wasn't loyal."

"In your heart you were. Nobody else mattered until you'd gotten David out of your system. I used to think monogamy was an awful lot of work, and not worth the trouble. But . . . well, maybe you're rubbing off on me. When you find somebody worth waiting for, they're worth waiting for. Right? Besides, Madam X goes berserk if I see anybody else."

"Do you?"

"No, and I'm afraid it's worse than that," he confessed. "I said I'd marry her."

This explained why money—and whether he had enough—had suddenly entered into our conversations. Madam X worried about how much her husband would want from her if they divorced. And she had kids, lots of kids, a detail that Dad managed to keep from me for most of the summer. "All daughters. Gorgeous little things. She's raising them very properly and carefully. Heading straight for cotillion and debutante balls." When I said nothing, he changed the subject.

"How are things with Tomas?"

"Good. Great."

"How's the sex?"

"None of your business."

"That's okay if you don't want to tell me," he said, "but just remember, it's supposed to blow you away."

I had been blown away at the beginning, and things were like that for a month or so—nonstop sex and not talking, just clawing at each other until, exhausting all newness, Tomas led us into a pattern of being together that allowed for maximum sex but minimum relationship, mostly due to an endless supply of dope to smoke.

Mornings, after a few tokes, I went to the beach and swam the length of Waimea Bay and back, a mile or so, to keep the birth control pills from making me fat. Then I drove Tomas's white pickup to get an ice cream cone before lunch—the sort of thing you do, I suppose, the first year you leave home. And after another few tokes, the ice cream tasted so incredible. "You're such a kid," Tomas liked to joke, and rub my head. But, in truth, I'd never felt more grown up or sophisticated or serious. The North Shore was filled with perpetual adolescents, with stringy-haired Californians who wanted to be cool forever and with people from the East who were in the midst of remaking themselves into cool Californians, or people from the Midwest who looked the part, with dark tans and sun-streaked hair, but never figured out exactly how to dump their good manners and stop being too nice. No matter what age, the entire female population wore bikini tops with wraparound skirts. If a guy wore a clean T-shirt with a fancy logo—Heineken Beer or an expensive wetsuit line—that was considered dressed up. So compared to the hordes of tanned and frolicking adults around me, taking acid on the weekends, eating mushrooms between swells, dancing to country music at the Ding Dong Palace and the Dakini Bikini, it was easy to feel cultured and extremely mature, even at seventeen.

In the afternoons when the light grew quieter, I took photographs and sometimes I tried to cook, except I only knew how to make pasta, my father's scones, Ooee's garlic-tarragon vinaigrette, and a vegetarian stir-fry that Whitman had taught me. An older woman cleaned the house, a Filipina who was short and stocky—and reminded me a little of Abuelita—so I didn't have too many household duties beyond keeping a vegetable garden going. Sugar had planted it the previous winter, and, with some advice from Whitman, I weeded, watered, fertilized, and then harvested a bumper crop of tomatoes and okra and eggplant and everything else. Hawaii made gardening seem easy. Everything I planted reminded me of the magic beans that Jack throws out the window—and the next morning a giant beanstalk appears. The word "jungle" was an abstract concept before I went to Hawaii, along with "fecund." When I chopped the buds and tops off the marijuana, the next time I'd look, the plants would be twice the size.

Tomas was home during the day sometimes—and gone others. He'd return with an old sign that he'd found in a junkyard, or a kitschy postcard to frame. He had art director's taste, a kind of theatrical love of old things cluttered together for effect. He had designed his house like a set, with a series of views. Less than a year old, it was almost ramshackle already, built with pieces of an old pineapple factory and salvaged yachts. Tomas had put up Hawaiian artifacts and signs everywhere, mostly old advertisements with images of hula girls and palm trees. In the kitchen there was a wall clock from an old diner, a jukebox with lights that flashed, and a ridiculous Lone Star beer advertisement from Texas—a clear plastic dome over a painted-plaster monkey who sat with a green hose. When Tomas got the motor of this thing working, water shot from the hose and splashed at the top of the dome while the monkey twirled.

Saturday nights we went out. The North Shore was eternal high school—people drinking bottles of beer in their cars while they drove around trying to find where the best party was. We made the rounds every week, to Jerry's house, to Leftie's house, to Whitman's—for a little dope, blender drinks, some dancing, or a few lines of cocaine. Tomas always had some on hand, probably the reason he was always greeted with great enthusiasm and affection wherever he went. Even by the standards of the day, and of the North Shore, Tomas was a cokehead. It wasn't disgraceful in those days, but mystifyingly glamorous. Cocaine made you funny and smart. Cocaine made you sociable and lively and as close to urbane as imaginable in a place like Hawaii. Everybody had that much figured out. Grass made you Zen-like and contemplative. Alcohol made you bold (sometimes obnoxiously so). Cocaine made you irresistible— particularly in your own mind, which turns out to be the only place that counts. By the time the summer ended and I turned eighteen, when I wasn't stoned or drunk or high, I was bragging about how wasted I'd been the day before—while desperately trying to employ as much island slang as possible. *Da kine* meant something was really good, or "the kind." *Ono* meant something was the best, or number one. *"Ono da kine bes pakalolo"* was the way an idiot haole (white person) would say they'd had some really great grass. Then, if you wanted to say, in simple druggie jargon, that you'd had lots of toot, there was always, "My nose was packed all night, bra." For my birthday Whitman brought me flowers and my father sent a check for $1,818.18. Tomas gave me an old movie poster and three grams of cocaine. It was gone in a week.

At the onset of October—definitely still summer, no matter what the calendar said—I began to fill out forms for college. I answered all the questions—crowding information about myself in the narrow blanks—signed releases for transcripts and SAT scores, wrote a pathetic essay about what my camera meant to me and how I could make the world a better place with it. (I even mentioned wanting to be a war correspondent.) After Whitman proofread it, I drove to the Haleiwa post office, a dilapidated green cottage with full trash cans and worn-out linoleum, and stood next to the mail slot marked MAINLAND. The white paper envelope disappeared into the dark slot. It felt like stuffing a note in a bottle, a long shot and a faraway dream that I wasn't sure was possible—or even mine.

The sun. The cornmeal sand. The blue waves. Even Tomas, and his sense of humor—his way of looking at life with a kindly, bemused, slightly out-of-it smile—was like a wonderful dream, and sunny, endlessly sunny and easy. Waves of good things kept coming to me, and pleasure, and I felt so good all the time that I couldn't make distinctions between my feelings anymore, because they were all much the same, almost as if the tropics had cooked the complications out of me. Any lingering anger and resentments seemed gone forever. Life was good. Life was easy. That's what I kept telling myself—the little inconveniences about living in Hawaii weren't going to get to me anymore. I'd gotten used to waiting for twenty minutes for the attendant at the gas station to fill up the truck. I'd gotten used to slow waitresses and bad food in restaurants, to melted ice in my mixed drinks and tepid beer in bars, to the laid-back shopkeepers who barely lifted a finger to help. Everything was *ono* and *da kine,* and everybody was on "Hawaii time," including me.

It seems crazy now, but I'd never thought about how Tomas had built the house—or where his money came from. Maybe he'd made a lot as a set designer, in the old days. Maybe he'd been a smart investor. How did I know? Money was mysterious and magical to me then—it came and went, had rules of its own that I didn't know about, that never made sense to me. So I guess it seemed natural for Tomas to have mysterious money. Like Whitman and lots of other guys on the North Shore, he rarely seemed to be working. Sometimes he made calls. Sometimes he drove around. He had "crews" of guys at his disposal, but I assumed they were gardening crews or stonemasons who were building fake waterfalls all over Oahu.

Whitman was the one to spill the beans. "He's a dealer, you innocent."

I chose to ignore that for a while. Not months. Not forever. But just long enough so that when it came back to me, this information seemed more like a recurring dream that might not be real. Everything in paradise felt negotiable anyway. Not quite real, not quite happening. Over the summer, when I heard from Abuelita that Robbie's father had died, I hadn't sent a note or even called. So far from home, and so far from what was considered civilization, the old rules didn't seem to apply.

Or maybe I was just too stoned. I'd go down the hill and smoke dope with Whitman, then run into Leftie, or Jerry, and get a pill of some kind, just for fun. And then I'd come back up the mountain and do a few lines of cocaine with Tomas. Sometimes the lower half of my face was so numb I wasn't sure if it was still there. Sometimes I was afraid to eat—worried I'd bite off my tongue or start chewing on my cheeks.

"So are you really a dealer?" I asked Tomas one night. I'd decided that I could live without him, I suppose, and that I wasn't interested in fixing him either.

He didn't miss a beat. He didn't seem stunned either. Being in Hawaii for six years had removed that option from his personality. "Who told you that, Little Girl?" he said, chopping another line.

"Whitman."

Tomas nodded and just kept nodding. Very slowly. He pursed his lips and then smirked. "Well, I guess, then, I'm supposed to tell you that he's a junkie. Or maybe you've figured that out already."

I didn't leave Hawaii right away. And I can't really say why—denial, listlessness, or indecision. Maybe I didn't have any energy left for consciousness. Winter came. The air temperature hovered in the mid-seventies, and aside from more rain clouds passing over my towel on the beach and occasionally drenching me, the days of sunshine and perfection continued. The humidity lessened, or I got used to it. The waves picked up and up and up—grew as tall and thick as buildings—and I barely recognized my old beach spots anymore. The storms took away the sand and a few other things, too. As Jerry had said on my first day in Haleiwa, there were supposedly seven guys for every girl on the North Shore—a nice ratio, if you could find the guys anymore. They were in the water at Pipeline or Sunset or just hanging out at any one of the beaches that ran the length of the North Shore. There were dozens of them, surf spots with informal names and shifting locations due to changing sandbars. One lazy afternoon, after Whitman had come back to his house all tired and worn out, almost nodding off, we ate dried cuttlefish and Maui Chips and drank beers and listed the nicknames of the surf spots in order: Velseyland, Secretspots, Backyards, Sunset, Kammieland, Rockies, Gas Chambers, Pipeline Lefts, Backdoor Pipeline, Off the Walls, Shit-Fucks, Bonzai Rocks, Leons, Log Cabins, Changes, Daystar, Rainbows, Avalanche, Haleiwa, Himalayas, Laniakea, Chums Reef, Marijuana's, All Rights, Waimea Bay.

That afternoon I remember feeling as though I'd lived in Hawaii my whole life. My skin was so dark, people asked if I was part Hawaiian. That pleased me. I'd nod vaguely. Maybe I was. Did it matter anymore?

By Christmas, like a true native, I'd even gotten bored of the beach. The waves were too big for swimming anyway.

"What are you reading?" Dad asked on the phone.

"Nothing."

"You haven't sent me a new batch of pictures in a long time."

"Haven't taken any."

"Are you worried about getting in?"

"Getting in where?"

"College."

"Oh." The application was something else I kept forgetting about. It seemed like years ago—another lifetime ago, before the big waves and the surfing tournaments and all the winter parties, which were now non-stop—that I'd sent the thing off. "I don't really care," I said. "I mean, I was into it when I sent it, I really was. But now I don't really see the point. Maybe I don't see the point of anything."

"You don't?"

"Not really. It's weird. But living here—the perfect weather just goes on and on. It almost creeps into your soul and bleaches it out. I mean, there's a wreath on the Star Market, and lights on a few palm trees, but it doesn't feel like Christmas. It doesn't matter. I hate Christmas anyway."

"No, you don't."

"I don't?"

"I'm the one who hates Christmas—not you," he said. "I know what the problem is."

"Please don't say I need to come home."

"No," he said. "You need to quit smoking pot."

His voice was very certain, had a kind of firmness that I hadn't heard since I was very young. When I didn't say anything right away, he lightened up. "For two weeks. That's all. Just try it."

After two weeks, he asked, "Feel any better?"

"What do you mean?"

"Your disappearing joie de vivre—and new hatred of Christmas. Your apathy."

"Nothing's changed," I said. "I'm fine anyway. I just don't feel anything. Well, maybe I feel a tiny bit better. I bought one of Madam X's books, the kind of thing I never read, and I actually liked it for a while."

"Oh, that's not a good sign. What else are you doing—besides the pot?"

"Not much," I said. "Whatever turns up. Sometimes a Quaalude here and there. Cocaine once in a—"

"*Cocaine?*" He raised his voice, almost to a shout. "How stupid. Who gave you permission to do that?"

I didn't say anything for a long time. I do remember thinking it seemed a little hypocritical for him to be complaining about my drug use.

"You're drinking, too?"

"Where are you going with this? You make it sound like *Lost Weekend* or something. It's not that bad. And I'm not depressed or anything. I just . . . The world seems flat. That's all. I'm flatlining and floating all the time. Nothing sticks. You know what I mean? I'm not hooked on anything—it's almost the opposite. I couldn't get hooked on anything if I tried."

"Another two weeks," he said. "You've got to go another two weeks. Stop everything—whatever you're taking or drinking or smoking. You'll feel better soon. You're just in a slog."

It might have been a week later—I was driving to meet Tomas at Kammieland for some bodysurfing, and on the way I saw a dark horse in a meadow. There was a young girl on the horse, and there was something about her, and the horse, and how they moved together, that made me start to cry. The next day, when I was shopping in the Star Market, I saw a newsmagazine with Jerry Brown on the cover and felt homesick, so terribly homesick. He'd been the governor of California for so long I'd forgotten about him too. That evening, as a test, I picked up Madam X's book again and tore through it in one sitting.

The next morning, when it was still too early to call my father, I went down to the rocks in front of Whitman's and took pictures of the local kids fishing for eels with their drop lines. They stood so proudly with their buckets and smiled so hugely for my camera. When Whitman wandered out, I took a sleepy picture of him in the morning light. Whitman—golden, so golden and brown and smiling at me.

In the next week, I had so many momentary epiphanies that it would be difficult to chronicle them. They came sporadically, in a rush, almost as if all the thoughts that I hadn't had all summer and fall were now desperately trying to find their way out. I was alive with thoughts, and reconsiderations, and feelings, and almost manic energy. Mostly I was just alive. I bought coffee and a newspaper at the café in Kua Aina, and while I was drinking the coffee, I came across an article with a New Delhi dateline, and suddenly I remembered, almost from the depths of my being, that there was a real place called New Delhi and it was still there, along with the rest of the world, teeming with stories and people, teeming with life, beckoning to me and calling me. I wanted so much to be there, in the world again, and not pacified in a tropical haze of adolescent dreams and decadence and stupidity. What was I doing with my life? I lifted my head from the paper and slowly looked around the Kua Aina café and felt, for the first time in a long time—perhaps ever—that I knew who I was. But how had I wound up in Hawaii?

In January, when the news came from University of California that I'd been admitted, I was capable of wild excitement. I couldn't wait to buy books and notebooks, to start classes, to feel cool weather again. I stretched out in bed and dreamed about needing to wear a sweater. I thought about Wolfback—its wonderful fog and gloomy microclimate. The gray sky, the chill, the dark clouds, the windswept beach. But how could I leave Tomas?

"You've got to be honest with him," Dad advised in the serious tone he always adopted when he was giving me love advice. "None of the head games you played on David. If you're going to enjoy the freedom and pleasures of adulthood, then you've got to act like an adult yourself. Even if it's just an act, or a rehearsal. Be an adult. Level with him. Simply tell the man how you really feel. Tell him it's hard to leave—but you have to—and cry if you feel like crying. He's a decent guy. He'll understand how you feel."

A few days later, a copy of James Abbott McNeill Whistler's *The Gentle Art of Making Enemies* arrived in the mail with a funny note. Dad called more frequently than before, asking if I needed anything. He seemed as energized and excited by my return as I was. "I've made the most perfect apricot scones," he said one night. "Too bad you're not here. My best batch ever."

And Whitman? Tomas could be wrong, I told myself. Was it my business anyway? But Whitman did seem thin, and distracted. He fell asleep in the middle of dinner and was out of money sometimes. When the swells came, sometimes he didn't bother going into the water. Why didn't I just ask him? In books and movies, people always ask direct questions and get direct answers. In life it always seemed too hard. I was afraid of losing him. Even though, in some way, I suppose that I already had.

I t was a long flight back to civilization. At the last second, I wasn't sure if I was ready. The airport felt too busy and hectic. The plane felt strange and futuristic and way too clean. I ordered a gin and tonic from the hostess, and then another, and moved to the back of the plane, to the smoking section, and pulled out a fresh pack of Camel cigarettes—and I smoked them. I felt sorry for myself, I suppose. I wondered what the waves were doing at Waimea. I wondered if the local kids were fishing on the rocks in front of Whitman's house. I wondered who'd look after the garden at Tomas's house now and whether I'd really come back over the summer like I said I would.

Getting off the plane at LAX, I looked around for Abuelita and my mother and remembered they were meeting me in baggage claim. I gathered up my things, wondered if my breath smelled like gin and how cold it was outside. I was wearing a pair of baggy white shorts with a red-wine stain that I couldn't get out, flip-flops, a skinny camisole that said DA KINE across my breasts, and a string of water-buffalo beads that Tomas had gotten me in Indonesia. My hair was loose, not brushed, and almost blond at the ends. My mother had said it was going to be sixty-two degrees in Los Angeles, but that number was meaningless to me. It felt like years since I'd been in weather that cold.

I entered an underground tunnel that was paved in turquoise-blue tile and lit by a long tube of fluorescent light. I felt a little drunk, and sad. Most of me was still in Hawaii, I suppose, or wishing I were. In an odd, dreamlike moment, I looked at the far end of the blue tunnel and saw Robbie and Mrs. Morrison coming toward me. They were talking to each other and walking quickly. Robbie was wearing something very wintry and collegiate, almost eastern—a plaid skirt and a hunter green sweater. She was wearing a pair of brown loafers, too, the kind of shoes I hadn't seen or thought about in ten months. They looked very leathery and strange and old-fashioned. Like shoes from another century. The whole getup was like a costume.

Her hair was still long, but darker and held back by an Alice in Wonderland headband. Then she saw me.

"Oh, my gosh!" Robbie called out. "Is that you, Inny??"

"It's me."

"Oh, my gosh! You're so tan. *Where have you been?*"

She was excited and almost hollering. I'd forgotten all about that—how people could be enthusiastic and jump around.

"Hawaii," I said, trying very hard to show a little spirit, too. "I've been living there—since summer."

"You have?"

"At the University of Hawaii?" Mrs. Morrison asked. And then I remembered that there were lots of Mormons in Hawaii—not that I met any. They ran a big tourist site called the Polynesian Cultural Center. The whole Morrison family had visited it years ago, way back in days of Mrs. Shockley and Camp Fire Girls.

I shook my head. A burst of good feeling was running through me, though, because I'd suddenly come up with a way to say everything I needed about the last ten months of my life—how to couch my experience in a nutshell. "I wish I'd been getting some school credit," I said to Mrs. Morrison. "But I'm afraid I've just been a degenerate instead."

Boo laughed very hard—exactly like she always did. Robbie was laughing, too. "Oh, Inny," they kept saying. "You're so funny. *You're so funny.*"

The next day, when I tried the old number, Boo answered. She seeming thrilled to talk to me again. "Hawaii! Oh, Inny, that must have been so wonderful."

I played up the photography thing, made it sound like I was verging on professional. "My mom got married," I said.

"Wasn't that a while ago?" Mrs. Morrison asked. "Last year? But I didn't know you were in Hawaii all this time. You clever girl—a year off. And all that healthy sunshine. I thought it might be too cold for Robbie at BYU, but she's learning to ski instead. Just shows you."

Boo made out like I'd been on a Mormon mission or something, like I'd been saving souls and making the world a better place, not culminating a sad, years-long descent into indolence and self-deception. She acted as if Robbie and I were still in touch, too, as if nothing were different, but I could tell she was wondering why I'd called. She acted happy about it, but curious. Boo liked me; she always had. No matter what I did. When Marguerite died, she'd sent a small basket of carnations and daisies that got lost in the grandeur of the tall lilies and topiary azalea of the San Benito types. ("Who are *the Morrisons*?" Aunt Julia wanted to know. "It's hard to write a thank-you to people in Van Dale you've never heard of.") Boo had a kind of faith in me, and high expectations. And I wondered why I'd thrown all that away so easily—a whole family of nice people, who knew me, who liked me.

"I was really sorry to hear about Dr. Morrison," I said finally. "That's the reason I'm calling, really. I meant to call last summer, Mrs. Morrison, but—"

"Oh, Inny, goodness gracious don't apologize. Gosh, I can't wait to tell Robbie that you called—do you need her number in Provo?"

1980

NINETEEN

Big Bang

I wish I could say that everything was smooth sailing after that, that I went to college and became a better person. That life stopped being confusing and I knew who I was, every day, and what the point of things was. But maybe nobody feels that way.

I'd been back in California almost nine months when all hell broke loose. It was after New Year's and my second quarter at Berkeley was starting. I missed the first week of classes and then wobbled for the next three. I suppose I might have dropped out, except I'd struggle home in the car traffic at night and climb the stairs from my apartment underneath Wolfback, and Dad would have all my textbooks out on the kitchen table, and he'd be reading them.

"Have you considered looking at some other explanations of the big bang—because this astronomy book isn't particularly well written. The book makes things more confusing than they need to be. The theory's very simple, actually, one of the reasons for its great success."

"We did the big bang. We did it the first week."

"I see that from your syllabus. But you were gone, and I worry that you didn't nail it in your mind. I don't care about your grade on the midterms, or any of your grades. I'm talking about the rest of your life, and when will you ever revisit the big bang? I've found a better chapter—over here, see? One of my books dwells mostly on the flaws of the theory but does a very nice job of explaining it, too, and how the planets were formed."

"All from the same matter. After a billion-year explosion."

"You've reduced it to a cartoon."

"I thought that was the point."

He was wearing beautiful dark pinstripe suits in those days, and always on the way to a museum board meeting, or the opera board, or some artificial-intelligence symposium, or to discuss investing in a new software company. He was busy, busier than he'd been in a long time, and always folding himself into the back of his restored Cadillac limousine (I was not allowed to call it a "limo") with Hector in front and looking less like a chauffeur than anybody on earth. A couple of hours later, he'd unfold himself and appear at Wolfback again. He was never gone for long. The house was his epicenter, his HQ, and he hung around the place like the fog. He'd set up quite a nice life there. He baked and cooked. He played piano—after a few years back at the instrument, he'd gotten quite good, playing Beethoven's *Pathétique* again and again, perfecting it the way he used to perfect a *soleares* on the guitar. Most evenings, if Evie was tied up, he was following the presidential campaign on TV with an intense interest that I'd never seen in him before. ("I'm ready for a whole new decade, Inez, aren't you?")

Mornings he spent an enormous amount of time in preparation for the day. The steam from his shower carried the smell of fancy unguents about the house, and Dad would stand before the tall mirror in his spacious master bath, combing his hair straight back like Count Dracula's or putting on one of his impeccable shirts. They were special-ordered— after a long debate over whether French cuffs were gauche or not, and then he'd succumbed. He was wearing handmade Belgian slippers from a small store in New York, something Evie had turned him on to, and I didn't mind the slippers or the fact that he wore them without socks like some kind of fraudulent prince. But the black velvet ones, with the monogrammed PNR in gold cord and a little gold crown, were way too much for me.

He was loyal to Wolfback, despite Evie's occasional outcries that it was too small or too cold or too remote. And he'd remained loyal to me, of course. That second quarter at Berkeley, when things were tough, he read the complete textbook of my ab-psych class in a night and highlighted all essential terminology. (Next to a paragraph on autism, he wrote in the margin, "This sounds like me, doesn't it?" Next to narcissism: "Me, too.") Although he wasn't pleased to learn that I'd declared psychology as my major. News of this, in fact, provoked a rare tantrum. "Oh, God," he cried out, "how awful to be draining emotional bedpans for a living!"

I'd been busy draining *his* emotional bedpan most of the year already. The previous spring, when I'd come back from Hawaii, he had entered a state of emergency. Evie—or Madam X, as she was still called then—was on the brink of leaving her husband, then not on the brink, and then brinking again, a roller-coaster ride that my father did not enjoy or ever get used to, in spite of all his advice to me about what fun love was. For my part I'd grown very tired of Evie and the special grip she seemed to have on him.

"She wants to meet you," he said.

"Sorry," I replied. "I know too much already." She graced the entire back jacket of her books, a super-close-up portrait with heavy airbrushing. The perfect, swept-back hair. The big eyes. The big half smile and overbite hanging there like a theater balcony.

It was probably infantile regression, but I found myself wishing Dad were with Justine again. When she'd heard that I was living with Dad and starting college nearby, she called the house and left a message for me.

"Justine?"

"We're still friends," Dad said. "You knew that. She'd like to see you."

She was living on a horse farm in Carmel Valley, a place Whitman had told me about the year before. He'd kept in touch with Justine in a way that I never had. They shared something—a bond of some kind. It seemed to have something to do with Dad.

"Won't you come for a weekend, and we can ride?" she asked me. I wasn't so sure—did I want to get started up with Justine again? Every memory of being with her seemed so intense. And did I want to sacrifice a college weekend? Soon enough I discovered that most of my Berkeley classmates, who lived in campus dorms or sororities, were reveling all weekend—smoking and drinking and staying up all night, exercising the assortment of freedoms that I'd already grown tired of. So one Friday afternoon, I packed the hatch of the MG with an overnight bag, riding boots, breeches, and a new helmet with a chin guard. It was nice to get away. And to leave college, and Wolfback, and to let my father be alone with Evie.

Justine was waving at the door of a small shingled cottage when I pulled up. The sight of Dad's old car brought nice memories, she said. Her house was one story and very modest—just three rooms and one bath, a tiny room with warped linoleum and a rusty sink where the porcelain had been eaten away.

"Conspicuous nonconsumption" Dad called it, but I could see right away that Justine was a different person, healthier and happier and more confident. Her gaze was steady—not confused or uncertain—and her daughter, Lara, who'd been almost invisible in the old days, taken up with a nanny, had grown into a tall teenager with an extravagant head of wavy hair. She and Justine wore blue jeans and sweaters and beat-up cowboy boots. Gone were the furs and rare beads. As Whitman had reported, Justine had even quit smoking.

Her old habit of honesty was still intact. "I never really left your father," she said, thirty minutes into our first hello. "I just decided to leave him alone. That's what he seemed to want—from everybody. But when I heard you were living with him, I thought it incredible. And it made me wonder if he has changed."

"He has," I said. "But it's hard to say exactly how."

It was a weekend of long rides through eucalyptus groves and along hilltops, a dinner by the fire in a nearby inn, and quiet talks—city life versus country life, my impressions of Hawaii, how school was coming. I went back to Carmel Valley fairly often after that. It was nice to be with Justine and Lara, and nice to share their peaceful, thoughtful life. I had a funny feeling, too, that I was meant to be there and that Justine was supposed to be in our lives again. Maybe I hoped to bring her back to my father, that she'd marry him. They were so alike—or so unlike anybody else, two rare fruit trees sprung up in the California soil. But I worried she had outgrown him. She seemed wiser, and calmer, and not fooled by things. Newness held little power or attraction for her. Was it all the time she spent alone? Was it Buddhism? In the past her religion had seemed an affectation to me, almost silly, but I was beginning to suspect that I'd been wrong about that. Somewhere along the way, parts of Justine had been brought forward, others erased or smoothed over. Her shyness and awkwardness weren't an obstacle to knowing her anymore, but an opening where you could see her heart. And when the Whitman thing happened, it was Justine who led us onward and seemed to know a great deal about how to rescue somebody—even yourself.

That's the funny thing. You think you're rescuing your brother, and in the end you're the one who's suddenly walking on solid ground. It wasn't brave or anything like that. Marguerite had more to do with it than anybody else. I did for Whitman what I hadn't done for her.

I couldn't reach him—that's how it started. Since leaving Hawaii, I'd gotten into the habit of calling more often. A few times a week, usually at night. I said that I was homesick for the North Shore and wanted to hear how things were. What was going on, what parties I'd missed, how the waves were. What Waimea was doing. "Same old, same old," Whitman always said, reassuringly. But I was really calling to check on him. He couldn't be that bad if he was getting up at six in the morning and tying his surfboards onto the roof of the Valiant, I told myself. He couldn't be that bad if he was answering the phone and making jokes. "You're not missing much," he said cheerfully. "Jerry's still drowning women in his hot tub. I hear the moans every night."

And when a new girl moved into Tomas's house—just a couple months after I'd left Haleiwa—Whitman treated this development carefully and thoughtfully, filling in the blanks that Tomas had left. "Her name is Kennan. I kind of knew her in Ojala," Whitman said. "She's the stepdaughter of a woman who used to live with a guy my mom dated for a couple months." It bothered me a little that Kennan was a photographer, or said she was. And it bothered me a little when she turned out to be older than me, twenty-four, exactly the golden age difference from Tomas. But I was always happy that Whitman was okay, and I hung up the phone relieved. It was as if Hawaii didn't exist anymore, and Tomas was gone, and who cared about Kennan?

I'd lived with Abuelita over the summer before college, working at Bob's again. He and my mother were at Abuelita's for long stretches, too, while renovations were being done on their house in La Cañada—a staircase was coming out, a courtyard being put in, all new bathrooms. They seemed so happy, and absorbed with protein shakes, weight training, and fitness. On weekends they dressed in matching tennis warm-ups and headed to the gym. I didn't do too much that summer. I read a lot. I got ready to move up north. I worked.

To be honest, I wasn't thrilled at the prospect of living with my father. But he'd gone to the trouble of building an apartment for me, getting another remote control for the gate out front, and he seemed so excited. I felt like I had to move in—even if the commute was a nightmare and the apartment was kind of dark and cavelike and when I was taking a shower it felt like the entire city of San Francisco could see me.

When I complained to Whitman, he called it the "subterranean Wolfbackean lair," which made me laugh. And made me think, all over again, that he was okay. But I started college and began calling Whitman's house at night and never getting an answer. Or I'd call and get some tenant, some unknown person, who was almost incomprehensible on the phone. It was only late September—and the waves were probably still bad. So where was he? But then, a few days later, Whitman would finally return the call and sound great, and we'd pass the phone back and forth over the dinner table.

"What's his day like, Inez?" Dad asked one night. "I mean, what does Whitman really *do*? Is he really working?"

I shrugged. "He has a couple hotels—fern-grotto places, indoor gardens with fake waterfalls, that kind of thing. He feeds and prunes the plants. The trunk of his car is full of chemicals and wands and clippers and plastic buckets. But I have to say, his heart doesn't seem in it."

"Where is it?"

I shrugged again, not wanting to say what I thought.

"I can't believe," my father said, "that kids are allowed to live so far away from their parents." And then he laughed. The funny thing was, he wasn't kidding.

Not long afterwards Evie left her husband. Dad had pressured her—given her an ultimatum. But almost immediately she'd begun to wobble and regret her decision. She worried that Dad couldn't be faithful, that he wasn't considerate enough or kind enough, that he wouldn't be able to "take care" of her feelings, as she put it to him in a letter. She suggested that they see a therapist together. He agreed, a concession on his part that seemed larger and more significant than his proposal of marriage, which was still apparently on the table.

How to explain the people we fall in love with? Freud said it was a decision made so far into you, in the dark, that it wasn't the result of reason. Love was a thing of urges, and needs, and fears. My father liked to pretend he knew the answers to all the human riddles—as though there were equations that could be worked out, laws of nature that governed all. He had theories about how to start an affair. How to choose the proper person. How to keep it going. How to end it. Why it was necessary to leave eventually, and find somebody else. "A relationship is like a potted plant," he told me once. "At some point the plant gets too big and needs a new pot. And if one of you doesn't have the energy to switch pots and make the necessary changes, it's time to move on."

But his kind of romance seemed like a dying thing. His kind of romance depended upon a magic trick, a veil that wound up hiding everything worth seeing. I'd done the equation in my head and projected myself into time. According to his golden rule, when I was forty-five, the perfect man would be seventy-six. When I was fifty-two, he'd be ninety.

Evie had been separated from her husband for a month or so when Dad began wobbling, too. He wondered whether he could really marry her—or anyone. It meant giving up Wolfback, most likely, and giving up the freedom that he'd made so many other sacrifices for, sacrifices like Cary and Justine, Gretchen and Shanti and Lauren. Wonderful women, all of them. Sacrifices like Patricia and my mother, too. "And besides," he said one night after dinner, "it wouldn't be fair to you kids."

"What do we have to do with it?" I asked.

"I wouldn't have as much time to spend with you, would I? Who'd read with you? Who'd make you scones in the morning? I couldn't be as hovering and devoted, could I? Evie would have to be number one."

"I'd get by," I said. But he had a point. Now that I had him all to myself finally, why should I share?

The battle in his mind waged on. "Maybe she's right," he said one morning. "This house is impractical. It's leaking. There's a smell of sewage coming from the septic field that we can't figure out."

"What smell?" I said. "I don't smell anything."

"I know," he said, flip-flopping again. "There's no smell of sewage. She's out of control. I'm tired of all her demands and complaints."

Just before Christmas, before I was able to meet her—something Dad kept trying to arrange, and I kept dodging—Evie returned to her husband. The air in the house was lighter and breezier. The storm had passed. Dad seemed himself again, relieved the ordeal was over.

Not long afterward I walked into his bedroom to look for something and noticed a cluster of framed pictures leaning against a wall of his dressing room. Four or five frames—old, covered with chipped paint and dust. Curious, I flipped through them. A diploma from Caltech, another from Stanford. A math award of some kind. When I came across two photographs of a nude girl, I remembered that I'd seen her before: in my father's old closet in San Benito. Whitman and I had looked at them the day we met.

In one photograph the girl was standing in a shallow pond or lake. She was bent over, admiring the water. The picture was hand-tinted and almost campy—her skin was as pink as a doll's and the water too blue. In the second picture, she was lying on a chaise or bed. Her arms were very long and thin—like sticks—stretched over her head. Her face was long and familiar. And she was looking directly at the camera.

Marguerite. Suddenly I could see that. Her eyes were the same. And so intense, so alive and immediate. It was strange that hadn't been obvious before.

"She was so lovely, wasn't she?" Dad said when I carried the pictures out to the kitchen. "Don't you love those poses? I was just looking at them again last night."

"Where have these been?" I asked.

"What do you mean?" he said. "I've always had them. Since Mother died anyway. Aren't they fantastic? She was such a beautiful woman, wasn't she? I was thinking it might be nice to put them up—maybe in my bedroom. Make a little memorial. Why not? I've been missing her lately and thinking about her. That's all."

I called to ask Whitman about the photographs—and if he'd known that Marguerite had been an artist's model in New York before she met N.C. It wasn't a secret, Dad insisted, just a piece of information that, by coincidence, nobody had mentioned to me before. "She had to make a living," Dad said. "Her family was completely broke and had nothing. She worked for a photographer, an older man. He probably kept her, God only knows. Or maybe he was just in love with her. He wrote to her for the longest time. Even when I was a boy. What's the big deal?"

I tried Whitman twice and got no answer. Later that night, when we were making dinner—some stir-fry that made me think of Whitman again—Dad and I tried his house one more time. "You're obsessed with turning this Marguerite thing into *a big secret*," Dad said, sort of mocking me, but nobody picked up the phone. Before going to bed, we tried again. No answer.

The next day, on Christmas Eve, I tried yet again. My mother and Bob were in Baja, at a Mexican resort for people who needed to play tennis constantly. Abuelita was working through the holidays—Mr. Feinman had droves of family members arriving. So I had wound up with Dad, even though he was aggressively antiholiday and refused to have a tree, or put up lights, or do anything remotely festive. There'd been some talk about Whitman's coming to Wolfback to join us, but he'd never bothered to let us know for sure. That seemed a little weird, too.

"I can't imagine that nobody's home," I said after the third attempt to reach him. "This time of year, the house should be full of people— particularly at night."

"Maybe he's got a new girlfriend," Dad said.

"Yeah," I said, shooting him a look.

"That's just pie in the sky, isn't it? Santa Claus talk."

I waited until the next morning before deciding to call Leftie or Jerry or John—had they seen Whitman? I figured it wouldn't be too intrusive to call them, except it was Christmas Day. But I didn't have their phone numbers and couldn't obtain them from information. I didn't know their last names. Nobody on the North Shore seemed to have one.

When I called Tomas, a woman answered the phone.

"Kennan?"

"Oh, no," the voice said a little awkwardly, in a decisively laid-back way, as if she were working it really hard. "Kennan doesn't live here any-more," the voice said. "This is Chris."

"Hi, Chris," I said. "This is Inez Ruin. Is Tomas there?"

"No," she said. Her voice had hardened, and the edges were sharp. "He's out."

"Can I leave a message?"

"Sure." She knew who I was.

"I'm looking for my brother," I said. "For Whitman. I was wondering if Tomas had seen him lately."

"Oh."

"Have you seen him?"

Quiet. "I'm not sure," she said. "But I think he got hurt—there was some kind of accident. I heard that somewhere." But I got nothing else out of her.

When the hospitals had no record of him, Dad and I started calling the Ke Iki house every thirty minutes. Early the next morning, I almost gave up.

"Hello, Tomas?"

"What? Who's this?"

"I'm sorry to call in the middle of the night," I said. "I'm sorry to wake you up. It's Inez."

"Oh."

"Did you get the message that I'd called?"

"No." His voice sounded sleepy.

There was a pause. I could hear sheets rustling, movement. Tomas was getting out of bed, walking somewhere.

"I'm looking for Whitman. He's not at the house." I stopped and waited for him to say something.

"Yeah," Tomas said, "there was some kind of accident. But hey, you know what? I don't want to get involved. He's *your* brother. You know the story."

I arrived in Honolulu at eleven in the morning. It was still the day after Christmas. And it seemed to have been eleven o'clock for two days already. During the five-hour flight, I could bring myself to think about Whitman only sporadically, in fleeting moments of dread—where he might be, how I might find him. Then my mind would rest again on Marguerite. Christmas always made me think of her, and the way the house in San Benito smelled like pine trees. The way things were decorated. The way the long dining room table was set with pressed white linen place mats and the dull shine of old sterling. She put bunches of holly with red berries in little silver cups of water. And white candles. She served turkey with stuffing and side dishes that never changed: shrimp cocktail, carrot and turnip ring, squash pie, chocolate steamed pudding. There were tiny stockings on the mantel in the living room for all six grandchildren with a check for fifty dollars inside each one. The tree was ablaze with lights. New candy was piled inside the tiny covered dishes.

I thought Christmas at her house would never end. A whole world without end. Marguerite seemed so solid, and tradition-bound, and completely changeless. She fooled me, maybe all of us, with that. In the four years since she'd died, I'd come to see how stupid I'd been—how fooled and ungrateful. I regretted all the moments I'd spent with Marguerite that I hadn't bothered to notice. I regretted all the things that I thought would be forever, the things that Marguerite brought into my life and took away when she died. The big house in San Benito, the veranda and the garden, the afternoons at the Arroyo, tea in her living room. The feeling of her looking after me—and paying attention. People always say that you take things for granted when you're a kid, but it never stops, does it? When I thought about it on that plane ride, weeping in my cozy airplane seat, I saw that there were things I was taking for granted right now—just by pondering how much I'd taken Marguerite for granted—things that would eventually pass away or die or just stop. Things I'd lose someday. Things that would never come back. The long talks with my father. The books we read together. The stupid TV shows we watched, and all the movies we'd analyzed and fought over. The way he'd always asked for my opinion, for my thoughts, and treated me like a grown-up. The way he'd never sugarcoated things or lied. The freedom that gave me, to speak my mind. And the presents he sent, which were always too nice and too expensive. He bragged about me to his girlfriends, made me feel loved, and then he'd play the *Pathétique* endlessly, almost as if trying to drive me mad with the song. And his ridiculous questions—the way he'd hang on the phone and was impossible to get off. Wolfback. I loved that house, didn't I? And Whitman. Whitman, of course.

I wondered if I'd find him, the way Marguerite was at the end—in the dark woods, the birds flying from tree to tree. Curled up on her side in a ball. In the past few weeks, though, I'd stopped thinking of Marguerite that way. I had a new picture in my head. She was a girl about my age. She was naked on a bed and looking straight at the camera, fearless. I saw her face—almost felt her around me. It was almost as if she were traveling on the plane with me, as though she were inside me, urging me on. She was making me go back and get him, not letting me wait until it was too late. She was pushing me to stop being scared and hesitant, too late and too passive. *The way you do one thing is the way you do everything.* That was the phrase, wasn't it? Marguerite wasn't thrown from her horse anymore and on the ground. She was naked on a bed and looking at the camera. A girl like that wouldn't wait. A girl like that wasn't afraid. The way you do one thing is the way you do everything, Marguerite was telling me, until you decide to do it differently.

TWENTY

What Marguerite Left Behind

After I'd called Tomas, my father and I quickly made plans, worked out various scenarios—we'd imagined how I would show up at Whitman's house. We planned what I might say. How I would convince him to come back with me.

Then I tried to sleep. But what if Whitman were already dead? Or what if he were dying right then—right at that moment? We hadn't called my mother or Abuelita or Patricia either, for the same reasons, I guess, that Tomas was so unforthcoming on the phone. "You know the story," he'd said. Where did Whitman's personal business begin and end? Where do you draw the boundary lines in a family of people who weren't used to them?

Around five in the morning, I wandered into Dad's bedroom to see how he was. A bedside lamp was still on. He was just lying there, on his side, with his back to the door.

"Dad?"

His green silk robe was rumpled and wadded under his armpits. The black velvet slippers had been kicked off. The sky outside was dark orange, as if the earth were burning. I stood next to the bed, waiting for him to say something. He didn't move. "There's something I should have told you about Whitman," I said.

"Like what?" I could see only the back of his head on the pillow. His voice sounded angry. It was as if everything about Whitman made him sad or angry now, as if this night, and all we were going through, were the very thing that Dad had worked hard all his life to make sure would never happen. "*What is it, Inez?*"

"I have a bad feeling."

"About what?"

"I should have told you before. Something Tomas told me. I didn't want to believe it before, but maybe now I do."

"Oh, God. What?" He was shouting into the pillow—more angry than curious. When I finally told him, he stopped shouting, and then his back was moving in heaves, almost like he were sick. I'd never seen him that way—so sad, so overcome. Maybe what Tomas told me wasn't true, I said. Maybe it wasn't true—I'd been praying that it wasn't. But I needed to talk about it and not keep it secret any longer. Dad was very quiet after that. And still. Almost as though this new piece of information had killed him. And I remember looking at the back of his head and wishing he'd just say what it was, the thing he was so scared of. We were all afraid of something, weren't we, all terribly afraid, the kind of fear that drove us and pushed us toward things, and away from things. We were all terrified of something, and tried to wall it off, but pretending you weren't afraid just made it worse. Mom and Bob were always talking about fear, almost belittling it. They'd both gotten that tactic from est, I suppose, but it made sense to me. Fear fed on itself. Whatever Dad was afraid of, I knew that Whitman and I were a part of it. Something had already happened, maybe a long time ago. It happened when he wasn't paying attention. Whitman and I. We'd crept up on him. Hadn't we? We'd snagged him somehow. He hadn't figured on us, factored us in. And now we were everything to him—almost everything he cared about. We'd become al-

most as important to him as he was to himself. He'd figured out ways
to get out of being a husband, but he'd never been able to stop being
our dad.

"I know what I did," he said. "I know."

"What?"

"I crushed him, didn't I?"

"You—"

"He was so beautiful and strong, and he wasn't like me—didn't seem
to want to be. Didn't even try. I suppose that bothered me most of all.
And then I crushed him and crushed him and crushed him until he was
just a crushed boy. I knew what I was doing, and I went ahead with it anyway. That's what we do to each other, isn't it? Men. That's how it is."

I wasn't sure what to say. While he was talking, I wanted to comfort
him at first and say, Oh, no, you shouldn't feel bad about that. Whitman
was responsible for his own fate, wasn't he? He made his life the way it
is. Or maybe Patricia's money had wrecked things—left him purposeless
and lost, or just spoiled. But I stopped myself. I wasn't sure that it was
true either.

"I knew," Dad sobbed. "That's the worst part. And I still did it."

How easy it is, when somebody you love is suffering, to forget the
harder things, the miserable parts—what a fink he was, how suffocating
his selfishness and vanity could be, his coldness, his intrusions, the way
he seemed to put everybody else last and himself first. It's funny how ob-
serving another's pain can wash away things like that. You stop dividing
and adding up. He wasn't a white knight or a black knight anymore. Lying on his bed, he was overcome with worry and shame and almost a kind
of madness, and I guess I saw another man emerging. He loved us, and
we loved him, this gloomy, difficult, sweet, insightful, honest man. He
cared—maybe too much—and was always wrestling with some piece of
unhappiness, a man who felt like a failure unless he was lost in music or
love. Adoration was like a drug to him, a craving, a need so deep it was almost endless, and because of that he'd made himself a wooden merry-go-
round horse that rode in a circle while the women climbed on and off.

I sat down on the edge of his bed. And then I crawled over on my hands and knees to his side. He stayed still. I pulled myself closer, pressing against him, wrapping my arms around his back. He didn't move his head on the pillow, and for a long time he made no sound. Eventually—maybe fifteen minutes or thirty minutes later, I'm not sure—he spoke. It was completely real and not emotional, the way he usually talked—straight ahead: "What will we do if we've lost your brother?" he said. "That's where I get caught, Inez. I'm afraid I won't make it beyond that."

"Yes you will," I said.

The orange dawn was growing brighter. And I remember thinking that the edges of the windows seemed on fire.

I got to the North Shore a little after lunchtime, if I'd been marking the day in terms of meals, which I wasn't. Driving along the highway above the beach, I rolled down my window and tried to feel the beauty of the place, the sunshine, the deep blue sky, and the way the green cliffs hugged the road. The yellow sand at Waimea Bay was mostly gone, taken by storms, and the water was deep blue—the kind of luminous color that used to make me ache—and beyond at the horizon, a brilliant turquoise.

What did all that beauty do, exactly? What was it there for? Everywhere in Hawaii there was something lovely to look at. And something new, something fresh and young. The faces of the North Shore girls walking from the beach. The crowds of guys in their cool sunglasses—the styles changed every winter like clockwork, exactly as the baggy swim trunks got longer, and then shorter, or the way the cool T-shirt was this way, the cool backpack like that, or the cool Walkman was this color, or *da kine* flip-flops were nylon now, a certain brand, a certain stripe running along the bottom. New music was better than the old—and anything was better than the Beach Boys. The new boards. The new shapes and sizes. A fin was put here, then down there—or split into two fins. When something was new, it seemed perfect and untouched and beautiful. Didn't it?

The door was unlocked at Whitman's and slightly ajar. There were piles of dusty flip-flops on the porch, and it almost looked like a party must be going on. But it was quiet, except for the phone ringing. I wondered if it was Dad, seeing if I'd arrived. I went inside but didn't answer the phone. I didn't do anything or say anything, didn't call out anybody's name. I just walked into the dark house as quietly as I could.

Whitman's room was empty—the bed unmade, some sneakers on the floor. It was hard to tell how long it had been, except that the soil of the plants in his room was dry and pulled away from the edges of the pots. I walked out into the hallway, pushed open the door to the second bedroom, which Reggie, the marine, always rented, and it was empty. All the stuff that I'd seen last year—the bamboo bong, the ashtrays, the stacks of record albums that Reggie used to clean pot—was gone. Only a blue-and-white sticker was left on a bulletin board: RONALD REAGAN FOR PRESIDENT.

I went to my old bedroom door, and for some reason I looked at the ceiling first to check if the scarf was still there. In a moment completely disconnected from anything real that was happening, I found myself happy to see that it was. And to see the plants, and the curtains, and pretty much everything else, as I'd remembered them. I'm not sure why it took me so long to see the dark-haired girl in the bed. She was so skinny and motionless. I guess at first I thought she was a lump, a pillow. I wasn't sure she was breathing, so I walked up closer, but tentatively. Her eyes were shut. Her hands were closed up like the paws of a squirrel holding a nut. I reached out to feel her arm. It was warm. I felt a slow, faint heartbeat. She was alive, just asleep. I was glad of that. But when I tried to wake her up—and ask where Whitman was—she didn't even flutter her eyes.

What was going on? Who was she? In books and movies, people's faces are slapped and eyes open. Mouths speak. A confession tumbles out. But in life it was always too hard. You slapped and nobody woke up. You asked, but only yourself. People knew things but didn't speak of them—these weren't secrets, they were just pieces of neglected information. I left the girl with her beating heart and sat down on the sofa in

Whitman's dark living room and thought about what to do. Fleas were jumping against my ankles. Then I heard something scurrying in the kitchen—rats, mice, lizards, jungle things—and I got up and went outside, where it was midday and still beautiful. And the sky was clear and the palm trees were glistening and shiny, and the breeze was clean.

I walked out to the bench at the ridge of the property. Two kids were fishing on the rocks. There were more kids down the beach, carrying their pails and buckets. They were a mixed lot, those kids, all those locals—a quarter Hawaiian or half Japanese or half Filipino, or half something else: Portuguese, Chinese, Tongan, Samoan. They were jabbering in their halfspeak. *"Da kine. Da bes. You nah like de kine eel—tas so fine."*

"Inez?"

Whitman was a ghost—more of a shadow of a person, an outline, a frame without contents or flesh. Against the beauty of the scene, he looked like a superimposed figure from hell. His body was gangly. His eyes were droopy, his fingernails dark. The side of his head was black and purple, almost as if it had been spray-painted, and his nose was swollen and scabbed on one side—a grotesque black scab. "A bad wipeout," he explained. "Last week. Or maybe the week before." Then he managed a pathetic smile.

I tried to think of something to say that wasn't immediately harsh and negative, that wasn't "Why didn't you call?" or "What the fuck's wrong with you?" or "How could you do this to me?" but the only thing I could come up with was:

"What did the doctor say?"

"No doctors." He shook his head.

I grabbed his hand. He began to pull away, almost unconsciously— and I wondered how long it had been since somebody touched him. With my other hand, I felt the swelling on his arm that looked like a fresh insect bite. "What's that?"

"I've been shooting into my eyebrows mostly, so that won't happen," he said. "But I guess I got so fucked up I forgot."

No attempt to hide anything. That was good, I thought.

"Who's the girl in my bedroom?"

"Don't worry. She's okay."

"I'm tired of not worrying."

Out of the corner of my eye, I saw movement next door. Somebody had come out of Jerry's house and was standing on the deck. "Jerry," I whispered to Whitman. "I think he saw me."

"Let's go inside," Whitman said right away. "If he comes over, we'll say we're busy. We'll tell him there's been a family emergency. We'll say Dad died or something."

He was already colluding with me, I thought. He was thinking ahead. He had a story. He was glad I'd come. Maybe he'd even been waiting for me.

We walked back to the house and sat down in the living room. We didn't bother putting on a light. I found a pack of cigarettes on a sofa cushion and lit one up—something I never did anymore.

"You're still smoking," Whitman said.

"Not really."

"It's a method of keeping people away from you—with odor," he said. "It's like a form of bug repellent." I wondered when he'd last brushed his teeth.

"You're reminding me of Dad," I said.

"Thanks."

"It wasn't a compliment," I said.

"I know."

"Well, you know what Ooee says."

"What?"

"The best people have the worst parents."

"Do they?" he said. "I like that. I think it might be true."

"He didn't want us, that's all," I said. "Either of us."

"I know that."

"When we were born, he thought his life was over. We wrecked the perfection."

"I know that," he said again. "I've always known."

Was I supposed to charm him into the car—or scream and threaten him? Was I supposed to be happy and jolly and make the whole thing look like fun, a big adventure, and tell him what a great brother he was— and how he'd saved me so many times that I couldn't begin to count them? Could I love-bomb him into the car? I would have done anything that worked. But for some reason I decided to take Dad's advice and just tell him the truth.

"I came back to get you," I said finally. "I never should have left Hawaii without you. But I was too afraid of what you'd say. And I was too messed up myself."

"You're bringing me home?"

"Yeah."

"Wasn't it Christmas already?"

"That doesn't matter."

"Home where?"

"Wolfback."

"Wolf bane."

I didn't laugh. "Who's the girl in my room?"

"You."

We didn't call Dad—we decided not to. Maybe that was the final payment we extracted after enduring a lifetime of him. At the airport we got tickets for the next flight, for later that night, a red-eye. We checked a few bags—the only thing Whitman cared about was his backpack and the stuff in it that he thought was keeping him alive. Tickets in hand, we drove into town, to a big Marriott to kill some time. Whitman kept cranking the window down on the old Valiant, like he needed the wind on his face to stay awake. He was drinking a beer, too. "Drinking and driving is a Hawaiian tradition," he said.

"I remember."

At the big Marriott, there were umbrellas in the colored drinks and soft Don Ho–type music, half-Hawaiian and half something else— watered down. Maybe that was a good thing. The whole world could use some watering down.

"That was Sugar in my room," I said. "Wasn't it?"

"Kennan."

We went to Tin Tin's in Chinatown for dinner, and Whitman went into the bathroom with his backpack, then nodded off when the food came. "I like it here. I'm happy. Hawaii . . ." He could barely finish a sentence. "Of course, I'm needing more and more junk to keep that feeling going."

"I think you need a divorce," I said.

"From who?"

"From junk."

"I thought you were going to say from Dad."

"That, too." And then he laughed—a horrible new laugh. Only junkies laugh like that, or old drunks, almost as if something happens in their throats and disconnects their laugh from anything real inside them. The throat laughs. But it's an empty-shell sound, unfeeling, not even attempting authenticity, a big show, a big fake machine gun of a laugh. Nobody should ever have to hear a brother sound like that. "Tell you what," he said, really fake but with a serious face. "You go to college and I'll get clean. Think how happy Marguerite would be."

"I'm already in college," I said.

"Oh, right."

It wasn't hard getting him on the plane, except he'd wander off at the airport and I'd have to bring him back to the gate. The backpack somehow became my responsibility, and I was guarding it, and worrying about it, and wondering if I was going to be arrested, and always fretting that Whitman would need it, like one of those shaking people on TV. But it wasn't really like that. He didn't shake. He mostly slept. As it turned out, the flight home was the easy part. The rest was worse—the treatment programs that didn't work, the halfway houses that couldn't hold him, the dour predictions of specialists, and the sadness, the horrible sadness in

Whitman's eyes, like he'd lost everything that he cared about. The way my father fumbled around and couldn't keep up the act anymore that he didn't care about anybody but himself. When he gave up the act, he was mostly mad. But all his rage couldn't really make a dent in Whitman.

Eventually Justine got through. I'm not sure how. Or what she said, exactly. But Whitman spent a weekend with her in Carmel Valley and immediately checked in to a hospital in Santa Fe, and whatever happened at Justine's or that hospital worked. He came back—alive again, all the ingredients back together, whole but arranged in a slightly different way. He talked about heroin as if it were an old love that had been left and replaced with something else, something enduring—not a person or even a passion, really, but almost a sense of timelessness and space, a place that Whitman could always get to because he and Justine had cleared a path to it inside him. After that, he stayed with Patricia in Ojala for a while and seemed to mend whatever had broken between them. Then, in the late spring, he arrived at Wolfback, to be with me and Dad. We laughed a lot, cooked for each other. Whitman and I took hikes, and he told me the names of all of the plants. My father talked about building a guest cottage, away from the main house. He wanted Whitman to stay there. I didn't say too much or try to steer Whitman toward that or away. At the end of the summer, he found a small house to rent in an olive grove in Napa. His friend Ross came to visit, and then stayed. Whitman and Ross seemed happy together, and suited, like good friends. Were they gay? It seems strange now, but in those days we didn't ask. And it didn't matter. They were settled and comfortable and committed in a way that my father never had been.

"I knew you'd wind up living here someday," Dad said to me in late November. He'd seen Evie for dinner and then come home early to help me study for midterms. He was shuffling around in his horrible monogrammed velvet slippers and green silk robe—and was still so handsome that it didn't seem fair. He was cheerful, as happy as I'd ever seen him, and he buzzed around his kitchen with the espresso machine making all those sucking sounds, fiddling with a new recipe for brioche as though he were experimenting on a nuclear bomb. Maybe he was happy because Whitman was nearby, in Napa, and gardening again, and talking with a kind of firmness and resolve that he'd never had before. Maybe Dad was happy because I was imprisoned in my subterranean lair, studying for exams and playing his old flamenco records too loudly. Or maybe he was happy because Apple was going public and he'd make another fortune that he'd spend as fast as he could. Ronald Reagan was going to be our next president—and Dad seemed to feel this was a diabolically enchanting turn of events. Things with Madam X had stabilized. They were outlaws again, loving in secret—in hotels and friends' yachts and borrowed pieds-à-terre, always on the fly. She was still married. He seemed to like her better that way. And it would make the whole thing easier when he met somebody new.

"I've known since you were little," he said. "Remember that walk on the beach, when we came to the ridge for the first time? You were so tiny and wearing those white corrective shoes that must have weighed ten pounds each. You were so adorable with those two braids on the sides of your head. And you looked up at me like I was a god, like I was the greatest man you'd ever know. I knew we'd live together someday—right here on the ridge. Or I dreamed we could. And I pulled it off. I'm very proud of that. Ours is a great love story, isn't it, Inez?"

I smiled.

"I don't deserve you, do I?"

I made a harrumph sound. "You didn't deserve any of us," I said, grabbing a coffee and one of his experimental brioches to take down to my lair. "But that's life."

Later, when I was tired of studying, I called Robbie's number in Provo—the number that Boo had given me two years before. "She doesn't live in this dorm anymore," a young girl's voice said. I recognized something familiar about the voice—a kindness, an openness, a willingness to help me. "Let's see if I can find her in the BYU directory," she said. There was a short pause. "Yep, here she is. Robyn Morrison. At Deseret Towers."

I dialed the number right away.

"Robbie, it's Inez."

"You're kidding! Hello!"

She acted like it was nothing, like she'd just missed me. She acted like I'd never dumped her, or replaced her with Shelley, or grown up too fast, or tried to throw my life away. "I'm so glad you called!" she cried out. "My gosh! You sound exactly the same."

"I am."

ACKNOWLEDGMENTS

A nn Godoff, my editor, is as elegant and bright as a lit match. I hope books aren't like cigarettes—and that lighting three of mine in a row is okay. My debt to Ann, in any case, is now so profound it's beyond my ability to describe. Thanks to Liza Darnton at Penguin Press, too, for logistical assists and great manners, and to Maureen Sugden for copyediting and amazing soap-opera connoisseurship.

Alan Rifkin read this book in draft and his comments were astute and invaluable. Judith McBean inspired me in many quiet but significant ways, as did Sandra Anderson, Linda Cannon, Jeffrey Chin, Adelaide Gore, Robert Hemmes, Mark Hougard, Leo and Marlys Keoshian, Leah Levy, Tom Lubinski, Danielle Mirabella, Dana Osborn, Michael Phillips, Rochelle Racchi, Sonie Richardson, and Albert Schreck. I'd like to thank Barb Mehner for being unforgettable. And Barbara Keller, a.k.a. Blue Icon—I'm sad we never met. I'd also like to thank my husband, Bill Powers, who bursts with good ideas and kindness, and our son, Liam, for his creativity and good cheer. Tess Batac has taken care of me through many pages now with patience and a sense of fun.

Flip Brophy, my agent at Sterling Lord Literistic, doesn't come to visit me anymore since I moved to the hinterlands, but I still love her. The Sinclairs and the Spiegels, along with Nora Gallagher, are new friends but have the grace and understanding of old ones.

In addition to my immediate and extended family (of Sherrills, Boninis, Easons, Powerses, and Shallcrosses), I've been buoyed by various unofficial support groups, especially The Glams (Clara, Geraldine, Sally, Elsa), who make me laugh hard at lunch and express interest in my characters long after I've grown sick of them. I'd also like to acknowledge my debt to the Parlayers (Julie, Stebe, and U.U.), who remember the TV grid on Thursday nights in 1975 and who have taught me how to bet exacta boxes and wheels. And as always, without my cousin Leslee Sherrill in my life, where would I be?

MARTHA SHERRILL is the author of *The Buddha from Brooklyn*, a work of nonfiction, and *My Last Movie Star*, a novel. She was raised in Los Angeles and now lives in Massachusetts with her husband and son.